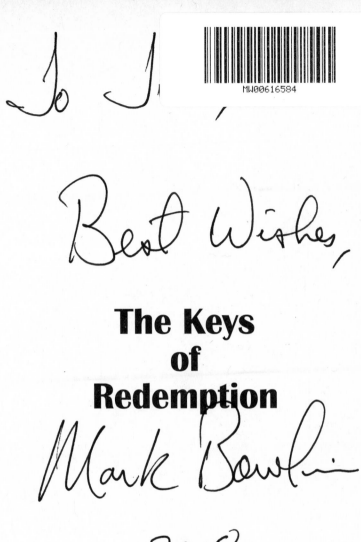

To J...,

Best Wishes,

The Keys
of
Redemption

Mark Bowlin

2018

Also by the Author

The Texas Gun Club

Victory Road

For God and Country

Ghosts of the Mountains

The Keys
of
Redemption

A Texas Gun Club Novel

Mark Bowlin

The 1630 Press, LLC
Flower Mound, Texas

The Keys of Redemption
A Texas Gun Club Novel

This is a work of fiction. Names, characters, places, and
incidents are the product of the author's imagination or are
used fictitiously.

Cover art by Billy Tucci
www.crusadefinearts.com

Manufactured in the United States of America

For information, please contact:
Mark Bowlin
The 1630 Press, LLC
P.O. Box 271683
Flower Mound, Texas
75027-1683
mark@markbowlin.org

ISBN-13: 978-0-9908904-2-3
ISBN-10: 0-9908904-2-2

10 9 8 7 6 5 4 3 2 1

The Keys of Redemption is dedicated to Bob and Toni Rose...three decades of friendship and still going strong.

Acknowledgments

I would like to thank Susan and Alex Bowlin for their support during the writing of *The Keys of Redemption*. I would like to thank my father, Stan Bowlin, and Shannon Chawk for being my readers. Many thanks to CAPT Doug Grossmann, USN (Ret.) and Toni Bernardi Rose for lending their names to such scoundrels.

I'd further like to express my appreciation to COL Joachim Strenk, TXARNG (Ret.); LTC Ross Davis, TXARNG; LTC Kevin Smith, TXARNG; Lt Cdr Robert Hawkins, MBE, RN; Capt Fin Jones, USMC (Ret.); SFC Aaron Hodgson, USA; Gary B.G.E. Beams; Chuck Carter; Joyce Gilmour; Michael Higgins; Michael Renzine; Scott Taylor; and Billy Tucci.

I want to acknowledge my friend and fellow author, Jim Pepper, who sadly passed away last year. I met Jim many years ago when our first books had just been published, and within a minute of meeting, we discovered that our respective families had been friends and neighbors outside of Weston, Missouri, long before I was born. Jim was a Marine infantry officer, a graduate of the U.S. Army Ranger School, and a veteran of the Vietnam War. His advice on warfare was always on the mark and his enthusiasm for writing and, well, everything else under the sun was inspirational.

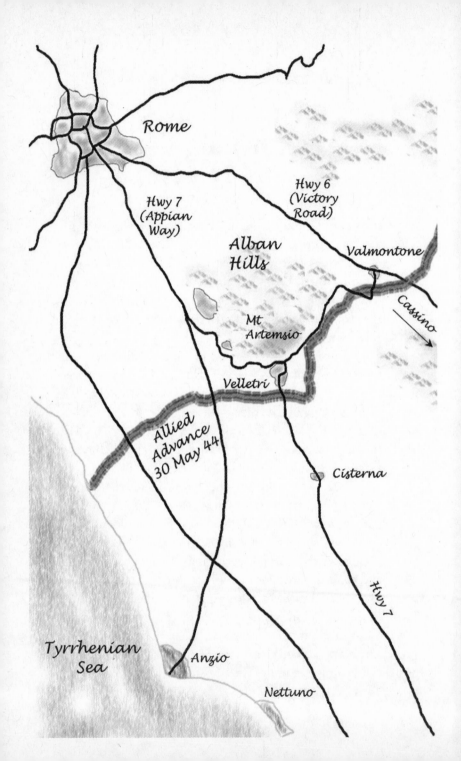

Prologue

June 4, 1944
0930 Hours
Rome, Italy

The three men sprinted up the last flight of the white marble stairs. They halted on the landing, and before an ornate wrought-iron door. The door itself was a work of art, although its beauty was lost on the three men. Their prey was not far ahead.

The senior soldier was a tall captain with a dark brown tan, black hair, and incongruently ice-blue eyes. He held his hand up to stop his party behind him and he cautiously peeked around the corner of the landing. Before him was a long empty hallway dotted on either side with heavy wooden doors each leading to a luxury apartment. The officer knew which apartment their prey would have likely gone to, and he silently motioned for his companions to follow him. He slipped around the door, raised his Thompson submachine gun to his cheek, and walked as softly as he could down the richly carpeted hallway.

Both of his companions mimicked his movements, although neither of the other soldiers carried a submachine gun. They were both armed with M-1 Garand rifles, which were carried in a ready position: cheek against stock, and rifle butt against shoulder. No safeties were on any of their weapons, and fingers rested with gentle competency on triggers.

All three men were breathing heavily, not just from the exertion of the chase, but also from the excitement of the hunt. Months of effort had led to this moment, and although all three men were veterans of the hardest fighting America had seen in the war up to that very week, they could barely control the adrenaline, the breathing, and the rapid pulse.

The smallest man was a scarred and bespectacled sergeant. He was seemingly too young to be a soldier, let alone a sergeant, yet he was the coolest killer in the small company of killers. The young sergeant was the first to regain his composure. He had been paying attention to the iron numbers mounted on the doors to either side of him, and he knew they were getting close. He gently put his hand on the shoulder of the soldier before him, and when he had his attention, he held up two fingers and mouthed the words, "Two more on the right." The tall captain nodded.

The last man was an even taller captain. He was fair with light blue eyes, and his frame was heavier and more muscular than his cousin's—the leader of the group. He was regarded as something of a gentle giant, but today, he had a dangerous angry look in his eyes. He had come on a mission of vengeance.

Captain Perkin Berger, the leader, halted his party when they were still twenty feet from the apartment doorway. In the softest whisper he could manage, he said, "Sam, you kick the door in and move to the side. Eddie, toss a grenade in. I'll move in first."

His companions, Captain Sam Taft and Sergeant Edwin Kulis, barely heard the words but they knew what to do. They had dreamed of this moment for countless days and nights, and while their dreams had seen themselves capturing and interrogating their prey or making him beg for his miserable life, they all knew subconsciously that those dreams were silly flights of fantasy. Their history with their prey had been far too costly for such indulgences.

They would kick the door down, and then they would kill everyone in the apartment without mercy.

Chapter One

May 15, 1944
0900 Hours
141st Regimental Bivouac Area, Qualiano, Italy

"Have you ever eaten a fig?" asked Perkin Berger of his cousin Sam Taft.

"What?" Sam replied with a measure of irritation.

"Have you ever eaten a fig?" Perkin asked again.

Sam looked his cousin over with a mild degree of disgust and asked, "You sent a runner to find me, to tell me that you needed to see me, and the issue of the day is fruit?"

Perkin shook his head. "No. That's a generalization. I know you've had fruit—I've seen you eat a watermelon like a hog at the trough. No, I'm asking specifically about figs. Have you ever had one?"

Sam sighed and said with a touch of resignation, "Well, some would say that a watermelon's a vegetable, but no, Perk. I ain't ever had figs. Other than the cookies, of course. Does that answer your question?"

Perkin thought for a moment and shook his head.

"I don't think so. I ain't sure that the cookie captures the essence of a fig. They're wonderful and all, but I don't think they answer the key issue."

Sam looked with puzzlement at his cousin and then realized where the conversation was going. Sam grinned, and said, "Ah...I see. I'm guessing that the key issue is you don't know how to eat one."

"Exactly. Eddie gave me some spring figs—I don't know how they're any different from summer, winter, and fall figs—and I don't know how to eat them. Do you pop the whole thing in your month and eat the outside or is that poisonous or something like a rhubarb leaf?"

Sam shrugged and said, "How the hell should I know? You've got a Ph.D. and you're afraid of a fruit? Why don't you just take a bite and find out? If you have a seizure or something, I'll probably call a medic for you."

Perkin laughed. "Maybe that's why I called you over—to take me to the medic in case I start foamin' at the mouth. But now that I think about it, you've had a medal for bravery since yesterday's award ceremony, and I ain't seen you do anything brave since. I think you should try it first."

Sam shook his head. "Well, once again, you think wrong. I could do it, but I have no curiosity about figs. You could truthfully say I don't give a fig about figs. Why didn't you ask Eddie how they're eaten?"

"You astonish me sometimes...because it demeans the rank—asking an enlisted man about fruit. Seriously, how can you be a captain in the United States Army and suggest something like that?" Perkin looked at his cousin with mock seriousness.

"You have an odd calculus on life, cousin. You didn't ask the obvious person how to eat the fruit out of some concern for the sanctity of your rank, and instead you troubled an enlisted runner to come get me, which says you don't give two hoots about the sanctity of either his rank or mine. Does that sum it up?" Sam shook his head as he looked at the roof of the large tent Perkin shared with Major Bill Spaulding, their battalion commander.

"In a nutshell. Why do you find it odd that I'm less concerned about your rank?"

"I don't know why I should," Sam said. "Well, since you've never given a second's thought about either decorum or self-embarrassment, I assume you forgot to ask Eddie how it's done."

"Yeah. I got distracted and forgot." Perkin took a small brown fig out of his left pocket. "The real reason I sent Dombrowski for you is that we're going to have a battalion all-officers meeting at 1100 in the schoolhouse over yonder. Thought you might want a heads-up."

Sam nodded. "Thanks, although I suppose Dombrowski could've told me that. Well, Perk, if we've exhausted the subject of our mutual experience with fruit, I'll just head back to the company. The last of my replacements came in this morning—just before the great fig crisis of '44 erupted. I'm gonna go meet them, and then I'll see you at the schoolhouse."

"Are you sure you don't want one of these figs? C'mon. Try one. I'll eat one if you do." Perkin held the fig out for his cousin.

Sam shook his head in resignation and took the fig with a dubious look. "At the same time?" he asked.

"At the same time," Perkin confirmed, and he pulled a fig out of his right pocket.

"On the count of three, then," Sam said. He counted to three and waited until Perkin honored his side of the agreement by popping his small fig into his mouth, and then Sam did the same with his own fig and cautiously bit into it.

Perkin watched as Sam's face lit up with pleasure, and when Sam noted they tasted just like the cookie and asked for more, Perkin gave him another six figs from his left pocket. As Sam ate figs while walking back to his company, Perkin pulled a ripe fig from his right pocket, pulled it apart longitudinally, and ate the flesh of the fig with delight. After eight months in Italy, he long ago had found he loved the fruit. Curious to see if Sam would react to the unripe figs stored in his left pocket, Perkin pulled another fig from his right pocket and ate it as well. Perkin had learned the hard way that eating the skin of unripened figs sometimes had a delayed reaction not unlike a mild jellyfish sting in the mouth.

0930 Hours
Rome, Italy

Douglas Grossmann, a lieutenant colonel of the SS Security Service known as the SD—the intelligence arm of the SS and the Nazi Party—lit an American cigarette with a Zippo lighter bearing the painted image of Betty Boop. As he inhaled the smoke, he tipped his chair back against the stone building and closed his eyes against the light and warmth of the sun. He was wearing a light gray civilian suit and sitting at a sidewalk table at a small café and restaurant on the edge of the Piazza del Popolo. There was an awning stretched over the tables, but Grossmann had pulled his chair around so he could sit with his back against the stone building while both watching the people crossing the piazza and enjoying the sunshine. Italy was finally warm again, but Grossmann couldn't get enough. It had been a long terrible winter, and the spring of 1944 was only better because of the warmth.

He reached the end of his cigarette and lit another. Grossmann watched as a very thin but attractive woman led a young child by the hand across the piazza. Both the woman and the child looked clean, and Grossmann wondered where they found soap. It was hard to come by these days.

So was good food and drink, which was why Grossmann liked this café. The owner was a Fascist and was also sympathetic to German officers, which wasn't always the case. Naturally, the Germans were able to pay higher prices for his drinks and fare, and consequently, he was able to procure coffee beans and wheat flour from the black market for his fresh bread and pastries. Dealing on the black market was a crime punishable by severe penalties including death, but as the man's would-be judges and executioners were his frequent customers, allowances and exceptions were made.

The restaurant owner personally waited on Lieutenant Colonel Grossmann, whose identity wasn't widely known in Rome, but those Romans who knew who he was feared him greatly. He found that it led to wonderful service. The restauranteur set down a small plate with two chocolate-filled cornetti that had been dusted with powdered sugar, and then inquired if Grossmann desired anything else. The German intelligence officer pointed wordlessly at his empty coffee cup, but as the owner turned to fetch a pot, Grossmann stopped him with a hand on his arm.

"No, Signore Alessio. Bring me a *caffè corretto* if you would," Grossmann ordered in fluent Italian. "If you have any of the bourbon left, I would like that. If not, grappa or brandy. Whatever you have."

The Italian smiled obsequiously and nodded his head. "Sir, just for you, I keep a bottle of the American whiskey hidden away so that even if my wife or the Pope should look for it, we have none." The owner bowed even more obsequiously and scurried away to prepare Grossmann's coffee. In the few cafés in Italy that still had real coffee, a caffè corretto was usually a small cup of espresso with maybe a tablespoon or two of alcohol to "correct" it, but based on experience, the owner knew Grossmann was looking for a full shot of whiskey to supplement his espresso. A few minutes later, he set two small glasses in front of the German officer and as he saw that Grossmann needed nothing else, he moved away to leave the German alone.

Grossmann wasn't alone for long. A short man in a dark civilian suit walked up to Grossmann's table and without invitation sat down. Grossmann looked at his new companion and after a few moments, he pushed the plate of cornetti across the table with the observation, "I think you need this more than me." The newcomer was older than Grossmann with black hair that was beginning to turn white at the temples. He normally had intelligent and attentive brown eyes, but this morning, they were severely bloodshot with dark circles underneath. He waved off the cornetti.

"I'm hungover," Major Friedrich Kemmerling announced in Bavarian accented German. "The Vichy trade attaché kept me out too late last night." Kemmerling looked again at the pastries, changed his mind, and with a shaking hand picked up one of the croissants and tore off an end. He contemplated the piece of pastry before shoving it into his mouth. The older man forced the food down and then closed his eyes and said, "I think I shall vomit soon, but lest I disgrace the SS, I hope to wait until an ugly *Katzenfresser* woman passes first."

Grossmann grinned at his companion, shook his

head in mock sorrow, and said, "Fritz, despite your debauched state, you do the Fatherland proud. While he may disapprove of referring to our allies as 'cat-eaters,' I'm sure Reichsführer Himmler would be happy to reward your zeal with a combat command in the East."

"Indeed. Nothing would make me happier than to bask in that chicken-fucker's approval." Kemmerling groaned slightly and slouched in his seat. "Christ. Can't we move under the awning or inside? This light might kill me. It's unnatural. I've endured more sunlight in the past two months than in a year in Bavaria."

Although Grossmann had spent considerable time in Rome, it was a new posting for Major Kemmerling. The two officers had met at the Waffen SS training grounds at Bad Tölz in Bavaria. They had both been Abwehr officers who were now enrolled in the SD, but they had not known each other in the Abwehr. As they already held commissions, they were spared the full SS training regimen. Instead, they went through a three-week course designed specifically for army officer accessions into the SS. It was three dreadful weeks of Nazi indoctrination, intense physical training, and sadistic hazing made worse for the two officers who were considerably shorter than the SS standard. Each man had to document that there was no Jewish ancestry for the last two centuries, which was easy enough for both men. Grossmann's mother was American, but first generation and of German stock. Grossmann and Kemmerling were both members in good standing of the Nazi Party, and were considered to be reliable officers unlike many in their old organization. The two former Abwehr officers, known as the Lilliputians by their SS instructors, then formed a bond through misery over the course of the three weeks. At the conclusion of the course, Grossmann had requested that Kemmerling be assigned to Rome to work for him. As Grossmann was a minor hero in SS circles following his testimony leading to the arrest of Admiral Canaris in February—testimony that earned an Iron Cross First Class personally awarded by Reichsführer Himmler himself—it was a request that had been immediately approved by SS headquarters in Berlin.

They arrived together by train in mid-March, but Grossmann was surprised to find that his primary responsibility was no longer intelligence collection in the SD office of foreign intelligence as it had been during his posting in Rome for the Abwehr. Both men were immediately assigned to General Wolff as special projects officers. It was a billet that both men loathed at first, but had come to appreciate.

The beginning was the worst. Two days after they arrived in Rome, Italian partisans attacked members of the German Bozen Regiment as they marched through central Rome. It was a simple homemade bomb of TNT placed in a stolen cart parked along the side of the road. A long fuse was lit as the German soldiers came into view and as the soldiers passed the cart, the bomb detonated, killing thirty-three and wounding scores of soldiers and watching Italians. It was a massacre that outraged not only the German military command in Italy, but the Nazi leadership in Berlin as well.

Grossmann had been told the Führer was so outraged that he demanded a quadrant of Rome be razed in retaliation for the deaths of the German soldiers. The Führer evidently had a change of heart but whether he changed his mind following personal introspection, calmer heads prevailed, or it was simply deemed infeasible, Grossmann didn't know. Instead, a simple formula was established for retribution. Ten

Italian citizens would be killed for every German life lost to partisan terrorism. Grossmann and Kemmerling were in agreement that such a ratio was a reasonable solution until they learned that Reichsführer Himmler personally directed that Grossmann be placed in charge of this special project. Nearly two months later, Grossmann was still undecided whether he was assigned by the SS commander in Berlin to be a mass murderer as a test of his loyalty or in recognition of it.

There had been no way to dodge the orders, and Grossmann gave little thought to disobeying in any case. He and Kemmerling had crossed the Rubicon together, and there was no way to return to previous lives as simple soldiers. Kemmerling had been a pre-war policeman who joined the Wehrmacht during its expansion in the late 1930s, and while he turned pale upon hearing of their new orders, he never voiced concerns about the legality of the orders. Over several drinks, he told Grossmann the night before the retaliation was carried out, "War is distasteful, my fellow Lilliputian…but you heard the briefings in Bad Tölz. This is a plush assignment compared to the East. We should be grateful we're not there. Speaking for myself, I am, and if killing a few cat-eaters will protect German lives and keep us out of the East, then I ask, 'When do we begin?'"

Grossmann had raised an eyebrow and nodded. It wasn't the most honorable of sentiments, but it was one that he shared wholeheartedly. "Damn right," he said. "What's going on there is an order of magnitude worse—we might end up in some hellhole like that dump in Plaszow. Or worse. Besides, someone should pay for this in any case. Listen, I have a few ideas."

Grossmann had spent the better part of an hour and two bottles of wine detailing his plan to Major

Kemmerling, but that night and the day that followed were in the distant past for the two men sitting at the café on the Piazza del Popolo. Grossmann watched with amusement as his companion stood up, belched loudly, and said, "I can't wait for an ugly woman. Be right back."

While Kemmerling staggered around the corner of the building to vomit, Grossmann drank his caffè corretto and ordered two more. If Kemmerling couldn't drink his while they planned their operations for the week, Grossmann would. If other duties permitted, they would meet at the same café for a late breakfast and would spend the morning drinking and talking. Sometimes coffee, but always alcohol. As Grossmann objectively told himself, it was becoming necessary to drink just to get through the day—and the day went by faster if he started drinking earlier.

1000 Hours
141st Regimental Bivouac Area, Qualiano, Italy

Perkin watched as the officers filed into the makeshift briefing room—one of the few standing rooms remaining of the Francesco Crispi Lyceum. Before an American 250-pound bomb errantly destroyed much of the schoolhouse in September of the previous year, the classroom had been the daily home of twenty secondary school students who learned and studied between air raids. Attempts had been made to repair the school, but following the calculated destruction of Naples by the retreating Germans in September and October of 1943, the efforts had been abandoned and other arrangements made for the students.

American soldiers had been posted outside the

building so briefings could be conducted without the
use of blackout curtains, and a nice warm breeze blew
through the room. Perkin stood at the front of the room
in a natural position for a would-be professor, but the
situational irony escaped him as he prepared to deliver
the 1st Battalion briefing.

In attendance were the four company commanders
of the battalions and all of their subordinate officers as
well as the battalion commander, Major Bill Spaulding,
and Sergeant Edwin Kulis, who was Perkin's assistant
in the battalion intelligence shop. Other staff officers
from the battalion were present, and everyone shuffled
around, looking attentively at Perkin while finding
their seats.

Perkin wasn't the first to speak, however. Major
Spaulding indicated to everyone that they should take
a seat as he walked to an open window and spat a
long stream of tobacco juice into the dusty schoolyard.
Perkin moved aside at the head of the classroom, and
Spaulding cleared his throat before speaking.

"Well, shit, fellas. Here we are again. After the past
two months of training, everyone knows everyone else,
so no need for introductions. We got some newcomers,
but we're mostly all old hands at this business now."

While Spaulding talked, Perkin looked at Sam
and suppressed a grin. Sam's face was red and he had a
trickle of sweat dropping along either side of his neck,
although the room temperature was moderate. Perkin
saw that he had a canteen resting in his lap, and Perkin
suppressed another grin as Sam took a long sip of water.

The effect of the unripe figs on Sam was lost on
Major Spaulding who scratched at a mosquito bite just
above a long lateral scar across his face—a memento
from the battle at Paestum. Spaulding said, "We got
our alert order last night. It's the usual thing, 'On

order be prepared to redeploy, etcetera, etcetera.' No surprise there. We knew that the vacation was coming to an end..." Several of the men grinned and shook their heads. The previous two months had been the most intensive training in anyone's memory. "...So...I suppose everyone's wondering where we're redeploying to? Well, I got good news and bad news for you boys, but first, I'd like to remind you that the battalion slush fund gets a cut from any betting pools that may be running."

Everyone shifted expectantly in their seats, but they didn't have long to wait—Spaulding wasn't the type to dramatically draw out an announcement of this magnitude. "All right, boys. The good news is that we aren't going back to the Gustav Line. There's no more Cassino for us but the bad news is we're headed to the meat grinder at Anzio. I expect the movement order tomorrow with a shipboard embarkation no later than forty-eight hours after that."

1005 Hours
Rome, Italy

Major Kemmerling's purge of the previous night's excess of bad Italian wine seemed to help. He had been steadier on his return to the table, and after a few minutes, he tentatively tried the cornetti again. Signore Alessio brought out a carafe of water for the two officers, and before long Kemmerling was functional again.

There had been a time when Grossmann would never have tolerated such behavior from a subordinate. The successes of the German Army were forged on the anvil of discipline, but those days were gone for Grossmann, and he certainly wasn't going to hold another officer accountable for transgressions that he himself was committing more and more frequently.

"Okay, Fritz. What did you learn from the French attaché last night?" Grossmann sipped appreciatively at his bourbon, but at Kemmerling's request, he set his glass on the empty table next to theirs so the major wouldn't be subjected to the fumes of the whiskey. His recovery was still tenuous.

"I learned that he has no scruples. He's a whore-chasing crapaud who probably likes boys as much as girls. But, judge not lest ye be judged, right? The important thing is he likes money, and he is a collector of information." Kemmerling picked up a glass of whiskey, tentatively sniffed it, and put it down with a grimace. The time wasn't right yet.

"So, he's willing to run some things to ground for us?" asked Grossmann.

"Yes. After I picked up the tab for drinks and dinner, he gave me a tidbit as a sample of his wares," Kemmerling said.

"Like what?"

"He gave me the name and address of a cat-eating businessman who imports industrial tools…taps and dies or something like that. That's it, he imports taps and dies from the Frogs. I went to the toilet and wrote his name and address down so I wouldn't forget." Alcohol was a wonderful lubricant, but sometimes the details were less than clear the next morning. Grossmann often did the same thing.

"Good," said Grossmann. "What's the hook on the Italian?"

"He's hiding a family in his house. He approached our Frenchman just a day or two ago and asked for help. Mama and Papa, and four little Jews. Italian Jews. Speaking of which, do we want to have the Italian police search the house, or do we want to do it ourselves?"

"Do they have any money? Gold? Jewelry?" Grossmann asked.

Kemmerling shrugged. "He didn't know."

"Let's do it ourselves in case they have anything, you know…worthwhile. Besides, if the Italians were competent, these Jews would have been transported to Fossoli by now." Grossmann motioned to the restaurant owner to bring another shot of whiskey. He had toured the Italian concentration camp at Fossoli, taken over by the SS in March, and much of the alcohol he had drunk since was to help ease the discomfort of the memory. It was better than the camp they had toured at Plaszow in early March, but not by much. "See? Since, we're doing their job, no sense sharing the wealth. We should see what the host family has as well. They might have a little gold tucked away, and maybe some food that we can sell on the black market. The usual deal: a share for the troops, a share for you and one for me, a share for Wolff, and if there's any left over, a little remembrance for the Fatherland. No sense sharing with the Italians."

"No, of course not," Kemmerling smiled. This had been a wonderfully lucrative posting so far. "When do you want to do the raid?"

"Tomorrow morning at 0500. I hate getting up early, but it's best to catch them asleep. Anything else from the Frenchman?" Grossmann asked.

"No. He just offered this as proof of his bona fides but he says he has more. He also says he has the address of a black-market warehouse that we could raid, but it's Camorra owned." The Camorra was the Neapolitan mob.

"Camorra?" Grossmann looked doubtful.

"Yes. No. Well, I don't know. That's what he told me." Kemmerling shrugged.

"It's unlikely to be Camorra here in Rome, I think.

Who knows these days? I'd love to hit their warehouse and confiscate the contraband, but we have to be careful about tangling with the mob. Any idea what they have? American goods? British?"

Kemmerling shrugged again. "He wouldn't say... probably a mix of things. He'll want a good price, of course. But if we decided to do so, we could take what we want, and then sell the rest back onto the black market."

Grossmann nodded. "Interesting thought. It could be very worthwhile...but I'm thinking that the timing's key. In any case, we don't bring Monsieur La Whoremonger on as a partner. Strictly fee for service. If he gets too uppity, we'll have to put him in his place."

"Speaking of uppity, he wants to be paid in dollars, sterling, or gold, which tells you who he thinks is going to win. Asshole. I told him reichsmarks but he wasn't happy. I said he'd be lucky if we don't pay him in zlotys but I don't suppose he can complain much if we pay him in francs or lire."

"It doesn't matter whether it's marks, francs, or lire. But if he insists on hard currency, I can requisition some of the sterling forgeries from the camp at Sachsenhausen. That would serve the bastard right." Grossmann paused and thought for a moment. "In fact, let's do it this way. I'll requisition, say, a thousand pounds...no, let's make it two under Wolff's name, and we'll pay the Frog a token to keep him happy, say, twenty pounds. We should hang on to the remainder for a rainy day. But let's not give in too easily. It'd make him suspicious and we might want all those bills for later anyway."

"Okay, boss. Anything from Signorina Bernardi?" Antoniette Bernardi was a dedicated Fascist who had worked as an agent for Grossmann since his arrival in

Rome two years before. She was his lover and confidant. Outside of his father and Kemmerling, she was the only person he almost trusted on the planet.

"No. She suspects that a convent north of the city is hiding Jews, but she can't confirm anything yet." Antoniette had brought him more Jews than any other source, but she hadn't had any names for Grossmann for nearly ten days.

"We're going to catch some heat from the general if we can't increase our numbers. He's under pressure from Berlin," Kemmerling said unnecessarily. Both Grossmann and Kemmerling were well aware of the political pressures.

"I know. I'm seeing him today. In forty-five minutes, in fact. I'll delay him as best I can but let's keep working the Jewish problem…that's where the payoff will be. I have to go. Wolff has someone coming in from Berlin that he wants me to meet."

Grossmann stood, signaled to his driver to bring the car around, and he nodded to his security detail down the street. It was time to go to work.

1015 Hours
141st Regimental Bivouac Area, Qualiano, Italy

Major Spaulding concluded his remarks, nodded to Perkin, and took a seat at a wooden desk that had students' initials and images of genitalia carved into it. Perkin walked back to the front of the classroom and picked up an olivewood pointer that was custom made for him by an Italian woodworker in Naples. Engraved in the side of the pointer in small letters was the inscription, "1st Bn Egghaids." Perkin was delighted with the misspelling, and he considered the pointer a treasured memento of the Italian campaign. As he was collecting his thoughts, the door opened and an officer in the uniform of the Welsh Guards walked in with a somewhat odd gait.

"Waller!" Perkin exclaimed in surprise. Sam and Spaulding stood and walked to greet the officer with broad smiles and outstretched hands. The Welsh officer, Captain Waller Finley-Jones, was just as delighted to see his old friends and Perkin was struck once again by the closeness of the brotherhood. Here was an officer with little in common with his American counterparts other than shared campaigns and shared dangers, which were sufficient to make the Welshman and the Texans friends for life.

"By God, Waller, it's good to see you!" Sam said with deep feeling. "How's your foot?" A fragment of a booby-trapped grenade had sliced through his boot in a house in Ortona in January and Captain Waller Finley-Jones had been evacuated to Britain for convalescence.

"Would you believe they had to take off my hallux and the next one as well? Bloody butchers! It shortened my foot enough that I am obliged to wear different sized shoes. It's embarrassing. Although on the other hand, it's improved my kicking in rugby. All in all, then, you would think that it cancels out, wouldn't you?"

Sam and Perkin looked at each other and Sam opined cautiously that they thought it might. Finley-Jones shook his head and said, "Well, you're wrong then, old boys. It doesn't. It doesn't even out at all, and I've learned the wisdom of the words of Friar Laurence."

"Well, I can't say I've met the fellow. What'd he say?" asked Sam.

"It's from Romeo and Juliet, and he said, 'Wisely and slow. They stumble that run fast.'"

Sam looked at Perkin again, saw no help in his

cousin's face, and he asked, "What's that mean?"

"It means…sometimes, I just fall over for no reason." Finley-Jones laughed. "It's the damnedest thing."

"I'd fall over too if they took off my bollocks," offered Perkin with a grin.

Finley-Jones was about to explain that it was not his bollocks that were removed, when Spaulding took him by the arm and introduced him to the others in the room. The Welsh officer shook the hands of the officers he knew, nodded to the rest, and when he got to Sergeant Kulis, he smiled warmly and said, "Sergeant now, is it? When I left you were just a lance corporal, no, I mean a private first class."

Sergeant Kulis smiled shyly and said, "Yes, sir. It was a busy couple of months and I got promoted 'cause I was the only one left, sir. Another battle or two, and maybe I can take over the division."

"God help us all." Finley-Jones stepped back, looked at the young soldier, and said, "My lord, I think you've grown. That reminds me, did you ever get to shoot that cannon we took in Ortona? The Mauser antitank rifle?" Without waiting for an answer, Finley-Jones said, "I say, is Private Fratelli around? I'd like to say hello."

Kulis shook his head, his smile gone. "No, sir, he was kilt on the river, and Sergeant Kenton lost that Mauser there too, I'm sorry to say."

Finley-Jones's face fell and he sighed. "Oh dear. I'm dreadfully sorry to hear about Fratelli. Was Kenton lost there too?"

Sam answered for Kulis. "No, Waller. We were captured, and escaped. I made it back, but he didn't. I was going to take your advice and steal a boat and sail to Swansea, but our path out got shut down. He's with Lieutenant Beams in occupied Italy and I think they're in good hands. I'll tell you about it after the briefing."

Spaulding nodded and said, "We'll get you caught up on everything in a little bit. Are you back for good, or just stopping by?"

Finley-Jones's smile returned. "Since I'm still as mobile as Gimpy McHenry, I had no trouble convincing my British regiment to allow me to return to my liaison job with my American regiment here. They're convinced that the American Army is one hundred percent motorized, and I shouldn't have to do much walking. I checked in with the regimental staff last night, and they told me that Perkin here had a briefing scheduled and would bring me up to snuff."

"Well, that's the best news I've heard since we left Cassino. Have a seat next to me, and we'll critique Perkin as he briefs. He told me he's got a great pun prepared but the Aggies wouldn't get it." Spaulding nodded at Perkin as he sat down.

Perkin walked to the front of the room again and said brightly, "Good morning, gentlemen, Aggies, and Welshmen. Major Spaulding asked me to do a few things in this briefing: talk about the gains being made on the Gustav Line, give an overview of the battle of Anzio to date, and then a few words about what we can expect there."

Perkin walked to a map that was tacked to a large corkboard courtesy of the school, turned to face his audience, and said, "As most of you know, we are four days into a major offensive that had three components: one which has been executed, one which is underway, and one which is yet to come. The component that is completed is the transfer of the bulk of Eighth Army to the Cassino area of operations. Over the past few weeks, they've put a holding force on the Adriatic and in the central mountains, and moved at least two corps into our old stomping grounds. As that was being effected, Fifth Army slid to their left into the Aurunci Mountains and onto Highway 7 along the coast. It was neatly done, and they're on a rough line abreast of the Eighth Army." Perkin used his pointer to show the new disposition of the Allied armies on the map. "Once this massive redeployment was completed, the second component or phase kicked off. That was the resumption of offensive operations along the Gustav Line from both armies: the Fifth along the Tyrrhenian coastline and in the Aurunci Mountains, and the Eighth Army across the Rapido and in the mountains north of Monte Cassino. This operation is called Diadem, which I think is a name that lacks both verve and pluck, but no one asked me. If they had, I would have told them it's hard to imagine winning a war by naming our operations after tiaras or any other form of bejeweled headgear for that matter."

Those that knew Perkin grinned while the newer officers seemed somewhat confused by the turn the briefing had taken. Sam leaned over and whispered to Major Spaulding, "I must've fallen asleep. That wasn't the pun, was it?"

Spaulding grinned and shook his head as Perkin continued. "Starting with some generalities, the Allied nations have some twenty-five to thirty divisions in Italy...the number I hear most often is twenty-eight. As I was alluding to, we're divided into two armies, which are split into four areas of operations: the Adriatic, the Liri Valley approach, the Aurunci and coastal roads, and, of course, Anzio. In the Eighth Army portion of Diadem, four days ago, we resumed the assault. Eighth Army is commanded by General Leese, and he's got ten divisions crammed up in the approach to the Liri Valley: three armored divisions and seven infantry divisions with just about every nationality under the sun represented. This includes a two-division Polish Corps, and them poor sons-a-bitches drew the short straw and have assaulted across Snakeshead Ridge towards Hill 593 with the goal of taking the Abbey. In their first drive, they came across what we believe are two German battle groups in the process of a turnover in the mountain defenses, and as a result, found themselves facing a combined force of at least ten battalions of infantry and panzer grenadiers. That assault began on the eleventh, last Thursday, and by Friday, the Poles were forced to pull back and regroup." Perkin sighed and looked much older for a moment at the memory of his own regiment's failed attempt to take Hill 593. He shook his head to clear the memory and said, "There's some good news to tell about Diadem. First, the Poles aren't out of the fight yet and I understand they'll assault again soon. Also, down in the valley, the Eighth Army established a beachhead across the Rapido River."

Several officers who had been present at the Rapido River assault sat up straight and stared at Perkin with a fierce intensity. Seeing this, Perkin nodded and said, "Yeah. Eighth Army's doing it right...or at least better. We tried crossing with two understrength regiments. The Brits have thrown two divisions plus across the river—the Indian 8th Division and the British 4th Division. Again, their assault began Thursday night and they ran into many of the same problems that we did—lost most of their boats, ran into minefields, and, unfortunately, a lot of soldiers drowned. Like us, their casualties for the first night were high—in the hundreds. But, unlike us, they had a dry valley floor and were able to get bridging equipment up to the riverbanks. On the first night, they got two bridges across on either side of Sant' Angelo supporting the Indian Division, and another across up by our battalion crossing site in January. That bridge is supporting the British 4th. Since then, they've been able to get six more bridges across and have established an actual beachhead of several miles."

"By God, they better hold it!" Sam said vehemently. Several other officers nodded although their mixed feelings were evident. It hurt that someone else succeeded where they had failed, but they also knew that the circumstances were different. Overriding all other concerns were the desires to make the Germans pay dearly at the Gustav Line, and for the Allies to never have to cross that river again.

Finley-Jones spoke up. "Perkin, if I may? I understand that it was the Gurkhas, which took Sant' Angelo. If you chaps don't know them, they're brutish little wogs who know killing better than anyone in the empire. Wonderful fellows to have on your side. Terrifying to face. Their specialty is killing people while they sleep, and like your red men, they count coup. I suppose there are more than a few Jerry corpses missing their ears this morning. But, their crossing was quite dear though. I was told the Gurkhas lost some two hundred soldiers at Sant' Angelo."

Perkin nodded to Finley-Jones and said, "So, the battle for the Liri Valley continues, as does the fight for the Cassino Massif. While this might break down to an old-style trench war, I think that unless the Wehrmacht is able to reinforce in great strength, the weight of metal being applied here will win the day. Before long, the Germans will have to abandon the Gustav Line and fall back to the Hitler Line to the north, and eventually above the Caesar Line just south of Rome."

Perkin shifted his body so he could indicate a different portion of the map. "This is the Fifth Army's area of operations in the south. The Aurunci Mountains

are more of the same crappy mountains as we were in…
full of rocks, ravines, and Germans. Actually, they're
worse. Elevations up to five thousand feet with very
sharp ascents and lots of rocks and little cover. The intel
indicates, however, that the enemy is stretched pretty
thin in the mountains, although the troops are from
Senger's XIV Panzer Corps. Tough troops and a very
good combat commander. Speaking of good combat
commanders, on our side, the mountains will be taken
by the French Expeditionary Corps commanded by
General Juin. They've got four divisions in the corps—
one of Free French, one of Algerian infantry, a Moroccan
infantry division, and a Moroccan mountain division.
The Berber and Arab soldiers of the North African
divisions are known as Goumiers, or Gooms for short.
Since last Thursday, they've made good progress in the
mountains under some very trying conditions, and
they believe they will control the highest point in the
Auruncies, the Petrella Massif, no later than tomorrow.
So…" Perkin paused to make sure everyone was paying
attention, and he said, "…you know what that means
for the high ground of the Fifth Army sector?" Perkin
paused again, and then said with a grin, "Heer today,
Goom tomorrow!"

Sam knew from years of experience that Perkin was
building up for his pun, and when he heard it, he paused
and thought for a second, and then started laughing—a
deep infectious laugh that had others grinning more
than Perkin's pun. "Hey, that's good, Perk!" he said, as
he laughed some more.

Perkin bowed slightly as he accepted the boos
and the laughter of those who caught the joke, and
to one puzzled lieutenant from Charlie Company,
he explained, "We say the Wehrmacht to refer to the
German Army, but their proper name is the Heer. Get

it? Heer today, Goom tomorrow?"

The lieutenant looked doubtful, and Perkin was tempted to explain further, but knowing that a joke that must be explained in depth isn't funny, he started to resume his briefing. He was interrupted by Major Spaulding.

"Hang on, Perk." Spaulding walked to the window and spat again. When he returned, his smile was gone and he stood alongside Perkin at the front of the classroom. "I want to say somethin' about these Gooms. They have a reputation of being good fighters, but bad soldiers. They've left a trail of destruction in their wake—looting, murder, and above all, rape. When they were north of us on the Cassino massif, they went through the villages like barbarians. They raped young and old women and girls, men and boys alike, and I seriously mean the children weren't spared. They even raped a priest or two. I heard rumors yesterday—I cain't fathom it—but I heard that Juin told his Gooms that anything goes for the next week as long as they drive the Germans out of the mountains. I feel right sorry for these Dagos that are in their path—their liberation is gonna be worse than the occupation, I'm afraid. Now... we have good soldiers, but let's not kid ourselves. We have some bad apples too."

Spaulding spat unconsciously on the floor, barely missing Perkin's boots, and then he said firmly, "On this subject, I want to be crystal clear. I won't tolerate rape. Commanders that come across this will deal with it or I will deal with them. Without exception, soldiers that rape will be remanded in custody, tried by court-martial, and I will do everything in my power to see they're executed in accordance with Article 92. They can then justify themselves to their maker. There will be no turning of a blind eye to this crime. Understood?"

There was a chorus of "Yes, sir," from the assembled officers, and Spaulding turned back to Perkin and said, "Your floor, Professor."

"Yes, sir. So the French Corps operation up in the mountains is coming along, and it's the most crucial piece of the puzzle. The U.S. II Corps isn't doing so well. They've been hung up in heavy fighting south of Formia, and their progress is slower. It's disappointing. I was hoping they'd take Gaeta by the time we pulled out, but it ain't gonna happen."

"What's so important about Gaeta, sir?" asked Second Lieutenant Alex Ryan, one of Sam's platoon leaders in Able Company.

"Well, I suppose it has military value and all that. You know, the gateway to the Pontine Marshes and the southern flank of Anzio. But, there's a famous church there on the water that I'd like to see where Pius IX came up with the notion of the Immaculate Conception, and a restaurant next to it called Emilio's, which Gianina said had the best *sauté di vongole* in Italy." Perkin frowned and added, "That's assuming, of course, that it's still there."

Sam rolled his eyes and said, "Perk…"

"Yeah, well, as I was saying, II Corps is moving slowly but should Diadem pan out, II Corps will take Gaeta, Sperlonga, and then Terracina. Once we're past Terracina, the coastal strip widens dramatically and we have room to maneuver. The plan is to effect a link-up with the Anzio lodgment, and as there's a lateral highway between Terracina and Frosinone, we should be able to maintain communication with Eighth Army as they move up Victory Road…if they succeed with their breakout."

1045 Hours
Rome, Italy

Doug Grossmann showed up in uniform fifteen
minutes early for his meeting with General Wolff, the
senior SS officer in Italy. Instead of waiting, Wolff's
aide ushered Grossmann into the magnificent office,
complete with rich mahogany furniture, and a massive
portrait of Adolf Hitler behind the general's desk.

The general wasn't sitting at his desk, however. He
and another SS officer were seated on leather chairs
pulled up before a small coffee table. Both men were
drinking coffee and smoking cigars, and they had the
familiar air about them of old comrades.

"Ah, Grossmann! Come in!" General Wolff casually
returned Grossmann's party salute and waved him to a
third chair at the table. "Grossmann, I'd like for you to
meet Colonel Wilhelm Mueller. He's a friend from the
Freikorps days. He was a medical student and I was a
demobilized lieutenant. We had nothing in common
but good times breaking the bones of Bolsheviks." Both
men smiled at the memory of the rough and tumble
days following the end of the Great War.

"Herr Colonel," Grossmann said as he took a seat.
He looked over Colonel Mueller and saw a man who
had gone soft over the years—his uniform was too tight
and fat bulged over his tight collar, but Grossmann saw
signs of intelligence and perhaps anxiety in his eyes.

As Grossmann began to pour himself a cup of
coffee, General Wolff said, "My friend Colonel Mueller
is a member of the SS Medical Corps, and has some
requests of us here in Rome. I would like for you to
help make arrangements. I have a meeting to attend, so
Grossmann, take care of Colonel Mueller's needs. You
can use my office."

Grossmann and Mueller stood up as General Wolff departed the room, and when they had taken their seats again, Grossmann asked, "What can I do for you, sir?"

Mueller laid down his cigar and leaned forward in his chair to talk. It was then that Grossmann recognized what he had seen in Mueller's eyes was not mere intelligence, but intelligence imbued with fanaticism. It was common in the officer corps of the SS.

"Yes," Mueller said. "Yes. I understand that are the general's special projects man. Yes?" When Grossmann said that he technically belonged to the foreign intelligence directorate but he took care of special issues for the general, Mueller nodded his fat head several times and again said, "Yes. I am a special projects officer too. I work for the SS Surgeon General on projects. Special projects. For the Führer and the Reichsführer. Projects that will help the Fatherland and humanity."

Grossmann nodded again as if to say, "Go on," while his nod was an outward reflection of his inward acknowledgment that he was right: the doctor was a fanatic.

"I am standing by to help of course, Herr Colonel. What do you need?"

The SS doctor didn't answer directly. Instead, he asked, "I'm glad to hear that. You know of Herr Professor Hans Eppinger? Yes?" When Grossmann replied that he did not, Mueller pursed his lips in disapproval. "He is one of the most renowned physicians and professors of medicine that I have ever met. It is an honor to work with him. Why, before the war, he even successfully treated Joseph Stalin and half the royalty of Europe."

Grossmann was tempted to say that perhaps it was regretful Eppinger was apparently competent, but he kept those thoughts to himself, and instead said, "Yes, sir. Now that you mentioned it, I think I've heard of him. He's Austrian, is he not?"

Mueller brightened, the disapproval gone. "Yes! He was born in the old Austrian Empire during Franz-Joseph's reign and he spent many years in Graz. He is a brilliant man."

Grossmann had never heard of the man, but most of the famous doctors he had heard of either came from, studied in, or practiced in Vienna, so it was a safe bet. "Indeed, that is the reputation I've heard." As Grossmann wasn't going to ask for a third time how he could help, he crossed his legs and sat back in his chair expectantly.

"Yes. Brilliant. Indeed. Yes, so here is what we need. Herr Professor Eppinger is doing experi...well...uh, studies. Yes. Studies."

Grossmann suppressed a smirk and decided to make the fat man sweat a little more. "Studies, Herr Colonel? Did I hear you right? Did you say experiments?"

"Yes. Well, yes. The professor is doing some brilliant analyses to further military medicine out of the medical sub-camp at Dachau. You've...you've heard of Dachau?" When Grossmann affirmed he had indeed heard of Dachau, Mueller said, "Herr Professor Eppinger is working on many, many projects, two of which you may be able to assist."

"Of course," Grossmann said. Just for fun he asked, "Are my services required in Germany? I am on the next train."

"No, no. Nothing like that. One experiment is straightforward. We are looking to test anti-malarial medicines, and I've brought a team of entomologists to do the collection of mosquitos and their contaminated water. All I need there is a security detail to escort them to the Pontine Marshes and back."

Grossmann jotted a few notes in a pocket notebook.

He smiled at the colonel and said, "Mussolini drained the marshes, you know, but our engineers restored it to, well, its natural state. I'm sure we can find you all the mosquitos you need. Consider it done. The team will have to skirt past the Anzio pocket, but we control the lines of communication to the south. Shouldn't be a problem, although we might be able to get your mosquitos from a safer area like Civitavecchia. I read a report the other day about rates of malaria among the troops west of Rome. Whichever you prefer, sir. What was the other project?"

"Civitavecchia? Yes. If you're sure. My other project...well, Herr Professor Eppinger is working on an experiment whereby humans can adapt to drinking saltwater...seawater..."

Grossmann was astonished. "Really? That's amazing. How's it going?"

"Amazing? Yes, it is. Indeed. Yes. Well, here's the problem. Many of the, uh, test subjects that we work with, that Herr Professor Eppinger works with, don't have the, uh, physical stamina to endure prolonged, you know, testing. Yes. Our test subjects have all died, and while we have a, uh, limitless subject population in the camps, they are simply too weak—I mean, let's face it: Jews aren't particularly healthy or robust to begin with, and the population in the camps are, well, disease ridden. Scurvy, rickets, pulmonary disorders everywhere one turns. It's quite disgusting. No, as every subhuman Jew we've tested has, uh, expired, we need to explore other avenues."

Grossmann shrugged, "Have you tested on Allied prisoners?"

"Yes. There's been some testing on Russians, but without success there either. But, they're half-starved by the time they make it to us, and it wouldn't be ethical to test on West European, British, or American prisoners." Mueller's eyes focused on the remaining coffee in his cup.

Grossmann suppressed a shiver and said, "No. I imagine it wouldn't. Are you looking for me to provide Italians?"

"Not yet. We discussed it of course, but we feel that might be impolitic. So, we have a bit of a conundrum. None of the prisoners can withstand the testing, and, unfortunately, we're limited to undesirables like Jews and Slavs. We could test on German homosexuals, of course. That would be ethical, but Herr Professor Eppinger is collaborating on a cure for that affliction as well, so we need them, you know, intact for other experimentation. So…we thought we might try Jews who haven't been confined yet and see if that produces better results, and perhaps Italian Jews might fit the bill better than Northern European Jews. Better diet, climate, that kind of thing. I would love to have access to American Jews, but we only get their soldiers, so even they are off-limits. So, Italians Jews, perhaps. Yes? It may not work as the obstacles are prodigious, but we must try, mustn't we?"

Grossmann nodded and said, "Yes, of course. If it's in the name of science…if we can, we must. It's my motto for wine and women as well, Herr Colonel. So, how many do you need? Test subjects, that is. Our capture and deportation of Jews is just a trickle, but I'm sure I can find you a dozen or so to ship to Dachau within the next couple weeks."

Colonel Mueller slumped in his chair, disappointed. "No. Herr Professor Eppinger said he required no less than one hundred subjects of good health and constitution. Some will have to serve as a control group, you know. I was really hoping you could help…

Reichsführer Himmler said you were a problem solver."

Grossmann suppressed another shiver, and looked at the glaring portrait of Adolf Hitler on the wall. He smiled without feeling the smile, and said, "Give me forty-eight hours, Herr Colonel. There may be a couple things we can try. In the meantime, I will arrange for a security detail to escort your scientists to malarial paradises, and if you like, I could recommend a few wonderful restaurants or cabarets to try during your stay."

1110 Hours
141st Regimental Bivouac Area, Qualiano, Italy

The briefings had taken longer than anyone wished, but Major Spaulding uncharacteristically got sidetracked by a discussion of combat loading for the ships. It was a subject that had to be covered but Perkin had hoped to wrap up his portion of the briefings first.

Major Spaulding had called for a ten-minute break to allow for coffee refills and latrine visits. Refreshed and more comfortable, Perkin once more took his position at the front of the room. "All right, gents. Major Spaulding made me promise to keep this short so we can finish up with the company assignments and operational planning."

Spaulding nodded his assent, and Perkin continued, "Everyone knows that Anzio is, as the boss said, a meat grinder. And we all know what happened: The initial landings took place while we were attempting to cross the river. They met little resistance coming ashore, and instead of seizing the high ground of the Alban Hills or pushing to cut the German inland lines of communication to the Liri Valley, or even sending troops to Rome, General Lucas, the VI Corps commander, decided to consolidate the beachhead first. I think it's fair to say that historians will be debating that decision for years to come."

"How do you feel about it, Perk?" asked First Lieutenant Frank McCarter, who was Sam's 1st Platoon Leader and as his senior lieutenant was his acting executive officer.

Perkin shrugged. "I hate to judge without being there, but for what it's worth, I think it was another Salerno but against better prepared forces. The expectation seems to have been that VI Corps would be aggressive and audacious, and once they severed Victory Road, the Germans would be forced to abandon their position at the Gustav Line for fear of encirclement. Okay, that sounds great in theory, but so did Gallipoli. I think pretty highly of Winnie, but neither Gallipoli nor Anzio were among his best ideas. Knowing what we know about the Germans, the thought that they would abandon their position without contest seems unlikely to me even if fortune favors the bold. If VI Corps extended too much too soon, they could have been split like we almost were at Salerno, and that would have been that. If they'd had sufficient forces, it might have worked, and the enemy might have been forced to withdraw from the Gustav Line. But, we didn't, so they didn't. The Germans were able to reinforce quickly and contain our landing, which makes the decision to consolidate under the umbrella of naval gunfire support seem wise. But, the decision to consolidate isn't without critics as well. An argument can easily be made that Lucas waited too long before moving inland...that his slow consolidation cost us the initiative and led to a four-month stalemate."

Spaulding interrupted. "We won't ever know which

was right. But I agree with that last statement of the professor's. It took too long. That might not be Lucas's fault, but he was the man on the scene, so Clark and Alexander shit-canned him, and VI Corps is now commanded by the professor's bridge partner, General Truscott."

Captain Finley-Jones sat up and said, "Excuse me? Bridge partner?"

Perkin laughed. "I hate to contradict the battalion commander, but Truscott wasn't my partner. I was playing against him. Helen and I arranged a furlough together on Capri, and Truscott was there on a medical R&R. While we were watching Mount Vesuvius erupt, we played bridge with General Truscott and Peggy Bourke-White. Peggy wanted to play strip poker, but Truscott was surprisingly modest for a corps commander." Helen was Perkin's girlfriend and an English nurse working at a British field hospital near Presenzano.

"Oh, sweet Jesus!" Finley-Jones looked around the room in disbelief, and when he saw that no one else understood, he sighed, "So, you know Margaret Bourke-White as well?"

"Oh yeah. Eric Sevareid too. He wasn't much fun, but Peggy's great. She took a bunch of pictures of Helen and me, and said she'd try to get us on the cover of *Life*." To groans from his audience, Perkin added, "I'm very photogenic, you know."

Finley-Jones leaned over to Sam and whispered, "He's got the prettiest girl England has to offer, he plays cards with our new corps commander, he got to watch a volcano explode, and now he knows the most famous photographer in the world. What I wouldn't give to be Perkin for just one day."

Sam grinned and replied, "Your ego ain't big enough

to handle a day in the life of Perkin Berger. Your head
might explode."

Perkin collected his thoughts and began again, "I'm
only going to give you the basic rundown now since
we don't know what our assignment's going to be yet,
and where we'll be placed along the line. As you know,
the Anzio-Nettuno lodgment is only about twelve to
thirteen miles deep at its farthest point from the sea.
If you were to put a compass on Nettuno and draw
an arc with a radius of, say, twelve miles, that kind of
describes the pocket the lodgment forms. The Germans
hold the high ground in the Alban Hills, also known as
the Colli Laziali, which is a group of smaller mountain
complexes, no higher than one thousand meters, to the
north-northeast of Anzio. It allows them observation
over the entire pocket, and they have some very heavy
artillery tucked away in caves in the hills, including, we
believe, two K5 rail guns of 280mm. Those monsters
hit the beach daily. They have a barrel about the length
of one of the main guns on the Iowa-class battleships
but with a smaller caliber and payload—roughly 500 to
550 pounds of high explosive. However, with their max
range of 40 miles they can cover the entire pocket. They
roll them out of the caves, fire, and then truck them
back in before we can begin counter-battery fire."

Realizing he was getting sidetracked, Perkin took
a sip of water from a canteen and said, "Going back to
the course of the battle, we landed there on 22 January,
pushed aside the area defense forces, carved out our
pocket and began to build defenses of our own. We
landed on D-Day with two divisions: the British 1st
Infantry and our 3rd Infantry, along with our 504th
PIR and British commandos. The Germans had about
the equivalent of a reinforced battalion in the area but
moved more than twenty-thousand troops into place

within twenty-four hours of D-Day, including an armored regiment of the Hermann Goering Division. By D-plus two, 24 January, the Germans had elements of two armies, the Tenth and the Fourteenth, in play with more than forty-thousand troops committed. In other words, while we're digging in, they're reinforcing and quickly. By D-plus seven, they had brought in seventy-thousand troops, and added another twenty-five thousand in the next three days. Some of the units were committed wholesale, others as pieces of ad hoc kampfgruppen, or battlegroups, like we saw in Salerno. Some of them, like the 29th Panzer Grenadiers, are units that we've faced ourselves. Others, like the 1st Parachute Corps and the Hermann Goering Division, are among the most highly rated units in the German Army. Furthermore, we believe that the Germans committed at least two Waffen SS regiments in those first few days. All of this was to hold us in check, and then prepare for the inevitable: a massive counterattack to drive us back into the sea."

Perkin looked out over the grim faces of the soldiers before him. Most were combat veterans, and had an appreciation of the ferocity of a German counterattack—he had lost count of the number that he had faced and repelled. "We tried beating them to the punch with an attempted breakout from the beachhead although where they thought they were going is beyond me. By the end of January, when Sam was feasting on squirrel nuts..."

"Acorns," Sam corrected.

"...during his vacation in an Italian palace..."

"In a derelict castle," Sam corrected again.

"...and Sergeant Kulis and Lieutenant Ryan were snoozing in the vineyards of Mount Trocchio..."

"In a mud-filled foxhole," groused Lieutenant Ryan.

"...and I was on death's door..."

"In a houseful of lonely women," Sergeant Kulis added, and the group started to laugh. The atmosphere was beginning to lighten.

Perkin sighed dramatically. "Hey, y'all...it's impolite to correct the briefer. The rules are when I've got the pointer, I do the talking." Perkin held his wood pointer out like a magic talisman. "So, where was I? Yes...VI Corps went on the offensive first, and while it was unsuccessful in gaining desirable ground, it disrupted what we believe was an intended German attack on the beachhead scheduled for 1 February."

"How do we know that, Perkin?" asked First Lieutenant James, the commander of Charlie Company.

"A couple different ways. Initially, the Germans were able to build up quicker than us. The disposition of their forces suggested offensive operations, not defensive, meaning their intent was to destroy us, not contain us. We confirmed that with prisoner interrogation. Our offensive didn't last long and we shot our bolt in two days. While supporting the 3rd Division, the Ranger Force under Colonel Darby was ambushed in an attempt to take the town of Cisterna. As I'm sure you know, the 1st and 3rd Ranger Battalions were completely lost, only six Rangers total escaped, and the 4th Ranger Battalion took fifty percent casualties in a relief effort of the other two battalions. Both the U.S. 3rd and the British 1st Infantry Divisions took heavy casualties, and our 1st Armored wasn't able to make much of an impact with only one regiment ashore. Our offensive was over in forty-eight hours, and forty-eight hours after that, the enemy went on the offensive and tried to collapse the beachhead from the center."

Major Spaulding interrupted and said, "It looks to me like all of the German offensives have basically been within forty-five degrees or so along the center of that arc that the professor described. They've conducted reconnaissance in force along the flanks, of course, but if they get too close to either the northern or southern coastlines, they become vulnerable to naval gunfire support—and we believe that after Salerno, they have a pretty deep respect for the volume of high explosives the fleet can throw ashore."

Perkin nodded and continued, "During the month of February, the enemy launched three offensives, each lasting less than a week. By the second and third offensives, it seemed they'd largely given up on a run to the beach, but were instead trying to force a reduction in the pocket. They had a few gains, such as the elimination of a British bulge in the lines west of Aprilia, but after some close calls we kept the lines largely intact. Meanwhile, we put more troops ashore. Our friends in the 45th landed and were pretty instrumental in holding the 2nd and 3rd offensives, and the 34th Division relieved the 3rd towards the end of the month. The remainder of the 1st Armored Division has come ashore as have more British infantry and a considerable amount of Anglo-American artillery. It's largely been a stalemate since the beginning of March and instead of large scale operations, it's more of a static campaign of small skirmishes, colliding patrols, and massive use of artillery."

Spaulding spoke again: "The professor and I went to the beachhead at General Walker's direction a week ago, along with some division staff officers. While they worked out port operations and our onward movement, Perk and I talked to some buddies from the 3rd Infantry, and Perk ran into a friend of his from the 1st Special Service Force. What they told us…well, I'm not going to pretend that this is somethin' it ain't.

It's gonna be rough there. Anzio is a little war of its own, and it's a war of attrition. The artillery is ungodly, and most of the work seems to be done at nighttime in underground bunkers like the first war. We have an advantage in the air, but it's contested. We've been able to use heavy and medium bombers in a battlefield support role—hundreds of sorties. I don't know if that's ever been done before but the good news is the air force is givin' 'em hell. The bad news is the Luftwaffe is still able to get through our pickets and bomb us at the beachheads and attack the fleet. Almost the entire pocket is under observation from one point or another, and the Germans have become very good at directing fires onto the slightest movement. And, just for fun, they shell the beachhead daily and the clearly marked hospital areas—whether on purpose or by accident, I don't know, but they call the hospital zone, 'Hell's Half Acre.' It's not an exaggeration to say that in the first time in military history, a wounded soldier would rather be in a filthy foxhole than on a cot with fresh sheets and nurses."

1245 Hours
Rome, Italy

Reposo, the Italian siesta that runs from one to four o'clock in the afternoon, was nearly ready to begin, and many Italians were heading home for lunch. They would sit around a sparse dinner table with their family and eat a simple meal with some kind of pasta lightly drizzled with either olive oil, or if they were lucky, a canned sauce. It had been a long hard winter, and Rome was now cut off from the hard wheat of the south, which was the best for pasta, and the citrus fruit of Sicily and Campania. Fresh vegetables were long sold out, but would hopefully be ready soon, and many families had optimistically planted small home gardens wherever the land was available. The more pessimistic Romans just assumed that should their little crops come to fruition, the Germans would merely confiscate them or their neighbors would steal them. Meat was likewise difficult to find. Beef was nearly impossible to come by, and when a meat was called beef, the odds were just as likely that it was horse, mule, or donkey. Poultry, pork, lamb, and mutton were also occasionally available, but not in great quantity, and only at vastly inflated prices. Those without means, sometimes, as Major Kemmerling suggested, resorted to eating the ubiquitous street cats. In the spring of 1944, Rome was slowly starving.

Douglas Grossmann had shifted from his uniform back to Italian middleclass clothing—his light gray suit with white shirt and a black tie and hat. He was sitting on a stone wall with his back to the Tiber River while he munched on a thick prosciutto cotto and mozzarella panini washed down with a black-market Coca-Cola, stolen from a U.S. supply depot in Southern Italy the previous fall.

The sun was still nice and warm, but not too hot, and Grossmann was still enjoying its bounty although it wouldn't be long before the sun was in his eyes. As he ate his sandwich, he kept an eye on the front entrance to the *Ospedale di Santo Spirito*, the Hospital of the Holy Spirit. There were actually two hospitals bearing that name that were side by side—the older of the two having been started the previous millennia, and the newer one was its modern replacement. Grossmann liked the architecture of the old hospital, but even the new hospital had an old world charm that the American in Grossmann appreciated. His eyes kept darting away from the entrance of the newer ospedale to admire the arches of the older when he saw his target leave the building and walk down the sidewalk toward the river.

Grossmann tossed the remains of his sandwich and the empty soda bottle into the river. He picked up his newspaper and scanned the front page. It was a local newspaper from Dusseldorf that was only two weeks old. He had taken it from General Wolff's headquarters as the headline read "Bombs on the Population, Prepare for the Invasion" caught his eye, and he was curious to read about the Allied bombing campaign. He read the classified reports daily, of course, and he was fairly surprised that the Dusseldorf paper's account of the recent bombing was relatively accurate. The disasters on the Eastern Front were being downplayed in the heavily censored press, but as every German was acutely aware, there was no sense pretending that the skyborne apocalypse wasn't unfolding.

Grossmann casually glanced around the edge of his paper from time to time, but there was no need to worry, his target was as dependable as a Swiss watch. Unless it was raining, he would walk to the stone wall at the steep bank of the river and smoke a cigarette. Then he would head to his aunt's home for lunch and reposo, and end his day in the Vatican.

Grossmann folded his newspaper, and walked up behind the man in a black cassock. He paused for a moment, and then a broad smile crossed his faced as he boomed out, "Hiya, Father!"

The SS officer's hail-fellow-well-met attitude wasn't reciprocated. The Italian priest started at the unexpectedly loud voice seemingly right behind him, and in the same instant, a very unpleasant association crossed his mind. When he whipped around to look at the unknown person, his face was already draining of blood.

"You!" the priest gasped. His normally intelligent visage had been replaced with a look of sheer terror.

"Yes, Father, it's me!" Grossmann's jovial attitude even deepened as if the man's horror was as amusing as a good joke told over a drink at a Bavarian beer hall. "I'm glad you haven't forgotten me. I don't know about you, but I hate to meet someone only to have him tell me we've already met. It's so awkward. How have you been doing all these weeks?"

"I...I can't help you," the priest stammered. He looked cautiously to either side and started to back away from Grossmann, but he stopped when the SS officer put a gentle restraining hand on his arm.

"Father!" Grossmann exclaimed. "I haven't asked you anything, other than, of course, to inquire about your health."

The priest said nothing, but looked around again, this time more anxiously.

Grossmann looked around dramatically as well, and then sighed. The smile returned. "Oh. I figured maybe someone was sneaking up behind me, but then I thought, for just a second, that you were going to run away. That would have been a mistake. I mean, don't get me wrong. You look fairly fit for a man of your profession, but let's face it. I'm an officer in the SS. I have to remain in peak condition at all times, and even if, say, I twisted my ankle or my shoe was untied or in the unlikely event you're actually faster than me, I doubt that you're faster than my soldiers who are watching us."

The priest looked around again, and shuddered as Grossmann casually put his arm around his shoulders. Grossmann pointed out a black sedan to his left, and then he gave a friendly wave to another sedan to his right. A blond man in civilian clothes offered a friendly wave and a smile in return.

"You know, I think I figured out what you're looking for. You're looking for my brother—he was with me the night that we first met. Yes?" The brother that was referenced had been an Abwehr officer named Gerschoffer, another German-American soldier fighting for the Reich. The night the priest had met Grossmann and Gerschoffer had been the very worst night of the priest's life. Captain Gerschoffer was killed at the battle of San Pietro in December at the hands of Captain Perkin Berger.

The priest looked at Grossmann and nodded silently.

"He's not here if you were looking to say hello. He's taken a posting at our barracks in Siena. My God, that's a beautiful city. Has he been by to visit your mother yet?" Grossmann asked brightly.

Again, the priest said nothing, but he stared at the ground and shook his head mutely.

Grossmann took the priest by the arm and nodded his head toward the path of the river walk. "Let's just chat while we walk, shall we?" As they began a slow stroll to the south, Grossmann asked, "We haven't seen each other for a while, have we? My associates have stopped asking you for information, and I suppose you believed that our collaboration was over. Yes? Well, I'm sorry to say that our working relationship is coming to an end, although I hope to remain friends to the end. I have no more need of political gossip from your colleagues in the Holy See, and, well, the thing is I think your usefulness has just about run its course. I'm just here to tidy up a few loose ends."

The priest stopped abruptly and looked at Grossmann with growing alarm. "You're here to kill me?" he whispered.

"What?!" Grossmann said in mock astonishment. Then he started laughing gently. "Father, you're not the loose end—what an imagination! No, it's just an administrative task, actually. Nothing more. Well...one thing. A little errand. Do you think you could run a little errand for me, and then, I'm sorry but I would have to say farewell."

"Do I have a choice?" asked the priest with just the slightest edge returning to his voice.

Grossmann looked at the priest and saw intelligence coming back to his eyes—the priest was regaining his composure. "Of course you have a choice. God granted us free will, did He not?" Without waiting for an answer, Grossmann opened up his newspaper and showed the priest the title of a front page article. It read "*Zu allem entschlossen.*"

"You can read German, can't you, Father?" Grossmann asked.

"Yes. It says 'Ready for Anything.'"

"Ready for anything? That's close, perhaps, but don't fret. German isn't my first language either. Let me ask you, do you doubt that the Reich is ready for anything? That the Führer hasn't considered every single path to victory? Every variable? All the permutations of fate? Of course...of course he has! All of Europe, the entire world knows that of course, we are ready for anything." Grossmann squeezed the shoulder of the priest—the very image of one friend offering advice to another. "But that's really a misreading—of both the man and the words. The real point is, and I want you to listen closely...the real point is Adolf Hitler isn't ready for anything. That suggests he's waiting for history to unfold before him, that he is some peasant soldier who is waiting behind the wall for the barbarians to arrive at the gate. No...to understand the Führer is to know that he is not a man to wait for the enemy to come to him. He isn't ready *for* anything—he's ready *to do* anything. He's determined *to do* anything. That's a better translation, I think. You must understand that the Führer has seen the destiny of our people, and nothing, not God nor man nor the daughters of Nox and Erebus, will deny him or Germany that destiny. So…if a man as great…a man of such historical significance as the Führer is prepared to do anything to win, how can I as an officer in the SS do less?" Grossmann offered another smile and a friendly pat on the back. "There lies the answer to the unasked question that is stalking you like a wraith in your mind. So…when I ask for your assistance…oh, here's your aunt's building…so when I ask for your assistance, don't assume that I'm not ready to do anything either. Don't think I won't be as resolute as the Führer. How could I in good conscience be less? Understand, my dear Father, and I must speak frankly to you now… understand that if you cross me, or fail in any way…I will kill your aunt, her children, their children, and my brother in Siena will most surely gut your mother and feed her entrails to the trash can kitties. I will publish the photos showing you raping my teenaged niece, and I will make sure the Pope himself has copies to keep as mementos of German friendship. And if you doubt my word or you think perhaps I'm bluffing…well, let me just share with you a little secret. And I have to insist as a friend that this remain between us…two months ago, at the end of that terrible winter, I was the commanding officer at the Ardeatine Caves."

Grossmann was unsure if the priest knew of the caves, but he was gratified to see the color fade from his face again. Grossmann then explained to the shaking priest what he needed and when, and as Grossmann looked back when he walked away, the Italian was on his knees in prayer, tears streaming down his face.

1600 Hours
141st Regimental Bivouac Area, Qualiano, Italy

The briefings had finally run their course, and the meetings broke up. Every officer present had a comprehensive understanding of the dispositions of both enemy and friendly forces, loading and off-loading procedures, the battalion's initial destination upon debarkation, and a thousand communication and logistical requirements. Everyone was mentally exhausted, but there was still work to be done.

"Waller, I'll see if I can track you down tonight at regiment," said Sam. "Bill, Perk, and I try to meet for chow every night, although it's usually hit and miss. But until then, I want to go over all this one more time with my platoon leaders and bring the NCOs into it as well."

"Sounds splendid, Sam. I'll head out now with you if you don't mind and maybe you can point me in the right direction back to regiment," Finley-Jones said.

Sam smiled. "Happy to. Just follow the smell of the latrines until it takes you to the mess tent, and then turn left. If you don't mind, let's head out now. Hey, Sergeant Kulis, why don't you walk with us for a minute and we'll get caught up?"

"Sir?" Kulis asked. This was directed to Perkin, who nodded his approval.

When everyone had departed the small classroom and Perkin was folding his maps, Spaulding sat on an old table and swung his legs like a child in a big chair. There was a long silence, which was broken when Spaulding said, "You know you can go if you want."

Perkin looked at his friend and shook his head.

"No, Bill. We knew this day was coming and Helen and I said our goodbyes a week ago. She'll be too busy to see me in any case. I plan to use the next day or two to talk to each platoon one at a time."

"What about?" Spaulding asked.

"Well, this is the first opportunity, really, since Paestum where we might see a real armored attack. I want to go over the tank profiles again and review the best tactics against each. I'd like to cover enemy aircraft profiles and make sure we don't shoot down any more friendlies. I just want to convey some of the lessons of the past six months with them. You know, crack-thump and that kind of thing."

"No," Spaulding said.

Perkin looked at him in surprise and asked, "What do you mean no?"

Spaulding shook his head. "I mean no, Perk. You've done your job; now let the company commanders, the platoon leaders and the sergeants do their jobs. You and I, our whole staff, spent a great deal of time going through the personnel assigned to this battalion. Every company commander I have has seen combat—at least one battle, and Sam has seen more than his share. A little more than half of our platoon leaders have as well. Our NCO corps isn't what it used to be, but all of our top and platoon sergeants have been there, and even if it's only a PFC, every squad has at least one combat veteran."

"I know but..."

"Let me stop you there. We can always be better. We can always find time to train, and new subjects to train. We can clean weapons, practice marksmanship, throw grenades on the range. We can plant mines and disarm them again and again. We can look at pictures of Tigers, Panthers, and Mark IVs and just to be complete,

Shermans as well. We've done all that." Spaulding walked to the window and stared out at a distant mountain. He cleared his throat, and said, "Although the boys that we landed at Salerno and the boys we lost since then will always be my boys, I'm lying to myself if I think that the Able Company that I commanded at Salerno was better than the Able Company commanded by Sam. You know, Perk, we made a lot of mistakes, and I regret every one that led to someone getting killed or hurt, but learning from those mistakes has been more valuable than the Louisiana Maneuvers or any of the training we did at Camp Bowie or Blanding. We had no fucking idea what war was about before we landed at Paestum, and some of the morons at 5th Army ain't figured it out yet. But, this battalion has had better, harder, more realistic training in the ten weeks since we left Cassino than we had in the nearly three years between when we were federalized and when we found ourselves first in combat. Don't you agree?"

Perkin was silent for a second, then he shook his head and answered, "Yes. Yes, sir, I do."

Spaulding looked back at his friend and walked back to the table. He sat and started to swing his legs again. "Do you remember the first question I asked you when we got off the line in February?"

"How to meet girls?"

Spaulding laughed, and the seriousness was gone. "Whether I asked for that or not, you keep explaining it to me, and I keep telling you that the Berger method only ends up with me gettin' slapped. No...I asked you whether you thought the combat effectiveness of the individual German soldier was better than ours."

Perkin nodded. "Sure, I remember."

"That's a hard question to answer because nationalism and pride affect objectivity, but you gave me the most thoughtful answer I could expect. You told me that you thought the Germans were overall better than us, and I asked you if that was simply due to combat experience."

"Yeah. My belief is that after you adjust for combat experience, that after we equalize for that variable, we're still playing catch-up to the Krauts. They're still better soldiers. I hate to say it, but that's my theory. It sure didn't make me popular." Perkin remembered the conversation well. Major Spaulding had vehemently disagreed, and another officer that Perkin had known for years called him a "goddamned defeatist."

"Well, hell, Perkin. Nothing you say makes you popular. But, I spent a lot of time thinking about that conversation. There were three things you said that stuck with me: Most importantly, you told me that you believed without a doubt that we were going to win the war and you explained it using the analogy of the Civil War. The South had better soldiers and generals at the beginning and the advantages of defense and interior lines of communication, but the North had the men and the resources, and the quality of the soldiers and generals surpassed the South over time. The second thing that stuck with me was your commentary on counterattacks. The Germans simply do that better, more automatically, than we do. They've driven us off every foot of ground we've taken from them more than once and they made us pay dearly to retake the same ground. We not only have to be better at preparing and defeating counterattacks, but we need to be better at doing them ourselves. Finally, the thing you said that really differentiates the German Army from the U.S. Army was leadership down to the lowest level."

Perkin laughed. "Boy howdy, that one agitated some folks. They thought I was saying Hitler was better than

Roosevelt or something, but I was trying to explain that the professionalism of the German Army was better than our own, even though our expansion began only a couple years after theirs. It's as if the German Army never lost the lessons of history in their collective memory, but somehow we have to keep relearning it. The American Army is almost all citizen soldiers. The Germans are just soldiers, even though we both started with an army of 100,000 in the thirties. Isn't that telling? We know they're not ten feet tall. They sure ain't Aryan supermen. They're not smarter than us, not more physically fit, and outside of tanks and machine guns, I think we have better equipment across the board. So, where does the specific difference lie? Well, I think it has to come down to leadership. We choose select people for leadership. I think the Germans prepare everyone for leadership. We give it lip service but they do it. We've seen Kraut companies effectively led by corporals and battalions led in combat by sergeants and junior lieutenants. They all seem to know just what to do when they suddenly find themselves in charge. I think that the adaptability and ingenuity of Americans in combat is unequaled by any army I've seen, but I've felt for a long time that we could be better in this regard."

Spaulding nodded. "After some soul searching, I agreed with you. You helped develop the training plan. We worked on all those things over and over again: sergeants commanding companies, corporals commanding platoons, privates commanding squads, and God help us, lieutenants commanding the battalion. Based on your recommendations, our boys aren't afraid to take command, and they know when in command, be in command." Spaulding stood and stretched. "Where were we? Oh yeah. I was just telling you your work is done for now."

"Thanks, Bill. I appreciate that." Perkin stretched as well, and then said, "I'd love to go up to see Helen, but no one else gets to see their girlfriend, so I can't really justify it."

"You don't have to. I got a note from the Division G-2 this morning. You're requested, but not required, to attend a meeting at Caserta at 1000 with the squid and spook crowd, I'd imagine. Take a jeep and Kulis, and if you have enough time, you can shoot up to Presenzano and maybe say hello to Helen."

1615 Hours
141st Regimental Bivouac Area, Qualiano, Italy

The three soldiers took their leave of Major Spaulding and Perkin, and as they walked away, Sam asked his Welsh friend, "Waller, do you know anything about figs?"

"I know everything there is to know about figs, Bear," Captain Finley-Jones said. "Why do you ask?"

"Do you know why they burn your mouth so?"

"No. No one knows that. It's one of the great scientific mysteries of the world, I'm afraid. I just know that you need to ensure that the fruit is ripe." Finley-Jones spied a familiar trail and not willing to be engaged on the subject of figs any further, he arranged to have dinner with Sam, said his goodbyes, and left.

As Sergeant Kulis and Sam walked along, Kulis observed, "It ain't exactly a challenge like time travel, sir. It's has to do with the uh…oh hell, I cain't remember the word for it, it ain't acid exactly, but…well, the Cap'n's right. Make sure they're ripe. Did you aholt of some that ain't?"

Sam didn't answer the question. Instead, he looked

down at the sergeant and asked, "When did you learn about figs? Back home?"

"No, sir. I ain't ever had figs before Italy. Cap'n Berger and I learnt about them while we were driving down the boot in September. He's become quite the aficionado, sir. He can tell you what type they are and the size of the tree they come from. You want me to ask him if he knows the answer to the mystery of figs?"

"Nope. That's okay. I might ask him myself sometime. Hey, have you seen Jim Bob?" The person in question was a twelve-year-old Italian boy who made a good living running errands for the soldiers of the 1st Battalion. He had been orphaned in Naples, and had attached himself to the Texans after their redeployment off the Gustav Line in February. Every time the battalion moved to a different training ground, Jim Bob had to be left behind, but he showed up a day or two after they had established a new bivouac. No one remembered his real name, but the boy thought that an all-American moniker like Jim Bob was heroic.

"He's usually around about this time. You want me to send him to you, sir?" Kulis asked.

Sam shook his head. "I'm gonna be pretty busy. Would you mind sending him on an errand for me?"

"Sure. Whatcha need?"

"I feel like some steamed crabs. Would you send him down to the bay to collect as many live crabs as he can?" Sam asked.

"That's a bit of a hike, ain't it, sir? There's a fishmonger down yonder who usually has some on ice. Want me to get some of them?"

Sam shook his head again. "No. I want them fresh—and I mean alive. However many he catches and whatever size will be just fine as long as it crawls with claws."

Chapter Two

May 16, 1944
0800 Hours
Highway 6, Four Miles South of Caserta,
Italy

The drive from Qualiano to the Fifth Army head-quarters rear element at Caserta Palace was only about twenty-five miles, but Captain Perkin Berger knew from experience twenty-five miles would take well more than an hour if the highway was clogged by the endless line of supply trucks heading from the port of Naples to the battlefields of Cassino.

At Sergeant Edwin Kulis's suggestion, they had taken a series of back streets through the slums and bombed out industrial areas north of Naples. Even though both men had taken this route before, it required a strenuous exertion of attention on both their parts to remain faithful to their route. They had gotten lost twice leading to recriminations, counter-accusations, and apologies.

"Ain't this the pink house, sir?" asked Kulis. "Shouldn't we have turned here?"

"Well, it's pink, ain't it?" replied Perkin. He was in an uncharacteristically grumpy frame of mind, and even though he knew the gist of the sergeant's question, he was being willfully and fractiously unhelpful.

"Sir," Kulis said with the dogged patience of a sergeant experienced in dealing with fractious officers, "Every third fucking house or apartment in this country is pink or faded red. Is this the right one?"

"I don't know. Is it the one with the broken door on the shithouse?" Perkin realized his unhelpfulness was in danger of become actively counterproductive. He sat up, looked hard at the pink house, and sighed loudly. "Yeah, this is the one. Turn here."

"Sir? What's wrong? Didn't sleep again last night? You ain't feelin' crapulous, are you?" Kulis had a pretty good idea of Perkin's ongoing struggle with the harder memories of the war. He wasn't the only one with those struggles that Kulis knew, and sometimes the encampment could get pretty wild when men woke up from a bad dream in an unknown land and reached for a weapon.

"Crapulous?" Perkin asked with the faintest of smiles.

"Yes, sir. I learnt it from Cap'n Finley-Jones. He said it's a more precise word than hungover."

"I know what it means, Eddie. No, I'm not feelin' crapulous. I didn't sleep well."

"Was it that scream about midnight? Jesus Christ, have you ever heard anything like it in your life? It gave me chills." It was indeed a bone-chilling scream that would have had the camp's roving patrols running to inspect the source had they not been warned in advance by Captain Sam Taft.

"No. I must have slept through that," Perkin said rather vaguely. Inside, however, he shuddered at the memory. He had been sleeping face down on a cot when he felt the crab crawling up over his blanket, up his neck and onto his head. That event had not produced the scream, but it had led directly to a vertical leap from a prone horizontal position, and when gravity exerted its will and Perkin came to ground, he landed on a fig, overbalanced, and fell onto an open gunnysack, which had almost completely discharged its load of crabs. Almost. That event produced the scream, and by the time the forewarned Major Spaulding had turned on his flashlight, Perkin was sitting in his underwear in a mound of mashed unripened figs while engaged in a full-scale battle with four foul-tempered crabs.

0905 Hours
Rome, Italy

Douglas Grossmann sat at his usual café and enjoyed a caffé corretto while he picked at a croissant, dunking the bread into a soft-boiled egg. Even with the connections on the black market that Grossmann enjoyed, fresh eggs were hard to come by.

He wasn't thinking about food or even about a drink or two. Antoniette Bernardi was on his mind. He hadn't seen her since last week, and he was getting lonely. Antoniette had gone with her parents to spend the weekend at a relative's lakeside villa in Umbria, and while she was due back that evening, he was unsure he would see her again.

It was just nervousness, he told himself. The war changed everyone's lives, and for some, it changed as randomly and as quickly as the toss of a coin. There was Allied bombing of the highway and rail bridges north of Rome and although rare, sometimes the bombings effectively reduced traffic from north to south down to a trickle for days at a time. Grossmann had needed to acquire a pass for Bernardi and her family to travel on the main roads as they were completely controlled by the German military and their Fascist allies, but that was an administrative task that had taken him just thirty seconds to accomplish. He even signed the pass himself. General Wolff's special projects man was a man to be feared and respected, and he had on occasion overridden more senior officers of the Wehrmacht when it conflicted with SS priorities. Or at least his own priorities.

Grossmann knew his anxiety wasn't just for Antoniette's physical safety. He worried deep down the time would come when she simply disappeared and was out of his life forever. He had seen her play targets like that—seemingly deeply in love and then gone without a trace the next morning. No note. No farewells. Grossmann had never been sure whether he was being played by Antoniette, but the majority, or a strong plurality at least, of both his heart and his intellect told him she was as much in love with him as he was with her. They were truly a couple, professionally and romantically, and they had begun making long-term plans over the past months—not matrimonial plans, but plans that kept them together nonetheless, and that was the most important thing in Lieutenant Colonel Grossmann's mind.

It would be difficult in the future. Grossmann believed strongly to the point of near certainty the days of the Third Reich were numbered. Even if the cross-channel invasion of the Anglo-Americans failed to materialize or just simply failed, the Soviet juggernaut could not be stopped. Not while Hitler called the shots in any case. Just as certain that Germany would lose the war, Grossmann was convinced that not only was the Führer insane, but his vaunted genius was a myth. The words Grossmann had spoken to the priest the day before were merely for show. Nothing provoked terror quite like an SS officer fanatically extolling the virtues of the Führer.

The key to surviving the war, and most important-ly, surviving the war with Antoniette was timing. He didn't know when the day would come—it wasn't close yet—but later this year or early next year, they would head to Switzerland. It wasn't easy to cross the border, and of course, he would be shot if caught attempting to cross without permission, but there were ways to get to the sanctuary of the Swiss Republic. Indeed, Switzer-land was infested with foreigners seeking to escape the war. American and British pilots on bombing missions over Germany regularly reported engine problems to justify an emergency landing at a Swiss airfield. The Swiss would duly impound the aircraft and intern the airmen until the war's end, but the internment was in name only.

Senior SS officers had maintained lines of com-munication to Switzerland, and Wolff's chief of staff, a full colonel, had explained some of the methods over schnapps one night. "We've been doing it since the be-ginning of the war. Illegal bank accounts of Jews were seized and the proceeds of the sale of Kike properties have been transferred to Swiss banks. Most went into the Treasury, but sometimes, it just seemed prudent to move monies to Switzerland. You know, for safekeep-ing. Much of the art we took into safekeeping has been further moved outside of the Reich as has much of the gold taken from the enemies of the Reich. The Swiss are accommodating, of course, and many a Swiss banker can rest easy knowing his family is financially secure for generations, thanks to this war." After a few more drinks, the colonel suggested, "You should get a Swiss account if you don't have one already. Come see me tomorrow and I can make arrangements for you, if you like."

The colonel had been very helpful—the SS was a brotherhood after all—and Grossmann had given him several bottles from his own personal stock of the wonderful '24 Chateau Haut-Brion in return. It had taken some work to convert his reichsmarks into dollars on the black market, and he had paid what he considered to be an unfairly exorbitant exchange rate. While his Swiss account was an investment in his and Antoniette's future, it was apparent his savings and his pay would not go far with such an exchange rate.

As Grossmann sipped his caffé corretto and he thought about Antoniette, he mused over the fact he couldn't remember if it was his idea or Antoniette's to make the move into criminal territory. The shakedowns and the outright theft of property and accounts were alien to him, but, morals aside, it had been a good idea. Kemmerling was a ready partner and being a policeman and a trained interrogator, he was good at telling when their targets were lying. That talent had led to several hidden caches over the weeks since Grossmann had been in Italy. Initially, they kept the fruits of their labors to themselves, but then the chief of staff stated openly that the Rome SS headquarters would be happy to share in their acquisitions. So, Grossmann and Kemmerling made sure a reasonable share was given back to the front office, and so far, it had been a mutually bene-ficial plan. Occasionally, interesting pieces of art had been confiscated and were passed to the general, and the colonel had a penchant for fine wines. In exchange, the SS headquarters resolved a few disputes with the Italian authorities, and they made it known Grossmann was beyond the reach of Italian law. It wouldn't have been possible in the old days, thought Grossmann, but the times were indeed changing. No one dared mention the impending loss of the war, but everyone could feel it even as they prayed for a miracle from the Führer. Catastrophe was coming to all, and only those who prepared would survive.

0930 Hours
Caserta, Italy

Perkin and Sergeant Kulis were led by a clerk to a smoke-filled office in one of the outbuildings of the magnificent Caserta Palace. Perkin always felt uneasily in awe of the building every time he went to the compound, and he hoped the building would survive the American occupation. Already, miles of telephone wire stretched from window to window of the palace and thousands of boots crossed its threshold every day.

Lieutenant Commander Jimmy Cardosi was sitting in a corner desk in the intelligence office. Although it was a space belonging to the Fifth Army, Cardosi had occupied the same desk since last November. He came and went largely as he pleased, and as far as Perkin could tell, Cardosi had no apparent chain of command.

"Perkin! Damned good to see you rednecks!" exclaimed Lieutenant Commander Jimmy Cardosi with an outstretched hand. "How are you, shipmate?" This question was directed at Sergeant Kulis who beamed at the recognition.

"Good, sir. How are you?" Kulis replied.

"I'm doing great," said Cardosi. "It's been a good week or two."

As Perkin shook Cardosi's hand, he noticed the naval officer did seem to have a lighter air about him than was normal. "What's up, Commander? You have the look of a man who is itchin' to tell a secret."

"I am indeed, Perkin. You guys come with me." Cardosi put out his cigarette, and he led Perkin and Kulis to another room in the same building. An American soldier was standing guard outside the room, and he came to attention and saluted as Lieutenant Commander Cardosi approached. The naval officer, being uncovered, did not return the salute but nodded instead.

The soldier, who seemed unfazed by the strange ways of sailors, knocked on the door, opened it, and said, "They're here, gentlemen."

Perkin couldn't hear any response, but the soldier opened the door and ushered them into a room with two desks, a large table covered in maps and photographs, and a collection of ancient folding chairs. Sitting on two of them were other acquaintances of Perkin and Sergeant Kulis.

The taller of the two men was a former FBI agent named George Hill, who was currently in the employ of the Office of Strategic Services. His shorter companion was an Englishman named Charles Ackernly, a representative of His Majesty's Special Intelligence Service, more commonly known as MI-6. Both men greeted Perkin and Kulis with broad smiles and handshakes.

After the pleasantries were exchanged, coffee was poured and the five men sat at the table. Hill spoke first: "Commander Cardosi, I think you get the honors."

Cardosi nodded, and said, "Thank you, George. We asked you to come here to share some information about our common friend, Douglas Grossmann. He's in Rome these days, and while you may think you've heard it all, you won't believe what that son of a bitch is doing now!"

0930 Hours
141st Regimental Bivouac Area, Qualiano,
Italy

Sam had returned to the Francesco Crispi Lyceum for a meeting with the battalion commander and his fellow company commanders. Major Spaulding was the last to arrive, and he walked into the classroom energetically and in a good mood.

"Listen up, fellas," Spaulding said. "No orders yet, although I was told to expect a tentative movement order sometime today. It should read along the lines we discussed yesterday. Be prepared to redeploy within twenty-four hours. When the day and hour is locked down, trucks will arrive at the battalion bivouac and we'll be carted over to the Naples port. We'll embark onto LSTs and LCIs, and God willing, the world's finest Navy will get us there safely. I still don't know where we'll be deployed once we disembark in Anzio, but I expect us to go into reserve initially dependent on the battle. Any questions?"

There were few questions for Spaulding. Everyone had prepared for movement, everyone was confidently sure of their orders, and everyone was waiting for the word to go. It was a familiar drill to everyone. Prepare and wait. It was the way of the army.

Spaulding dismissed the meeting but motioned for Sam to stay. When the room was cleared, Spaulding threw his head back and laughed. "Sam, I'll always be indebted to you for last night. I ain't laughed so hard since the incident in Agropoli. The professor was just gettin' a little big for his britches, and it was about time he had a good old-fashioned hobo beat down, and you know, I think it teaches a man humility to fight crabs in your underwear. Oh Lord, you should have seen the battle he had with them crabs—you don't think he'll reenact it for us, do you? It was truly more heroic than… uh…well, shoot, I'll have to ask him what it was more heroic than. I'm sure he's got an example tucked away already."

Sam grinned and said, "Well, it was worth a sleepless night for me then." Sam hadn't slept much out of fear of retaliation even though in the cousins' fluid code of ethics, they both knew Perkin had it coming.

0930 Hours
Caserta, Italy

Perkin, unaware he was the subject of a discussion twenty miles away, listened intently as Lieutenant Commander Cardosi began to talk.

"It shouldn't come as any surprise to either of you that we have elements in Rome, both OSS and MI-6. In addition, I have contacts in the Camorra that were willing to put me in contact with, you know, some of their colleagues in Rome that share ties to a family in Campania."

"You went to Rome, sir?" asked Kulis.

The naval officer nodded but offered no details. "After the massacre at the Gildardino farm, the decision was made in Washington and Whitehall that Grossmann couldn't be a top collection priority, but would be considered a target of opportunity. His name has been added to a growing list of assholes to be investigated after the war for war crimes, and so there's no longer any interest in trying to turn him. However, if we have the opportunity to kill or capture him we should take it, and my understanding is that D.C., at least, is indifferent to his survival—personally, I don't think they're anxious to try an American citizen as a Nazi war criminal.

Our personnel in Rome were told his name, rank, and description and were directed to collect whatever they could on him as other priorities permitted. Of course, military movement and intentions are the top priority and we had a blank spot of some weeks before we picked him up. There was a growing sense it was possible he'd been reassigned after the arrest of Admiral Canaris, or even detained himself. But that wasn't the case."

Charles Ackernly spoke, "Yes. Professor Berger, while Whitehall and your Pentagon might have other priorities, after the Gildardino incident, we weren't inclined to move on. We kept looking as the commander said, but we ran into a brick wall and all of our leads were dead ends. I don't mind admitting to a spot of disquiet when we couldn't locate him. Our chaps in Rome found plenty of Italians who could identify Grossmann, including the doorman at a flat he maintained, but none had seen him recently. We were getting ready to call off our assets, but based on some things that his doorman said, we decided to change the focus of our effort and look at his relationship with Antoniette Bernardi... kind of 'if the mountain won't come to Mahomet, Mahomet will have to go to the mountain' type thing. The doorman, who admitted to one of Commander Cardosi's underworld contacts that he had been in the employ of the Germans, said Major Grossmann was fanatical in his devotion to Miss Bernardi. He reckoned Miss Bernardi had him wrapped around her finger, and it was his opinion, that of the two of them, Bernardi was the more dangerous. So, based on that, and some corroborating accounts, we believe Miss Bernardi is his weakness, and he can always be found through her."

"Charles," interrupted Hill. "This is Jimmy's story, I think."

"Oh dear, yes!" Ackernly exclaimed. "Accept my

apologies, Commander."

Cardosi didn't seem perturbed at all. He smiled and said, "Don't worry about it, Mr. Ackernly. It's a team effort and you're certainly more eloquent than me. Please continue."

Ackernly turned back to Perkin and nodded. "It has indeed been a team effort, Professor Berger, and it's been a most invigorating project, I must say. So...we shifted our focus to Miss Bernardi, and it was a fruitful return on our investment. A few words about her first. We believe she is about nineteen or twenty, give or take a year, and I don't wish to sound judgmental, but she has a shocking degree of independence for a woman of her age. She maintains her own apartment in an expensive section of Rome, and, if you can imagine this, has her own bank account."

"Shocking," agreed Perkin with an inward smile.

"Indeed. Anyway, we put a surveillance team in the area. Actually, they were criminal associates of Commander Cardosi, who were willing to contract out to your navy. He keeps the worst company, doesn't he? Because they weren't professionals and we wanted to limit our exposure, we couldn't get twenty-four hours coverage, just six or seven hours of tracking Miss Bernardi per twenty-four hour period, mostly in the daylight, but after a week or so, Grossmann came round in the wee hours and knocked her up."

Kulis sat bolt upright, and exclaimed, "Holy cow! You must have a great source."

Ackernly frowned and said, "Come again?"

Although Ackernly seemed somewhat puzzled by Kulis's sudden interest in a fairly benign event, Hill understood and explained, "It's not what you think, Eddie. After months of working with Charles, I've found it's only the same language on occasion and then usually by accident. He means he went to her apartment and woke her up, not, that she's...uh..."

"Gravid," Perkin offered helpfully.

"Yes..." said the amused Hill. "As far as we know, she's not...gravid. Anyway, we picked up Grossmann for the first time early in the morning of March 22nd, and after that, our associates in Rome focused on him and dropped the coverage of Miss Bernadi. The next morning, Grossmann didn't return to his office in the Abwehr, but instead went to the Rome SS compound, where he has reported to work nearly every day since then. At best we have a periodic tail on him...we can't do it all the time because we don't have access to enough qualified Italians to do a tail without being detected, and he travels with a security detail in any case. But we've enough visual contact to know he usually moves about Rome in civilian clothes. We know his favorite cafés and restaurants, we understand his Italian is reportedly fluent with a perfect Roman accent, and, hold on to your knickers, when our teams have seen him in uniform, he now wears the uniform of a lieutenant colonel in the SS Security Service, the SD."

Perkin raised an eyebrow and said, "Huh...that's interesting, isn't it? He betrays Canaris and is rewarded with a promotion and a commission in the SS intelligence service?"

"Interesting indeed, Professor Berger," said Ackernly.

"Do we know what he's doing now...what portfolio he holds?" asked Perkin.

Ackernly and Hill's eyes turned to Lieutenant Commander Cardosi, who nodded and said, "Yeah. Grossmann's one bad California hombre. He holds the mass murder portfolio."

0945 Hours
Caserta, Italy

Perkin and Kulis stared at Cardosi in silence, and after a moment, Perkin asked, "Okay. How's that work? What are we talking? Not prisoners, surely?"

Cardosi shook his head. "Not that we know of. The SS doesn't have a stellar record of supporting the Geneva Conventions, but I've not heard of any involvement of Grossmann."

"What then? Jews, I suppose? Italians?"

"Bingo. Both, we think..." Cardosi was about to say more but Ackernly interrupted him.

"Taking the Jewish problem first; as you may be aware, Mussolini was resistant to deportations of Italian Jews prior to being deposed, and Italian officers refused to deport Jews in their areas of occupation in France and the Balkans. You can't deny that both of which required a significant degree of courage in the face of Nazi terror. But since the German occupation of Italy subsequent to our landing, Italian Fascist officials have cooperated with their Nazi masters. The deportation of the Jews is not on the scale of elsewhere in the occupied territories, but Italy had a smaller population to begin with. We believe there's been some assistance to Jewish citizens from the Church—not officially, of course, but similar in aspect to your cousin Sam. Altruistic and brave priests and nuns have risked everything to put Jews into safe homes and provide them with food and other necessities," said Ackernly with a touch of emotion in his voice. "I admire those people greatly, but for every good Italian, it seems there's one that cooperates with the Germans—out of fear I'm sure, but for some, I'm equally sure it's out of conviction."

"Do we know where they're being deported to?"

asked Kulis.

"For certain? No. Our speculation, though, is the Italian Jews who've been deported have been sent to extermination camps in the East, most probably in poor old Poland or maybe one of the larger concentration camps in Germany or Bohemia. The simple fact they're being deported from Italian concentration camps to elsewhere in the greater Reich says to me they are destined for either a death camp or a labor camp, which is effectively the same thing."

Perkin sat quietly as he processed the information, and then said, "It's unimaginable these things are happening in modern Europe, or it would have been unimaginable a few years ago, but from the things we've seen and heard, I have no doubt it's true. It was one of the things Patrick Riley and I talked about many months ago. I don't..." Perkin paused and shook his head as if he were trying to clear an unpleasant thought. He looked at Ackernly and asked, "So what's Grossmann's role in this?"

Ackernly shrugged and said, "Once again, old boy, we don't know for sure what Grossmann's doing, but our Italian sources believe he's possibly coordinating the roundup of Jews and their deportation. Rumors spread quickly in wartime, and perhaps even faster in Italy since they never seem to stop talking, but our sources say they believe soldiers under Grossmann's command have raided dozens of homes in and around Rome looking for Jews who've gone into hiding. The fugitive Jews are arrested and deported. Again, to where, we don't know. Their protectors, the Italian families, are either arrested or, and this is very interesting, fined."

"Why's that interesting, sir?" asked Kulis.

"Well, it's not the reported pattern that we've heard of from the undergrounds in Holland and France where families hiding Jews are treated quite harshly. They're classified as enemies of the Reich and sometimes executed on the spot or most frequently arrested, interned, and sent to a work camp. But, that's not what we're hearing about Grossmann. It appears their punishment is financial if they have means. They're given a certain amount of time to meet the fine, perhaps 24 to 48 hours. Normally, as enemies of the Reich, their property is simply subject to forfeiture and confiscation. The property would be liquidated and the proceeds would be returned to the Reich treasury," Ackernly said.

Perkin shuffled through the file on Grossmann resting on the table, and pulled out two photographs. The first was a distant photo of Antoniette Bernardi. She was walking out of what looked like a hotel or an apartment and she was tying a scarf around her neck. Perkin had forgotten what a stunning woman she was. He looked at the second photograph. It was an enlarged copy of Grossmann's senior picture from his high school yearbook from Coronado, California. He saw a happy, intelligent teenager—a good-looking all-American boy. It was difficult to square that picture with the emerging portrait of Douglas Grossmann.

Perkin tossed the pictures down and said as he stared at the smiling face of Grossmann on the table, "He's pocketing the money himself. It's a shakedown operation."

"Right again, Perkin," said George Hill. "The Jews are deported, presumably to execution camps, their belongings seized, and then the squeeze is put on their protectors. So far, it appears the only Italians arrested are those who can't meet the Grossmann fee, but we don't know for sure. That's supposition. We also don't know how much he's pressing them for, but I'd imagine it's close to their life savings."

"Okay, so the son of a bitch is a thief…it's not what I expected, but all right. How can we use that to our advantage?" Perkin asked.

Ackernly shrugged and said, "I don't know we can. It's just another datum for us to consider."

"What else do you have for us?" asked Perkin.

"George?" prompted Ackernly.

The former FBI agent had been standing listening to the conversation, but he pulled a chair up to the table and sat directly across from Perkin. "Well, there's one last thing, but it's the most important. On March 23rd, the day after we picked up Grossmann's trail at Bernardi's apartment, there was an attack on a unit of SS policemen marching down a street in Rome. One of the partisan organizations probably conducted the attack. We don't know for sure, but the Germans went berserk. A declaration was made that for every German killed as a result of partisan action, ten Italians would be executed."

"Go on," Perkin said intently.

"Over thirty Krauts were killed in the attack, so the Germans decreed over three hundred thirty Italians would be killed. And they were. Grossmann was the officer commanding the executions."

"Holy cow! Do we know this for sure?" asked Kulis.

"No. The information we have is third hand at best, but it was specific and there's even a slight irony in it as well. Grossmann and Bernardi came to our attention because they were running a honey trap against Allied officers in the areas we controlled. This came to us the same way. We have a source in an upscale brothel in Rome that has a mix of Italian and northern European prostitutes, and it's a favorite of locally stationed and visiting German officers. The girls themselves don't work for us per se, but the madam considers herself to be an Italian patriot, and she's on our payroll. She, in turn, has a Dutch girl and an Alsatian who are very good about getting their regular clients to talk—I think the Germans feel comfortable with blue-eyed blond girls, and they're lonely, and invariably drunk. So they like to talk about home or brag or complain about the war, but it's usually low-key stuff. When the madam brought this to us, she was excited and with good reason. One of her clients was an officer that was part of the execution detail, the revenge squad, if you will, and he spent a talkative night with the Alsatian girl. He was drunk and distraught and started crying in bed with this girl. Unmanly behavior to be sure but pure intelligence gold—a drunk German with a guilty conscience and no discretion."

Hill stopped, opened a file, and referred to his notes as he spoke. "Here's what reportedly happened… Grossmann was given the task of carrying out the executions. He had the SS jail in Rome emptied of political prisoners, and he rounded up as many Jews as he could find. When he didn't have enough, the Italian Fascist government coughed up a few prisoners of their own. But that still didn't bring him to his quota, so the Gestapo or the SD arrested several suspects for the bombing, and that wasn't enough either. In the end, Grossmann just snatched people off the street until they had their number including a fifteen-year-old boy. They were put into trucks and carted off to some caves where the SS carried out the executions. Interestingly, according to the madam, the execution squad was comprised entirely of junior officers, not enlisted men. When they got to the site, the trucks were emptied, and returned to pick up the next load. Grossmann established a rotation of officers to carry out the executions, and he ordered that the victims be brought into the cave five at a time. They were forced to kneel and were killed with a pistol shot in the back of the head. The original source of information, our drunk, guilty, indiscreet officer, confessed to his girl that he fainted the first time he went into the cave and had to be carried out. I don't know if he told her because it was true or because he thought it exonerated him somehow. He wasn't the only officer with qualms apparently. He told the girl about the commanding officer, Grossmann, who had brought a case of cognac to steady the nerves of the executioners, and he himself, reportedly got blind drunk before shooting several of the victims."

There was a long silence in the room. Perkin was deep in thought and Kulis watched the smoke come off his cigarette as everyone digested the news. Cardosi poured coffee into a heavily stained mug that was marked with "CA-35" in blue lettering on one side and the U.S. naval officer crest on the other, while Ackernly and Hill waited expectantly.

"When did we get this information?" Perkin asked.

"Within the last two weeks," Cardosi answered. "Evidently the girl was so spooked by what she heard, she didn't think it would be safe to repeat it. But she heard that the officer in question was transferred out of Rome, and then she brought it to the madam and from there to us. It's a slow process."

"And this doesn't change the calculus in Washington or London?"

"No. Their concern right now is really on the channel crossing and the establishment of a second front—as though you rednecks haven't been fighting here since last September. To the extent anyone outside of Italy thinks about this theater anymore, it's to wonder when Rome is going to fall, which brings me to the main reason that we asked you to swing by before the division redeploys to Anzio." Cardosi smiled.

"Why's that, Jimmy?" Perkin asked.

"Out of our little club here, I think you and Eddie are most likely going to get there first. The navy has other plans for me, and George and Charles don't go in on the first landing craft anymore. Therefore, if any of us can get to Grossmann in the near term, it'll be you. So, the real reason that we asked you here today is to give you this." He passed over a slip of paper.

"What's this, sir?" asked Kulis.

"It's a long shot—a real long shot—but it's the best we can do for right now," Cardosi said. "It's three things: the name and address of my mob contact in Rome, Grossmann's address, and Antoniette's address is there as well. Memorize and burn if you would. The army group staff is divided over the issue of whether Hitler turns Rome into a Stalingrad. You know, fight to the last man, but if there's a chance to get in before the Eternal City is turned to rubble, that's your best chance to find him. Like I said, a long shot, but speaking for all of us, capture the girl if you want, but for God's sake, gut Grossmann."

1335 Hours
Rome, Italy

Lieutenant Colonel Grossmann was angry, and was getting angrier by the minute. The priest was to have met him by the river walk at 1300 sharp, and not only was he late, but Grossmann had a growing conviction the priest was not coming. He thought absently about whether he was losing his touch, and he decided the priest was nothing more than a coward. Grossmann had explained in sufficient detail what would happen to the family of the priest if he either failed to deliver on

Grossmann's demand or if he simply failed to show. All Grossmann had asked for was a list of religious institutions or safe houses that were hiding Jews. He knew from his time with the church's underground railroad that Jews were being protected, and on church property. Vatican City grounds, of course, were off limits for the time being, but Grossmann thought if he could probably get away with a nonviolent raid on a monastery or a convent if pressed to do so.

Grossmann felt the priest's action, or inaction as it seemed to be, was putting him in an unfair position. He didn't want to hurt anyone, and he had nothing in particular against the Jews—he had never bought into the party's anti-Semitism. But orders were orders. He was the man not only tasked with finding the remaining Jews in Rome, but he was under implied pressure from Himmler himself to provide bodies for Herr Professor Eppinger.

Austrian, Bohemian, or German, it didn't matter where the lunatic came from, thought Grossmann. The illustrious professor was either a madman or a sadist—perhaps both—but Grossmann knew it didn't take a doctorate in biology or chemistry to know people couldn't adapt to drinking seawater.

He sighed as he thought about the complications this posed. Grossmann had no access to a cohort of healthy Jews that he could draw upon to meet Eppinger's requirements, but he knew where he could get at least a handful of test subjects.

Grossmann tossed his cigarette butt into the river and motioned to the head of his protective detail who in turn motioned to an unseen entity. A black staff car emerged from a side street, and to Grossmann's surprise, Major Kemmerling was sitting in the backseat.

"I figured you might be down here, sir," he said with

an honest smile. "I thought I'd come join you for the fun. I take it he didn't show?" Kemmerling slid over to make room for Grossmann in the back of the sedan.

"No. The asshole. Who the hell does he think he is?" Grossmann said with righteous indignation.

"Maybe he thinks he's protected from above?" Kemmerling offered.

"I'm losing count of the priests I've killed," Grossmann said. "What makes him special?"

"I don't know, boss. We have teams staking out both his aunt's home here, and his mother's house in Siena. No one warned them by the way…do you want me to send in the teams and eliminate them?"

Grossmann was silent for a moment, and then pulled a flask from his suit pocket. He took a long drink of the superb cognac, and handed the flask to Kemmerling. "Yes and no. Send the team into the house down here and arrest everyone. I want a photographer on site to take pictures of the arrest. Beat the hell out of any men that might be present, but if none are, choose the oldest woman. Get a picture of that as well. I liked the priest's mother in Siena so let's leave her alone, but I do want to take her one of the pictures with the caption, 'Your son did this.' Then, let's issue a warrant for his arrest and send a copy to the Holy See."

"What charge?"

"I told him I'd charge him with rape, so let's use that. I'll give you some edited pictures to have the Italian authorities take to the head of Vatican security. I doubt they'll give him up, but let's see," Grossmann said.

Kemmerling jotted down a few notes, and said, "What about the people we arrest here? A visit from the knackerman or a trip to prison?"

"Neither. They're headed to Dachau to volunteer for

an experiment that might benefit all humanity. I envy their sacrifice, and I plan to honor them by going to the office and preparing the extradition order myself. Before I kick you out of my car, do you have anything for me?"

Kemmerling smiled. "As a matter of fact, I do, Herr Colonel. I have an answer to a related problem. Fraulein Bernardi sent a note to the office with both our names on it. She sends her regards and wants you to know she'll return to Rome tomorrow evening. But in the meanwhile, she has a favor to ask. It seems her uncle discovered a large encampment of Romanis on the back side of his estate—hiding in the woods. It seems some kids came and begged at the villa, and ruined a dinner party. So she asked if we could send someone to take them away."

Grossmann's day was beginning to look a little brighter. He nodded and said, "Anything for Antoniette. How many?"

"She said it might take a lot of soldiers to get them to move. Her uncle's groundskeeper thought there were at least a hundred or more," Kemmerling said. He slapped Grossmann's leg with the back of his hand and said as if an idea had just occurred to him, "Say…now here's a bold thought, sir. You don't suppose that Herr Professor Eppinger would have any objections to doing some humanity testing on Gypsies, do you?"

Smiling for the first time that afternoon, Grossmann shook his head and said, "I doubt he would, Fritz. Want to meet for dinner tonight? My treat?"

1345 Hours
Caserta, Italy

Perkin and Kulis had concluded their day at Caserta. They had talked more about Grossmann and what their options might be, although those seemed limited to Perkin. They had then spent a couple hours with the Fifth Army intelligence team, and they left feeling more knowledgeable about the stalemate at Anzio if not more optimistic.

After lunch, Hill and Ackernly had said their goodbyes and left together to attend a meeting with the Fifth Army staff. Before leaving, George Hill had pulled Perkin aside and said, "As always, it's good to talk to you and get your thoughts on things. As Charles says, you have a quick mind. Here's the thing, Professor, both Charles and I would like very much for you to move past the tactical side of the war, and come work for me in the OSS. Look...I'm an old friend of General Donovan's. We worked together in the Justice Department back in the day and he recruited me specifically for this assignment. I know that he'd make your transfer happen on my word alone. What would you think about that?"

Perkin didn't hesitate. "George, I appreciate the offer and the vote of confidence more than you can imagine, but I can't leave the Gun Club. It'd fall apart without me." Perkin added with a smile, "I'm going to run for treasurer next year."

"Is that a fact? Well...other than being surprised by your organizational ambitions, I told Charles that'd be your answer. I was in the Great War, and I understand entirely. But I also know that the trenches lose their romance quickly. If you change your mind, it's an open offer." Hill gave Perkin a fatherly clap on the back, and then he headed off for his meeting.

Perkin walked out into the cool fresh air with Lieutenant Commander Cardosi while Sergeant Kulis brought their jeep around. It was a beautiful day, and the palace was the more magnificent for the sunshine and clear blue sky. The historian in Perkin looked at it in wonder, and he thought perhaps he'd never see its like again. The war always intruded, and even though he couldn't take his eyes from the palace, he had a question to ask Cardosi.

"Jimmy," Perkin said, "what were you doin' in Rome?"

"Between us girls?" Cardosi asked as he looked at the palace as well.

"Of course."

"My specialty so far in this war seems to be checking out beaches for amphibious landings..." Cardosi said, but he was interrupted by Perkin.

"Are we looking at Civitavecchia or something closer to Rome?" Perkin asked.

"It's a possibility, but I doubt it. We've lost most of our amphibious transport for the channel crossing whenever that might be. We've barely got enough to support Anzio's needs for now. We'll get you rednecks moved up there in a couple days, but it's mostly a supply, transport, and fire support operation for the fleet these days. The assault craft aren't sufficient to support another landing, and they probably won't be until we've established a lodgment along the west coast of France." Cardosi took his eyes off the palace long enough to find a pack of cigarettes in his shirt pocket. "No, I had another mission there. Meeting with some mob contacts about Grossmann, I already told you about, but that was just icing on the cake. The real reason was there's a professor that I went to visit in Rome. He taught oceanography at the Italian naval academy in Livorno until his retirement last July."

"Why did you need to talk to him?" Perkin asked.

"He's the expert on assaultable beaches in the Mediterranean," Cardosi said. "It's odd how little areas of expertise arise. I mean, even though Italy was hardly an amphibious powerhouse, he's the man. Even the Limeys, who think the Med is their personal lake, agree. You see, amphibious operations are very complex—maybe the most difficult thing the navy does, and my job is to identify beaches that have value and meet the requirements for amphibious warfare. It's not just a question of finding a good strip of sand. We have to look at enemy defenses, the seaward approaches—hopefully we have nice deep water up until we hit the beach—and then the beach gradient itself is important. Not too steep and not too shallow, and we need to know about reefs and sandbars and underwater obstruction and tidal ranges. Even if we find the perfect beach for naval operations, it still has to meet the landing force requirements. It's got to have good exits from the beach, and then access to areas of maneuver or lines of communication. If it doesn't have military utility, then it doesn't matter how good the beach is."

"So, if we're not lookin' to do a flanking landing around Rome, what were you talkin' about?" Perkin asked.

"Well, there are beaches in the Mediterranean with military utility other than beaches near Rome," Cardosi offered. "And I'll give you a hint. I'm headed to Sardinia for a two-month refresher course for a language. Any guesses?"

"Hmm." Perkin thought for a moment and said, "Well, you already speak Italian like a native. And you've hinted that it's in the Med, so, which is it? French or Serbo-Croatian? If you need a Spanish speaker, you can take me. Sam tries but all he can manage is border Mexican, which only sounds like Spanish."

"I'll keep that in mind should the need arise, but I'm

getting my French dumbed down to a regional dialect. I speak the Parisian dialect pretty well, but even there my accent needs work. I sound like an American Wop when I speak French, although oddly enough, not when I speak Italian." Cardosi laughed. "The professor didn't believe that I was American—he thought I was from Naples. He was a lot happier when he found out I came from New York."

"Was he helpful?"

"Very much so," Cardosi replied.

"Landings in the south of France then?" Perkin asked. "But this can't be the great cross-channel landing though, can it? I don't think we can wait a couple more months."

"I don't think it's the invasion. I think it's a subsequent operation. Possibly. Probably shouldn't even talk about it. All I know is that the navy is sending me to Sardinia to get some quality one-on-one time with a Frog émigré who was a former linguistics professor at the Sorbonne."

As Kulis drove up in the jeep, Perkin was imaging a massive pincer movement surrounding the German Army in France in a great battle of annihilation. He thought it would be the campaign that ended the war, and he said a silent prayer asking God that he be allowed to see it.

Kulis called out from the jeep, "Sorry, sir. But we need to get movin' along."

Perkin nodded, turned and offered his hand to the naval officer. "Well, enjoy Sardinia, my friend. Maybe we'll meet down the road," Perkin said.

"I hope so, Professor. You rednecks take care in Anzio, and for God's sake, keep your head down, shipmate."

1400 Hours
141st Regimental Bivouac Area, Qualiano,
Italy

Sam and Bill Spaulding stood a dozen yards apart in the deserted schoolyard and threw a baseball back and forth. They had been doing so for the better part of an hour. They'd toss the ball for a few minutes and then stop to talk. It was one of the few times that Sam enjoyed being a soldier.

All around the encampment, soldiers were checking and rechecking their gear. Sam had cleaned his rifle twice in the past two days even though it was spotless to begin with—it was force of habit and nervousness combined.

The order to load the division was delayed. Sam didn't know why, nor did he care. Part of him was anxious to move on because every battle won was a step closer to home, but another part of him was fine with the delay as if magically the war might be over before they went into combat again. There were soldiers who were itching to fight, mostly new soldiers, but Sam had never been one of them. He had seen hard fighting at Salerno and San Pietro, and he'd been taken prisoner on the far bank of the Rapido River. That experience alone was enough for a lifetime, he thought.

The confusion on the Rapido had weighed heavily on Sam's mind since the failed crossing four months earlier. He understood the notion of the fog of war, but this was something else. The soldiers weren't trained for a nighttime river crossing, let alone while under fire, and Sam thought the division had shown weakness in night fighting. He was by no means the only officer to come to that conclusion, and while the division dramatically intensified its nighttime training, the battalion had pushed even harder.

Over and over again, the battalion trained small unit tactics in the dark, up and down the Italian mountainsides. Scouts from the exceptional 91st Cavalry Recon Squadron were brought to their training areas and soldiers who had little experience in fighting at nighttime were taught how to move silently and with confidence by battle-hardened professionals. Sam believed confidence was the key. The division had gained a reputation as a hard luck unit, and Sam had heard from Bill Spaulding that the 36th was not highly rated by the Fifth Army staff. He would have given a month's pay to see one of those staff officers armed with a rifle, trying to cross that bloody river on a single footbridge while under preregistered artillery fire, or up on the mountain in the weeks following where the conditions and the fighting were as bad if not worse. The 36th had been ordered to do the impossible in the hardest fighting in the European theater, and men who were safely out of harm's way now had the balls to criticize their performance? Sam got angry every time he thought about it. *I'd like to see them say something directly to my face*, he frequently thought, and just as frequently he told himself, *we just need one hard fight on our side of the ledger to redeem ourselves and it won't be an issue ever again.*

"Bill?" Sam asked.

"Yeah?"

"Do you think Rome will be an open city?"

"Nope," Spaulding said. "Do you?"

"Some people relax a little as they add on years but I ain't seen any sign that Hitler's gettin' any more reasonable with time," Sam said.

"No. I don't suppose he is." Spaulding tossed the ball back to Sam. "Is there anything in particular on your mind?"

"Well, other than thinking I'd rather go to a rodeo in Fort Worth than see Rome in peacetime, I was thinking about Ortona." Sam had been a member of a small party that witnessed the end of the Canadian battle for the Adriatic town.

"What about Ortona? That it's supposed to be lovely this time of year?" Spaulding stuffed a huge wad of tobacco in his cheek, and then wound up and threw the ball to Sam like a pitcher.

"I ain't heard that, but I was also thinking about our training these past two months," Sam said. Spaulding looked attentively at Sam, so he continued, "Since comin' off the line, we've been training to fight in the mountains again...not just a little bit either. It was the hardest training we've done and mountain warfare was to the exclusion of just about everything else."

Spaulding threw Sam a grounder, which he fielded and returned. "So you're afraid that Ortona, a street fight, is what we should have been training for?"

"Well, it seems to me that we never train for the next fight, we train for the last fight. Look, we were in the swamps of Louisiana and then the North African desert training our asses off, so when we were finally deployed we fought in so many ranges of the Southern Alps, I've forgotten their names. Now we've trained our asses off in the Southern Alps and we're headed for the Anzio plain—and maybe a street fight in Rome." Sam caught the ball and threw a pop-up for Major Spaulding.

"When you say it like that, you make it sound like the army doesn't have your best interests at heart there, Bear," Spaulding observed. He lost the ball in the sunlight and ducked as it almost hit his head. Sheepishly, the major picked up the ball and threw it to Sam.

"Well, that's hard to believe, ain't it?" Sam laughed

as he caught the ball and returned it to Spaulding. "It's kinda like what we're doing now...practicing baseball when our next game is going to be football."

"Well, it's baseball season. Got any thoughts on street fighting?" Major Spaulding asked.

"Yeah...maybe. I was thinking we need to find the sweet spot," Sam said.

"Whaddya mean, sweet spot?"

Sam collected his thoughts and said, "Well, we haven't been in a real street fight yet...and that pretty much goes for the whole U.S. Army, since...well, I don't know, I'll have to check with Perk. The Canadians and Brits have a bit more experience, but not much. The Russians have a lot more, and unfortunately, the Germans have the most of all. When the Canucks took Ortona, I don't think they had any particular city fighting doctrine, but they did pretty well in a pickup game because they were innovative and aggressive and weren't afraid to destroy everything in their path. But they took heavy casualties. When Fifth Army tried to take Cassino with the 34th, they got bogged down because there was no element of surprise and we were pretty methodical and straightforward in our approach. I'm thinking that slow and cautious, waiting for supporting fires to come to bear, gives the Krauts time to adjust their defense and forces us into a battle of attrition—like the Russians did at Stalingrad or the Krauts at Cassino. The pictures I've seen of those places looked like any of them towns that was in the way of the fighting in the first war. But if we come screamin' in like Comanches on war ponies, we open ourselves up to ambush and German supporting fires, and I'd think, a rapid loss of command and control. I'd like to think there's a sweet spot between the two."

There was a long silence between the two men while

they tossed the ball back and forth. Major Spaulding had many of the same concerns about urban warfare as Sam, but it seemed there was never enough time to work out the problems. Finally, Spaulding said, "When Perk gets back, let's put our heads together and think through how we might do this if necessary."

Sam nodded. "Sounds good. I reckon we're gonna have to deal with it sooner or later. Waller told me last December that Ortona was like a laboratory of urban warfare, and he said there was a million hamlets and villages and cities between us and Berlin."

"What's a hamlet?"

"I asked Waller the same damn thing but he said it's just a small village. It's an unnecessary distinction if you ask me but I just said it to sound smart." Sam smiled as he threw the ball back to Spaulding.

"It's workin' for you, Bear." Spaulding caught the ball and held onto it as he said, "So, now you got me worried. Why can't we just fight like civilized men in a nice wide-open space like between Amarillo and Lubbock?"

1430 Hours
British 8th Field Surgical Unit, Presenzano, Italy

It had been several weeks since either Sergeant Kulis or Perkin had made the drive up the peninsula to Presenzano, but the little village perched on the hillside had changed. In January, when they had first come to the village, it seemed the war was in the past for Presenzano. It had been damaged in the fighting as the armies headed north along Victory Road, but the damage was not nearly as extensive or permanent as in San Pietro only a few miles to the north.

The British Eighth Army was now established firmly in the plain that ended at the foot of Presenzano, and Perkin could hardly navigate through the congestion of trucks, tents, and anti-aircraft batteries. An Indian sentry barely glanced at Perkin's travel orders, which he had written to include Presenzano, and their jeep was waved through with a tired salute from the turbaned Sikh guard.

The location of the 8th Surgical Unit was unchanged since it had moved into the area in February, but it was busier than he had ever seen it—and he had made the trip north at every opportunity he could manage. Sergeant Kulis was careful to stay out of the way of the ambulances constantly moving in and out of the hospital area, and when he found a place to park, it was more than one hundred yards distant.

"Do you want to come along?" Perkin asked of Kulis.

"I'd like to, sir, but I'll stay here. I don't trust any of these fuckers. They'll steal our jeep, allies or not. Besides I can stay busy." Kulis reached into the back of the jeep and pulled out a book from his gas mask bag—the mask usually being the first discarded item of every soldier who found himself in wartime Europe.

"Whatcha readin'"? Perkin asked.

"*A Ship of the Line* by C.S. Forester," Kulis said. "It's about an English sea captain in the Napoleonic wars. I think it's the second book in a series, but it's the first one I've read."

"Is it any good?" Perkin asked.

"Yes, sir. I like it a lot, although I got a British version so about half the words are spelt wrong. Listen to this, 'God damn and blast all you ham-fisted yokels!' That's damn good writing! I'm thinking about trying that out on some of the new soldiers and seein' how it works," Kulis said with a grin.

"Let me know how it goes," Perkin said as he slung his Thompson over his shoulder. "I won't be long, then we'll head up to the house."

Perkin looked back at the jeep after a few steps and Kulis was already deep in his novel. He stopped to let two green Katie ambulances speed past him, and as he approached the large surgical tent where Helen worked, Perkin saw a scene of seeming disorder, although he knew better. Ambulances were pulling up and four stretchers would be lifted out of each ambulance and laid on a shaded grassy area, where nurses were triaging the patients—deciding where and in which order wounded soldiers would be treated.

Perkin approached slowly and watched the medical machinery in action while his professional ear listened to the distant boom of artillery. A hell of a fight was going on just ten miles up the valley and it was obvious that the field hospital was simply trying to keep up with the wave of casualties. Perkin knew he would only get in the way if he tried to see Helen and he was turning away to head back to the jeep when he heard a sharp whistle followed by a New Zealand accent: "Hey, Yank! Give us a hand here, mate!" It was an orderly who was waiting for a partner to lift a stretcher from the back of an ambulance.

As Perkin jogged over to the ambulance, he moved the sling of his Thompson over his head and across his chest so it wouldn't fall off, and he hopped into the back of the ambulance with the orderly.

"Take that side, mate," ordered the New Zealander. He indicated with his head that Perkin should head toward the front of the ambulance.

As Perkin walked forward he saw that the ambulance held four stretchers on racks with two on each side stacked up like bunk beds. The floor of the vehicle was wet with blood, and Perkin noticed a steady drip of blood from one of the wounded men. Perkin looked at the orderly and said, "This one first."

They lifted the stretcher off the rack and the orderly managed the transfer of the stretcher to two more men on the ground who had run over to help unload the wounded. Perkin could see the fatigue on their faces, and although it was a cool day, both men were in shirt-sleeves and sweating. Perkin helped lift the other three stretchers from the back of the truck, and he hopped out with the orderly as another ambulance pulled up.

"Lend us a hand with this one," the New Zealander said. "Appreciate the help. It won't be long. My mate has the trots and had to find a long-drop."

Perkin thought for a second and then laughed as he deciphered the meaning.

The orderly laughed as well, but said, "It's not funny. Poor bugger's got it so bad he's thinking of cutting the seat out of his trousers to make it easier. Why he's...oh Christ, you're an officer."

"Hard to believe, but that's what my paperwork says. Cap'n Berger, 141st Infantry." Perkin offered his hand.

After a moment's hesitation, the soldier from New Zealand shook Perkin's hand and said, "Good to meet you, Captain. Lance Corporal Thompson. I'll get one of the blokes to help me." Thompson looked around until he saw some other soldiers smoking cigarettes, and he called out, "What the fuck are you standing around for while this American officer does your bloody job?"

One of the soldiers called back, "He can have it, I don't mind!" The soldier tossed his cigarette on the ground and trotted over. He offered Perkin a smile and a casual salute and hopped into the next ambulance to arrive. Other orderlies came by to assist, and Lance Corporal Thompson gestured with his head for Perkin to move out of the way.

"Is there anything I can do for you, sir?" Thompson asked.

"No, thanks. I have a friend here that I came to say hello to…Lieutenant Langley," Perkin said.

Thompson's faced dropped and he shook his head. "She left yesterday morning, sir, for England."

Perkin's heart fell. They had said their goodbyes already, but he was hoping to see her for at least a moment. "Oh shit," Perkin said. "Do you know if she's…"

He was interrupted by a woman's voice. "Perkin?" He turned around and saw the tallest woman he'd ever known, Captain Sylvia Midgley—Helen's best friend. Perkin was shocked at her haggard appearance. She was wearing fatigues that barely reached the top of worn boots and her clothes were splattered with blood. She had deep circles under red eyes, and she looked as if she'd been crying.

"Sylvia…," Perkin started to say, but he unexpectedly choked up. He hadn't realized how much he was looking forward to seeing Helen.

"Oh, Perkin." It looked like she was going to say something and then she changed her mind. "You came for Helen…you've heard she's gone home then?" Sylvia gestured to Perkin to join her as she walked along a row of stretchers laid on the ground. "Tommy…this one first." She pointed to a young German soldier whose stomach was covered with a mass of bloody towels. "We opened up a wounded Jerry yesterday. Abdominal wounds. We found a score of worms—five or six inches each—just twisting around his abdominal cavity. He was just filled to the brim with parasites."

"Jesus Christ!" Perkin exclaimed. He wanted to

hear more about the worms, but he had to ask about Helen first. "Is Helen okay? She wasn't evacuated, was she?"

"No, dear, her father was wounded in the Baby Blitz last month, and then had complications this past week. She arranged an emergency leave to go home to see him," Sylvia said.

"Is he going to be okay?"

"I don't know. It was serious enough that our chief of staff let Helen leave during all this…" Sylvia glanced at the men on the ground. "She wasn't going to go at first, but we talked her into requesting an emergency trip home. It's important to see your loved ones while you can." Sylvia's face hardened for a moment as she looked at a wounded soldier on a stretcher.

"What happened?" Perkin asked.

"There was an air raid and he didn't get to a tube station in time. The poor man was trapped under a collapsed building for a day—just dreadful. The injury itself wasn't so bad, not by these standards anyway." Sylvia gestured to the soldiers lying before her on the ground. As she knelt to look at a soldier in a British uniform, she said, "He had a concussion and a broken femur. Nothing to be alarmed about at first, but he developed an infection in the bone. If they had access to penicillin, he would be all right, but it's all diverted to us. But without antibiotics, it's a toss of the coin. It was all very fast, Perk. She found out one day, and was gone two days later. Helen tried several times to ring you but they just couldn't make the connection. She was so sad she didn't get to tell you she was leaving, but she told me that she would write from London."

"Oh hell," Perkin said. "Every time we said goodbye, it was with the understanding that it might be months before we'd see each other. I know y'all are busy, but I just hoped…oh hell, what am I saying? What can I do to help?"

"Nothing, Perk. We'll manage—one foot in front of the other, you know. It's what we do here." Sylvia pointed to an unconscious soldier and spoke to the orderly. "Tommy, move this one up to next and we'll see if we can save that leg."

"Yes, ma'am. What about these blokes?" Lance Corporal Thompson looked at two badly wounded soldiers in a uniform Perkin hadn't seen before. They were both unconscious and the blood-soaked sheets covering their chests barely moved from their shallow breaths. Perkin had spent enough time on the battlefield and at field hospitals to suspect from their pallor that their time was drawing close.

Sylvia lifted the sheets and looked briefly at both men. She shook her head slowly, a silent conversation with orderlies that she'd had many times before, and said, "Let's keep them comfortable, the poor dears."

The orderly responded, "Yes, ma'am," but he moved to help those he thought might live. Sylvia didn't correct him.

"Sylvia, are you doing okay? How bad's it been?" Perkin asked as he watched more ambulances drive up, the whining gears not quite drowning out the far-off sounds of combat.

Sylvia ducked her head so Perkin couldn't see her face, and she said with a slight tremor in her voice, "It's been…it's the worst week. But, I'm fine, thank you for asking. It doesn't matter about me. It's only these boys who count, God bless 'em. Our chief of staff said that Eighth Army casualties have been over four thousand this week alone."

"My God! Are you sure I can't help…hey, wait, what about a blood donation? I have the magic blood, you know," Perkin said and then added modestly, "Sam does too, but mine's better of course."

"Magic blood? What are you talking about... are you O-negative?" Sylvia asked as she deciphered Perkin's meaning. "Absolutely we could use it. When did you last donate?"

"They wouldn't let me donate after I was wounded," Perkin said. "They said I'd lost more than a couple donations worth, but I should be good now. That was back in January."

"Orderly!" Sylvia called out, and another soldier walked tiredly over. "Take Captain Berger in for a blood donation. Tell them to type it, but he says it's all-American type O-negative." She looked at Perkin with a wan smile and said, "Jolly good. We're almost down to plasma. If you do nothing else today, you might save a life. That would mean the world to me."

1515 Hours
Presenzano, Italy

Chairs had been brought outside and Perkin sat with what he called his "extended Italian family" in the sunshine. The nominal head of the family was old Dr. Bonucci whose blindness prevented him from enjoying the view from the mountainside village, but the house belonged to his daughter, Angela Frattini.

"I'm so glad you were able to find a new home," said Perkin. "I absolutely love it." The Italian family had been living in caves beneath the village of San Pietro when Perkin had first met them. When the battle had passed their village, the people of San Pietro had emerged from the caves to find everything destroyed. Not a house emerged unscathed, and the village, which had thrived in the shadow of Mount Sammucro for more than a thousand years, was given up as lost by its citizens. A new village bearing the same name was being planned for several hundred meters away, but no one was confident enough in the fortunes of war to begin building their new homes quite yet. Some people had moved to displaced persons camps. Others, like the Bonucci family, had moved in with relatives. Only a few months earlier, the Bonucci family had been refugees living in a relative's home in Presenzano with twenty other people. Now, they had bought a home of their own in the village overlooking a sea of medical and command tents.

"We wouldn't be here without you, Capitano," Stefania Frattini said. Stefania was a precocious thirteen-year-old who had adopted a handful of American soldiers, including Perkin and Kulis, as her own. She was sitting on the ground playing poker with Sergeant Kulis.

"Honey, I didn't do anything," Perkin protested. He had in fact introduced Stefania's mother to Helen Langley, who was able to persuade the 8th Surgical Unit to hire Angela as a nurse working the mid-watch at the field hospital. Angela was getting ready to go to work.

"That's not what Mama says," Stefania said. She was about to say more to Perkin when her attention was suddenly diverted back to the game. "No! You no can cheat me, Eddie Kulis. You told me a full house beats a flush. Give me back my centesimi!"

A grinning Kulis tossed several small stainless steel coins back into the kitty. "My mistake," he said, and he grinned even more when she leaned across the cards and punched him on the shoulder. "I guess I forgot."

"You forget nothing except to no cheat an Italian woman!" Stefania grinned back. "Don't forget that! Capitano? When will the war be over?"

Stefania's smile was gone, and Perkin knew she was thinking of her father who had been involuntarily conscripted into a German labor battalion.

"I don't know, honey. A year or more I would think. The generals always tell you it'll be over by Christmas, but they don't tell you which one," Perkin replied.

Dr. Bonucci had been listening and he smiled at the exchange between the card sharps. He lit an old meerschaum pipe and said, "We have this conversation every day, my friend. We want the war to be over so we hope it'll be tomorrow or at least by Christmas. I don't think the Germans will lose that quickly."

"No, I don't either. But they'll lose." Perkin was about to say more on the war, but Angela had walked out of the house and joined the group on the front lawn.

Angela Frattini had always seemed careworn to Perkin, but there was a new radiance about her now that she was working. "Perkin, will you walk with me down to the hospital compound?" she asked with a smile.

"I'd be happy to. Eddie, bring the jeep down in fifteen minutes. We need to get back to Naples." Perkin walked over to Dr. Bonucci, reached down, and took his hand. "Sir, I don't know when we'll be able to come back, but I will try. Please take care of all these women for me."

"At my age, they are here to take care of me," the old man cackled. In a voice so low that no one but Perkin could hear, Bonucci said, "I can tell you're leaving from the tone of your voice. Please be careful, my friend, and come back when you are able. Thank you for all you've done for us."

"No, sir. Thank you for all you've done for me. I'll see you when I can." Perkin shook his hand, and turned to Stefania. "All right, sweetie, give me a hug."

Over the months, Stefania was always stoic about

their goodbyes, so she hopped up and kissed him on both cheeks. Stefania stepped back, looked Perkin in the eyes, and said in a stern commanding voice, "Kill every German and bring my papa home."

"That's the plan, darlin'. Eddie, fifteen minutes sharp."

As they walked down a road toward a steep set of stairs, Angela held onto Perkin's arm. It was nice for both of them to have a little friendly contact with the other sex. There was no talking for a few minutes, and then Angela said, "I'm sorry that you missed Helen."

"I am too. I hadn't counted on a visit up here, but it seemed like a nice chance to see her. Did you have much of a chance to work together?" Perkin asked.

Angela shook her head. "No. I'm not a surgical nurse like she is. I just take care of the men after surgery, so I didn't get to see her much. But she was always very nice to me. Did you know that every man in the hospital is in love with her?"

Perkin laughed. "I don't doubt it. I get four or five death threats a week by mail."

Angela looked at him in alarm and then smiled. "You kid?"

"Yes, I kid," Perkin said.

"Well, you should be flattered. She's in love with you. You're in love with her. The doctors are jealous of you, and the other nurses are jealous of her. You're a favorite with the nurses, you know. All the other girls ask about you or Cugino Orso all the time." Angela smiled. "I'm married and I miss my husband so much, but I wish the girls could see me on your arm. A little jealousy can make a woman feel good about herself."

Perkin laughed. "You want me to carry you into the OR and plant a big kiss on you in front of all the girls? It's the least I can do for you."

Angela laughed back at her friend. "No, Perkin. Not today."

"Whew…thanks for letting me off the hook," Perkin joked. "I was afraid I'd have to explain myself to Sylvia."

An intense sadness came over Angela's face. "Poor Sylvia. I feel terrible for her."

Perkin stopped and looked at Angela. "Why's that?"

"Her husband was killed in India during the Japanese invasion. She found out yesterday."

"Oh, my God. I just saw her a little bit ago. She didn't say a word." Perkin was saddened once again by the personal costs of the war. Almost everyone he knew had lost someone close, and he knew how devoted Sylvia was to her husband. "Oh, Jesus. I should go talk to her."

"No, my friend. She is so very English. An Italian woman would still be crying to God, but the girls said she cried for a few minutes and then went back to work. I don't think she has any family now except the army, so I think she's getting as much help as she can, but it might not be good for you—a soldier—to make too much of this."

"I don't understand," Perkin said.

"She's very fond of you and Bear, and maybe she wouldn't want you to be shotted either. Maybe she wouldn't want to worry about that too. Maybe she just wants to, *come si dice*, mourn her husband by herself. The English are very strange like that."

Chapter Three

One Week Later

May 23, 1944
0530 Hours
Anzio, Italy

Anzio was hell. There was no other description the men could assign to it. Anzio was death and destruction on a scale that matched Cassino with total indifference to the cost of life and human suffering. In some respects, many respects, Anzio was worse. At Cassino, a soldier could hop in a jeep and in fifteen minutes could theoretically find himself in a peaceful and serene place where the dangers of war were out of sight, if not out of mind. There was no escape at Anzio. The entire pocket was within range of German guns, and that was evident from the moment of arrival.

The seaside towns of Anzio and Nettuno, separated by a few miles of coastal highway, were shattered remnants of the resorts that existed before the January landings. Divisions were brought to Anzio and thrown into the grinder until they were as shattered as the towns and villages that surrounded them. When the units were rendered combat ineffective, as they inevitably were, the wreckage of the units would be pulled off the line for a few weeks. With rare exception, they weren't evacuated from the Anzio area of operations, however, and they put their remaining manpower to work building a vast network of ammo dumps, trenches, bunkers, command posts, hospitals and more hospitals, and even a baseball diamond and an underground theater—all under the dubious protection of barrage balloons. Eventually, they would receive enough replacements to fill the diminished ranks, and would be rotated forward as another shattered division needed replacement along the line. The more cynical soldiers called it "the cycle of death."

The Texans were familiar with the soldiers in the Anzio pocket, and it seemed as if the 36th was just the last to arrive at the party. The American divisions that had spearheaded the landings were the regular army's 3rd Division and the Oklahoma National Guard's 45th Division. Both had fought alongside the Texas 36th since the battle of Salerno nine months before. Other units in the pocket, including the 34th Division of Guardsmen from Iowa, Minnesota, and the Dakotas, and the American-Canadian 1st Special Service Force, had fought next to the 36th in the mountains fronting the Liri Valley.

The division was brought piecemeal onto the Anzio battlefield over the span of several nights. Navy amphibious ships, LSTs and LCIs, moved companies to the port during hours of darkness where they were off-loaded as quickly as possible so the ships could be out of the port by daylight. Under the light of flares and fires, the soldiers were greeted by the familiar smell of death and the sight of endless destruction including the remaining fragments of homes that had been quite grand and expensive before the war arrived to Anzio's shore. When trucks were available, the soldiers of the

36th were transported to a bivouac four miles to the northeast of Anzio. When trucks weren't available, the soldiers formed into two columns and marched to the bivouac.

Able Company had marched to the site, and Sam Taft was glad they did. He wanted to stretch his legs from his time aboard the nameless LCI—Landing Craft, Infantry—that had brought Able from Texas Beach in Naples. The short transit was uneventful even if many of the soldiers were near panic—the army had shown the movie *Action in the North Atlantic* to the soldiers the night before embarkation, and the level of anxiety about U-boats was running high. Sam didn't worry about the U-boats. He just welcomed the opportunity to breathe air that didn't carry the all too familiar stench of Naples. It had been a clear night, and Sam had spent the transit looking at the stars and thinking of home. Several officers or old comrades had moved to talk to Sam during the ride north, but they were blocked by the new company top sergeant, First Sergeant Jimmy Donohue, who felt Sam deserved some time to himself.

After marching to their bivouac at the edge of the Padiglione Woods, the soldiers were told to dig in, but it was actually more of a question of finding an existing bunker, trench, or foxhole. It seemed every inch of the pocket had been occupied by someone at some point over the past few months, and tired soldiers fumbled around in the dark until they could find a place to hide safely when the unknowns of daylight arrived.

The intelligence reports from the Fifth Army indicated the Germans were low on artillery ammunition and the rate of fire had decreased dramatically over the months, but soldiers who had spent time at Anzio told the Texans that it didn't take much to inspire the

Germans to fire a round or two at any activity they observed. Discretion was the better part of valor at Anzio.

Through the course of the first night and into the next day, Sam established a command post in an underground bunker that had been built by engineers six weeks earlier. Although relatively new, Sam found they weren't the first occupants of the bunker, and while linesmen ran telephone wires to the battalion and regimental command posts and to the company's dispersed platoon leaders, Sam and his headquarters element cleaned out the trash and excrement left by the previous inhabitants.

It was miserable. Although Sam wasn't claustrophobic by any means, it was an extremely unpleasant experience to a man who spent his peacetime days on horseback under the broadest skies of God's kingdom. The engineers who designed the bunkers were dwarves, he decided, or trolls, or whichever miserable damn mythical character that did such work. They were most certainly not his size of six feet seven inches tall from the bottom of his shoes to the top of his helmet, and he was only able to walk around slumped over while simultaneously minding his head from the heavy beams that served as his roof. It was one of the disagreeable aspects of the command, he thought, that he was as miserable as any other soldier in the Anzio pocket, but he wasn't allowed to complain. Plenty of officers did, of course, but Sam felt the need to set an example and he refrained from a soldier's favorite pastime except on one occasion when a collision with a beam in the dark necessitated two stitches in the forehead from one of his medics.

This was Sam's third day in Anzio, and as much as Sam despised Naples, he found himself wishing he was back in Qualiano. At least Perkin was close by and they could meet daily. When Perkin broke away from his duties and came to Sam's CP, they would sit on ammunition crates that had been converted to furniture located under two droplights electricians had hung, and play cards and tell old stories. It was all a matter of waiting for the orders to move, but the division was in reserve. Soon, but not now.

It had taken four days to sneak the entire division into the pocket, and as far as any soldier of the 36th was aware, their presence was undetected. Radio intercept operators heard no indication the Germans had noticed the addition of a new division, let alone a fresh veteran division, and perhaps more reliable than the lack of radio intercepts was the fact Axis Sally had not yet gloated about their imminent demise. The soldiers with access to radios listened to her religiously. Few paid attention to the taunts and threats, but she was popular with the troops for the music she played.

As Sam sat in his bunker watching the previous night's rainwater drip between beams, he waited for the Fifth Army offensive to begin the breakout of the Anzio pocket, and he thought, *she'll know of us soon enough.*

0550 Hours
Anzio, Italy

The great breakout from the Anzio pocket had begun as all of the great breakouts seemed to do: the boom of artillery for hours upon hours. At least that was what Captain Perkin Berger expected. He could hear the big guns dug in by the shoreline, and the smaller field pieces closer to the line. He even identified the deep rumbling coming from the northwest as the heavy guns of the assembled fleet.

"Well, that's it," Perkin said to Major Bill Spaulding.

"Yep," Spaulding agreed laconically.

"Would you mind if I went over to Able Company and woke Sam up? He has no sense of history, and he might opt to sleep through this."

"I'll keep you company, if that's okay," Spaulding said. Without waiting for an answer, he picked up his helmet and said to his communications NCO, "Do a comms test with the Able CP."

While the communications check was in process, Spaulding chatted briefly with Major George Morris, the battalion executive officer, and Perkin grabbed several Spam and egg sandwiches. After it was established that communications were working between the two command posts, Perkin and Spaulding picked up their weapons and headed to Able Company.

When they had navigated through two hundred yards of trenches and open ground, they arrived at Sam's bunker. Sam was sitting cross-legged on top of the bunker next to First Sergeant Donohue. Both men were staring to the northeast with field binoculars. There was a large bag between them and a thermos of coffee, and Sam was setting down his binoculars and reaching for the thermos when Perkin and Spaulding walked up.

Spaulding saw that Donohue was preparing to spring to his feet, and he waved for him to keep his seat as the two newcomers sat down. "Is there any coffee left?" Spaulding asked.

"Yes, sir," Sam said, and he poured coffee for both Perk and Spaulding.

"Whatcha got in the gunnysack, Sam? Figs?" Perkin asked brightly.

"This is normally my crab bag, but it's got cornbread if you boys want some," Sam said with a smile. It was generally an agreed upon point among those who knew the cousins that Sam had won a rare round with Perkin in the war of fruits and crabs. There were no hard feelings.

"Sounds good. We brought some sandwiches. Here…," Perkin handed a sandwich to Sam and Sergeant Donohue, and then he pulled his trench knife and cut the third sandwich in half, which he shared with Major Spaulding. Donohue started to protest, but Perkin cut him off and said, "We have a French chef on retainer in the battalion headquarters. He was trained at the Cordon Bleu and his specialty is Spam sandwiches."

"Well, ain't that some coincidence, sir? Our cook is a private and he has the same specialty." Donohue took a bite and quickly washed it down with coffee. He had been a soldier for over a decade but still thought powdered eggs were unnatural.

Perkin grabbed his own binoculars, a very fine set of German field glasses, and stood on the bunker and surveyed the horizon for several minutes.

"Well, what'd you see, Professor?" Spaulding asked as he poured himself another cup of Sam's coffee. "Got it figured out which way we'll go?"

"Hell if I know," Perkin replied. "It just looks like a lot of dust and smoke around the pocket. I can't see anything worth seeing. Maybe I'll see about getting up in a Grasshopper today and take a closer look."

"The hell you say!" Sam exclaimed. "What good's that gonna do?" He held a dim view of his cousin taking a flight in a Piper L-4 Grasshopper.

"Well, Bear, it might give me a better understanding of the battlefield to start with," Perkin said with some asperity.

"Bullshit," Sam said. "It'll just give you an aerial view of dust and smoke. There's no need to take the risk. If you haven't heard, the Krauts have got triple-A all around Anzio."

Perkin shrugged. "That's why the army gives me ten bucks a month in badge pay."

"No, the army gives you ten bucks a month to be an infantryman, not Buck Rogers."

"Shit, Sam, if someone's gonna be in a coma for five centuries, I'd reckon it'd be you," Perkin said as he looked through the glasses again. He then muttered dryly under his breath but loud enough for all to hear, "Not that anyone could tell the difference."

"Oh, shut the hell up," Sam said with rising anger.

"Both of you shut up," Spaulding said mildly. He was used to Sam and Perkin's arguments. "Y'all are like an old married couple. First Sergeant, have you ever seen anything like this?"

Donohue shrugged and said, "Not exactly, but my little brothers tied a tomcat and an old coon by the tails and tossed them over the clothesline once. It's almost the same."

Sam and Perkin stopped their arguing and looked at Sergeant Donohue with incredulity. "Damnation!" Sam said. "Who won?"

"My ma. We was in the house when we heard the commotion and ran outside and saw it. I ain't ever seen a fight like that, nor heard nothin' like it. Ma was right beside herself though. I swear she wore them boys out, and then she set Daddy on 'em. He wore 'em out too. The coon kilt the cat, which was Daddy's favorite, but Daddy made me kill the coon with a shovel. I don't have no truck with either cats or coons, but that was just downright mean." Donohue shook his head and said, "They're my brothers, but they's dumb sons-a-bitches, and mean through and through. I cain't say that I miss 'em—I'm glad they was sent to the Pacific instead of here."

The conversation strayed to cats that they'd known, and from there to coons, then the conversation made the jump to coon dogs, which was followed by racing dogs and bird dogs. While they talked, both Sam and Perkin cleaned their respective weapons—an M-1 Garand for Sam, and the Thompson for Perkin. First Sergeant Donohue left to check on the soldiers, platoon by platoon, and over the course of the next hour, each of Sam's platoon leaders came by to check in with him while the battalion's company commanders did the same with Major Spaulding. There was nothing to do but wait.

0925 Hours
Rome, Italy

Lieutenant Colonel Douglas Grossmann lit another cigarette and watched the people walk past his favorite café. She was late, but she was always late, and it didn't bother him much on this wonderful spring morning.

Grossmann had spent the previous night with Antoniette at her apartment in Rome—it had been an evening of wine and love, and he was right with the world. He had kissed her cheek while she slept, and had gone to the SS headquarters early to read the morning's intelligence reports. Properly speaking, he wasn't doing intelligence work any longer, but old habits die hard. The news was potentially grim, but it didn't matter to Grossmann. The night before, Antoniette had told him she loved him, and that was all that truly mattered.

It was unexpected. He had never told her that he loved her, although he knew it was plainly written on his face. Grossmann had always been secretly afraid that she would laugh at him, or use it to her advantage somehow. He had always been afraid of the vulnerability that those three words exposed. "I love you," might be the most dangerous words in the collective human experience, Grossmann thought, and yet Antoniette had spoken those very words to him. It was so unexpected that he thought perhaps his heart had stopped altogether, and despite his misgivings and fear of vulnerability, he had gushed the same words back to her. He knew he looked and sounded like a teenager at that moment, but she hadn't laughed. His fears weren't realized. His dreams were.

When the laughter came later, it was the laughter of young lovers who were happy to be together—a couple who wanted and needed each other—two people who were made for each other. It had taken them nearly a year to come to this point, but Grossmann had never felt so complete. So happy. He thought as he sipped his caffé corretto, that he would do anything for Antoniette.

0930 Hours
Anzio, Italy

"Lieutenant, do you know how long I've been in the army?" First Sergeant Donohue asked of Second Lieutenant Alexander Ryan.

"No, Top. I don't think I know that." Ryan grinned. He had found that sometimes when a sergeant asked questions like that, it would lead to a condescending explanation of what the young officer was doing wrong, but Ryan and Donohue had formed a friendship based on shared Irish ancestry and farming backgrounds.

"I've been in this man's army since nineteen thirty-three," Donohue said.

"Okay. What's your point?"

"No point, really. I was just thinking that in eleven

years of active service, the best thing to happen to me was gettin' malaria."

"That was the best thing?"

"Yes, sir. I was on the back side of my second tour at Camp McKinley, that's in Manila, when I caught malaria and almost died. Other than the occasional pestilence, McKinley was a good post. They had a big swimmin' pool, a nice PX, cute local girls if you like Oriental women, which I do, and they even occasionally had cold beer. While Manila is damn hot, it was a good place to be. Unless you got malaria, and then it was terrible, and they told me that if I got it again, it'd be worse. So, I tried to figure out where I could go where there'd be no malaria, and I requested a transfer to Fort Riley in Kansas, which was askin' to go from an exotic Oriental shithole to a dusty Midwestern shithole, but that was okay with me as long as there wasn't malaria. The army countered with Fort McClellan, which probably had more damned mosquitos than the Philippines, and I decided I was going to separate. Finally, we settled on Fort Lewis after some give and take, and I shipped out to Honolulu in November of '41—my orders had me changing ships there and then I was to carry on to the West Coast. When I got to Hawaii, I was lucky and wound up with two weeks of no duties while I was waiting for my troopship to depart. All I had to do was check in every morning at the transient barracks and I was done for the day. It was my first vacation ever. Some vacation…while I was there I got to see the Japs attack Pearl Harbor."

"What'd you do? You know, that day?" asked Ryan.

Donohue shook his head. "Not a damn thing, sir. Not until it was over. I just watched. On the worst day of my life, I just watched. I wasn't close to any armories or batteries. I just watched," he said again. "Crossing the Rapido was the second and third worst days. So, I spent a month manning an observation post at Kaena Point while we waited for the Jap invasion. Of course, they didn't attempt to land at Hawaii but they attacked the P.I. next. I volunteered to go back to defend Manila, but the army said, 'Orders is orders,' so I eventually got shipped out to Washington State and then I made my way to the 144th, and from there to the 141st when the 144th went to California. To close the circle here, if I hadn't caught malaria, I wouldn't have been sent to Hawaii and while I wouldn't have seen Pearl Harbor, I'd have been taken prisoner or killed on Corregidor and I wouldn't be here to see this."

Ryan looked at the sergeant, who was only a few years older than himself and said, "That's a touching story, Top, but I don't see anything other than dust and smoke off in the distance." To emphasize his point, a gust of wind blew acrid smoke from a distant smoke generator across their faces.

"I'm sure we'll get to see something, Lieutenant."

1005 Hours
Rome, Italy

Douglas Grossmann was still sitting at his favorite café when he saw her walking across the piazza. She was stunning. There was no other word to describe her. He had known many beautiful women in his lifetime, and not one of them could compare to Antoniette.

She was aware of her beauty, of course. Her sexuality was her weapon—a weapon Grossmann had seen used to devastating effects in the past to absolutely destroy the lives of men, but she looked completely unassuming as she walked toward the café. Antoniette was dressed in a cream-colored skirt with a matching suit jacket and a wide-brimmed hat that framed her face perfectly. There was no sign of worry or concern at all, and an uninformed observer could be excused for not knowing a war was raging only some tens of miles in the distance.

Antoniette's face lit up when she saw Grossmann, and when she picked up her pace to hurry to his table, his heart missed a beat. He stood up as she arrived, and the light in his face matched hers. Grossmann kissed her on the offered cheek and held her chair for her as she sat down.

"You look beautiful today, my dear," Grossmann said as he sat down across from her.

"Thank you, darling," Antoniette replied with a graceful smile. "I think being in love agrees with me."

Grossmann's heart skipped another beat and he was searching for the proper words to express his feelings when she gave a playful laugh. She had seen his struggle, known what it represented, and it amused her. Antoniette's laugh prompted laughter from him, and he said, "I think it agrees with both of us."

Grossmann waved the restaurant owner over to the table, and said, "Signore Alessio, do you have any champagne? I know it's a little early, but on a beautiful spring day like this, it somehow seems appropriate."

The restauranteur bowed and said in reply, "Signore, it's never too early to drink champagne with a beautiful woman. I have champagne but I also have a delightful prosecco if you would prefer." The offer of the Italian variant implied that the champagne was expensive.

"No prosecco today. We'd like a bottle of your best champagne, please, and maybe some cornetti and any fruit you might have."

"Of course, right away. Today, I have something that is unique in all of Italy."

"Signore Alessio?" asked Antoniette. "Would

you take our picture for us, please?" She produced a German-made Certo camera, a gift from Grossmann, and quickly showed Alessio how it worked.

Alessio snapped a picture of the beaming couple, handed the camera back to Antoniette, and scurried off with a barely concealed smile. This might be a day he could close early.

"It seems so extravagant—having champagne for breakfast," Antoniette said with a smile. "We should fall in love more often."

Grossmann smiled back. "We should, my dear."

They made happy small talk for a few minutes until Signore Alessio returned with a waiter in tow. The waiter was carrying a large silver tray, which he placed on a nearby table, and then he departed. Alessio was carrying an unopened bottle of champagne, and he showed the label to Grossmann for his approval.

Grossmann was stunned and delighted. It was a bottle of the 1928 Krug, considered by many to be the best champagne of the past one hundred years. Grossmann, who considered himself a wine connoisseur, had never had it before. It was beyond his means and in normal times, it would have cost a month's salary. Today, it was still a considerable sum, but not out of reach.

"Signore Alessio, you never fail to surprise me!" Grossmann said with a genuine smile. "Absolutely! If we're to drink before noon, it should be only the finest, am I right?"

"Yes, signore, you are correct." Alessio opened the bottle and poured a sample for Grossmann to taste.

"It's as wonderful as I expected. Thank you." Grossmann beamed. It was a great day.

Signore Alessio poured champagne for Antoniette first, and then filled Grossmann's glass. As he set the bottle down into an iced champagne bucket, he said to

Grossmann, "I have another surprise for you, and please don't get angry with me."

"Why's that?" asked Grossmann.

"Before the war, I had a customer—an English diplomat—who missed his home food. Why? I couldn't say. English food is abysmal. But he would ask me to make some dishes for him, so I would. The only one that was worth keeping was this one: scones, with clotted cream and fresh strawberries."

"Strawberries?" asked a delighted Antoniette. "Are the strawberries ready? They're my favorite!"

"Yes, signorina. They are the *fragolina di bosco* from Nemi, the best strawberries in Italy." Signore Alessio smiled. "They are a real treat...I don't know how long I will have access to them, so please enjoy."

"We will," Grossmann said. "I don't remember anything so nice." He looked at Antoniette and asked, "Where's Nemi?"

She bit her lip as she thought, a trait that Grossmann found endearing, and then shrugged. "I don't know. Signore Alessio?"

"It's in the Alban Hills south of Rome. Not far from the town of Velletri. They have a strawberry festival every year at the beginning of June, but I don't know if there will be one this year."

"Velletri's pretty close to the fighting," Grossmann said. "Nemi's loss is our gain though. Why the scones now?"

"There's an Irish priest at the Vatican who helped a cousin of my wife's, and she asked me to make the scones and clotted cream as a present for the Irishman."

Signore Alessio offered his customary bow and was turning to leave when Grossmann said, "That was nice of you. Is the priest Monsignor O'Flaherty, by any chance? I've seen him at the opera...I understand he's a great man who helps many in need."

Signore Alessio offered a very Italian shrug. "I don't know about the Irishman, signore. I wasn't told his name." The Italian then laughed and said, "You young people don't know how marriage works yet. My wife tells me her cousin, he's a priest too, needed some help, and this Irishman helped him. I'm told to make scones and clotted cream for some Irishman, so I make scones and clotted cream." Alessio bowed and said as he departed, "That's how marriage works."

Grossmann was about to pursue the coincidence of the priest in need possibly being his priest and the Irishman possibly being O'Flaherty when Antoniette interrupted his thinking by saying, "I liked how he said you don't know how marriage works...yet." She smiled sweetly with a mock innocence, and all thoughts of errant priests left Grossmann's mind for the day.

1015 Hours
Anzio, Italy

"Anything?" Perkin asked as Bill Spaulding returned to the Able Command Post following a quick visit to regiment.

Spaulding spat in the drying dirt and shook his head. "Nope. The information is pretty sparse at this point, as you might expect. Some advance in the 3rd Division sector towards Cisterna, but casualties are heavy and there's no breakthrough for us to exploit. I did find this leaflet though." He handed a dirty piece of paper to Perkin, who saw a drawing of a G.I. getting dressed while a topless British woman on a bed pulled up her stockings. The caption was, "While You Are Away."

"Huh. Look at that. Well, at least someone's taking

care of business." Perkin briefly thought of Helen, wadded the paper up and threw it into the nearby trench. Jealously was seldom an issue for Perkin and he easily turned his thoughts back to the fight. "So no notion of when we'll move?"

"Nope," Spaulding grunted as he looked at the crumpled leaflet in the trench. "Regiment's got a pretty clear eye on things I think, and they reckon that unless something unexpected happens, we'll be in place until one of the other divisions is ground down, or the geometry of the battlefield expands enough for us to move into."

"Did you ask them to keep it down like I asked? It's going to be hard to sleep with all this racket," Perkin said. The artillery continued to pound German defenses ahead of the advance, although it had slackened somewhat compared to earlier that morning. Perkin had seen several flights of attack aircraft and the bombs they dropped simply added to the cacophony.

"Professor, I ain't your messenger boy, but I'd be happy to make an appointment for you to meet with the regimental commander yourself. He might enjoy hearin' your complaints."

"He just might. Of course, I don't view it as a complaint as much as a matter of military efficiency. I need my sleep you know—a brain as big as mine needs both sleep and food. Speaking of which, is it lunchtime yet?"

"Not yet. I hate to disappoint a big-headed man like yourself…"

"Big brained," Perkin corrected.

"Whatever. I do have some good news for us all," Spaulding said.

"What's that, Bill?" Sam asked. He had taken his shirt off and was lying in the sun hoping to even out his farmer's tan.

"General Clark flew in last night to personally take charge of the battle."

"Our air defense guys sure picked a bad time to quit shootin' down friendly aircraft," Sam observed dryly.

"What makes you think it's friendly?" Perkin asked. His hatred of Mark Clark ran deep and intense. Had he been at a 40mm battery, he wasn't sure he wouldn't have opened fire.

"Perk, I heard somethin' else that might interest you," Spaulding said. "I gather there's some kind of fallin' out between Alexander and Clark over what this breakout is supposed to accomplish."

"Whaddya mean?" Perkin asked.

"General Alexander has issued orders that the Fifth Army objective is to sever Highway 6 and prevent the German Army from escaping from Cassino."

Perkin nodded. "Sure. Doing so will allow us to encircle and annihilate the German Tenth Army before they escape. I've been waiting for that opportunity since we landed in Italy last September. Where's the fallin' out?"

"A friend at regiment has heard that Fifth Army doesn't like that. They think when we break out we need to turn north to Rome along Highway 7." Spaulding lifted an eyebrow as if to say, "Can you believe that?"

Sam rolled over onto an elbow and looked at Major Spaulding, "Why would they do that? Kill the Krauts and the city automatically falls. Take the city and the opposite ain't true. I…"

Perkin interrupted and said caustically, "I'll tell you what this is about. I'll give ya two choices—a charitable reason and then my own suspicions, and you tell me which one's right." When Sam gestured for Perkin to continue, he said, "Ever since Clausewitz came up with the notion of a center of gravity, military theorists have seen capitals as the center of gravity. The North thought it was Richmond. The South thought the Yankee center of gravity was Washington. I suppose you could make an argument that when Alaric's Goths sacked Rome they were destroying the Roman center of gravity, but..."

"I wouldn't make that argument," Sam said.

Perkin grinned and replied, "Likely you wouldn't, but maybe that was true then. It ain't true now. In the age of instant communications and battlefield mobility, it don't matter if the emperor's in the capital or not. It's like the bombing campaign of Berlin. I'm pretty sure Hitler ain't gonna die in a bombing raid, so why are we doing that instead of focusing on the war-making capabilities of Germany? As for down here, Rome certainly isn't the Germans' center of gravity in Italy. It's their forces in the field. But the problem is there are still people who buy into the nonsense—that Rome has so much symbolic value that if we take Rome, it shortens the war in some dramatic way. Maybe it'll help, but not nearly as much as capturin' or killin' a hundred thousand Krauts."

"Okay," said Spaulding. "What's the uncharitable version?"

"It has nothing to do with military necessity. It's ego and nothing more. Clark is more committed to headlines than victory. Capturing the first enemy capital is a good headline. Beating the British Eighth Army to Rome is a good headline. And the military justification is secondary. But, I can't believe even Clark's that stupid. The good news though is if what you said is true, it don't matter. Alex is callin' the shots, not Clark."

1325 Hours
Anzio, Italy

The first day of the breakout continued with marginal success along the line demarcating the Anzio pocket. Small inconsequential gains were made by all the Allied divisions, only to be lost in the inevitable counterattacks. Artillery dominated the day, and the soldiers saw more airpower come into play than in any other battle of the Italian campaign to date, but small desperate battles were fought at close range between the infantries of the respective combatants.

The soldiers of the Texas Gun Club were still in a holding pattern. Officers monitoring the battle at the VI Corps headquarters occasionally saw glimpses of an exploitable success only to have the window closed before the reserves could be even notified of impending action.

Some of the Texans had gone below ground again in the trenches and bunkers of the Anzio battlefield. Many soldiers continued to improve their quarters even though they knew that their residence in the bunkers would be temporary. Discarded trash of previous units was sifted through and occasionally items of some value were discovered—boot laces, mess utensils, or gunnysacks for pillows.

Some Texans stayed above ground and watched the battle from afar. Beyond the smoke, dust, and ceaseless noise, no one knew how the battle progressed. This lack of knowledge only facilitated the rumors, each of which spread through the encampment like a wildfire: that the 3rd had broken through at Cisterna was matched only a few minutes later by the 45th being bogged down and the First Special Service Force entering Rome. While some of the experienced soldiers listened and laughed at the rumors, other experienced soldiers crafted increasingly more fantastic and utterly improbable tales motivated by a mix of boredom and orneriness.

A softball game took place in the battalion area even though men were fighting and dying mere miles away. A battered American helmet bearing a faded Thunderbird insignia was used as first base; second base was a bullet-ridden 55-gallon drum; third base was originally laid down with a skull of unknown nationality until a horrified chaplain from Seguin replaced it with the first item he came across—a splintered half-moon of a toilet seat. Home plate was simply a home plate. A partially collapsed trench intersected the second to third baseline as it carried into the outfield, and the shortstops were selected on the basis of their long-jump capabilities. Base runners had a choice to make: either to attempt the leap across the trench or to hop into the trench and emerge on the 3rd base side. Although the initial rulings on playing the trench were fairly contentious until the chaplain brought order to the game by decreeing that a ball hit into the trench was still in play, and not a ground rule double as some advocated, and that base runners falling into the trench were allowed to emerge at any point in the trench and not just along the base line. Two base runners in the trench at once was ruled an automatic out for both base runners, but the increasingly dictatorial chaplain decreed that while one base runner was in the trench, the following base runner was allowed to pass him but only if he successfully jumped the trench. While such an approach was harshly criticized by some of the players as illogical and capricious, others agreed that trenchball was the most fun they'd had outside of a Neapolitan whorehouse. Meanwhile, the war raged on.

1745 Hours
Rome, Italy

Doug Grossmann sat at his desk in the SS headquarters in a small office he shared with Major Kemmerling. Grossmann stared at an obligatory picture of Adolf Hitler hanging on the wall over his desk. He felt from time to time like asking the Führer what the hell he was doing to Germany, but Grossmann half-suspected that his office was bugged and so he always kept his feelings to himself. Both he and Kemmerling had searched many times for listening devices, and had never found one, yet Grossmann always proceeded on the assumption that they were there. Grossmann had selected a black and white portrait of a younger Adolf Hitler that had a film noir feel to it. It was one of the favorites among the SS officers because of the supernatural power suggested by the glowing eyes emerging from the darkness of the background. Grossmann liked it for its artistic value, and wished he could take pictures as competently as this photographer could.

Grossmann was contemplating a course of action, and he couldn't decide which way to go. The Führer's portrait was unhelpful in resolving his dilemma, but he stared at it anyway the way one might look at a page in a book but not read it.

"Afternoon, Boss..." Kemmerling walked into the office and dropped into the chair behind his desk. "Oh, sorry. You're thinking about something?"

Grossmann looked over at the major with a puzzled smile. "As a matter of fact, I am. How'd you know?"

"You have a few tells. I'm not going to share all of them with you in case you want to lose money to me in cards again, but when you're trying to reach a momentous decision, you seek guidance from the

Führer." Kemmerling snorted. "I tried it once. Thinking it worked like an Ouija board and could dispense
advice, I asked it what to do with my career."

Grossmann grinned back in anticipation. "Is that a
fact? What'd he say?"

"He told me I should invade Poland."

"Really?"

"Yeah. It's an old picture." Kemmerling laughed
at his own joke, looked at an empty coffee cup on his
desk, and then pulled a flask from his desk drawer. "It's
cognac. I got it from the Frog whoremaster." He took
a deep swallow and passed it to Grossmann who did
likewise. "So what has you seeking guidance from the
almighty?"

Grossmann took another long drink of Kemmerling's
cognac and shrugged. "Before I answer, what's your
assessment on the Allied efforts at Cassino and Anzio?"

Kemmerling scowled and said, "It's going too well
for the Amis and the British for my liking. The danger,
of course, is that Clark cuts off the line of communication to von Vietinghoff's army as it moves back from
Cassino." Kemmerling stood up and closed the door.
As he sat down, he said with a raised eyebrow, "This
is very dangerous, you know. We're used to slow and
methodical Allied advances, but if the breakout from
Anzio is successful, we could be routed and von Vietinghoff's Tenth Army annihilated."

"That's what's got me thinking. I think our time
in Rome is growing short. We could be pleasantly
surprised, but the Allies will win this fight in Italy. If
not through maneuver, then certainly through attrition."
Grossmann pulled out his cigarette case, offered one
to Kemmerling who accepted, and Grossmann lit both
cigarettes with his Betty Boop lighter.

"I don't think these clowns win a war through

maneuver. Clark? Leese? But, they'll push through, I suspect, on sheer numbers and airpower. So, what's on your mind?" Kemmerling leaned back in his chair and inhaled deeply of the American cigarette.

"Well, I'm thinking that timing may be critical for us. We want to squeeze the last drop out of Rome that we can before we leave. But timing's everything." Grossmann looked at the picture of Hitler again.

"You'd be surprised the number of women who've told me that very thing. Ach…just like a woman, if we squeeze too hard, we get slapped in the face, yes? That is what you're concerned about?" Kemmerling asked.

"Something like that." Grossmann was silent for a few minutes while he collected his thoughts. His morning with Antoniette had been delightful, but she had brought up this same subject. Her concern was that once the Fascists fled Rome, there might not be anything waiting for them on their return. Her parents were preparing to become refugees of a sort, but rather than fleeing from the German Army, they would be retreating with it. Much of Signore Bernardi's personal wealth had either been transferred to banks in Milan or to Swiss banks, and Antoniette had given Grossmann a considerable sum of lire to hold for her in his safe at work. The Bernardi family had slowly and quietly moved out of Rome in increments even though Signore Bernardi continued to manage his holdings from his Rome office.

That wasn't Antoniette's concern, and so it wasn't Grossmann's. As they sipped champagne and enjoyed the strawberries and scones, Antoniette had brought up one of her concerns for the future.

"Darling," she had said, "the window of opportunity is closing here, is it not?" When Grossmann gave her a resigned shrug, she continued. "We have put away some money for the future. Some in your accounts and some in mine, but we don't have enough yet."

Grossmann had nodded. "I agree."

"Some would say that Milan is the jewel of Italia. It is richer than Rome and richer than Venice. But it's a city controlled by Fascists to an extent unequaled here. It will be harder for us to reestablish our business there unless the SS occupies it, and then we'll run the risk of bringing the partisans down on us."

Grossmann agreed with her line of thinking. The partisan movement was nascent but was becoming active against the Fascist party organs in Milan. "It will be more challenging to set up operations there, and there's no guarantee that once we withdraw from Rome, if we do withdraw, that General Wolff will still be in command of the SS in Italy or that we'll be relocated close to Milan. We'll have to adapt to whatever location we go to next."

"I think so too. Papa will move all of his business to Milan as a prelude to relocating to Switzerland. He has property in Bellinzona and a company apartment in Zurich. You and I will have to decide where we'll go in Switzerland after the war. I don't think we can stay in Italy, and there may not be much of Germany to go to." Antoniette took a cigarette from Grossmann's pack and looked at him while he lit it for her.

That evening while Grossmann was staring at the face of Adolf Hitler, Antoniette's image came into his mind. He had seen every side of her personality from playful to murderous. He had never before seen such anxiety—and it almost broke his heart. Grossmann shook his head to clear the image and shifted his gaze to his subordinate. "Fritz," he said softly, barely above a whisper, "I want us to step up our operations and bleed Rome dry. I mean every last pfennig. We'll continue to share the wealth, but if we're working overtime, we take a larger cut than usual. I also think we're going to have to be prepared to evacuate on a moment's notice, so we'll have to have some way to transport or transfer money out of Rome. When do you come back from Siena?"

"If the transport's available, tomorrow evening. The trip shouldn't take long." Kemmerling grinned.

Grossmann grinned back. "Good. Give it some thought, and meet me at the café for breakfast the day after tomorrow. We'll plan our final days in the eternal city."

Chapter Four

Two Days Later

May 25, 1944
0445 Hours
Anzio, Italy

Most soldiers had slept poorly since arriving in Anzio. The boom and crash of artillery continued ceaselessly throughout the night, and even though it was not directed at the soldiers from Texas, it kept many men awake, particularly the replacement soldiers. Some men, again, the newcomers mostly, gathered atop the bunkers, crawled out of their slit trenches and foxholes, and watched the distant fireworks for hours on end.

For two days, it had seemed like most of Italy was on fire. The veterans of Salerno, San Pietro, the Rapido River, and Monte Cassino told the newcomers to listen to the booms and many men became experts on identifying German from American artillery and British ground artillery from naval gunfire. Flares from miles away filled in the shadows left from the reflection of the fires off the clouds, and traces of smoke occasionally blew back to the 36th bivouac in the nighttime offshore breeze. Trucks moved back and forth across the Anzio plain taking men and supplies to the front lines, and evacuating the wounded. There were many to evacuate.

Captain Perkin Berger sat in the rear seat of a Piper L-4 Grasshopper, which had a cowling painting of a foul-looking raccoon with oversized buttocks. Perkin fiddled with his German-made binoculars and nervously looked out the long rectangular window at the ground crew. He had only flown once before, and while he had enjoyed the flight, it was in Texas and as far as he was aware, no one was shooting at him.

"Seriously," he called out to the pilot, a first lieutenant named Maurice Badeaux, "Aren't we supposed to have parachutes?"

"And I already tell you, Cap'n, as low as I plan on flyin' you gonna have no time to open no chute," Badeaux explained in a thick South Louisiana accent. "You be surprised how fast you fall. I saw a boy jump out of a burnin' Focke-Wulf 190 at three hundred feet and he bounced off a barn roof about four seconds later. He must've hit a rafter 'cause I swear I thought he was goin' straight through. Dat was the damnedest thing I ever seen."

Perkin pictured it in his mind, shivered, and said, "I reckon it was. What happened to him? Ground fire?"

"No, sir. He was shot down by one of dem nigger pilots from the 99th, a boy named Ashley. Not like dat fairy in *Gone with the Wind*, dis was his last name, you know. Lieutenant Ashley. Saved my life...I think dat Kraut pilot comin' for me. I tracked Willie down at Capodichino and shook dat boy's hand and give him a cigar. He's a hell of a guy in my eyes, whether he's colored or not."

"Well, I'm sure that fucking made his day," muttered Perkin to himself.

"What's dat, sir?" asked Badeaux.

"I said you were sure lucky he saved the day."

"You don't have to tell me twice. I've been tellin' anyone who listen that dem nigger pilots is good, and I don't care who knows it! If you asked me before the war if der should be colored officers, I say 'hell no' but I changed my mind." Badeaux shook his head emphatically. "I swore I wouldn't say nothin' bad against niggers ever again."

"That's pretty forward thinking of you," Perkin said with an inward grin. "What about Indian officers?"

"Why, I've never heard of such a thing. Is there?"

"Sure. Of course."

"I don't think I could endorse dat, do you?"

"I don't know why not. It's a modern war. Did you know there was an Indian general on the Confederate side during the War of Northern Aggression? A Cherokee named Stand Watie?" Perkin said.

Badeaux had only been half paying attention as he watched the ground crew move out of the way of the Piper. He turned around and gave Perkin a quizzical look. "Is dat true or are you makin' fun of an ole coonass?"

Perkin shook his head. "It's true. General Watie was the last Confederate general to surrender in the field. He made it longer than Lee, Hood, or Longstreet."

"I'll be...nigger pilots and an Indian general fightin' for the South. Who'd a thought dat?" Badeaux turned back around and gave the aircraft some throttle. The small Piper began to taxi through a maze of fortified walls made from wine kegs and sandbags escorted by two ground crew who made sure the wingtips didn't hit the walls. Once the aircraft exited the fortification, the two airmen saluted Badeaux, and the Piper taxied unescorted to an improved dirt runway. Badeaux didn't hesitate when he reached the runway. He simply gunned the engine, and after a very bumpy but short takeoff, Perkin was flying for the second time in his life.

0450 Hours
Anzio, Italy

The great Anzio breakout was both confusing and amazing from the air. The Grasshopper had banked and headed out to sea over the multitude of ships off the Anzio coast. Badeaux took his small plane up to two thousand feet and gave Perkin a quick lesson in the geography of the battlefield. After they had flown the length of the coastline, Badeaux circled back out to sea again and dropped his elevation to one thousand feet as he crossed over the Anzio airfield heading inland.

Even an elevation no higher than one thousand feet gave Perkin a completely different perspective of the battlefield. In the dim morning light, Perkin could see the flashes of Allied artillery tucked back throughout the pocket, and as the Grasshopper continued to drop in altitude and moved toward the perimeter fighting, an amazing range of colors greeted him. In the span of only a few minutes, he saw both red and green Very flares and the white eruptions of explosions.

"You see dat town over der?" Badeaux pointed due east, which was slightly to the right of the aircraft's nose.

"Yeah. Is that Cisterna?" Perkin answered. He couldn't see much from their distance other than the vague outline of the town.

"Yep. I'm supposed to give that a looky look. Hang on, we gonna skip over dem rooftops. Keep you eye off to da right."

Badeaux dropped the nose of the small aircraft and lost altitude while gaining speed. "We no Mustang here. We ain't built for combat, so we keep our distance."

"What does distance mean?" Perkin asked.

"We stay on our side of the line, or at least where I think it is, and when the shootin' starts we turn right back."

"That's comforting," Perkin mumbled to himself. In a louder voice he asked Badeaux, "Are those the ditches where the Rangers were shot up?" Perkin tapped the pilot on his shoulder and pointed to his right.

"Yeah. Dey got encircled and that was all she wrote. Just over der, do you see dat burned-out tank?"

"The Panzer IV?" Perkin answered. "What about it?"

"A Ranger major named Dobson got hisself on top of it, killed the TC, and dropped a phosphorus grenade down da hatch before getting his ass shot up. Who be dumb enough to get on a tank in an open field like dat?"

"I don't know," Perkin replied absently. "It probably takes a special kind of stupid."

"Speaking of special kind of stupid, hang on and keep your eyes to da right. I'm counting on you to tell me what you see." Badeaux pushed the nose down even farther and the Grasshopper dropped until it was no more than two hundred feet above the battlefield. Perkin watched as American soldiers of the 3rd Infantry Division invariably looked up at the Grasshopper and waved. Seeing that, Badeaux said, "I'm dey best friend, you know. Not those peeshwanks in da Liberators. Me. I've lead to the destruction of more artillery pieces on the battlefield than all the strategic bombers combined."

As the Grasshopper approached what Perkin assumed to be the forward edge of the battlefield just to the west of Cisterna, Badeaux banked sharply to the left, and Perkin saw two M-10 tank destroyers in a hull-down position in an excavated pit. Crewmen were busy pulling netting over the tank destroyers, and Perkin saw one crewman sleeping in a slit trench next to the M-10s. He looked as though he was lying in a grave.

"So we've advanced some thousand yards since yesterday morning. They bulldoze out dat positions overnight for the TDs, and dey be in place in case of a German armored counterattack. Get your binoculars. We pop up for a look."

Badeaux gunned the engine and the little aircraft quickly gained another two hundred feet in altitude. Perkin looked hard through the binoculars for signs of moving armor but saw none. All he saw was the familiar wreckage of the battlefield: shredded and smoking vegetation, shattered homes, and burning hulks of vehicles.

"Whoa! Der we go now!" Badeaux banked sharply to the left and dropped in altitude. In a flash it seemed as if they were just feet over the battlefield. Grinning soldiers on the ground waved while others ducked as they watched German tracer fire track over their heads in search of the Grasshopper. Perkin saw a soldier hop onto a mound of rubble and motion frantically for the plane to get lower. Maybe he was just telling the plane to clear the area. Perkin couldn't tell. Fascinated by the soldier for some reason, Perkin twisted in his seat and watched as the man shouted at the soldiers around him and then pointed toward the unseen German machine gun. He was still directing fire against the German line as he faded from Perkin's view.

0635 Hours
Anzio, Italy

Lieutenants Alex Ryan and Frank McCarter ducked instinctively as the heavy artillery screamed over their heads toward the port of Anzio. The shelling of the port

The Keys of Redemption 133

had been underway for twenty minutes and while they were more than three miles from the port, the noise and smoke from Anzio reminded them that they were closer than they cared to be.

"Anzio Annie," Frank opined. Annie was the nickname for the 280mm railway cannon that was periodically wheeled out of a tunnel tucked back into the Alban Hills near Frascati. It would fire briefly and then return to the protection of the tunnel before Allied air strikes could be brought to bear.

"Maybe," said Ryan. He didn't want to commit himself on the subject so early in the morning even though he thought McCarter was right. Both men ducked as a massive explosion to the north of the port rattled the bones of every living creature in the Anzio pocket. Although both men had seen artillery explosions in their respective time in Italy, neither had seen anything like this. A wide fireball reached up to the sky, and the initial blast was followed by subsequent explosions and then a massive black cloud that drifted over and encompassed the port of Anzio.

"Holy cow," said McCarter. "That was an ammo dump, I'd bet you. Perk tolt me that they were destroying fifty to sixty tons of ammo *a day*. I swear that was worse than when the *Savannah* caught one at Salerno."

They ducked again as the burning ammo dump gave up more secondary explosions but they were on a mission. After determining that the artillery posed no direct threat to them, they straightened up and continued on their course to the Able Company bunker. Each man carried a thermos in one hand and a bucketful of slightly green powdered eggs and dried sausage in the other. Resting on top of the eggs was a handful of hard rolls and small cans of orange marmalade that Sam's supply sergeant had received in trade for cans of

C-ration beef hash from a British supply sergeant.

Sam had a field kitchen set up in a trench less than one hundred yards from his command post, and normally he would have gone through the chow line like any other soldier in the company, but the two lieutenants were paying off debts incurred in a marksmanship wager with their company commander the day before. Both lieutenants were acutely aware that Sam was a far superior shot than they were but they had mistakenly believed the additional 75-yard handicap that Sam had accepted would even the match. They had been wrong by an embarrassing margin, and so they were bringing what Sam referred to as "breakfast in bed."

Even if Sam had possessed a bed, he wouldn't have been in it. The lieutenants found him in the company of Major Spaulding, and both men were sitting cross-legged on top of the bunker and scanning the sky with binoculars.

"You're late," Sam said with an uncharacteristic terseness.

Frank McCarter was preparing to explain that the eggs weren't done yet but he saw in the corner of his eye that Major Spaulding was waving the explanation off with a slight shake of his head. McCarter had served with Sam since before Salerno, and he knew Sam was worried about Perkin. Instead, he said, "Any word, Sam?"

Spaulding answered for Sam, "Not yet. What do we have this morning?"

"Eggs Benedict and croissant, sir," said McCarter, whose East Texas speech was so slow that eggs Benedict seemed to have more syllables than was possible.

In spite of himself, Sam smiled. "Have you ever had eggs Benedict, Frank?"

"No, sir. Our diner in Atlanta didn't serve it."

McCarter shook his head as a memory popped into his mind. "But I was in a bar in Texarkana and had a pickled egg on a dare once but it was the most repulsive thing I ever ate. That was on the Arkansas side, you know...Bowie County's dry."

Sam began to dish out scrambled eggs to Spaulding and Ryan but when he got to McCarter, it seemed the lieutenant had lost his appetite. Sam smiled and saved some greenish eggs for McCarter should the lieutenant's memory of the Arkansas bar fade.

The breakfast progressed and the officers discussed the legality of executing the company cooks, their disparate opinions of marmalade, and baseball. Sam tried to steer the conversation to cattle, but found no takers. Another attempt was tried with horses but he had no success there either, and the conversation remained centered on baseball. The New York Yankees were the reigning World Series champions, but Alex Ryan offered a bold opinion that the St. Louis Browns were the team to beat this year. Ryan became the subject of intense derision and he was trying to explain that he was really a Cubs fan when more heavy artillery thundered overhead and every officer turned his head to see that the port was taking another hit.

"Goddamnit, where's Perk?" Sam exclaimed in equal parts exasperation and anxiety.

"Sam, he'll have to go through a debrief, won't he? Be patient," said Spaulding, who was getting anxious himself. Perkin had told the group that he would be back by 0600.

0855 Hours
Anzio, Italy

Perkin was overdue by almost three hours, and Sam

couldn't wait much longer. After breakfast had broken up, he had sat on top of the bunker with First Sergeant Donohue. They had gone over the company manning and Sam was particularly irritated to find that one of his soldiers had apparently deserted overnight. He wouldn't be considered a deserter for now, just absent without leave, but the soldier in question was a replacement soldier who had quickly gained a reputation as a troublemaker. He had tried to talk other soldiers into deserting with him, and when they wouldn't, he slipped away during the darkness of night. He wasn't the only soldier in the Anzio pocket to desert, but he was the first in Sam's command. Sam sent notification to battalion and resolved that unless the soldier returned quickly and of his own volition, he would be court-martialed. There would be no company punishment.

After Sergeant Donohue left, Sam drank another cup of coffee as he sharpened his new Bowie knife on a small stone—his old one had been taken as a souvenir by a German corporal when he surrendered on the banks of the Rapido River. His wife Margaret had sent him a new one, which had just arrived the week before. Sam contemplated a letter to Margaret, but he was too anxious to write. When his knife was razor sharp, he had a field desk set up on top of his bunker. While he sat and waited, he attended to the thousand details requiring his attention that morning. Sam hated the administrative details of command, but he found managing a company of nearly two hundred men was no more demanding than managing his ranch of several thousand head of cattle—it was just less rewarding, in his opinion. Leadership, on the other hand, was surprisingly rewarding to Sam, who had never coveted command. He found that he enjoyed mentoring his officers and soldiers, and he quietly delighted in watching the ongoing transformation of civilians into competent soldiers under his guidance. Sam had no use for the army, but unknown to him, the army had a use for Sam.

On this day, however, while Sam felt no delight in anything having to do with either leadership or management, there were advantages to command. He pushed his chair back and stood up. Immediately, two privates who had been detailed as runners for the day stood up and looked at Sam attentively. To one he ordered his jeep to be brought around, and to the other he directed that Lieutenant McCarter and Sergeant Donohue be notified that he was heading to the airfield. As he moved to jump down from the top of his bunker, he heard the whine of a jeep in low gear.

"Hang on!" he ordered and both men paused. Sam saw a jeep driving slowly along the dirt path to the bunker—too much speed raised a cloud of dust, which might come to the attention of enemy artillery spotters. It was Perkin in the passenger seat, and when Sam saw the broad grin on his face, he waved his waiting soldiers off.

"We got shot down!" Perkin yelled as soon as he was close.

"What?" Sam said. Sam looked Perkin over closely as he climbed out of the jeep and thanked the driver. His cousin seemed whole and uninjured, but the excitement in Perkin's eyes was real.

"We got shot down!" Perkin said again. "We had done a quick recce over Mount Artemisio and we were skirting past Velletri when we took some machine-gun fire from the town."

"Good God," Sam said with a shudder. "What happened then? Is the pilot okay?" Sam looked Perkin over again for good measure.

"He's madder than hell, but he's fine. I guess they didn't miss him by much. Or me for that matter. Our engine block evidently took some rounds and just quit running. Bam! Just like that. And then they shot through one of the horizontal stabilizers and part of the vertical stabilizer—that's the little wings and tail to you—and maybe through the right wing as well. Evidently having holey control surfaces makes it hard to fly without an engine...I don't know if that's true, but Lieutenant Badeaux seemed kinda concerned about it all."

Sam looked at his cousin to see if he could divine whether Perkin was telling a tall tale. He decided that Perkin was mostly telling the truth and he shuddered again. "Jesus Christ, Perk. Where'd you land?"

"We came down about six or seven hundred yards inside our lines in a little pasture. It was hard to tell the distance really 'cause it all happened kinda fast. I gotta say that Badeaux is a hell of a pilot—the plane was moving in ways that I don't think Wilbur and Orville intended, and he got it stabilized just before the wheels touched down."

"What was that like?" Sam checked his cousin over again.

"Stop lookin' at me like that, I'm fine. Well, to be honest, the landing was a little rougher than I'd hoped for. Do you remember when you drove your daddy's car into that palm tree along the bay? It was a lot like that." Perkin gave Sam a mischievous grin.

"Don't start with me, Perkin," Sam warned with a shake of his head. It was a forbidden subject of discussion between the cousins. Sam had been driving his father's '34 V-8 Ford Cabriolet when Perkin stood straight up on the seat to wave at a car full of pretty girls. Perkin overbalanced and when Sam lunged to catch him, the car veered to the left, went over a curb and hit a palm tree head on. Perkin went flying over the windshield barely missing the tree but suffering nothing worse than an abrasion on his arm while Sam's nose was broken on impact with the steering wheel. In the entirety of Sam's memory, the car had been his father's sole self-indulgence and wrecking it had bothered Sam for the past decade. But Perkin had been in an airplane crash only hours before and while he hadn't gotten to that point in the story yet, he and Badeaux had been mortared for several minutes while being evacuated by the Thunderbirds. He was too full of adrenaline to be frightened by his cousin.

"I can understand you not wanting to talk about it. I reckon you feel guilty after blamin' them Mexican girls," Perkin said with a grin.

"I do feel guilty but I didn't blame them Mexicans. I blamed you. I swear Dad was madder at me than Hitler was at Russia, and you got off scot-free, you asshole…" Sam was on the verge of grabbing Perkin and making him swear allegiance to Texas A&M and the Republican Party when Major Spaulding walked up.

"I see you idiots are engaged in more intellectual discourse," Major Spaulding said. "Hullo there, Professor, me and Bear were gettin' a little worried. What kept you?"

Perkin smirked at Sam, recounted the shoot down for a second time and this time he added the mortaring. When he was done he looked at the concerned faces before him and shrugged. "Hey, they told me comin' to Europe might be risky. By the way, when do I get my Air Medal?"

Spaulding shook his head at Sam, grinned and asked, "Did you do anything other than your crab scream on the way down?"

Perkin looked wounded. "No, but I hardly see how that's germane."

"I'm not surprised," Sam said dryly, his anger gone. "Leavin' aside your heroics for the moment, while you were toolin' about up there, did you happen to see anything of interest?"

Perkin's wounded looked was replaced, and Sam saw the excitement in his eyes flare again. Perkin looked around to make sure there wasn't an audience, and he said in a low voice, "Who said my Air Medal was for heroics? It should be for what I saw…or better yet what I didn't see."

0905 Hours
Rome, Italy

The morning's intelligence reports had reinforced Lieutenant Colonel Grossmann's conclusion that it was time to consider folding up operations in Rome. Although there seemed to be some optimism in Field Marshal Kesselring's headquarters that both breakout attempts could be contained, Grossmann read an eyes-only report to General Wolff that morning from an SS field commander that he assessed a successful Allied breakout as inevitable. It was an assessment that Grossmann concurred with, and the only remaining question was when the collapse would occur. When Grossmann asked Wolff whether the field report was to be shared with Kesselring's headquarters, the general shook his head and merely remarked that it was SS business and not the concern of the army.

General Wolff was unprepared to commit to moving his headquarters yet, but his chief of staff had quietly informed senior officers to prepare contingency plans. It was important to be discreet about such preparations.

If the troops in the field caught wind that the SS and Gestapo commands were preparing to evacuate Rome, it would undermine their morale. Even worse, if higher command in Berlin thought defeatism ruled the day in Rome, heads would roll.

Grossmann had spent the previous day shipping his Gypsy detainees to Dachau for experimentation after he had seen Colonel Mueller and his team of entomologists to the remains of the bombed-out Rome train station for their return transit to the Reich with their malarial specimens. The deportation of the Gypsies was extremely unpleasant. The Gypsies were far less compliant than the Jews who would obediently form lines and climb into the cattle cars. The Gypsies argued and cried and it wasn't until one of Grossmann's soldiers shot an angry woman and her husband that the rest of the Romani fearfully complied with his orders. During the embarkation of the Gypsies, he received so many death threats and evil eyes that he later told Kemmerling that he was surprised to have survived the morning. However, with that distasteful task off his to-do list, Grossmann was free to think about projects closer to his own heart, namely Antoniette and their future together.

Although Grossmann offered to take Antoniette the night before to an exclusive restaurant that overlooked the Colosseum, she had insisted on cooking for him at her apartment. It had always surprised Grossmann that Antoniette was an extraordinary cook, but rather than the gourmet fare that he had come to expect, she had prepared what he considered to be a whimsical home-style dinner. With an uncertain smile, she had placed a plate of veal cutlets and roasted potatoes before him with a tall German pilsner to drink. He had laughed delightedly—after the day he'd had, he was in need of a familiar home-cooked meal and the cold beer was the perfect accompaniment.

"Mein Gott! Wiener schnitzel! Oh, it's my favorite," he had said. "I couldn't think of anything better."

Her smile changed from uncertainty to pleasure, and Antoniette said, "We call it *cotoletta alla milanese*, but I prepared it more in the German style. I thought you might need a taste of home."

The next morning as Grossmann sat at his morning café waiting for Major Kemmerling to arrive, he realized how badly he had needed something just like that—a familiar taste and a remembrance of home and normality. His mother had prepared schnitzel just like that and he had unexpectedly choked up as he thought of her. That Antoniette instinctively knew he needed a small gesture like a good home-cooked meal touched him deeply, and if it was possible, made him love her even more.

0915 Hours
Anzio, Italy

The three officers had moved from the top of Sam's bunker to the interior, and in the indirect light, they looked at a map of the Anzio-Nettuno battlefield. Perkin traced his morning's flight and as he calmed down, his explanation of what he had seen became more organized and detailed.

"The first thing, the 3rd Division is on the verge of taking Cisterna. There are American troops in the town and it looks like we're about to encircle it. I understand that they drove off or destroyed a dozen Tigers this morning during a counterattack. God bless those boys—they've been trying to get Cisterna for four months now. I only got a brief glimpse of it but there ain't nothin' left. It looks like those pictures of Ypres from the first war. Secondly, talking to Badeaux, it looks like our lines have extended roughly a thousand yards around the perimeter of the forward line. It's uneven, of course. There have been some small setbacks, and smaller gains, but the fact remains that the geometry of the battlefield is changing." Perkin pulled a small green notebook from his shirt pocket and did a few calculations. "Look, where we're at today...if we assume an equal outward extension of a mile around the arc of the battlefield where our current radius is fifteen miles from Anzio, it adds three miles to the VI Corps perimeter. It's like an expanding balloon. It also adds an additional fifty square miles of territory that we control. If we don't achieve a breakthrough at a specific focal point, we can't sustain this. We certainly can't go much farther without the commitment of additional divisions like us."

Sam and Major Spaulding nodded. Spaulding said, "Sure. We get committed on the basis of one of four things: a collapse of our line at some point; a break-through to be exploited; to relieve an exhausted division; or, as you say, the simple change in the geometry of the battlefield. But, we know that, so what's your point?"

Perkin shrugged. "There's no particular point other than noting that while we're having success, it's not sustainable unless we puncture the balloon at some point, which brings me to what I wanted to show you. As our geometry expands, so does the German geometry. We're on the interior of the expanding balloon, and they're on the outside. Right? So, their manpower requirements increase just as ours do."

Sam studied Perkin's face for a moment and said, "I assume that you're not giving us a basic lesson on ground operations because you think we're in need of remedial instruction."

Perkin grinned. "I wouldn't ever say that about you or Bill to your face. But...what do you do when your defensive line becomes too extended to manage with the resources at hand? You either try to reduce your lines or add additional resources, but if you can't do either of those then you look for ways to safely minimize your risk. In our time in Italy, we've seen the Germans do this over and over again. They are the masters at using the terrain to their advantage, and to our great disadvantage, and I think that's what they're preparing to do here. In the north-northeast corner of our balloon is the Colli Laziali also known as the Alban Hills. If you look at this southern massif here, it's called Mount Artemisio. It's not exactly Mount Sammucro, but it's a terrain feature that poses a formidable roadblock."

They looked at the map again. As with most of the mountains climbed by the Texans so far in the war, Artemisio wasn't a single mountain, but rather was a peak on a long ridge of many peaks. The massif extended five miles east to west with some of the peaks exceeding three thousand feet. Although it was volcanic in origin like many of the mountains of Italy, it was no longer active and was heavily forested.

"Well, that makes sense, but as we've crossed every mountain that we've come to, why would this one be any different?" Sam asked.

"I think it's an allocation of resources. It provides greater challenges than the flat plains to the south or north of its ends, so maybe they are hoping that our effort is the lines of communication—Highways 6 and 7." Perkin paused and looked at his comrades. "Everywhere we flew I could see signs of military presence: troops, barriers and fortifications, equipment, and even flags. I didn't see a damn thing on Mount Artemisio."

0935 Hours
Rome, Italy

"I was beginning to wonder if you were going to join me," Lieutenant Colonel Grossmann said to Major Kemmerling.

"Sorry, boss, I overslept," said Kemmerling. "I had a rough time coming back from Siena. Our train was strafed by Allied pilots just as we were leaving the station. No one killed, but there were casualties and it took some time to get them evacuated. Then we went to the nearest tunnel and parked there for several hours. I didn't get back to my quarters until 0200." Kemmerling motioned a waiter over and ordered a breakfast of a soft-boiled egg, a roll, and a caffè corretto.

"Well, I'm glad you're back. I got rid of three pests while you were gone: the priest's family, the Gypsies, and Colonel Mueller. How was your visit with the priest's mother?"

"Traumatic. I've never known women to cry and carry on as much as Italians—Miss Bernardi notwithstanding. Thank God, German women are made of sterner stuff. You're a fortunate man, boss." Kemmerling stared at the espresso and glass of grappa that had been placed before him. He reached for the grappa and downed it in a single swallow. His visit to the priest's mother had been one of the most distasteful things he had done in his time in the service. Kemmerling had understood why Grossmann was carrying out his threat to show the compromising photos to the old lady, but comprehension of orders didn't always make them palatable.

"I am fortunate indeed," Grossmann said. "What are your thoughts on the Gestapo office in Siena?"

"Fanatics. Hard core Nazis. Every last one of them. There was no way I could broach any business with them. If they're running any black-market operations, and I doubt that they are, we won't be able to move in as outsiders. And if they're not, it's because they're too busy being the master race. I needed to take a shower after leaving. If we relocate to Siena, it may be a while before we could set up shop…so I'm thinking it might be better to work on the boss to relocate to Milan. It's much bigger and more opportunity in any case. You know, if evacuation is necessary." Kemmerling motioned for the waiter to bring another grappa. His espresso remained untouched.

"I'm thinking that it might be," Grossmann said. He told Kemmerling of the eyes-only message for General Wolff.

"Shit. I was afraid of that. You said that Kesselring still thinks it's possible to contain the breakout attempts. Is that a serious assessment or is that for Berlin's consumption?"

Grossmann shrugged and said, "I don't know. Two divisions, the 362nd and the 715th, were mauled yesterday by the Americans at Anzio. Ach…Kesselring's brilliant, but you know what? We're pretty smart too, and I don't see how things can be contained—particularly if the Allies conduct the cross-channel landing in the next thirty days or so. Berlin will have no reinforcements left for Italy, and if we can't move to another fortified defensive line, the Allies could be at the foot of the Alps by fall. Maybe sooner. I'm particularly concerned about Von Vietinghoff's army. There's a significant danger there of encirclement."

"I know. But there is hope," Kemmerling said with a smile.

"What's that?"

"We always have General Clark on our side. So... on to more optimistic subjects. While I was stuck in that damn tunnel last night, I gave some thought to our business operations," Kemmerling said.

"Excellent! Let's hear your thoughts." Grossmann waved the waiter over and told him to leave the bottle of grappa.

"Okay...I think that we, and by we, I mean you, should put together a trigger list or a decision matrix," Kemmerling said as he lit a cigarette. "What I mean by that is we don't want to get ahead of ourselves here. We can't afford to raid the mob warehouses too early or we risk getting the Italian authorities involved. As you said the other day, timing is everything. You're better at this than me, but if we were to put together a list of indicators of enemy activity it might help us judge when the time is right. For example, I think that if Fifth Army cuts Highway 6 and traps von Vietinghoff, we might have no more than five days to conduct our raids and either ship the goods out of Rome to our next station or to find another buyer. Personally, I think we should find a buyer in advance. Not the biggest, but not the smallest boss either. Someone with cash reserves, ambitions, and not afraid to take risks."

Grossmann smiled. "Great minds think alike. I was thinking the Occhiato family would fit nicely. According to the criminal reports I've seen, they've been aggressive in their protection rackets and the market. They've got ties to the Calabrian mob, not that it should matter, and I suspect they'd welcome the opportunity to acquire new stocks in the coming chaos of the battle for Rome—and we need to make them aware that we intend to drag the battle out for months like Stalingrad."

"Are we going to?" Kemmerling asked.

"I don't think so, but they don't need to know that," Grossmann replied. "Who knows what Hitler will order?"

Kemmerling nodded. "Hmm…I hate to even guess. As for the Occhiato family, I think they'd be a good fit for us as well. Do you know any of them personally? I don't."

"No, I don't. We've done business with them but via middlemen, but I'm sure it'd be easy to set up a meeting as a businessman or something as a front. I'd like to do that sooner rather than later. I also like the idea of a trigger list. I'll give that some thought. You're probably too conservative in your guess on cutting Highway 6. I would think that even if the Tenth Army is in retreat or encircled, they'll be able to hold the Allies at bay for a minimum of ten days. The danger to us is a breakout that's directed at Rome and not a military objective. I can't see why they'd do that, but if they did, our timeline might shrink from ten days to, say, three. Speaking solely as an entrepreneur, I hope that's not the way this plays out."

0940 Hours
Anzio, Italy

"I think we should request permission to conduct a reconnaissance patrol on Mount Artemisio," Perkin said.

"No. We're not at that point yet," Major Spaulding replied. Spaulding walked to the doorway of the bunker, ducked under the railway tie that served to frame the top of the door, and spat a long stream of tobacco juice into the dust.

"But, Bill…" Perkin started to say, but he uncharacteristically stopped when Spaulding held up his hand.

"Hang on, Professor," Spaulding said. "You know what I'm gonna say, don't you?"

Perkin looked at Sam and shrugged. To his cousin he said, "Bill's gonna tell me that someone else is going to get the fun." In an exaggerated movement, he dropped into a chair and slumped as he placed the back of his hand against his forehead and exclaimed, "Oh, the unfairness of it all!"

Spaulding shook his head. "Do you see what I have to put up with?" he said to Sam.

"Bad acting?" Sam grinned and said, "I've seen better, Perk. I think your skills need a little polishin'… one of your weaker performances, I'd reckon. It lacked… what'd you say the other day? Pluck and verve?"

Perkin sighed dramatically. "Do you think so? Gosh, guys…I get shot down while saving humanity and all you can do is deny me my just desserts of leading the patrol and then you criticize my thespianism."

"That ain't a word," Sam said. He opened a thermos and sniffed at its contents.

"It is so," Perkin countered.

"Maybe in Austin, but nowhere in the civilized world is thespianism a real word." Sam poured some coffee into his canteen cup and sniffed it again. "Bill, leaving aside the feelings of the most sensitive man ever from Texas, what do you want to do?"

"As soon as Professor Thespian has recovered from his swoon, I'll have him draft a report to the intelligence officer at regiment, and then I suspect he'll make the G-2 rounds at division and corps. I'd love to take a look-see up there myself, but since Mount Artemisio is about twelve miles from here and we'd have to cross either through the 34th or the 45th sectors as well as the German Army to get there, I think it's somewhat lacking in practicality. For now."

1005 Hours
Rome, Italy

"I think we have a workable outline. Do you want me to recap, sir?" asked Major Kemmerling.

"Go ahead." Doug Grossmann took a sip of espresso. He was beginning to get lightheaded from the grappa and he wanted his mind to remain clear.

"First, I'll talk to my contact with the OVRA. He can get us some names to start with from the Division of Criminal Police." The OVRA was the Organization for Vigilance and Repression of Anti-Fascism. It was the Italian Social Republic equivalent of the Gestapo, and both Grossmann and Kemmerling had a cordial working relationship with several senior members of the headquarters staff. The Division of Criminal Police had the organized crime portfolio but neither German had any solid contacts there.

"I'll get some of the Sachsenhausen counterfeit notes to open some doors for us. Tell your guy we'll need the information immediately, and there's a bonus in it for him if he can get what we want by the close of business tomorrow," Grossmann said.

"I bet he could do it by close of business today, sir. He's motivated. Second, we'll arrest and interrogate the names that OVRA provides us. Third, we'll conduct a reconnaissance of the black-market warehouses identified in the interrogations. Fourth, on your command, we'll raid the mob warehouses, confiscate their inventory, and fifth, we'll sell the entirety to the Occhiato family at wholesale prices—and if I may, perhaps we should charge a…uh…protection fee to the Occhiato family in the meantime. I'll set up a preliminary meeting for this afternoon, if possible. Sixth, we'll divide the prize money between us and our partners, and speaking for myself, I will transfer the majority of my proceedings to Switzerland."

"I intend to do the same," said Grossmann. "Do you want to do the interrogations or do you have someone in mind? He doesn't have to speak the language. He just needs to be persuasive."

"Funny that we were just speaking of Sachsenhausen. I think I know just the man to do the questioning." When Grossmann raised his eyebrows, Kemmerling smiled and said, "You'll love this. The SS guardhouse just got a new trooper in named Fleischer—a transfer from Sachsenhausen."

"So?"

"So...he's a brute of a man. Just the sight of him will have these cat-eaters pissing their pants." Kemmerling smiled. There was obviously more to the soldier Fleischer than he was saying.

Grossmann looked at Kemmerling in anticipation and said, "Okay. What else about this man aren't you telling me? You're sure he's up to the job of interrogating the Italians—off the record interrogations?"

"I'm sure. He was the guard that killed Yakov Dzhugashvili at Sachsenhausen for walking too close to the wire," Kemmerling said. "He ordered Dzhugashvili to move away from the wire, and when he didn't comply, Fleischer killed him on the spot. He was entirely in the right, but it took balls nonetheless."

Grossmann frowned. "I must be getting tired. The name is familiar but I can't place it. Who was...uh... this Dzhugashvili guy?"

Kemmerling offered a nasty smile. "Stalin's oldest son."

1230 Hours
Anzio, Italy

The day was continuing to drag on, and most of the soldiers congregated in small groups, smoked countless cigarettes, and talked about home or women. Sergeant Kulis had jogged over to the Able Company encampment and helped himself to a lunch of Able Company beef stew and potatoes. Kulis walked around until he saw Private First Class Roscoe Pfadenhauer, and he sat down next to his old friend.

"Hey, Howie," Kulis said. He looked at the sniper's mess kit and observed, "If you ain't gonna eat that stew, I'll trade you a chocolate bar for it."

"It's a deal," Pfadenhauer agreed and the swap was made. "I can't bring myself to eat any more stew. I'm going to go hunting through these woods and see if I can rustle up a deer or wild hog. I'd love to have something other than canned army food for a change."

Kulis shrugged. "There's no wildlife left for twenty miles other than skeeters, but good luck. Didn't you get some fresh food down in Naples?"

"Yeah, but I ate some of them little octopuses and mussels in that *frutti di mare* you talked me into and it gave me the screaming scours real bad." Pfadenhauer shook his head and shuddered at the memory. "Christ, that was bad. Let's not talk about that now."

Kulis nodded and happily ate both his stew and Private Pfadenhauer's. He enjoyed army food, army company, and he was happy to move on to the next phase of the operation. Whenever that might be.

"Eddie, do you think there's some way we can get over to the hospital?" Pfadenhauer asked.

Kulis looked at his friend with some concern thinking that the subject was back to food. "You feelin' poorly? I can call a medic."

"No. That ain't it. I'm fine since we left Naples. But I'd like to see some girls that ain't whores for a change. Or at least American girls. When I was in the evacuation hospital back in January, them nurses were real nice to me," Pfadenhauer said.

"Of course they were. You're the famous war hero Roscoe Pfadenhauer—you've got a Purple Heart *and* a Good Conduct Medal. I can see why they'd be nice to you." Kulis smirked at his friend. "Did you ask any of them nice nurses out?"

"No. They're officers. But I like to look at 'em and they smell nice. The only thing to smell around here is smoke, dust, diesel, mildew, farts and more farts. I prefer the nurses." Pfadenhauer finished his chocolate bar, looked to see if an officer was nearby and when he saw none, he tossed his wrapper behind the shredded remains of a bush.

"You want me to see if I can scrounge a jeep?" Kulis asked.

"No. You know they ain't gonna let us get a jeep just to look at nurses. Shit, I'm bored. You wanna see if we can get a game of trenchball going?" Pfadenhauer unconsciously wiped his hands on his trousers and then cursed as he saw the chocolate stains left behind.

"Sure. But only if we play the plank rule," Kulis said as he stood up.

"I don't know that one. What's the plank rule?"

"They put a plank over the trench. I can't jump the trench and those assholes have dug it so deep since we got here I can't climb out without following it to left field. The first time they tried was just a little plank that lasted until Cap'n Bear broke it and fell into the ditch." Kulis started laughing. "That was the funniest damn thing I ever seen. So a fella from Baker Company found a two-by-four, which the chaplain said was okay to use, but he banned Cap'n Taft for life from the plank."

"That chaplain's a little dictator." Pfadenhauer scowled.

"Chaplin was the little tramp but a great dictator," Kulis replied with a smile.

"Huh? Oh. Ha ha. I'm too bored for your humor." Despite himself, Pfadenhauer smiled at the play on words. "What were we talking about? Two by fours?"

"Yeah, the plank rule and dictators. So, I ain't gonna argue the rules of trenchball with a man of God, but it does seem severe. Have you noticed them religious tyrants want to ban everything good? Whores, cards, liquor, smokes, and now trench planks for big people." Kulis offered his hand to Pfadenhauer and pulled him up as he said, "Where's it all end?"

Pfadenhauer was about to remark that he didn't think regulating planks was comparable to disapproval of prostitution when Sam emerged from the company command post. Spying Kulis, he called out, "Sergeant Kulis! You're to head over to battalion now. Grab Cap'n Berger if you see him, and tell the battalion bubbas I'm on my way."

1300 Hours
Anzio, Italy

Major Spaulding had been pacing in front of a small collection of officers and enlisted staff members in the confines of the bunker serving as the battalion command post. He had been waiting for the last of the company commanders to arrive, and when the commander of Dog Company ducked through the doorway and embarrassedly said, "Sorry I'm late, Major." Spaulding merely nodded in acknowledgment.

Spaulding did another mental count of heads in the bunker although he already knew everyone was present. As he collected his thoughts, he looked at the faces staring back at him. The officers had their suspicions as to why they'd been summoned, and they were just waiting for Spaulding to formally give them the news. In those faces, he saw a mixture of excitement, anxiety, and hard professionalism. They were all veterans at this point, and no one had any remaining illusions about honor and glory in general, or about their enemy in particular. Everyone expected a tough fight.

Spaulding was a hard professional as well and he inwardly shook his head to clear any emotions. He spat a stream of tobacco juice in the general direction of the door, and said, "The movement orders are in the works. I don't have them in hand at the moment, but they're solid. We'll clear this bivouac beginning at 2045 and we'll be hauled to our new position by the 3606 Quartermaster Truck Company."

"Where's that gonna be, sir?" asked the Dog Company commander who thought that perhaps he'd missed part of the briefing.

"I was just comin' to that, Jimmy. The general plan is this: the 141st will establish the regimental CP northeast of Cisterna. Quartering parties are heading up later this afternoon, but figure roughly a mile or so beyond the outskirts of the town to the northeast. Second and 3rd battalions will move beyond that to a defensive position aligned north and south and we'll remain in reserve for the time being. Perk?"

"Sir?"

"Bring everyone up to date on what we know," Spaulding said.

"Yes, sir," Perkin said. "Today's been a good day. The II Corps advance from the south is moving through and around the Pontine Marshes and there's actually talk of a linkup today between II and VI Corps. In the Anzio pocket, the Germans are being pushed back in some areas and holding in others. The 3rd Division took Cisterna this morning and has successfully defended against the first rounds of counterattacks and continued their own advance. The 3rd is pushing hard and has reportedly shredded the German 362nd Division, although they're not out of it yet."

"Tell them what you know about the 362nd," Spaulding directed.

"Yes, sir. The 362nd is a relatively new division that G-2 believes was formed in Northern Italy from the remnants of several divisions that were shattered on the Eastern Front. So it's a mix of veteran and new units that's task organized into three grenadier regiments, an artillery regiment, one fusilier battalion, and the usual engineering and support units." Perkin looked at Spaulding who nodded, and then continued, "Not all of the fights are going well. The 1st Armored and the 34th are bogged down to the left of the 3rd in their drive towards Velletri, and the 45th to their left hasn't made much headway yet either. Still, Cisterna is the good news. You control Cisterna and it's another piece of Highway 7 in our pocket as well as a minor but paved road heading to the northeast towards the Lepini Mountains. The task as I see it is to hold Cisterna while the drive on Velletri and or Valmontone continues."

Spaulding walked to the doorway and spat outside this time. He nodded and said, "I think that's how this unfolds in the next day or so. We're being moved up to consolidate our gain at Cisterna. It took us four months to capture it, so there's no way we're giving it back. Velletri must fall to secure our flanks should we or the 3rd continue to move to the northeast towards

Valmontone. I look at Velletri as being another unfortunate town that we have to move past, and the Krauts seem determined to hold it. We may see a repeat of San Pietro, and we all know how that turned out. But after seeing what happened there, I hope like hell I'm wrong. I sure don't want to be part of it."

1845 Hours
Rome, Italy

Douglas Grossmann and Friedrich Kemmerling sat at a small table in a bar belonging to an undistinguished hotel off the Via Principe Eugenio. The bar itself opened onto a large courtyard formed by the six-story walls of competing apartments and hotels with one wall a dirty white and the other three various shades of dirty pastel yellow. Over their heads in the courtyard was a rickety pergola either supporting or being supported by a single gnarled grapevine that originated in the sole square foot of dirt in the courtyard. Grossmann couldn't decide which was holding up which.

The courtyard had various other amenities. Another hotel used the courtyard for its bar, and two boys wearing matching green shirts and ragged black shorts kicked a soccer ball back and forth with no great enthusiasm. Two of the bar tables, one at each hotel's bar, hosted a two-man SS security detail—hard men in civilian clothes with machine pistols under their coats. They stood out in any environment, but in the courtyard where no Italian man was taller than average height, they were particularly visible. Another table under the pergola was taken by an Italian couple—a young man and his wife. They also worked for Grossmann. Virtually everyone else in the courtyard, with the possible exception of the soccer playing boys worked for the Occhiato family—or at least Grossmann thought.

Sitting across the table from Grossmann was Salvatore Occhiato. He was middle-aged, medium height and medium build. He looked like virtually every Italian man Grossmann had met. As Grossmann saw it, there were only two features about Occhiato that stood out. His eyes were particularly sharp and his gaze darted constantly about the courtyard as he continually assessed his environment. The black eyes of Occhiato reflected intelligence and shrewdness without a drop of humor or wit. The other feature that caught Grossmann's attention was a pistol resting in a shoulder holster under Occhiato's left arm. It appeared shaped like a Luger but Grossmann assumed it was a Glisenti 9mm. Not a particularly well-regarded weapon, but good enough to be the service pistol for the Italian Army for over twenty years.

Grossmann opened up his cigarette case and offered a cigarette to Occhiato and Kemmerling. Both accepted. He took one for himself, and lit all three with his Zippo lighter. There had been some small talk when they had all sat down at the table a few minutes before but now that the drinks had arrived, it was time to get to work.

"Signore Occhiato, I would like to discuss a small business matter with you," Grossmann said in Italian as he inhaled of his cigarette.

"So I understood," Occhiato replied. He looked at Grossmann and said, "Is this a business deal between you and me, or is this a business deal with the SS?"

Grossmann was surprised. He had been introduced to Occhiato as Herr Schmidt of the German-Italian Business Council, an organization that didn't exist as far as Grossmann was aware. "The SS?" Grossmann asked with a faint smile. "Why would you say that?"

"Tenente Colonnello Grossmann, I'm a busy man. I know who you are. Please let us not play games. Is this a business deal with you and Maggiore Kemmerling?" Occhiato struggled with the pronunciation of the major's name. "Or is this a deal with the SS?"

Grossmann looked at Kemmerling who raised an eyebrow. "I don't know yet, Signore Occhiato," Grossmann said. "Let's say for the sake of discussion that it's one and the same." Occhiato looked puzzled and Grossmann clarified, "It's business with me unless I'm unhappy. Then it becomes the business of the SS."

Occhiato snorted, and then looked at Grossmann with wry amusement. "Yes. Business with you but you must be happy. Pardon me for saying that's a very German way of doing business." Before Grossmann could respond, Occhiato asked, "What business do you have in mind, Colonel Grossmann?"

"I'll explain in a minute, but first...I don't think we've met. How do you know my name?" Grossmann doubted that he would get a straight answer, but he wanted to ask.

"We've not met, but we've bought things from you. Through middlemen. I like to know who's acquiring quality goods, and so I made inquiries. I know who you are, Colonello," said Occhiato.

Grossmann didn't divine anything untoward in the Italian's matter of fact account, so he nodded and said, "We know you as well, Signore Occhiato. It's our belief then that we can do business more directly and openly without the use of middlemen."

"Yes. I think we can, Herr Schmidt." Occhiato's face showed the slightest trace of a smile, and Grossmann thought perhaps he had missed the humor in the man's eyes. "What are you proposing?"

"From time to time, we come across items that have

value in the current Rome economy. You know this...
everything from food to jewelry to furniture to art to
fine automobiles..."

Occhiato smiled more broadly and said, "Yes. We
got a very good deal on an American Stutz Victoria...
the 1933 convertible."

Grossmann returned the smile. "I remember the car
well. DV32 engine, beautiful burgundy—hand-rubbed
lacquer. A marvelous ride. I didn't realize that you were
the buyer."

"Like I said, we use middlemen sometimes. In
truth, I was a middleman myself. I wanted the car for
my mistress or maybe my wife, but in certain circles,
it was well known in Rome. There were probably less
than a dozen cars like it in all of Europe before the war.
Well...after the war, I didn't think I'd be able to explain
how I came to possess it, so I found a buyer in Monaco."
Occhiato looked impassively at Grossmann and asked,
"How did you come to own it, Colonel?"

Grossmann was tempted to ask Signore Occhiato
how he transported the vehicle to Monaco, but he wasn't
going to waste his time asking questions that he knew
wouldn't be truthfully answered. Instead, he answered
Occhiato's question truthfully. "We confiscated it from
a Jewish enemy of the Reich."

"Those Jewish enemies have proved to be very
profitable I think."

Grossmann nodded. "Yes. For both of us." When he
saw Occhiato nod thoughtfully in return, Grossmann
added, "It's profits like these that I wish to discuss."

Occhiato caught the attention of a waiter and called
for more grappa. When the three small glasses came,
he drank his without waiting for the Germans and said
dryly, "I thought I should brace myself before hearing
your proposal."

Chapter Five

May 26, 1944
0900 Hours
Northeast of Cisterna, Italy

Although tens of thousands of men were engaged in a desperate struggle to live mere miles away, the Texas Gun Club remained out of the fight. There had been small skirmishes since the division moved forward, but they were incidental actions—patrols that collided in the night with little effect. With the 1st Battalion placed in reserve and held behind the two forward rifle battalions of the regiment, even this experience belonged to someone else.

Captain Perkin Berger and Major Bill Spaulding walked together as they moved from company CP to company CP. Sam's company had been the first they visited. It was hardly a formal inspection, just a friendly check on the spread out units. They stopped and chatted with Sam briefly, but they could tell he was impatient to get his soldiers squared away. They stayed long enough to share a somewhat stale cookie from a box of treats that his wife Margaret had sent, and then they moved on to Charlie Company.

Perkin and Spaulding had seen nothing during the course of their walk of any particular concern in any of the companies—many soldiers were trying to catch up on the sleep missed during the nighttime movement and others were writing letters or cleaning weapons or smoking and talking. It was all about waiting at this point. Waiting for an order to come down that would commit the battalion, the regiment, the division to that desperate struggle mere miles away.

"Bill, do you need Sergeant Kulis and me for anything this morning?" Perkin asked as they left the Dog Company encampment.

"Well, your company's wearing a little thin, and there's no trenchball here, so I don't think so," Spaulding replied. "Why do you ask?"

"I was thinking about grabbing a jeep and heading to Cisterna to give it a look-over, and then going to division and having a chat with the G-2 fellas."

"Anything on your mind?" Spaulding asked.

"No, not really. I just hate the thought of us being tucked away here and not knowing what's going on. I thought I'd snoop around some."

After a moment's silence while he thought through the request, Spaulding said, "Leave Kulis. Take Sam. I want him to get some more exposure to the G-3 section at division."

Perkin smiled with delight. "Great! He'll hate going, of course, but it'll give us a chance to get caught up on the news from home after yesterday's mail call."

Spaulding smiled in return. "Tell Sam this is coming from me," he said. "You'll know if something changes in our status before we do, so if there's a movement in the works, get back here ASAP. Otherwise, I'd like to see y'all back here no later than 1600."

0930 Hours
Rome, Italy

Lieutenant Colonel Douglas Grossmann and Major Friedrich Kemmerling exited the staff car and blinked in the sunlight. They were standing outside of a drab concrete building, a dingy stockade, at a German embassy property on the Via Tasso now occupied by the SS. They carefully adjusted their peaked hats with the SS death's head insignia, and both men straightened their jackets under their belts.

The *SS Rottenführer* who opened the car door for the two officers was also their driver. After closing the door of the Mercedes behind Major Kemmerling, he ran to the building entrance. Ignoring the two SS guards at the front, he opened that door as well.

The guards saluted as Grossmann and Kemmerling approached the doorway, and held the salute as the officers stopped and looked at the building façade. "I don't think I've seen an uglier building in all of Italy," Kemmerling remarked.

"It's the product of modern Italian architecture," Grossmann replied. "It's modeled after the public toilet that Mussolini was born in." He returned the salute of the guards and followed Kemmerling into the building.

Kemmerling led Grossmann down a hallway that smelled like sweat and fear, and another guard opened a door that led to a small office housing a desk, two chairs, a phone, and a single droplight from the ceiling. Kemmerling indicated that Grossmann should take the seat behind the desk and he took the other. Kemmerling nodded at the guard and said, "Tell Sergeant Fleischer that we're waiting for him."

After the guard departed, Kemmerling looked at Grossmann's face and decided that his boss was uncomfortable with the planned activities of the day. Without saying a word, he pulled a flask from his jacket pocket, unscrewed the cap and offered a drink to Grossmann, who accepted. Then he took a deep pull of the cognac before putting the flask away. He breathed deeply and said, "Sir, we have two, uh, volunteers here. A worker of the Esposito family, his name is Mario Russo. He's a driver and just a hired hand. He won't be missed, and they'll likely think he's been nabbed by a labor battalion. The other volunteer is a goon belonging to the Moretti syndicate. Our contacts in the Italian OVRA say that he's an enforcer for the Moretti family. A tough guy that's not afraid to break fingers or legs or to rough up women."

Grossmann looked at Kemmerling with a degree of curiosity replacing his previous discomfort. "Do you think he'll break?"

"I don't know for certain. I'm sure he will but I must admit that there's a bit of scientific interest in it for me," Kemmerling said.

"Oh? How so?"

"I want to see how quickly a German enforcer can break an Italian enforcer. I told Fleischer I wanted it timed. Would you care to wager?" Kemmerling took out a pack of British cigarettes and offered one to Grossmann.

"Well, Fritz, I normally would, of course, but I'm not familiar with either man. My position would be nothing more than speculation—a mere guess. Has he started yet on this Moretti fellow?" Grossmann asked. There was no sense in not making the unpleasantness interesting.

"His name's Conti, in fact. He works for the Morettis. No. I thought this might be the case. No one wants to take a bet in the blind. I told Fleischer to start with the Esposito truck driver."

They were interrupted by a knock on the door, and after Grossmann gave permission to enter, a tall lean *Scharführer* strode confidently into the room. He stood at attention and barked out, "Sergeant Fleischer reporting."

Grossmann took a look at the man who killed Stalin's oldest son. Fleischer was like many SS soldiers that Grossmann worked with: tall, blond, and a weathered face that made him look older than he was. As Grossmann told the man to stand at ease, he saw a set of blue eyes that seemed devoid of intellect or soul. Grossmann had been in the company of hard men for most of his adult life, and despite Fleischer's relatively ordinary looks, he believed he was in the company of a particularly hard man. As he suppressed a shiver, he thought to himself that this was a man with sang-froid who would kill without compulsion or guilt—a blunt tool to be used for blunt work. He was perfect for Grossmann's needs.

"Sergeant Fleischer," said Major Kemmerling, "this is Lieutenant Colonel Grossmann. You work for him, as do I, in General Wolff's special projects division."

Fleischer nodded, looked two inches over Grossmann's head, and said, "I am at your command, Herr Colonel."

"Excellent, Sergeant," Grossmann replied. "I understand you've already begun the interrogation of one of the men."

"Yes, sir," Fleischer said. "With an Italian-speaking soldier, we started this morning."

"When do you think you'll be complete?" Kemmerling asked.

"We're done. I have all the information that you asked for," said Fleischer. He said it with all the casualness that he might have used to remark on pleasant weather. "He gave us the addresses of seven warehouses. Two are major warehouses and hold food and household goods—things like soap, towels, sheets, and stuff like that. He said that one of the two major warehouses held nearly one thousand kilograms of sugar as well as American military pharmaceuticals. He admitted to stocks of German military goods including food, small arms, and vehicles."

"The bastards!" Grossmann exclaimed. Inwardly, he was delighted. That gave him all the cover he needed to conduct his raids. "Did he say there were any changes planned? Major movements in or out?"

"No, sir. He said that it was a steady stream of products to and from the warehouses. Much of the materials come from looted Ami and British stockpiles and then they're smuggled back into Rome where they fetch the best prices. He didn't say where the German stores came from but they must be from Wehrmacht supply dumps." He said "Wehrmacht" with a special contempt reserved for SS personnel.

"When will you be ready to interrogate the other man?" Grossmann asked.

"Right away, sir. I didn't break a sweat with this one," Fleischer said. "He was weak, and he told me everything he knew—I would swear to it. What do you want me to with him?"

Grossmann looked at Kemmerling who shrugged. Grossmann shifted his gaze to the tall sergeant and said, "We're going to put surveillance teams on these locations, and as soon as we've verified what he's given us, shoot him, and dispose of the body."

"*Zu Befehl, Herr Obersturmbannführer!*"

0930 Hours
Cisterna, Italy

The town was still smoldering even though the fighting inside the city limits had ended more than a day before. The smoke and the dust rose from the rubble and it reminded Perkin of the constant stream of smoke that he'd seen from Mount Vesuvius. It had an end-of-times air about it, and although both Sam and Perkin had seen total annihilation in both San Pietro and Cassino, it was still indescribably sad.

An MP stopped their jeep on the outskirts of the town. He saluted the two captains, and then asked, "Where are you gentlemen headed?"

"We're here to do an assessment of munitions effectiveness, Corporal," Perkin improvised. He wanted to see the town and suspected that they wouldn't be let in as sightseers. He didn't much mind lying to the MP as there was little love lost between the combat soldiers and many of the MPs that seemed to exist solely to make their lives miserable. Perkin had been fined five dollars in Naples by an MP for wearing jump boots while not being in an airborne unit and it still rankled.

The corporal turned and looked at the destruction of the ancient town of Cisterna and said, "It looks like they were pretty fucking effective to me, sir. You should put that in your assessment, Captain, and if you don't mind me saying so, you should stay out of the town for the time being. There's a shitload of unexploded ordnance all over the place, and some of the fumes coming out of the rubble are noxious. So, if you do go in, I'd recommend wearing your gas mask if you still have it. Besides, you can only go in by jeep about another fifty yards or so before it becomes impassable. Once on foot, there are too many booby traps and unexploded shells lying around for it to be safe. Up to you gents, though."

Sam looked at his cousin, saw that Perkin was preparing to go ahead in any case, and said, "You convinced me, Corporal. Our orders can wait. Can you direct us to the 36th Division headquarters?"

The corporal gave them directions back from where they'd come, and Sam put the jeep into gear and wheeled away from the town. Seeing the disgusted look on Perkin's face, Sam laughed and said, "You've seen one Dago town, you've seen 'em all. Reach into my pack there and break out the cookies. Let's eat 'em before they get any more stale."

Perkin did as he was told and pulled a cardboard box out of Sam's pack resting in the back of the jeep. When he opened it up, he saw a wide variety of unfamiliar cookies and bars. "What are these?" he asked.

"Other than the peanut butter cookies, these are all experiments," Sam said. "That one you're holding is called a tollhouse cookie, and that brown bar ain't a cake disaster, it's called a brownie. Maggie's letter said the magazines say these are all the rage for G.I.s."

"Wow, are these good," Perkin said as he tried a chocolate chip cookie. "It's an amazing thing when you think about it."

"Cookies?"

"No," Perkin said. "The fact that your lovely wife can cook these in South Texas, and the United States government can get them to you in Italy...in a combat zone in Italy...before they get too stale to eat. That's amazing."

Sam reached into the box and pulled out a brownie. He took a bite and said while he chewed, "It is amazing, but it's sad as well."

"Whaddya mean?"

"Maggie could have made these for me at home,"

Sam answered. "Or a pecan pie. Or a good chicken fried steak or Lupe could have made tamales. The point is that I would have been home to enjoy them. Instead, we're toolin' around the outskirts of a nice little town that's been totally obliterated…where there ain't a god-damned house that's still intact and we cain't even go in it 'cause it's booby-trapped. Some day in the near future some Dago boy or girl is gonna step on a mine or a 200-pound bomb is going to detonate in the middle of the night and kill a whole damn family. It's just sad."

"I know, Bear," Perkin said. "It is sad. I know you'd rather be home. I wish you were…I really do. But, more important than your concerns, I'm exactly where I want to be. I said all along that I didn't want to miss this, and I'm glad I ain't. This war is terrible, it's tragic, and it's fixin' to get worse any day now. But I think we're doin' somethin' wonderful here—we're puttin' an end to the worst tyranny the world has ever seen."

"I think I missed the wonderful part," Sam said with a slight smile. He wasn't going to let the conversation take a morose turn.

"That's not surprising but it's all been magic. The experience of a lifetime. Except for the crabs, of course. That was just downright cruel. But c'mon…have you seen any indications that the Germans would be content to leave us alone if we'd stayed in the States?" Perkin asked. He pointed to a collection of tents set in a small hollow about a hundred yards from a dairy barn.

"Nope. I ain't seen nothin' that suggests there's a single 'live and let live' German. Not one. So, I reckon that I'd rather kill 'em here than in Texas. But I don't have to like it." Sam steered the jeep toward the tents and said to Perkin, "Put that box away, would you? I don't want some dogface thinkin' he's entitled to my cookies."

Perkin laughed as he put the box back into Sam's pack. "You got it. Even if it's nothin' but bad business over here, ain't total war just a little more bearable with cookies?"

1005 Hours
Northeast of Cisterna, Italy

The division headquarters was set in the partially destroyed buildings of what had once been the most successful dairy farm in the Cisterna area. Sam breathed in deeply of the farm air, and while it sometimes brought tears to his eyes as it reminded him of home, today it made him smile. "Cow lots ain't for everyone, but it sure smells good to me," he said to Perkin who pulled his undershirt over his nose until he decided the cow lot might smell better.

Perkin wandered off in search of the intelligence section, and as Sam walked into the main barn, he smiled again, this time with appreciation. This was a modern dairy with a large 3000-liter refrigerated bulk tank. As Sam looked over the equipment, his smile faded. Someone, presumably German soldiers, had stolen the electric motor for the agitator and had dismantled the drain valve. It would be costly to repair but not nearly as costly as the farmer's stolen herd would be to replace. Sam had yet to come across an Italian farm that hadn't had its livestock plundered.

Sam pushed open a swinging door and walked from the storage room into the milking chamber of the barn. There were several American officers having a conversation at the far end of the large room, but Sam paid no attention to them as he looked over the rest of the dairy barn. It had three milking stalls that were framed by metal tubes that had once been painted orange but the paint had long since peeled. A runway with a rope and pulley-operated door brought the cows into the barn from the outside lot and the gates to the stalls opened with a hand-lever. A large trough held feed for the cows during the milking, and the stalls were elevated allowing the farmer to stand upright while putting the milker onto the cow's teats. The milkers were operated by vacuum and the hoses fed the milk into glass tubes that ran from the milking room to the bulk storage tank in the other room. Although there were obviously some years on the system, Sam was impressed with the modern setup. He spied a closed door and opened it expecting to find a feed room, which he did, although the grain that was used to feed the milking cows had been emptied long ago by German soldiers to feed their draft horses.

"Are you a farmer, sir?" asked a first lieutenant who seeing Sam's professional eye run over the setup limped over and joined him.

"Nope. I'm a rancher, although I have a few Holsteins for our needs. Nice outfit, here," Sam said.

"It sure is. We didn't have automated milking on our farm in Maryland until right before the war, but it looks like this has been in place for a while. I'm George Peterson, by the way," the lieutenant said. "I'm stashed in the G-3 section until my leg is back to a hundred percent."

Sam shook hands with the lieutenant and noticed the hard calloused hands of a farmer. "Good to meet you, George. I'm Sam Taft. What happened to your leg? Bloody river or Monte Cassino?"

"Neither," the lieutenant said, and then his face lit up as he recognized Sam's name. "Sam Taft? Were you on Mount Sammucro in November?"

Sam nodded. "Yep. I was on and off that rock for

over a month," he said as he tried to place the lieutenant. He wasn't great at names but he had an excellent
memory for faces. "Do we know each other?"

Peterson said with a smile, "Kind of. I lost my
footing on Mount Sammucro in November, fell ten
foot onto a ledge and broke my leg in three places. You
brought me down draped over an old mule."

Sam smiled broadly. "I remember. I was just up
there helpin' out. If I remember right, you had lain out
all day in one of them rainstorms and they couldn't get
to you until dark. Your boys had to use a rope and a
mule to pull you up off that ledge. But you had so much
morphine in you by the time I led your mule down, you
were out the whole time. I don't think I gave you my
name or even talked to you."

"I asked around. I wanted to thank everyone that
helped me out, but I'd been told you were taken at the
river."

"I had been, but I was able to get away and make
my way back."

"It was pretty lonely out there waiting for nighttime, and I'm still grateful for the rescue. So...thank
you!" Peterson offered his hand and said, "I appreciate
it more than you know, and I'll buy you a beer if we ever
see a bar again."

Sam shook his hand again and beamed with
pleasure. It was a rare day in the infantry when he'd
been thanked for anything. "By God, you're welcome!
I'm damned glad to see you're okay. Not all the boys I
brought down made it through the night. What are you
doing in the G-3?"

"I'm helping update our operational picture,"
Peterson said. "It's kind of boring compared to being
in a rifle company, but, you know...whatever I can do
to help out."

"Great! I was sent down here by battalion to get the scoop on what's going on. Maybe you could help, if you don't mind me fetching our battalion intel bubba. He'd like to hear it too."

"Sir, there's nothing I'd like better."

1145 Hours
Rome, Italy

The second interrogation was taking somewhat longer than the first, but Lieutenant Colonel Grossmann was under no illusions that it would be concluded in short order. Major Kemmerling had left to arrange the surveillance of the Esposito warehouses, and with a promise to faithfully record the time, Grossmann had stayed behind to watch the interrogation of the Moretti hard man.

The Italian stockade that the SS had taken over had a two-way observation mirror in a viewing room that allowed Grossmann to watch the interrogation in solitude. This wasn't the first interrogation he had witnessed in his career, but it was by far the most brutal.

Fleischer had evidently sized up both of his opponents and while the mere threat of force and a few hard kicks were sufficient to make the first man talk, Fleischer had taken a different approach with the second man. Using a police truncheon he had found in the Via Tasso stockade, Fleischer had thrown open the door, stormed into the interrogation room where the hard man from the Moretti syndicate was held, and slammed the nightstick down hard on his left collarbone. The Italian had instinctively tried to raise his hands to protect himself, but they were shackled to the table. The swiftness and the violence of the attack was so unexpected that Grossmann jerked back in his seat as if he had been struck as well. There was no doubt in Grossmann's mind that the man's collarbone had just been shattered and he was shocked at the brutality of the assault.

The man screamed in pain and fear, and as the tall SS sergeant moved behind the seated prisoner, he gracefully spun on a jackbooted foot and slammed the truncheon down hard on the gangster's right wrist. The nightstick crushed the Italian's wrist, but it also hit the edge of the metal gray table, splintered, and broke in two. Fleischer threw away the stump of the truncheon in disgust and stepped back out of view. For a moment, the Italian's eyes whipped wildly from side to side as he tried to see his attacker, but Fleischer moved carefully to stay out of view. Then Fleischer walked quickly up behind the man and clapped a gloved hand over the prisoner's mouth. With his other hand, he pinched the Moretti man's nostrils closed, and held on firmly as the man thrashed in his shackled seat.

Grossmann watched, fascinated and appalled. The Italian must have been in terrible agony from his broken bones, but he struggled to the best of his limited ability. Grossmann lost track of the time but felt that the prisoner had been deprived of air for several minutes, although in truth it was far less. As the man's struggles began to weaken and he was clearly close to passing out, Fleischer let go and stepped back. While the Italian gasped for air, the SS sergeant pulled out a black bag that was tucked into his belt and whipped it over the prisoner's head. He then slapped him hard on the head and the face for several minutes, and then without saying a word, Fleischer left the room and slammed the door behind him, seemingly in anger.

When Grossmann left the viewing room, Fleischer was lighting a cigarette. He came to attention when he saw Grossmann but relaxed as Grossmann told him to carry on. Grossmann looked closely at Fleischer's face as he inhaled deeply of the cigarette. It was completely impassive. There was no sign of adrenaline, fury, or even exertion, but neither was there any sign he had taken pleasure from the brutal beating. He had a vaguely benign air about him and Grossmann was reminded of a long distant colleague who had once used Grossmann's desk phone to call his wife to tell her he wanted spätzle for dinner. It was unnerving to see a man so calm after such violence.

It wouldn't do for the sergeant to see him unnerved, however, so Grossmann lowered his head as he lit a cigarette of his own and regained his composure. Inhaling deeply calmed him down, and he was somewhat surprised his hands weren't shaking. Deliberately deepening his voice, he asked, "What is your plan here, Sergeant?"

Fleischer looked at Grossmann with calm eyes and he nodded slightly. In a professional voice, he said, "Sir, I plan to let him suffer for a few minutes, and then I'll return and repeat the procedure. It's my intention to hurt him bad enough that he wants to die, but he can't. I'll double the near asphyxiations from here on and although he may desire death, he'll fear it more. I'll do this four more times, which is equal to the cigarettes in my case, and then I'll begin the interrogation. I'll have your answers two minutes after that—I used this technique many times at Sachsenhausen and it never failed. After that, with your permission, I'll kill him and dispose of the body. He won't lie to me, nor hide any information, and it would be pointless to let him suffer further."

1215 Hours
Northeast of Cisterna, Italy

The outbuildings of the Italian farm had been taken over by the various staff sections of the division, and Lieutenant George Peterson had led Sam and Perkin to a large stone smokehouse with a damaged red tile roof. Although the hams and sausages that once cured here had long since been consumed, the faint smell of decades of smoked meat made Sam's stomach growl.

As Peterson searched for a large area map of central Italy, Perkin told Sam about his meeting with the division G-2. "The German Tenth Army is conducting an orderly withdrawal from the Gustav Line, primarily along Victory Road. It's a textbook withdrawal that's allowing the bulk of their army to redeploy to this sector while select units hinder the advance of the British Army. Meanwhile, more forces are headed this way including the remainder of the Hermann Goering Division."

"They come to us. We go to them. I don't see that it makes a lot of difference," Sam said. He was about to ask Perkin about the German 1st Parachute Corps which had been in the Ortona and Cassino sector. He'd heard enough stories about the fighting qualities of the German paratroopers that he was curious if they would be committed to stopping the Anzio breakout. Instead, Sam was interrupted by Lieutenant Peterson.

"Okay. Here's where the operation stands as of this morning, and understand that this is a fluid situation." Peterson paused for a moment to collect his thoughts and said, "I guess I need to go back to last night. Clark issued orders changing the direction of the breakout, and VI Corps is in the process of moving the units to meet the new strategy of Emperor Marcus Clarkus."

Peterson ran his finger from west to east on the map just below the Alban Hills. "This was the main thrust of the breakout. First Armored, 3rd Infantry, and the Special Service Force were moving along this axis— Velletri to Valmontone and the idea was that they would cut Victory Road and stop that orderly withdrawal that Captain Berger was just talking about. Two divisions and a commando brigade should have been a good anvil for Eight Army's hammer to pound on, but Clark didn't like it."

Sam looked at Perkin who was paying intense attention to the young lieutenant. As Peterson started to say more about the original plan, Perkin put his hand on the lieutenant's shoulder. "Hang on, George," Perkin said. "This is Alexander's plan. Clark didn't change this on his own, did he?"

Peterson shrugged. "Sir, I have no idea. That's not how command relationships were explained to me at OCS, but there seems to be a consensus here that Alex might not even know what's happened yet."

Sam saw Perkin's face darken and before Perkin could explode, he interjected, "What's happened, George? What's the new plan?"

Peterson pointed back at the map. "There's only two ways around the Alban Hills. Either to the left or the right. To the right takes us towards Valmontone to cut the German retreat. To the left is the least complicated route to Rome. So, it looks like Emperor Clarkus is making a play directly for Rome. This is what I think is happening. Look here: the 1st Armored is going to redeploy across divisional lines in front of Velletri and slam into the fight going on south and west of the Alban Hills. The plan is to breach the Kraut lines on this side of the massif and take Rome using Highway 7 as the main line of advance. The 3rd Division is going to have to hold the German Tenth Army on its own. Them and airpower, I suppose."

"Huh," Perkin said with a frown. "Throw a couple understrength regiments at an army and let's see what happens. Sounds familiar, doesn't it?"

Sam stared silently at the map. The scale was sufficient that Sam could see dozens of side roads around the area of Valmontone, and there was a main road, Highway 82, that ran from Arce to Avezzano that would allow thousands more to escape. There was no way that a lone division would be capable of interdicting the retreat of the German Tenth Army. Sam shook his head, and asked of Peterson, "What about us, George? We're not committed and we're the closest full-up division to the 3rd. Are we going right to help at Valmontone, or are we going left?"

"We're not doing either at the moment. We'll move up closer today to Velletri, and maybe that's where we'll go. If not, we'll be well positioned to be a reserve for either effort."

1430 Hours
Northeast of Cisterna, Italy

Sam and Perkin had finished briefing Major Spaulding regarding what they had gleaned from division, and Sam was leaving to return to Able Company. Neither officer felt particularly enlightened by their time with higher echelon, and Sam remarked as he walked out of the bunker serving as the temporary battalion headquarters, that he would have learned more from the Italian orphan Jim Bob, who had recently made his way back to the battalion. No one could ascertain how he had made the transit from Naples to Anzio because his story changed every time he told it.

After Sam left, Perkin and Major Spaulding left their bunker and walked along a trench line while Spaulding smoked a cigarette. "So I gather that division really knows little more than we do. What's your best guess there, Professor?"

Perkin grinned at his battalion commander. "I don't guess, Bill. I'm an intelligence officer. I deal in the truth. I analyze cold hard facts and come to data-driven conclusions that escape all but the most astute."

"Huh," said Spaulding dryly. "Is that so?"

"Oh yeah. Of course."

"Leaving aside the implication that I must be in the less astute category…"

"Oh, you picked up on that." Perkin grinned again.

"Yes, I must be smarter than I look…so leaving that aside for the moment, I would note the last time I looked, your paperwork said you were an infantry officer."

As Spaulding lit another cigarette off the remains of the one he was smoking, Perkin said, "That's technically true, but I know the egghead handshake. I'm a member of the club now."

"Well hell, Professor. You must know exactly what's going to happen then…" Both men started coughing as they walked through a thick cloud of acrid smoke.

"No one does…Jesus Christ! I wish we'd get moving," Perkin said. "These pots are producing more smoke than Vesuvius."

Spaulding wiped his eyes and nodded. They hurried through the cloud until they found relatively clear air and Spaulding said, "To bring this stimulating discussion of your merits round full circle, when do you think that'll be? Or as importantly, where?"

Perkin vainly searched his pockets for a handkerchief, gave up, and wiped his runny nose on his jacket sleeve before answering. "I don't know, Bill," he said without the bantering tone. "The intelligence officer side of me doesn't have enough data, so my best guess as an infantry officer is tonight or tomorrow, we'll move towards the Velletri-Valmontone road. Once we cut that, it's a coin toss whether we go left or right. I think the smart money is that we go left towards Velletri. Finally take the town and secure the flanks of the attack towards Rome."

Spaulding nodded and said, "Yep. I think so too. Do you really believe Clark changed the attack on his own initiative?"

Perkin's face darkened. "I wouldn't put anything past him, but if it's true, why would Alex tolerate it? I'd relieve Clark for disobeying orders."

"You disobey my orders daily," Spaulding observed. "Maybe I should apply that standard to you."

"Let's not get ahead of ourselves here. Besides, while no instances of disobedience come to mind, I'm sure that I atoned for my mistakes. You know, if I'd made any."

Spaulding smiled, pointed out another thick cloud of smoke, and they turned back and headed for the bunker. They walked along for a few moments in silence and then Spaulding said, "I don't know about you, but I don't much care if the British get to Rome first or we do."

Perkin shrugged. "Well, I'd like to get there first. But to let von Vietinghoff off the hook for national pride don't seem right. Besides, we know that he didn't disobey Alex's order only because he had America's best interests in mind. It was personal for him."

Spaulding nodded but said, "Probably. But that ain't exactly a data driven conclusion, is it?"

"I don't see what that has to do with it." Perkin

paused for a moment, seemingly coming to a decision, and said, "Bill, have you heard any rumors about a group of Gun Club officers demanding a congressional inquiry into Clark's conduct at the Rapido?"

Spaulding stopped and looked around before answering. "God no. I would think that's a dangerous subject bordering on...I don't know...insubordination at best or mutiny at worst. Are you telling me this in an official capacity?"

Perkin shook his head. "Nope. It's just gossip as far as I'm concerned. A friend in the 143rd said that it was a bunch of University of Texas grads who met in a barn after the Rapido. My friend asked if I was one of the signatories—I think he suspected I was the ringleader. Shit...I might have been if I wasn't in the hospital. I still get angry just thinking about it."

They stopped and leaned against the dirt bank of the trench while Spaulding lit another cigarette. After he had inhaled deeply, he said, "I do too, Perk. Sometimes when I think about the men who were wasted there, the friends we lost, my hands start shaking. I can't hardly get 'em to stop."

"Really?" Perkin was carrying his own internal demons of war, but had no inkling that Major Spaulding might be as well.

"Really. The truth is I'm afraid the Rapido is gonna haunt me for the rest of my life. It's not something that, you know, just fades away. When I think about those boys who drowned or got burned alive or who were just left on the far bank to be killed or captured—not to mention your wounds or my half-finger—I can't hardly breathe. I wouldn't say this to anyone but you or Sam, but I don't sleep so good anymore. It takes forever to fall asleep because as soon as I lie down I start thinkin' about what I should've done different. I keep thinkin' that I should have disobeyed orders and brought 'em back. That I should have insisted to General Wilbur and Colonel Wranosky."

Perkin interrupted, "It wasn't your call, Bill. I was there when you asked permission to withdraw and they said no. There wasn't anything you could do."

"I actually know that but it's a terrible game of 'what if' that I seem to play every night, and all my options look better than the one we took. Then, if I get to sleep, I dream about it. Usually it's one of two dreams. It's either the Nebelwerfer attack and them boys burnin' alive, or me at the river calling out to the troops on the other side to come back and they cain't ever hear me. I'm pointing at a footbridge and just keep callin' and callin', and I can see that they know something's wrong and they're lookin' to me for answers but they can't hear me. Then while I'm standin' on one side and them on the other, the artillery comes. I lose my finger again and then I'm on the ground looking for it, and when I give up and look across the river, everyone's dead. And I can see them all. Hawkings, Fratelli…everyone. That's the worst one." Spaulding blew out a deep breath and shook his head before saying, "Not every night, but enough that I don't much look forward to hittin' the sack like I used to."

Perkin nodded and said, "Me too. I have this dream that I'm on Mount Trocchio with a sniper rifle and I'm linin' up on General Clark when Kulis interrupts me. It's more frustrating than the dream where I'm about to nail a cheerleader under the UT bleachers when a hailstorm blows in and she loses the mood because she keeps gettin' hit by ice balls."

Spaulding snorted, the somber mood broken. Laughing at Perkin's dreamed misfortune he said, "I haven't had that dream, nor, to my great disappointment, have I nailed a cheerleader. Maybe I can put that dream in my rotation to break things up a little. So, just on the off chance that your fellow Longhorns can pull this off and at least make that asshole Clark sweat a little bit, I'm going to pretend we didn't have this conversation so I don't have to report it. Not that it would go anywhere." He barked out a cynical laugh. "On the other hand, who knows? Maybe I should. It might get more signatures that way."

Perkin shrugged and said, "I would hope so, but we've got so many in leadership positions now that weren't at the river or on the mountain that you never know. It occurred to me the other day that we might fight until the end of the war—capture Berlin and Tokyo by ourselves—but they'll always be the guys who missed the river."

"They should be grateful," Spaulding said.

Perkin nodded. "I suppose so. You know, this petition is actually an odd coincidence. The other day I asked Sam if he'd written to any of his family about the river and his escape. Other than Margaret and Old Perkin, he hadn't. So, I asked him if he had let the Tafts in Ohio know—he's got a lot of cousins there, but I really had Senator Taft in mind. But Sam said he'd save that conversation for when he was out of uniform. I guess that's the right thing but I think that the conduct of this campaign in Italy could use some scrutiny from someone who'd like to be president. Even a Republican. Might bring some clarity to what we're doing."

Spaulding dropped the butt of his cigarette into the trench and ground it into the dirt with his boot. "If what you told me is true, I don't know how Alex doesn't relieve Clark. There's no atonement for insubordination like that. But if it doesn't happen, a little clarity now and then would still be welcome."

1545 Hours
Northeast of Cisterna, Italy

The bunker serving as the battalion command post had been swept as clean as soldiers without brooms could make it, but it was still dark and dusty. A lantern supplemented the little daylight reaching the bunker's interior, and a handful of officers stood around the sole piece of furniture—a field desk, the top of which held a map of the battlefield.

"Major Spaulding, gentlemen," began Colonel John Hamilton, "I wanted to give you a quick rundown on where we stand. We're likely in place for the night, but no guarantees. Second and 3rd battalions are conducting patrols between our position and the Valmontone-Velletri road. No contact reported so far. General Walker expects the regiment to advance tomorrow and cut the road. Unless there is a change, and there always is, plan on your battalion being on the right flank of the division. You'll establish and maintain contact with the 3rd Division—presumably the 30th Infantry. The divisional reconnaissance troop is moving into that area now, and you will relieve them in place tomorrow."

Perkin studied Colonel Hamilton's face. Although he'd had little exposure to the new regimental commander, Perkin had come to expect that Hamilton would be calm and matter of fact, and he was. The colonel was the fourth regimental commander they'd had since landing at Salerno the previous September. The first had been killed at San Pietro; the second had been scapegoated and relieved for the catastrophe at the Rapido River; the third had been killed a few weeks later on the massif behind Cassino; and the fourth didn't seem to worry much about the hazards of the job. Perkin respected that.

"Sir?" Perkin asked.

"Yes, Captain?"

"We were having this discussion just a little while ago. Any thoughts on whether we swing right or left after we cut the road?"

"If I were a betting man, I'd say that we head left. In my opinion, the Appian Way is the hard way to Rome as the enemy defenses are pretty extensive between the coast and the Alban Hills," Hamilton said.

The commander of Baker Company looked at the map and asked, "If it's the hardest way, why do you think we'll head that way?"

Hamilton frowned as if the answer was self-evident and said, "Because the bulk of VI Corps has been committed in that direction, and the advance of the other units is going to grind to a halt in short order. Then, we'll relieve one of the other infantry divisions— either the 34th or the 45th—on the line. The breakout from Cassino will change the equation here in several days, but until then, Anzio is still a meat grinder. You see what will be between us and our eventual position on the line?"

The officer from Baker looked at the map even though he knew the answer and nodded. "Yes, sir," he said. "Velletri."

"So, my estimate is that two regiments move forward to relieve either the 34th or the Thunderbirds, and one regiment takes Velletri." Hamilton lit a cigarette and pointed at the map again. "So, we have a one in three chance of being committed to a city fight."

"Sir?" Perkin asked again. When he had the colonel's attention, Perkin said, "There might be another way. Over the mountains."

Hamilton raised his eyebrows but said nothing.

"I did a reconnaissance flight over the Alban Hills

yesterday morning..."

Hamilton interrupted, "Ah...you're Berger, right?" When Perkin nodded, the colonel said, "I read your report. My intelligence officer seems to think there's merit in what you wrote. I do too, so I forwarded it to division with my endorsement and when we cut the road and approach the base of the hills, I'll definitely get a reconnaissance team up there to find out which is better, your eyesight or your imagination."

Perkin nodded, pleased, and he barely managed to suppress a grin when he saw Sam roll his eyes.

"All right, gents. I have to go. I'm heading to 2nd and 3rd battalions next and then I'm relocating my CP to your sector. So, let's keep it quiet tonight and get as much sleep as we can."

After the colonel had departed the command bunker, Sam grinned at his cousin and said, "My money's on your imagination. I'm pretty sure your eyes were puckered as tight as your asshole on that flight."

Perkin grinned back and said, "You have no idea." He caught Major Spaulding's eye as the battalion commander was saying goodbye to his company commanders. "Hey, Bill, when we get there, can I lead a patrol up into the mountains?"

Spaulding shrugged. "Maybe...it's a long shot, Professor, whether we'll be in the right position relative to the hills. But I imagine there's gonna be a bunch of patrols to determine where the German line of resistance runs in our path, so if possible, yes."

2125 Hours
Rome, Italy

The faint light from the desk lamp in Grossmann's office dimmed even further as an unknown perturbation disrupted the Rome power grid for the fourth time that evening. Grossmann looked over at the light waiting to see if there would be any additional fluctuations, and when there was not, he resumed looking at the papers on his desk. He studied the addresses again and finally looked up at Major Kemmerling. He handed the papers to Kemmerling and said with a pleased smile, "Fritz, Fleischer's worth his weight in gold."

"Yes, sir. I thought he might be useful."

Grossmann nodded. "He was. He not only got the addresses of the two families' warehouses, but also that of two more. Moretti's man was so terrified he gave up Moretti and the competition. He even confirmed the addresses of the Esposito warehouses."

"That was very generous of him. Boss, we have more warehouses on this list than we have resources for. What's the percentage of the total Roman contraband, do we think?" Kemmerling asked.

"I have no way of knowing," Grossmann said. "Probably a drop in the bucket. But assuming we get even half of this and even if we're generous with sharing the wealth, this should be enough to…I don't know… buy a house in Spain after the war."

"On the coast, I would imagine. Frau Kemmerling likes the water." Kemmerling pulled out a handkerchief and wiped a smudge off his uniform boots. "Me? I prefer the mountains."

"I would think you should be able to afford a house with both after the war," Grossmann said. "And a driver to take you to and fro." Grossmann borrowed the handkerchief and cleared a spot on his own boots.

"Sounds good. Perhaps I'll buy Frau Kemmerling a house on the water in Spain…" Kemmerling paused for dramatic effect and then said with a laugh, "…and I'll move to the mountains in Chile."

"Or Argentina or Brazil..." Stopping to collect the words in his mind, Grossmann then added in English, "'...Why then, the world's mine oyster, which I with sword will open.'"

Kemmerling rolled his eyes and said, "Ach...I don't know what that means."

"It's Shakespeare."

"Great. An incomprehensible Englishman. I still don't know. What does...never mind. Let me ask the boss. What do you think that means, mein Führer?" Kemmerling asked of the picture of Adolf Hitler hanging on the wall.

Grossmann answered for the picture in a passable impersonation of Hitler, "Invade Russia!"

Kemmerling laughed as he stood to leave. "You need a newer picture. The advice he gives is getting worse."

Chapter Six

May 27, 1944
0600 Hours
Northeast of Cisterna, Italy

Captain Perkin Berger alternated between humming and whistling as he walked along a shattered stone wall that in happier times had separated a pasture from a wheat field. "Big Noise from Winnetka" had been featured in a dream that was now gone to memory, but the song stuck with him through the course of his morning.

Some soldiers in the 1st Battalion hadn't slept well the night before, but Perkin had taken an early morning bombing run in stride and had quickly fallen back asleep in a coffin-sized slit trench he had dug that day. Slightly after midnight, German aircraft had dropped bombs within the regimental area and the dropping of flares shortly afterwards created some consternation, as many feared the bombing and flares were a prelude to a night assault. They weren't, and Perkin merely rolled over and started dreaming again.

He had been awakened again, this time at 0300,

by Staff Sergeant Taylor, his senior intelligence NCO. Radio intercepts had indicated that a German battalion reported its position as in transit through Valmontone along the Via Casilina. Perkin asked the sergeant if he knew which direction the battalion was moving. He was told they didn't know, and Perkin replied that it could wait until morning. Valmontone was more than ten miles away and the entire 3rd Division lay between the unknown battalion and Perkin's slit trench. Outgoing artillery from heavy 155mm howitzers to the southwest woke Perkin again at 0345 and yet again at 0500. None of the night's events seemed urgent enough to cause him to leave the comfort of his trench until 0530 when a full bladder prompted the start of his day.

After relieving himself, he checked in with Sergeant Taylor and glanced at the night's report under the light of a kerosene lantern. There was nothing of specific interest to the battalion, so he was moving along the rubble of the stone wall to the nearby battalion CP, which was set in the shattered remnants of a farmhouse. Although the house was somewhat obscured by the equally shattered remnants of trees, the windows and open areas were covered by heavy tarps, and Perkin was gratified that there was no light emanating from the command post.

Perkin pushed his way through a tarp acting as a door, and then through another tarp which was a light barrier, and walked into the kitchen which was the most intact room remaining in the house. The kitchen table had been pushed into a corner, and radio operators had claimed it as their own. Additional tables had been brought in and held maps and the battalion clerk's in and out boxes. In another room, previously closed to the kitchen but no longer thanks to artillery fire a month before, a field desk completed the furnishings of the battalion commander's office. Major Bill Spaulding sat with his feet up on the desk while tipped back in a rickety chair. His head rested against the corner of the walls and his mouth was slightly open as he snored gently.

Perkin looked over at an NCO that was manning a radio and asked in a low voice, "Has he been here all night?"

The sergeant shook his head and answered in Great Lakes accent, "No, sir. Just an hour or so. He…"

A harsh cough interrupted the sergeant and then a voice from the corner said, "Sergeant, you're givin' away my secrets. Whenever anyone asks, I've been here all night." Spaulding opened his eyes and blinked hard. The boots came off the desktop and the chair dropped onto all four legs. "Mornin', Professor."

"Good morning, sir," Perkin replied brightly. "How are you on this fine army day?"

"Hungry. You?"

"Peckish. What's for breakfast?" Perkin asked.

"Before I took my nap I was told it was bathtub oatmeal," Spaulding replied. "Before you ask, the stove is missing from this house—I guess the Germans stole it while they occupied this sector. But there's a heavy cast-iron bathtub that we're using as a substitute. There's a pot of oatmeal sitting in the tub."

When Perkin walked into what had been a nice bathroom, he saw that soldiers were using the tub to hold two large pots. One contained oatmeal. The other held boiled potatoes, and both had been cooked on a field stove set up outside the house. It was a self-serve operation, and while Spaulding poured coffee for both men, Perkin loaded the plates of their mess kits with oatmeal and potatoes. Spaulding poured a thick yellow fluid from a punctured can of sweetened milk into the coffee and over the oatmeal, and Perkin found salt for the potatoes.

"Do you think we'll ever eat normal food again?" Perkin asked as he sniffed suspiciously at the yellow milk covering his oatmeal.

"Does it smell bad?" Spaulding asked. "Kulis said it was fine. Just yellow."

"We're on the Kulis standard now? God help us," Perkin said as he pulled up a chair next to the field desk. "I've never known that boy to have even as much as indigestion or heartburn. I think he's like a puppy. He could eat tree bark, bugs, and small rocks with no ill effects. Moreover, he'd think it tasted good. It's unnatural. He's unnatural."

"Maybe the Nazis have it wrong," Spaulding observed. "Maybe Kulis represents the master race."

"Yet another reason we should keep him from reproducing," Perkin replied. He tentatively tried the oatmeal, decided it was safe enough, and as he ate it, Perkin said, "Did you ever study eugenics? I never put much stock in the notion of it, but they taught the hell out of it in college."

"Yeah, I studied it too," agreed Spaulding. "I never understood the feeling for it since there are so many counter examples. If you believe the Caucasian race is the acme of humanity, how do you explain Jesse Owens or Jim Thorpe? The exceptions that prove the rule? Whatever that means."

Perkin closed his eyes and sought the exact words before saying, "*Exceptio probat regulam in casibus non exceptis.*" He was about to explain both the historical origins of the phrase and that it didn't mean what most people thought when Spaulding raised his hand.

"Stop right there, Professor. When you speak Latin, I can see you're gonna enlighten me on one thing or another, but I really don't care to get smarter today. Let's stick to the subject. What about Owens?" Spaulding stared at the oily yellow film on his coffee and gently shook his canteen cup in a futile attempt to combine the fluids.

Perkin shrugged. "I don't know. A eugenicist might say he was the product of selective breeding. You know, slave owners breeding the biggest and strongest slaves to increase labor productivity like a draft horse. A Darwinian might call it survival of the fittest. All I know is that he's one hell of an athlete and FDR should've been ashamed at not invitin' him to the White House. Did you know Owens said Hitler treated him nicer than our own president?"

"I never heard that. What kind of sacrilege is this? I thought you were Roosevelt's boy."

"I am, but that don't mean he's perfect," Perkin said with a shake of his head. "How about a different example? One with the master race. How do the Germans explain all them Jewish Nobel Prize winners? Or for that matter, German Jewish laureates?"

"I think they pretend they don't exist. I suspect they've rewritten the history to give the accolades to Aryans, but that'd be your department. You know, anti-Semitism's a damn queer thing. I never met a Jew before coming into the army, and my grandpa never met either of the Jews in Texas, but he was as anti-Semitic as Hitler and Himmler. I reckon that if he were alive today, he'd have supported the ghettoes and the concentration camps. Of course, he didn't hold Republicans, Catholics, Negroes, or the Irish in very high regard either, and he'd probably be in favor of internin' them with the Japs. Particularly the Republicans." Spaulding finished his oatmeal and moved to the potatoes.

"Who did he like?" Perkin asked. "Anyone?"

"He didn't like many people to be sure, although he was surprisingly tolerant of Mexicans and Okies," Spaulding said.

"Huh. Well, ain't that somethin'. What about Yankees?" Perkin asked with a nod toward the communications sergeant.

"Oh, Christ, he hated them the most," Spaulding said with a wink to Perkin. As he lit a cigarette he added, "Probably his only justified prejudice."

"Fair enough. I'd rather have a sister in a whore-house than a brother that's a Yankee."

"Hey, gentlemen, I'm sitting right over here," said the communications sergeant from Ann Arbor. While eavesdropping on the officers, he was also writing on a notepad and holding a phone to his ear.

"That's okay, Sergeant," Perkin said with a smile. "We're broad-minded people. We won't make you leave the room."

"Well, biscuits and gravy...you're just too kind, Captain," the sergeant said dryly as he put down the handset. "Major, this just came in. Regiment wants all battalion commanders and key staff personnel at their CP at 0730."

Perkin looked at Spaulding and said, "This is it. I'll bet we're gonna be committed. It's survival of the fittest."

0830 Hours
Northeast of Cisterna, Italy

Captain Sam Taft sat through the briefing given by Major Spaulding and his cousin. Perkin had made a sound guess. The regimental commander had informed his battalion commanders that the regiment would most likely advance toward the town of Velletri, and it was a question of waiting for the order to come.

There really hadn't been much to brief. The companies were to prepare for immediate movement and the 1st Battalion would depart the regimental area and swing into the line alongside the 2nd Battalion to its north and east. Once that was executed, the regiment was to standby for the order to advance.

At Major Spaulding's nod, Sam stood and joined Spaulding at the front of the partial remains of an erstwhile bedroom. He looked at the faces of his fellow company commanders, and a handful of other officers who had hung back after the battalion commander had finished the briefing.

Spaulding spoke first. "Sam brought to my attention a few days back his concern that we might have been preparing for the wrong fight. The army had us fixin' to carry on in mountain warfare, and Sam pointed out that our next major objective was likely to be Rome. I cain't say for certain, but it's looking increasingly likely that our next major objective is going to Velletri. The army doctrine for city fighting is virtually nonexistent. Seriously, *FM 100-5* has a grand total of two pages on it. So, I asked Sam and Perk to come up with an approach that we can use. Both of them had the benefit of observing the Canadian fight in Ortona, and can speak to the lessons learned from there. Bear…"

Sam nodded and cleared his throat. "I'm going to keep this simple because we all need to get back to our companies. Our inclination would have us walking down Main Street led by armor. That might be fine for a wide-open Texas town where there's one main road and then a grid of supporting streets. But Italian geography ain't quite the same. For most of the smaller towns, our experience has been that there's elevation involved in the siting of the towns. They need the plains for agriculture so they built on the mountains. Or maybe they like the views, I don't know. But what we've seen is generally a narrow main road leading to and from the town, which is frequently surrounded by a medieval wall that also serves as a sufficient tank trap. A bunch of curvy side streets stem off the main road and they follow the elevation of the terrain. Italian towns aren't laid out in a grid that civilized folks can understand. Their towns are more of a three-dimensional spider web."

Spaulding nodded and said, "In San Pietro and Cassino, our tanks were picked off one by one as we led with armor. Even with infantry support, all the Germans had to do was destroy a single tank and the road was blocked for hours."

Sam continued, "Having said that, we need the support of armor. So what happens as we come down that main road? We run into the main line of resistance perpendicular to our advance. Along our main axis of advance, we can reasonably expect 50- or 75-mm antitank cannons, or maybe 88s in a direct fire mode, tank destroyers, and possibly Mark IVs and Tigers. On the rooftop, we can expect *panzerfausts* and antitank grenades and rifles. All of this, of course, supported by indirect and direct fires. Our response is always to plaster the area with artillery and then move in. It worked in San Pietro but not so well in Cassino. So, what we recommend, and this is hardly revolutionary, is instead of coming straight down Main Street or Elm Street or whatever, we come in slightly off-axis with an infantry infiltration, at an acute angle to that main road or roads, which will be most heavily prepared for armored fighting. Our thinking is that if we come in at an offset point, say 300 yards or less from the main road, we might be able to get access to rooftops and upper stories and clear those areas from above as our armor advances. The Krauts did a number on the Canadian armor from the rooftops, so it's critical that we control the higher elevations. A lot of these Dago towns are full of row houses but different than you might see in an American city. The streets are narrower, and the houses are tightly packed and not of uniform height. There's often a shared wall between the homes of families, and what the Canucks did at Ortona is gain access to a top floor, usually the hard way by fighting up the stairs, and then blow holes through the wall using satchel charges. Once the hole is there, they tossed grenades through and then sent in a two-man team to finish the work. They'd then move on to the next shared wall and then so on. That's what I recommend here."

Perkin spoke for the first time. "The infantry needs to clear the route for the armor to advance, which means we have to clear both sides of a street or road. The armor can clear directly forward, to an extent side to side, but it's up to us to control the vertical axis. We recommend a two-pronged attack coming in from the left and right to protect the flanks of the armored advance. It's going to be hot work and we'll have to use everything to clear the rooftops and barricades: rifles, BARs, machine guns, flamethrowers, and lots and lots of grenades."

Spaulding nodded and said, "We're going to be relying on a lot of personal initiative here. I expect command and control to break down pretty rapidly. So, while we'll go in with clearly defined objectives with delineated company boundaries, y'all will have to manage your fights as much as possible on your own. We don't know for sure that Velletri's a divisional objective, but it seems likely to me. We've got the 34th slugging it out to the southwest trying to come in under the Colle Laziali following Route 7 to Rome. We've got the 3rd slugging it out to the northeast towards Valmontone. It makes sense that we clear the middle ground between those two pushes."

0900 Hours
Rome, Italy

Lieutenant Colonel Douglas Grossmann sipped the first caffé corretto of the morning at his favorite café. He had spent a lovely evening with Antoniette, awakened early to check the morning reports, and headed to the Piazza del Popolo to meet with Major Kemmerling. It was a wonderful day, and he was in a great mood.

Kemmerling was on time and he sat beside Grossmann so he could look out onto the piazza as well. "You know, sometimes it's just fun to be in Rome. Other than the occasional raid on a switching yard and the distinct lack of commodities, you could hardly tell there's a war going on."

Grossmann smiled and nodded in agreement. He opened his cigarette case, offered one to his deputy, and lit both with his Zippo lighter. "Speaking of a lack of commodities, where do we stand? Oh, in case you didn't know, the general's aide sent word back this morning that the general plans to extend his stay at Obersalzburg for another forty-eight hours."

"What's he doing there?" Kemmerling asked. "I didn't even know he was gone. Nobody tells me anything."

"He flew up early yesterday morning," Grossmann said. "The Führer held a flag and general officer meeting at the Platterhof Hotel, and I'm guessing that between the altitude and the alcohol, the general has decided to stay in the Fatherland for a couple more days."

"Poor bastard. I had a boss that dreaded the meetings with the Führer. He said he would go on and on into the early hours of the morning on whatever subject popped into his fertile mind: Jews, Roosevelt—but I repeat myself—Stalin, art, culture, or whatever. He wouldn't stop until he got tired."

Grossmann laughed. "I've heard the same thing from officers who've served at the Wolf's Lair. I had a friend who was a Luftwaffe major who said the funniest thing he'd ever seen was all those old Junker generals pinching themselves to stay awake at two in the morning."

Kemmerling laughed and spread some rare butter on a piece of toast. "They won't have to stay awake much longer, Doug." The smile disappeared. "This thing is winding down. Another six months or a year and it's done. The barbarians are at the gate. The Amis and the British coming up from the south, soon from the west, and the Russians coming in from the east. I can't imagine what it will be like for our people in East Prussia when the Bolsheviks arrive."

Grossmann shivered as an old memory flashed through his thoughts. He was a teenager and visiting his grandparents in Germany. On a cool and rainy July afternoon, his grandfather took him to an exhibit of 16th century paintings at the *Hessisches Landesmuseum*. On loan from a museum in Spain was a piece by Pieter Bruegel the Elder entitled *The Triumph of Death*. To a bored sixteen-year-old, the museum had been preferable to working in his grandfather's garden, but just barely. Then he came across *The Triumph of Death*. More than four feet by five, the painting portrayed a grim assault by an army of skeletons across a burning landscape against a handful of people who were clearly losing. While skeletons blew trumpets in the background, others cut throats with knives or swept through the people with scythes. The background was filled with ships burning at sea and people hanged from trees and gibbets.

Normally, the only aspect of art that held Grossmann's attention as a teenager was the prospect of nudity—his appreciation for the arts didn't come until later in life—but Bruegel's painting was captivating. His grandfather, sensing a glimmer of interest, pointed out some of the symbolism of the art and asked young Grossmann to describe what he was seeing. They puzzled together over victims tied to breaking wheels atop bare poles, wondering how their torturers managed to get them there, and their eyes were drawn to a sword held aloft against the gray sky as a skeleton beheaded a man. They noted spilled wine, scattered cards, a backgammon board, and they argued whether a dog was protecting a child or preparing to eat it. Grossmann pointed to a scene on the right of the painting where a crowd of people was pushing to enter a giant box and he asked, "What are they doing there?"

His grandfather had stroked his chin and contemplated the box, which was about the size and shape of a railroad car. "I think it's a trap. They're lured to the cross thinking it means safety, but I think they're being fooled."

"And him?" Grossmann pointed to a skeleton sitting atop the box and beating on two drums. "War drums?"

His grandfather studied the painting and said, "I don't think so, although you may be right. I think he's a hortator—like the drummer on a slave galley. He's driving them to their deaths."

Many years later, Grossmann shivered at the memory. He was about to ask Kemmerling if the SS used hortators at Auschwitz but decided against it. Soldiers normally weren't opposed to gallows humor, but he didn't want to get too morose on a day that started out well. "You're right, of course," Grossmann said to Kemmerling. "But since there's not much we can do about that now, let's leave it alone."

Kemmerling nodded. Sometimes discussing the coming apocalypse with his boss was cathartic for both men, but often it was not. Kemmerling decided that on this day he would think optimistically. Like the night before, he would purposely daydream about surviving the Gotterdammerung and moving to Spain. Or Chile. He nodded again and said, "Yes, sir. Of course. To the subject at hand, I put a surveillance on all the main warehouses on our list. We'll see if we can get a notion of how many guards they use and how well armed they are. I don't mind robbing the cat-eaters blind, but I don't want any of our fellows hurt in the process."

"No. Me neither. We'll have to think this through carefully. In addition to troops to intimidate the Italians, we'll need trucks, forklift operators, etcetera. And we'll need to hit these places in a coordinated, synchronized way—as simultaneously as possible. Otherwise, the stolen goods will be gone before we have a chance to, uh, recover them."

Kemmerling laughed. "It shouldn't be difficult for us to plan. After all, we're German."

1345 Hours
North of Cisterna, Italy

Perkin was sitting on the front bumper of his jeep drinking coffee directly from a canteen. The battalion had completed a movement several miles to the north and now was at the farthest end of the division's new sector. While the remainder of the regiment complet-ed its own movement, and Sam and Major Spaulding were meeting their counterparts in the adjacent 3rd Division, Perkin was killing time. Patrols were already exploring the boundaries of the battalion's new territory, and Perkin's NCOs were setting up shop in an abandoned shed not far away. There was little for him to do but think.

As his eyes were drawn to the slopes of Monte Artemisio, still several miles distant, Perkin wondered where they would end up next and decided that he didn't see any good options. The notion of fighting in the town of Velletri concerned him as much as the prospect of being thrown into the grinder on the south side of the Alban Hills.

He was pondering the scant army doctrine on town fighting, particularly the question of infantry support and coordination with the tanks when one of his intelligence NCOs, Sergeant Taylor, walked toward the jeep with a dusty Italian in tow. The man was in his mid-thirties, terribly underfed, and had dark circles under his dark eyes. His black suit was torn in several places and had dirt and grease stains that would never be washed out.

Taylor brought the Italian over to Perkin and when he saw he had the captain's attention, Taylor said, "Sir, this is Signore Prazelini. Mario Prazelini. He was snagged wandering through our lines by one of our patrols. He just came down off the mountain, and I thought you might like to talk to him."

Perkin looked up from his thoughts and examined the Italian. His eyes were red-rimmed, but they were intelligent. "Good to meet you, Signori Prazelini," Perkin said. "Do you speak English?"

The Italian shook his head as Taylor answered, "No, sir, he doesn't. I'll translate if you like." When Perkin asked if the Italian had been fed, Taylor shook his head. "No, sir. Came here first."

Perkin nodded and said, "Just a second." He walked

to a nearby jeep where a large army pot rested in the back. He rummaged around through a box, found what he was looking for, and after a moment's preparation he returned to the front of the jeep with a tin cup filled with lukewarm oatmeal and covered with sugar and swimming in canned milk. As Perkin handed the cup to the Italian, he said to Taylor, "Please tell him our chef should be shot for this oatmeal but it's the best we've got for now."

A voice from a nearby trench called out, "I heard that, Cap'n."

Perkin grinned and called back, "Not you, I meant the other guy."

The voice called back, "Oh, well, you cain't shoot him. He's seeing the medics for food poisoning. Bon appetite, sir."

Laughing, Perkin turned back to Taylor and Prazelini only to find that the Italian had already finished the oatmeal. As Taylor watched with an amused look on his face, the Italian ran his index finger along the side of the cup and then licked the oatmeal from his finger. Suddenly, the Italian retched loudly, staggered a few feet and lost his meal. Both Perkin and Sergeant Taylor had seen many Italians on the verge of starvation vomit after a rich meal. Or any meal.

Sergeant Taylor rinsed the cup out, filled it with water from his canteen, and offered it to the Italian. After a brief conversation with Prazelini, Taylor said to Perkin, "I told him I'd let his stomach settle and then I'll get him something else to eat."

Even though he had lost his first meal in days, the Italian nevertheless looked a little better. He sat on the jeep's bumper while Perkin sat on a wooden crate filled with maps. Through Sergeant Taylor, Prazelini thanked Perkin profusely. Perkin was genuinely touched when the man started to cry and through his tears told Sergeant Taylor that he had thought he would not be treated like a man again.

Perkin waited until the man had found his composure and then asked, "What's your story, Mr. Prazelini?"

As Taylor interpreted, Prazelini said, "Signore, I'm an engineer. A civil engineer. I was taken prisoner by the Germans last October and forced to work in a labor battalion at what the Germans called the winter lines, and then two months ago, many of us were moved here by truck. I wasn't sure we would live through the ride, because our German guards were terrified. They kept looking at the skies but we didn't see any planes. Then we got here, but I didn't know where that was for the first month. We were just in the mountains building fortifications in the woods. It could have been anywhere in Italy as far as I knew, but they let some local women bring us strawberries and then I learned we were near Nemi. Then last night, a small group of us were marched to what I think is Monte Artemisio, and when it got dark, I just kept walking. I came down off the hillside, and I was picked up by your men this morning. Thank you, sir, for not shooting me."

Perkin smiled and said, "It was our pleasure to not shoot you, Mr. Prazelini. Did you have a hard time getting through German lines this morning? How did you do that?"

"I haven't seen any Germans since last night. I didn't pass any coming off the mountain. There was some razor wire, and I came across a minefield, but I walked around it."

"How do you know it was a minefield?" Perkin asked.

"It was marked on the far side of the field. The far side from here, that is. Besides, I laid so many mines near Cassino, that I know how the land looks when it's mined."

"Maybe you can teach me someday," Perkin said. "I see land and I think it's all mined these days. Signore Prazelini, if I promise not to take you too close, can we drive up towards Mount Artemisio and you point out the route you took?"

The Italian looked apprehensive for a moment and then nodded. "Anything I can do to help you drive the occupiers from our lands. You are the first Americans I've met, and you've treated me with more kindness than anyone else has since I was taken from my home in San Pietro last October."

Perkin looked at Prazelini and asked curiously, "San Pietro? Do you know Dr. Frattini, by any chance? Was he with you?"

Prazelini's face broke out in a broad smile and he said, "Yes. Yes. We were neighbors before the war came to our valley. He was with us in Nemi and then I heard he was sent to Velletri to be an orderly for the Germans. How do you know him?"

"I don't. I know his family. They're in Presenzano now."

Prazelini's smile faded. "Have you met Signora Prazelini? I've not heard a word from my wife or son since last October. I've prayed that they went to stay in Naples with my family."

"Sir, I'm sorry. I don't know your family. I was briefly in the caves but I can't say that I met her either then or after we passed by San Pietro." Perkin paused not wanting to say more about San Pietro. The village was destroyed so thoroughly that the townspeople decided not to rebuild. "Uh, Mr. Prazelini...where exactly in Velletri is Dr. Frattini being held?"

"I don't know. The last I heard, they had set up a

medical facility in the city hall. It was one of the few buildings still standing. Maybe there."

1430 Hours
Rome, Italy

Lieutenant Colonel Grossmann had intended to leave the SS headquarters at noon and join Major Kemmerling for lunch. They had a multitude of details to work out and Grossmann wanted to do his thinking over one of the pleasant Italian white wines. It was getting warm in the Italian capital and he thought a crisp white would be just the thing to sharpen his mind.

He had already changed into civilian clothes and had just walked out through the main doors when a running lance corporal caught him as he was reaching for the handle of the car door. His presence was requested in the chief of staff's office in ten minutes, and he just had time to change back into his uniform.

The chief of staff was a full colonel who had been wounded in an ambush by Yugoslav partisans in the Predil Pass in 1943. He had been a battalion commander at the time, but his wounds had relegated him to a staff position since his recovery. The colonel had a frightening visage due to heavy scarring around his right eye, but Grossmann had found him to be an amiable partner in his extracurricular activities. He assumed the colonel had gotten wind somehow of his planning to steal from Peter to sell to Paul.

An aide let Grossmann into the office. As he walked up to the colonel's desk, Grossmann offered a crisp party salute and a "Heil Hitler!" both of which were returned with equal fervor. One never knows who's listening, thought Grossmann. The colonel glared at Grossmann with his bad eye but Grossmann had learned the colonel had no other look to offer. An attempt at a smile could be equally disconcerting but Grossmann had no need to worry. The colonel gestured for Grossmann to take a seat.

"Douglas, you are aware that General Wolff went to East Prussia?" asked the chief of staff.

"Yes, sir. I heard it mentioned this morning that he was extending his stay in the Fatherland," Grossmann said.

"He sent an encrypted message about an hour ago saying that he was returning to Rome immediately, and he wanted you to prepare to brief him on your operations against the Vatican." The colonel tilted his head somewhat as if it helped him see Grossmann and asked, "Do you know what this is about?"

Grossmann answered truthfully, "No, sir. I don't. My work was in determining the Vatican's underground railroad for escaped prisoners of war and downed pilots. I had a pretty good handle on who the prime mover was—an Irish monsignor named O'Flaherty—and where some of their safe houses were. Perhaps it's related to that?"

The war-scarred officer shrugged. "Perhaps the Führer has decided to raid the Church properties we suspect might be protecting Jews. Who knows? We'll find out in another six hours or so, I would imagine. But, be prepared to talk to the general about your mission in general, and you might as well have specifics on which properties might be hiding Jews."

"Yes, sir," said Grossmann. "I can put together a list by this evening. Should I coordinate with the Gestapo and see if they have any sites that I might be unaware of?"

The chief of staff shook his head and mouthed the words, "Hell no." He followed that up a second later with, "That's a good idea, Colonel Grossmann, but let's wait and see what the general specifically wants."

"Yes, sir." Grossmann understood.

"I need some air and a cigarette. Will you join me?"

"Yes, sir."

They walked onto a balcony overlooking the SS motor pool—General Wolff had the good office, after all. Grossmann offered his chief of staff an English cigarette, which the senior officer accepted. After they had both inhaled deeply, the colonel said, "It's not that I distrust my staff, but I don't trust the Gestapo. It seems unlikely they would bug my office, but then again, it seems unlikely that there's an office in this country that's not bugged."

Grossmann nodded as he savored his cigarette. "I sweep my office all the time. There's nothing like the Gestapo for making an innocent man feel guilty."

The colonel laughed and said, "You're many things, Douglas. I'm not sure that innocent is one of them. Speaking of which…I have to assume you have plans made for the immediate future. And that you intend to take care of the front office."

"I do indeed, sir. I was planning to work on it this afternoon with Major Kemmerling."

"That's important in the long run, but I have to think General Wolff has something more pressing on his plate if he had to cancel his plans in the Fatherland."

"Yes, sir. I think so too."

1800 Hours
North of Cisterna, Italy

Sam and Perkin leaned over the hood of a jeep where a map was held in place against a warm stiff breeze by four large rocks. Perkin was originally going to use grenades, but Sam substituted the rocks.

"Bear, how far north have our patrols pushed?" Perkin asked.

"We've crossed the Valmontone-Velletri highway here and here," he said as he pointed at the map. "Our first patrol was engaged by a German patrol from about four hundred yards or so, and when we returned fire, they scampered off towards Velletri."

"Any casualties?"

"Nope. Not on either side. They didn't seem too inclined to mess with us, and our boys didn't want to chase them. Thought it might lead to an ambush," Sam said. "Our other patrol didn't come into contact with anyone, so they proceeded up to that minefield you told us about and marked it."

Perkin looked at the map again. "So, if we went along a line like this..." He traced a path on the map with his finger and continued, "...we should be able to get a patrol onto Monte Artemisio tonight."

"Yeah...assuming we don't hit a minefield on the slope or come across a pillbox ten yards into the woods. There may be a better route to the base of the mountain though. There's a north-south ravine that runs along the east side of my company boundary that I've got a patrol checking out now. It gives us better cover as we approach the mountain cuts and I want to control it. If there's any attempt to infiltrate our lines, that would be a good place to move through."

"How long is it?" Perkin asked.

"About a mile and a half, I'd guess," Sam said.

"What else do you have for me?"

"Our territory is all agricultural. We've got two large vineyards, what's left of the wineries up ahead, and a cornfield lying between us and Baker Company on my left. We've also seen a stream of locals movin' along the road mostly comin' from the fighting on the far side of Velletri." Sam shook his head and said, "I know they're just tryin' to find somewhere safe to hunker down, but I don't know where to send 'em, so I told the boys to just stay out of sight and leave 'em alone."

Perkin nodded. "I don't know what to tell you. Anyway, I'm going to ask Bill about patrolling on Mount Artemisio. What do you think?"

"Definitely. Sooner's better than later."

They didn't have to find Major Spaulding. As Sam was folding the map, the battalion commander drove up in a jeep with the regimental commander, Colonel Hamilton, following in his own jeep. Neither captain saluted their superior officers but nodded instead.

"Good afternoon, boys," Spaulding said. "The colonel and I are doing a quick inspection of the battalion positions. You're last and drivin' up, it looks like you're good to go. We already seen some antitank guns in Charlie's sector that were sited too far back to be any good, but I see that yours are up where they need to be." Spaulding grinned. "Charlie Company didn't give you a heads-up we were comin', did they?"

Sam shook his head and returned the grin. "No, sir. Assholes. I'll have to talk to them about that. Glad y'all are here though. Perk and I were just talkin' about gettin' some patrols up on the mountain yonder and wanted your permission to do it tonight."

Spaulding looked at Hamilton, who said, "Yes. I'll have my staff deconflict with the 143rd, which is going to do the same. They're farther west in the line towards Velletri and the 142nd's in reserve. Our orders are to patrol aggressively but avoid any major engagements. As I'm sure you're aware, the VI Corps attack has shifted directions. The 1st Armored is conducting a lateral movement behind us and is heading for the southern attack towards Rome. But we're in limbo. They still don't know which direction we're ultimately headed—whether we'll loop around to the west or east of the Alban Hills, so we'll hold where we are for the time being and protect the flank of the 3rd Division." Hamilton started walking back to his jeep. "Start the patrols as soon as possible. Captain Berger, if your notion pans out, I want to know as soon as possible." The colonel climbed into his jeep, spoke to his driver, and headed back in the direction of the regimental command post.

When the dust settled, Perkin looked at Sam and then Major Spaulding and said, "Bill, I'd like to lead a patrol if I could."

Spaulding said, "I thought you'd ask, but you're going to have to ask Sam if you can tag along. The 36th Reconnaissance Troop will be active closer to Velletri in the 143rd's sector, and we're going to do a company-sized patrol here in ours. Sam, grab your platoon leaders and Sergeant Donohue and meet me at my CP in, say, fifteen minutes and we'll figure out how to support you, should it turn sour up there."

2200 Hours
Rome, Italy

Douglas Grossmann sat stiffly in a soft leather chair in General Wolff's office as he waited for Wolff to re-appear. He had been summoned over an hour before by one of the general's aides and he had spent the better part of the last hour in the outer office waiting for the general to arrive. Finally, Wolff was driven up in his Mercedes staff car from a small airport north of Rome used by the SS.

After a soldier, who Grossmann had recognized as

an electronic technician, left the office, Grossmann had been escorted into the general's office. While he waited as Wolff changed into a fresh uniform, he mused about the technician. *Everyone's sweeping their offices these days...maybe it's time to sweep mine again.*

When Wolff came into the office, he waved Grossmann down as he started to stand and then told an enlisted orderly to bring a pot of coffee. After the general settled into a chair opposite the mahogany coffee table from Grossmann, he said, "I should have asked. Can you drink coffee this late or are you one of those that stops at noon?"

"It's never been a problem for me, sir," Grossmann answered. "How was the Wolf's Lair?"

The general grinned. "I wasn't there. The chief of staff spread that around as an operational security measure. I was in Berlin with the Führer. They're expanding the headquarters in East Prussia and nobody wants to listen to the construction. Besides, the Berlin staff believes that the Allies are going to level the Wolf's Lair any day now so we stayed in Berlin while the Allies bomb it instead..." The general sighed and said, "You passed through Berlin this spring, yes?"

"Yes, sir. A couple times."

"It's hardly recognizable these days. The March bombing was the worst so far, but we don't have time to rebuild before it gets hit again."

"I suppose that there's no chance of winning the war of attrition in the air, is there?" Grossmann knew the answer already.

"No. The Americans and British are taking terrible losses and are losing many more bombers than we are fighter aircraft, but we can't compete with American industry. I believe that if the Yankees were so inclined, they could rule the world. If Germany had half her might, we certainly would." Wolff offered a cigarette to Grossmann, who accepted, and after Grossmann lit both cigarettes, the general said, "The Führer remains optimistic, however."

"If I may ask, General, what is the source of his optimism?" It was a bold question for a subordinate to ask an SS general, but Wolff didn't seem surprised.

"Destiny. He feels our destiny will not be denied. He's a brilliant man, the Führer. There's a degree of defeatism in Berlin these days, not close to the Führer of course. Objectively, if a few things go our way, he might be right. He might save us all from the Götterdämmerung. God bless him if he can. The thinking in Berlin is that after the Allied landings are defeated at the Pas de Calais, we can hold the Allied armies here in Italy and move the forces in France and the Low Countries to the Eastern Front. The Bolsheviks are not invincible, but we can't have a third of our army tied down indefinitely if we wish to crush the Soviets."

Grossmann nodded. There was truth in what the SS general was saying. "And if we don't defeat the Allies at Pas de Calais or wherever they might land?"

General Wolff blew his breath out, raised an eyebrow, and then grimaced as he shook his head. "Things get more problematic."

"Do you think von Rundstedt is up to it, sir? You know him, don't you?" Grossmann asked. Grossmann had met the commander in chief in the West several times and believed he was past his prime.

"Yes, of course I know him. Is he up to it? Ach… that is the question of the summer, is it not? I think some officers dismiss the old boy at their own peril. His mind is still sharp enough, but the real question is whether we've given him the tools to succeed—the right subordinates, enough troops, and above all, good intelligence."

"He has von Rommel," Grossmann offered.

"Yes. He has Rommel. He's a brilliant man. So is Rundstedt. Does that mean they can work together? Only if there is a clearly delineated chain of command that subordinates the ego. Is there such a thing in the West? I don't know that there is." The general stood up and walked to a sideboard where he poured two cognacs, and as he walked back he said, "Let's forget the coffee. Rundstedt wants to fight the war as a defense in depth. He thinks that with our better armor and greater experience we can defeat the Allies when they come ashore. Rommel believes the enemy needs to be defeated on the beaches."

"What do you think, sir?" asked Grossmann.

"The beachhead is the answer. If a man like Clark can survive once he gets a lodgment, think of what a competent general can do."

"What do you think of their generals for the Second Front, sir?"

Wolff smiled wanly. "Not much but you're the intelligence officer, what do you think?"

Grossmann shrugged. "They're getting better. They've weeded out a lot of the weaker pre-war generals. For the current batch...starting at the top, Eisenhower is a politician—although I think he may be an amazing politician. If, however, the crossing fails, Eisenhower is busted back to his permanent rank of lieutenant colonel and goes to a desk job in Washington never to be seen again. Montgomery is methodical and competent, but may be too slow for a maneuver battle-field in 1944...a British Gamelin, perhaps. Bradley was a good corps commander in Africa and Sicily, but he inherited Patton's corps after Patton, well, straightened it out. We'll see if he can manage an army. But Patton?

Patton is a fighter. Better than any Allied general on either front. Should we allow Patton a toehold on the continent, we may never recover. Ach…if only they had more like Alexander and Clark."

"Indeed. So…I asked you here to talk about your work on the Vatican. Give me an overview while I freshen our cognacs." Wolff walked over the sideboard and simply brought the bottle to the coffee table. After refilling the glasses, he left it there.

"Yes, sir." Grossmann collected his thoughts and said, "I had three tasks while working for the Abwehr here in Rome on the Vatican portfolio. First, it was my job to analyze the workings of the Holy See and develop a predictive model of political insiders. Those that influence Pius, and what their political leanings are with respect to Germany and the Führer. Look for weaknesses and obstructions. Second, it was my task to infiltrate the network established within the Vatican to hide or repatriate escaped prisoners of war, downed pilots, and Jews and other enemies of the Reich. Finally, I was tasked to follow this network to its conclusion—its physical terminus—and be prepared to eliminate those involved. All of this data was to be prepared in a report to give German decision-makers the information they needed to take action against Pius if necessary."

"Thank you. That's the way I remembered your report after the Canaris affair. Yes. What type of action did you foresee as possible?" Wolff asked.

"That wasn't really for me to say, sir, but I would think at one end of the spectrum would be a démarche of the Pope. The other end of the spectrum would be occupying the Vatican and deposing Pius." Grossmann was curious where the conversation was headed. Perhaps it was the cognac or Wolff's friendly demeanor, he didn't sense any particular danger.

"Of the two ends of the spectrum, which would you have recommended if asked?"

"The lesser of the two, Herr General."

Wolff nodded thoughtfully, and asked, "Why? Why a diplomatic protest and not the removal of the Pope?"

"The Irish priest who ran their underground railroad, Monsignor Hugh O'Flaherty, told me personally that he had been ordered by Pius to cease his operations. O'Flaherty is a man of some great conviction, however, and he just continued anyway. Pius may have turned a blind eye to O'Flaherty's disobedience, but those orders did give him some political cover in case we responded. A rogue operator—that kind of thing. The main reason though was that stronger action didn't pass a cost-benefit analysis…"

"Explain," interrupted Wolff.

"Well, sir…I don't want to minimize the headaches that Pius has caused the Führer nor what O'Flaherty's done, but at most, we're talking a few thousand Jews and escapees. Probably far less. In any case, fewer than are being killed worldwide in a couple of days. I told the Abwehr command that in my opinion, a few thousand prisoners weren't important enough to justify deposing the Pope."

"What would you see as the consequences of us arresting Pius? Dismembering the political structure of the Church? Arresting O'Flaherty and the political insiders that you talked about?"

Grossmann looked hard at the general hoping to divine where the conversation was headed but Wolff's face betrayed nothing. "It would needlessly enflame the Catholic world. We would lose support that we need in Hungary and Croatia. Make Poland, Czechoslovakia, Italy, and France more difficult to govern as partisans—some who have no more use for the Pope than we do—use the issue to whip up the masses. It could end or at least tip the neutrality of Ireland and Spain. It might even arouse anti-government discontent in Austria and Southern Germany. To me, it never seemed worth it. But I thought that this was a dead issue...why are you asking me about the consequences of deposing the Pope now, sir?"

"Because that is what the Führer ordered us to do."

2215 Hours
Mount Artemisio, Italy

Second Lieutenant Alexander Ryan lay with his ear pressed to the concrete roof of a pillbox. It had taken Ryan nearly half an hour to work his way around the small semicircular fortification and while he had been moving slowly, his heart was seemingly pounding out of his chest. Distant machine-gun and artillery fire made listening difficult, and a dim flare from the direction of Velletri caused him to lie flatter than he was before if that was even possible. It wasn't but he tried anyway.

The patrol was Ryan's first action since the Cassino massif the previous February, although like everyone else in the regiment, he had trained nonstop in the mountains surrounding Naples. There was less than a quarter of a moon, but moving up an unfamiliar mountainside at night was almost second nature. Almost. They had found an old logging trail that headed up the mountainside with few cutbacks that Captain Taft wanted to follow to the top. Everyone was concerned that the trail would be mined, but the company commander had insisted they follow the old road. Their initial probes had come up empty, and then Ryan had taken the lead on the trail until a platoon scout reported the presence of the pillbox. Each step was taken gingerly and when there was no explosion, Ryan gritted his teeth and forced himself to take another.

He had dropped to his stomach and crawled until he could see the vague shape of the pillbox, and as he crawled so painstakingly slow around and above the pillbox while he probed fruitlessly for the mines that would protect its flanks, the thought crossed his mind that he would never be totally used to night operations, mountain fighting, or the army in general.

That he suspected the pillbox was unmanned didn't stop the pounding in his chest, the trickle of sweat running down his sides from his back, or the imagined shapes he saw in the forest. Suspecting a pillbox was unmanned was only slightly more comforting than knowing it was fully occupied—in wartime, the unknown threat is frequently the most frightening of all. Yet he had good reason to believe there was no one inside the small fortification. They had ascended more than five hundred feet of the two-thousand-foot mountain and it was clear the Germans were not preparing a defense in depth of the Alban Hills beginning at the base of the massif. It hadn't been entirely neglected by the Germans as the pillbox indicated, but there was not the strong enemy presence that the Texans' experience suggested they would encounter. After beginning their ascent, they had cut strands of razor wire, probed for mines, and listened and looked for the enemy. Nothing. Then the scout returned and told Ryan that there was a pillbox cut into the mountain on the far side of a man-made clearing. Maybe this was the first line of defense.

They had been moving in concert with the two other rifle platoons of Able Company in a wedge formation with Ryan's 2nd Platoon in the lead when the scout reported the pillbox. Sam, Perkin, Sergeant Kulis, and Sam's radioman followed closely behind while

Frank McCarter's 1st Platoon patrolled to his right, and Harold Balzac's 3rd Platoon to his left. Second Lieutenant Balzac, known in the company as Hairy Ballsack, was a replacement officer who was on his first actual wartime patrol and First Sergeant Donohue had chosen to ascend the mountain with him.

Assuming the pillbox was in a line of mutually supporting defensive positions, Sam halted the movement of the company, and scouts from the other platoons crept forward to examine their routes over a company frontage of 500 yards. As Ryan crawled around the pillbox, it occurred to him that Sam's whispered order to find out if the defenses were manned was not intended literally for him. Still, there he was lying on the rooftop listening for movement, voices, snoring, or anything that might suggest someone manning an MG-42 was only two or three feet beneath him. In these moments, Ryan truly hated the army. In a perfect world, he would sling a grenade through the broad firing slit and he wouldn't much care if the pillbox was manned or not. But they didn't want to reveal the patrol, so that course of action was not preferred. He had no way of knowing whether he was inches away from German soldiers because he knew the absence of sound wasn't good enough. He would have to take a look.

Even though he was lying on his stomach, Ryan crossed himself in the dark and said a silent prayer. Inching so slowly that it seemed he was hardly moving, Ryan pulled himself to the roof's edge. Grasping it with his left hand and pulling a grenade from his web belt with his right, Ryan inched out farther and peered down. His eyes stared into the darkness looking for a sign that the pillbox was occupied. Nothing. He leaned out even more. Still nothing. A brief flash from a distant illumination round dimly lit the front of the concrete pillbox. There was no MG-42 barrel protruding from the firing slit that he could see. Yet, he still didn't know, but he couldn't wait any longer.

He got ready to pull the pin from the grenade, made sure he had enough reach to arc his arm down and whip the grenade through the slit, and he whispered loudly, "Hey, you assholes! Wake the fuck up!"

Nothing.

2235 Hours
Rome, Italy

Douglas Grossmann gaped at General Wolff and then abruptly closed his mouth. He started to say something and then closed his mouth again.

Wolff laughed at the shock on Grossmann's face. As he poured more cognac, he said, "I was somewhat surprised as well."

Grossmann collected himself and asked evenly, "Did the Führer say how he wanted to resolve the, uh, disposition of the Pope?"

Wolff shrugged. "He said a lot of things. It was the most amazing flow of ideas seemingly off the top of his head. He talked nonstop for an hour, but I'll give you the short version. Resituate the Pope and his holy offices to a new compound in Lichtenstein was one possibility. The Reich will take the library, the art, anything of value into custody for safekeeping."

Grossmann nodded. The world of course wouldn't see Nazi seizure of priceless art and the irreplaceable documents of the library as anything other than cynical theft. "Yes, sir. I've heard of the Lichtenstein option. Do we think that their prince...what's his name... Franz Joseph would be amenable to hosting a modern Avignon?"

Wolff laughed harshly and said, "Who gives a shit what Franz Joseph thinks? Does he think his neutrality would be safe after we violate the neutrality of the Vatican? That Austrian pissant will do what the Führer tells him to do."

As will we, thought Grossmann. "What are the other options, sir?"

"Arrest Pius and send him and his godly courtiers to Dachau or Buchenwald. He can relax with Blum and Daladier...or half the German royalty, for that matter. A little vacation and some righteous work building munitions might do him some good."

It was Grossmann's turn to laugh. "Yes, sir. It might at that. Despite all I said earlier, I can't say that I would object to seeing his Holiness digging latrines or maybe because of his exalted status, he could be a *Funktionshäftling*."

"Indeed! Being a *kapo* might add some perspective to his notion of what 'Render unto Caesar' really means." Wolff's smile faded as he came back to the Führer's order to depose Pius XII. "But, there was a third option the Führer and I discussed. Arrest the Pope on the basis of your report—that the Catholic Church violated its status as a neutral entity by actively assisting the Allies. We would conduct a speedy trial here in Rome and then execute Pacelli and the entire Roman curia, arrest all the bishops, cardinals, and priests, and confiscate all Church property in the greater Reich."

Grossmann was silent as he thought through it all. It would add millions of enemies to the already considerable number of opponents facing Germany and would only hasten the speed of her defeat. He suppressed a shiver and asked, "Sir...why?"

"The Führer doesn't owe us explanations, Colonel Grossmann. He issues orders and, like the good

Germans we are, we carry them out to the best of our abilities." Wolff took a sip of cognac as he remembered his conversation with Adolf Hitler. He allowed the spirit to linger in his mouth and savored the pleasant burn in the back of his throat when he swallowed it. Facing Grossmann, he said, "The Führer is sometimes a contradiction and I admit I am not qualified to judge his brilliance, but as much as he has led the global fight against Bolshevism, there are some things about them he admires. Like Lenin and Stalin, he has no use for the Church. He believes faith in God diminishes faith in man and in turn that diminishes faith in him. People needn't look to God for guidance. We have the Party for that, and while we are clearly fallible, the Führer believes that it is up to us to chart our destiny. And it is up to him to guide us there…not this virgin man down the road."

"He sees the Pope as competition, then?" Grossmann asked.

"Of course. The Church has been the predominant power in Europe since the fall of the Roman Empire— arguably until the time of Napoleon. But it still has considerable vestigial power. The Church has been, well, neutral, in many respects towards our solution to the Jewish problem of Europe, but it's hardly cooperated with us. When the war is over and we've defeated the West and conquered Bolshevism, the Führer intends for there to be a day of reckoning for those who stood to the side and watched. Those that went to the Colosseum to witness the killing but didn't have the nerve or conviction to do it themselves. Perhaps he intends for that day to come for Pius before we are to leave this city never to return."

"What are you going to do, General?" Grossmann asked.

"As I said, carry out his orders, of course." Wolff fixed Grossmann with his gaze, the fatherly officer of only moments before gone. "You're my point man on this. All other projects for you, including any extra-curricular work, are secondary. Develop a plan that is flexible and allows us to meet either of the three courses of action that we just discussed. We'll talk tomorrow evening."

Grossmann stiffened. There was only one possible answer, but he decided to push his reservations as far as he could. "Yes, General. I hope it doesn't come to this. I think it's a mistake, but I'll take care of it."

Wolff nodded seriously. "I know you will. The Führer is counting on you."

2335 Hours
Mount Artemisio, Italy

They had been on the crest of Monte Artemisio for more than twenty minutes and Sam and Perkin were awaiting the return of scouts that had gone forward onto the reverse slope. Artemisio was like many of the mountains they had been on in the past nine months in Italy in that it didn't have a singular mountaintop, but rather it was a long oblong-shaped massif with multiple peaks. The crest, such as it was, was more of a ridgeline. It was narrow and irregular and it tipped over fairly sharply as it sloped downward to the north. The Texans knew from aerial photographs that what lay on the other side was the filled-in caldera of a massive ancient volcano that in turn was the home to smaller volcanoes and other calderas. Although neither man reflected in these terms, they were standing on the precipice of a volcano that had been dormant for a mere geological blink of an eye, yet it was unlikely any human had ever seen it erupt.

Sam and Perk walked just below the ridgeline on a path that had been carved into the soil by countless generations of Italians walking through the forests of the hills. Today, the only other sightseers on this part of the mountain were three platoons of American riflemen. The cousins walked silently side by side as they checked on the siting of a company observation post, and then they climbed a large rock to look hard into the distance at the lights in the coastal plains to their west. Rather than the lamps of peacetime, the lights were the flashes of artillery, the flares of soldiers seeking to illuminate their enemies, and the explosions signifying the destruction of men and materiel.

"Perk, I want to get off this mountain as soon as possible. You need to get yourself over to regiment and division and report this," Sam whispered in the dark.

"I know, Bear. It gives me chills just thinking about the possibility. If we can get enough bubbas up here, and with arty, we can break the German lines once and for all. You can't quite see to Rome, but I suspect when daylight comes, we'll be looking down on top of every German division engaged in the fight. It'll be like Cassino except we'll have the advantage."

They had seen signs of an extensive German presence, but like Lieutenant Ryan's pillbox, the remainder of the mountain seemed mostly uninhabited. They had come across a manned observation post, and soldiers from Balzac's platoon had taken the sleeping Germans prisoner but that seemed the extent of the German Army's presence on the massif.

"Do you think this is part of a German withdrawal?" Sam asked.

"No. I doubt it. Have you ever seen the Germans voluntarily give up wonderful ground like this without a fight?"

"No. Never. What is it then?"

Perkin thought for a moment and said, "It's one of two things. They're rotating units through and we're here during a gap, or, as I talked about the other day, the Krauts are resource constrained and they're using the geography as a natural defense."

Sam nodded thoughtfully in the dark, and said, "I'm no engineer, but the route we took could be dozed to get us up here. Heavy equipment. Maybe artillery and tanks. And men. Lots of men."

Chapter Seven

May 28, 1944
0715 Hours
Southeast of Velletri, Italy

Major Spaulding led Captains Berger and Taft into the farmhouse of the dairy that was serving as the divisional headquarters. Their regimental commander, Colonel Hamilton, had preceded them and was already in conversation with Major General Walker, the division's commanding officer.

Perkin yawned as he walked into a simple room adorned with field desks and folding chairs. General Walker and Colonel Hamilton were deep in discussion over a map spread out over a table. Hamilton's eyebrows lifted slightly when Walker smiled at Perkin and said, "Oh hell. You again. How are you, son?"

"Good, General. Thank you." Perkin was going to ask how the general was when Walker turned to Sam.

"Captain Taft...good to see you again. I have a letter from General Roosevelt that I received the other day that I need to share with you. He was asking me how you were doing since your return. I'm going to tell him that you're excelling. That was really good work with this patrol."

"Thank you, General," Sam said with an embarrassed smile.

"General Roosevelt?" asked Colonel Hamilton, who was unaware that Sam's extended family was American political royalty.

"Teddy Roosevelt, Jr., of the 4th Infantry Division," Sam answered. Seeing a puzzled look on Hamilton's face, Sam said, "A family acquaintance...I'll explain later, sir."

"Okay," said Walker. "I've heard Colonel Hamilton's account. He said your patrol went to the ridgeline, and that you sent scouts forward and they reported the same: little to no enemy presence on the mountain. Do you have anything to add?"

Perkin looked at Sam who nodded, and said, "Sir, we're not engineers but we think that a road could be carved up and over Mount Artemisio using an existing logging trail. It's not been used for years as far as I can tell, but unlike the rest of the mountain, it's not completely covered with trees. We're not talking about just an infantry infiltration but we think it's possible that tanks and artillery could be towed up. Unlike, say, Mount Trocchio or Mount Sammucro, there's soil here. It's not just hard rock. Having said that, in my opinion, the trail will need considerable work to support heavy equipment. Once we get to the top, the terrain offers plenty of defilade positions for artillery and we believe we could use this road to get the division behind the German lines west of the Alban Hills. It would break Anzio wide open."

There was a long moment of silence as each man contemplated the possibilities and then Walker nodded. "I saw your report from your reconnaissance flight, and the G-2 told me last night about your debrief of the

Italian fellow who came down off the mountain. To be honest, I didn't want to wait until your patrol was back, so I went on a reconnaissance flight myself first thing this morning. Good thing you didn't crash our last Grasshopper."

Perkin looked injured. "I couldn't crash it, sir. The aviation guys won't let me fly."

"I didn't know you could fly," said Walker with a puzzled look on his face.

"I can't, sir," Perkin said with a grin. "But I hardly see…"

"Perk…" warned Spaulding.

Only slightly chastised, Perkin asked of Walker, "Did you see anything, sir?"

Walker shook his head. "Like you, I saw a lot of nothing. No indications that the mountain's defended at all. No armored vehicles. No troops. No flags, no triple-A, no presence of any kind. I think we're about to catch them with their pants down." Walker paused and looked at Perkin before saying, "Well, so far you've been over this mountain more than anyone in the division. Once in the air, and then by foot. Would you like another opportunity?"

"Before or after my USO tour? I mean, I take it you want me to lead the assault?" Perkin suppressed a smirk at Sam who rolled his eyes.

Walker laughed out loud—a rare laugh for a division commander feeling the strain of months of combat. He turned to Sam and said, "Captain, do dumbasses run in the Berger family?"

"His grandfather's fairly sane, General. I think it's just Perkin," Sam said.

Walker shook his head. "I'm not sure. It must run in the family. I could have sworn that it was his father talking just then." Turning to Perkin, he said, "When we were at Camp Greene, your dad tried to talk me into fishing in the Catawba River from a hot air balloon. He wanted to drop British Mills bombs and have the second lieutenants net up the dead fish from rowboats. As attractive as the notion was, I had to tell him 'no.' Likewise, I'm going to have to disappoint you. No, Captain, you won't be leading the assault. I thought I'd get my engineer up there to take a look, and I'd like for you to lead him up the same pathway."

"Oh. Of course. I can do the USO tour some other time I suppose." Perkin grinned as he turned back to the map. He ran his finger along the topographic face of Mount Artemisio and said, "We came up a ravine along here until we hit the slope of the mountain. If you look here, sir, it's not on the map, but this is where the logging road runs. Sam, what do you think?"

Sam looked over Perkin's shoulder and said, "Based on what we saw, General, Perkin's laid out the best path, although we only covered a swath about five hundred yards wide as we moved up and back down again. It's a big mountain and there might be a better route but within the swath that we covered, this is the best option."

Walker nodded. "Got it. I'll leave the route recommendation to the engineers in any case. Captain Berger, can you take them up this morning? I know you haven't had any sleep, but I'd like for them to have some light to do their survey."

Before Perkin could reply, Spaulding said, "We'll get with the engineers and get moving, sir."

0930 Hours
Rome, Italy

Lieutenant Colonel Douglas Grossmann leaned

back in his chair and looked at Major Friedrich Kemmerling. He studied his subordinate for a moment and then looked back at the papers in his hand. They had completed the first draft of the plan to depose Pope Pius XII. It was little more than a skeleton plan, and they both knew there was much work yet to be done.

"Do we need to ask his advice?" Major Kemmerling nodded with his head to the brooding picture of Adolf Hitler.

"I don't think we're at that point yet, Fritz. However, should the time come when we need advice on how to invade a sovereign state, it's reassuring to know we have an expert in our midst." Grossmann looked at the papers again. "We have two big questions remaining. An exact order of battle for the Vatican guards, and any intelligence on secret passages that might be used to extricate the Pope."

Kemmerling shrugged. "The Gestapo has that information but the boss doesn't want us to bring them in. I wonder why…"

"Ours is not to reason why, Fritz. But since you brought it up, I'm glad we're not. They've been ass-holes to me ever since I got back. I think they hold Admiral Canaris's treason against me somehow. But it's an interesting question. The boss doesn't even want us talking to the rest of the headquarters about this either. Just you and me for now…" Grossmann frowned at the thought and then shook his head as if to clear any wayward notions. Continuing, he said, "Okay, so my understanding of the Swiss Guards is that the normal peacetime complement is about a company. Probably no less than two companies now plus their volunteer militia…the Palatine Guard, so maybe one or two battalions of light infantry and gendarmerie. Tops. In addition to their halberds, the Swiss Guard have replaced their bolt-action rifles with the Swiss version of the KP-31."

"That complicates things. I got to fire one of those in Finland—it's an excellent weapon. Kind of like a Tommy gun but 9mm. You can put a drum magazine on it and it has a rate of fire that must be close to 900 to 1000 rounds per minute." Kemmerling was about to say that the operation was going to be more bloody than would seem likely—the smallest state in the world versus the master of Europe—but he and Grossmann had already discussed it and decided should the Swiss Guard oppose their takeover, there would be casualties.

"I've never shot one, but I know it's held in high regard. I'd rather not send in Wehrmacht troops with Mausers. We can't have the world see us as being even slowed down by these clowns. The SS will have to do it, and we'll have to move quickly and without mercy." Grossmann shrugged. It wasn't going to be a difficult operation, but he would have to convince his superiors to give him the troops he needed.

"What if we can't find Pius? If he escapes or hides in the catacombs or something?" Kemmerling asked.

"We'll line up nuns, priests, monsignors, cardinals, or whoever against the walls or tie them to the basilisk and execute them one by one until he comes out. Or... maybe we'll hold a splendid auto-de-fé of our own," Grossmann said with the trace of a grin.

"Wait! I know that one! Don't tell me. That's from the French guy, right? Uh...Voltaire?" When Grossmann nodded, Kemmerling said with a laugh, "And you thought I was some dumb beat cop who only read dirty books."

"You're not?" Grossmann lit a cigarette and inhaled deeply.

"I was. Sometimes I wish I still was...now, that

was the best of all possible worlds. This one sure isn't." Kemmerling paused as another thought occurred to him. "What happens if we kill the Pope?"

"We either get medals or we get executed."

"I'd prefer medals. Seriously though. It's a risk."

Grossmann thought some and said, "We need to factor that into our planning. Off the top of my head, I think we announce to the world that his Holiness committed suicide rather than be captured. If the Führer is really serious about killing religion what better spike through their palm than the notion of the old boy committing a mortal sin rather than move to Lichtenstein. That should drive everyone crazy for at least a month or more."

Kemmerling laughed and said, "No one would believe it."

"No one's going to believe we killed him by accident either. Might as well give the faithful something to rend their garments over."

1140 Hours
East of Velletri, Italy

"Cap'n Taft? Cap'n Taft? Cap'n Berger's here. You asked me to wake you when he got back."

Sam was dreaming of sailing in Corpus Christi Bay in a small keelboat he owned as the hesitant voice drifting above him intruded. The sailboat was heeled over in a strong South Texas breeze and Sam was bracing his body against the ground in his sleep as he tried to maintain his balance in the dream.

"Cap'n Taft?" The speaker was Sam's company clerk, who hated waking his boss who frequently awoke in a foul mood, but he thought he might survive this day. "You've got some mail from home, sir."

The dream came to an end and Sam pushed himself up to a sitting position. He stared balefully up at his company clerk and then shook his head to clear his malevolent thoughts. He took the corporal's hand and allowed the much smaller soldier to help pull him to his feet. Conflicted about priorities, Sam hesitated for a second and then said, "Where's Cap'n Berger?"

"He's getting some chow here at the company. I made sure they saved you some—it's hash again—but I grabbed a can of peaches for you." The clerk handed the can to Sam and then gave him a letter. "Unfortunately, it's V-Mail so no perfume this time."

Conflicted again between priorities—thanking the soldier for the peaches and snapping at the same man for sniffing his correspondence—Sam merely grunted as he took the letter. That, apparently, was good enough for the clerk who wandered off to deliver more mail.

Perkin wasn't at the field kitchen any longer, and after helping himself to yet another meal of army hash, Sam went off in search of his cousin. He found Perkin sitting with his back to a stone wall on the edge of what had been a pasture. There was little of the wall remaining upright having been breached by multiple tanks only days before, but there was enough room for both officers to sit in what little shade it was providing in the late morning. Both men were tired and they sat in silence while they ate. Perkin's canteen had cold coffee with lots of sugar and they shared that to wash down the meat and potatoes of the hash eaten off of stale crackers.

"How'd it go this morning?" asked Sam. "Did you find a new road to Rome?"

Perkin smiled tiredly. "Maybe so. From the top of the mountain, we could see Highway 7 leading us all the way there. That's the old Appian Way."

"What's that?" Sam asked despite himself. He

wasn't in the mood for a history lesson.

"You've heard the phrase, 'All roads lead to Rome'?"

Sam nodded. "That's pretty much my observation. They just don't get there in a straightforward fashion."

"Indeed. Well, the Appian Way is the most famous of these roads. It runs all the way down to Brindisi and it was built three centuries before Christ. I talked to Colonel Barker about it while I was up there. You know what? For a roads scholar, he's pretty interesting. Get it? Roads scholar? No? Well anyway, he said it was an amazing feat of engineering—maybe second to Stone Mountain or the Great Wall of China. The foundation for it goes down about eight feet and is built upon layers of rock, mortar, and flagstone. He told me that he was pretty upset when he got here and found out the Fascists had paved over major stretches of it. According to him, there was no need. It was built so well that it could support modern traffic. Ain't that somethin'?"

Sam was impressed. "It sure is. I guess the Eye-ties forgot everything the Romans learned 'cause they can't seem to build a road strong enough to handle a dog cart. What'd Colonel Barker think about the mountain?"

Perkin said, "He's pretty fired up. He thinks we can build a road overnight up this side and down the other by widening the logging trail."

"Bullshit." Sam shook his head. "Overnight? He might want to give himself a little leeway, don't you think?"

Perkin took Sam's can of peaches and started to open it. After taking a sip of the syrup, he said, "He seemed to know his stuff. He even said we could winch some smaller bulldozers up over some of these little cliffs and bulldoze a road and cutbacks from the top and bottom simultaneously. Have our own Promontory Point, you know. He said it's doable as long as we keep the Krauts off his boys. He headed over to division as soon as we got back to talk to General Walker. Barker says he'd like to start in a day or two, but he said he could do it tonight if he had to."

"Well, that's a hell of a thing, ain't it? Goin' tonight? Don't you reckon you ought to get some sleep then—seeing as you're leadin' the assault?" Sam laughed. "Walker's right. You're a dumbass...I never really thought of Walker having much of a sense of humor, but for whatever reason, he seems to tolerate you."

Perkin grinned. "He knows good humor when he sees it. Hey...how about that story about my dad?"

"Fishin' with grenades don't seem real sporting, but I'd give a year of your salary to do it. Maybe we could try that when we get home. Get us a hot air balloon and drop ordnance on the gators in the Nueces." Despite his fatigue, Sam laughed. "I bet we could get Old Perkin to go with us. He'd love that. Hey! Save me some of them peaches!"

Perkin was holding the can away from his cousin with his left hand and was unsuccessfully trying to push Sam away with his right when Major Spaulding drove up in his jeep. Shaking his head at the sight of Sam choking Perkin with his left hand and going for the can with his right, Spaulding whistled and shouted, "Enough debate. Perk, you're with me. Sam, get your company ready to move. The division is going to take Velletri with the 143rd from the south and us from the north. Our battalion's in reserve—let's get ready to move!"

1430 Hours
Rome, Italy

"Lieutenant Colonel Grossmann," said the chief of

staff with a serious look on his scarred face. "I understand you are working a project for the general. What is it?"

"I'm sorry, sir, but I'm not at liberty to discuss it," said Grossmann uncomfortably. The chief of staff was one of his allies on the SS command staff in Rome, but General Wolff had been clear in his orders. No one beyond Grossmann and Kemmerling were to know.

"Ah...one of those that I don't meet the need-to-know criteria. That's fine." The chief of staff had a look on his face that suggested he really wasn't fine with the secrecy. Nevertheless, he said, "Generally, I'm happier not knowing. However, we received an additional directive from Berlin to accelerate our deportation of Jews and other enemies of the state from Rome. They won't say so, of course, but they're concerned we might have to withdraw from Rome and points south without having completed the Führer's wishes to cleanse Italy. Of course, you never can cleanse it entirely since it's peopled by the Latin race. Still, we have to do what we can in the limited amount of time we have left."

Grossmann said, "Yes, sir." He also knew he would say yes to what followed as well.

"General Wolff desires that you work both projects in parallel...simultaneously." The chief of staff lit a cigarette without offering one to Grossmann.

"Yes, sir." Grossmann was seething inside, but his face betrayed nothing. The deportation of additional Italian Jews was problematic. He had all the manpower at his disposal that he needed to conduct the raids, but the remaining Roman Jews were effectively dispersed. Italian families and the Church were hiding them throughout Rome and in the countryside. He would have to work his sources hard and time was slipping away from more important projects.

"Do you have any leads?" asked the chief of staff.

"I have a few but they aren't concrete and they're extraterritorial properties of the Holy See," Grossmann answered truthfully.

"I'd rather not raid the Church properties. Yet." The colonel slid a folder across his desk toward Grossmann. "The Gestapo has given us a list of homes that are believed to be hiding the vermin. It seems their sources are better than yours."

Grossmann looked at the list. There were more than two dozen addresses throughout Rome. "It looks that way," he said dryly. "What are my orders?"

"The Gestapo wants to use our assets and raid these homes in a coordinated operation. The Rome chief is going to be personally supervising their share of the operation. Why? Beats me, but if they're going to have a field grade officer in charge, then so are we. That's you, Colonel Grossmann."

"Yes, sir."

"One other thing. The Italians are spreading false rumors that we are preparing to retreat from the capital. That might encourage partisans or others to take action against us. Any resistance, and I mean any, is to be met with the harshest response. Is that clear?"

"Yes, sir."

1445 Hours
East of Velletri, Italy

The sounds of battle filled the Anzio pocket. Even though the soldiers of the 1st Battalion couldn't directly see the combat, they could hear the course of the war only miles to the east and even closer to the west of their position between the two towns of Valmontone and Velletri. Deep booms of artillery rattled the nerves of some of the soldiers hiding in the rolling foothills building to the Colli Laziali, particularly the replacements, but the veterans listened intently and then reassured their comrades that it wasn't destined for them. The 3rd Division to their east was still fighting yard by yard toward Highway 6—the Victory Road that the soldiers had hated for months—and the regiment's other two battalions were effectively halting an attack launched from Velletri to their west.

The push to the town had been interrupted by the battle. The regimental plan had been to move on Velletri at 1415 following a fifteen-minute artillery barrage. In preparation, the 2nd Battalion had pivoted neatly to the north and swung in line with the 3rd Battalion, while Spaulding's 1st Battalion remained in regimental reserve behind the 3rd Battalion. Moving through the forested hills and gullies, a German assault force of two companies of infantry supported by a platoon of four Panzer IV tanks had caught the Gun Club by surprise as it was preparing for its own attack. No American armor was forward yet, nor had the antitank guns been brought forward. Consequently, the German assault had been repulsed by infantry alone. The surprise ran in both directions, however. The German force had not planned to encounter two American battalions in an assault formation. The result was a relatively swift defeat of the German attack. Although it may not have been the German intent, their assault on the battalions of the 141st disrupted the momentum of the Gun Club attack on Velletri. While the battalions reorganized, the plan to liberate Velletri was shelved for the day.

Sergeant Edwin Kulis and Private First Class Roscoe Pfadenhauer were playing cards in the defilade of a bomb crater surrounded by shattered trees—the long forgotten air strike that had created the crater had intended to destroy a collection of German tanks that were refitting at the edge of the woods but had missed by more than a quarter of a mile. Both men had caught some sleep following the patrol from the previous night, neither were involved in the current fighting, and they were both waiting for something else—anything else—to occupy their time. Both had cleaned their respective rifles, an M-1 Garand for Kulis and a 1903 Springfield for Pfadenhauer; both had eaten hash for lunch while they listened to the guns; both had taken advantage of the last of the hot water to wash their mess kits. Neither had pressing assignments at the moment as the fight seemed well in hand, so they both waited. They weren't alone. To the men not of the 2nd or 3rd Battalions, the waiting was a form of cruelty—a torture that poked at the imagination of men facing the prospect of death. The longer they waited, the more apprehensive the men became. Except for Kulis and Pfadenhauer.

"So do you think you still want to be a Fuller Brush salesman after the war?" asked Kulis.

"What?" Pfadenhauer was concentrating on his cards. He needed another heart to complete a flush.

"Do you still intend to enter the exciting world of door-to-door brush sales?" Kulis had been dealt a full house, kings over threes, and was debating between betting heavily on the hand from the beginning or trying to draw his friend in first. He knew that Pfadenhauer would be spooked when he didn't draw any more cards.

"Why would I do that?" asked the young sniper.

"You tolt me when we were lookin' for Cap'n Berger on Mount Sammy that you were goin' to become a Fuller Brush salesman and get all the action you could handle from lonely housewives." Seeing Pfadenhauer pick up the deck, he shook his head and said, "I'm good. Nothin' for me."

As Pfadenhauer discarded his sole spade and drew another card, he said, "I'm too important to be a brush man. I've got a Purple Heart now." He rubbed his nose with the back of his hand as he contemplated his cards, and waited for Kulis to start betting.

"You're goin' on about being a war hero again? You fell off a riverbank and broke your arm. How that qualifies for a Purple Heart is beyond me. The army is gettin' soft." Kulis shot a glance at his companion who was still rubbing his nose while looking at his cards. He must have a good hand. The question was *how* good. Kulis decided to keep talking and see how long Pfadenhauer rubbed his nose while looking at his cards. "How does that make you important? I've got a Purple Heart and mine was a direct result of enemy action." Kulis pointed at the scars on his face.

"And who kilt them Krauts that shot *at* you? Me, and as I recall, they hit your windshield and not you."

"As I recall, I did the actual killing. You just wounded them. I issued the *coup de grâce*."

"Coup de grâce? You think speakin' Mexican or whatever makes you sound smarter? Trust me, it don't. And for the record, *mine* was a direct result of enemy action. I got blown up by artillery...I only fell in the river later."

"What difference does that make?" Kulis asked as he watched Pfadenhauer.

"What do you mean, what difference does it make? You brought it up." Pfadenhauer left his nose alone and scratched his ribs ferociously. That wasn't a tell but a reaction to a chigger bite.

"Oh. Never mind. Let's play." Kulis opened with five dollars which was far higher than their usual stakes.

"Seriously? You think you can bluff me after all this time?" Pfadenhauer picked up a brownish rock, which had been designated as a five-dollar chip. Then he chewed on his lower lip, picked up another rock, and tossed both into the pot.

The raises continued at five-dollar intervals until they reached their standard limit of twenty dollars each. "Damn! I thought for sure you was bluffing," said Pfadenhauer when the cards were turned over. He scratched again without satisfaction at the chigger bite, and said, "Let's do somethin' else. I can't afford to lose any more this month. I want to see if that doughnut girl wants to do somethin' when we get to Rome."

"D'ya think the regiment's gonna host a cotillion when we get there?" Kulis asked as he marked his winnings down in a green notebook. He handed the notebook over to Pfadenhauer for his review and signature according to their long-established protocols, and then he put the notebook back in his pack along with the cards. Had Pfadenhauer been on the black side of the ledger, he would have been the holder of the tally—that negated the risk someone in the red would "lose" the notebook.

"I ain't exactly sure what a cotillion is but unless it's more unnecessary training, I doubt it. So, what do you think about her?" Pfadenhauer asked.

"Other than that elongated tooth, I think she's a real peach. But I cain't stop staring at it. Maybe you could get a small ballpeen hammer and tap it back up in place where it belongs. Of course, if you fixed her smile, I reckon that'd put her out of your league, so you may just have to endure that tooth." Kulis laughed and asked, "Have you ever talked to her? You know, other than saying, 'I want a doughnut' or 'That's some tooth you got there.'"

"Of course!" Pfadenhauer said with mock indignation.

"Asking for coffee with your doughnut don't count."

"Then no." Pfadenhauer laughed at himself.

"Do you know her name?"

"Is it Stacy?"

"I don't know! Why would I know her name? She's got an extra-long tooth. Let's just call her 'Fang' until we find out." Kulis leaned back against the wall of the crater and pointed out dozens of contrails far above their heads. "I'm always amazed by them. I'd love to be up there."

"I'd give anything to be a gunner on one of the bombers for a day," Pfadenhauer said. "Could you imagine shooting down a Messerschmitt?"

"You'd be the best gunner in the air force," Kulis said sincerely.

"Thanks, Eddie," Pfadenhauer said, and then he smirked. "If there were any wounded pilots, I'm sure you'd coupe de grass their ass as well."

Kulis laughed. "We all have our modest role to play."

1625 Hours
East of Velletri, Italy

Sam and Perkin crouched next to Major Spaulding in the lee of his jeep, and all three men jumped as another round hit the opposite fender. They had been driving along the right edge of the battalion area when they started taking small-arms fire. The first round hit the hood on the passenger side of the jeep. Major Spaulding, who had been dangling his right foot out of the jeep, reached for his rifle only to have to use both hands to hold on as Perkin spun the wheel over hard and gunned the engine. The pleasant conversation the officers had been having about the separate subjects of women and baseball was quickly forgotten.

A second round blew out the driver's side rear tire of the jeep. As Perkin slid the jeep to a halt in a small copse of trees, the men bailed out and took shelter on the jeep's passenger side. The third round that had just impacted the opposite fender at least confirmed they were hiding on the correct side.

Sam, who had been riding in the back of the jeep, was the only one of the three men in possession of his rifle as both Perkin's Thompson and Spaulding's Garand remained in the jeep. When Perkin tried reaching for Spaulding's rifle, a fourth round smacked into the steering column of the jeep and he quickly withdrew his arm without the rifle.

"Don't try that again," Spaulding ordered.

"I won't. It's your turn," Perkin said, and all three men ducked as another round hit the far side of jeep.

"I think it's Sam's turn, actually." Spaulding reached for his pistol, changed his mind and pulled out his pouch of tobacco instead. After he shoved a wad into his cheek, he turned and looked back toward the Able Company position they had just left.

"The hell you say," said Sam. "I have my rifle...ah, here we go." Sam nodded toward a squad of soldiers from Able Company who were rapidly moving toward their position. When another round hit Spaulding's jeep, the soldiers started firing toward a clump of bushes about two hundred yards ahead of the three men.

Sam raised to fire as well and saw a gray figure jump up and sprint to the west—toward Velletri and the two forward American battalions. He whipped up his rifle, fired two shots at the fleeing soldier, and grunted in satisfaction as his target fell and lay motionless. Seconds later a machine gun opened fire from behind the jeep and Sam watched as twenty yards of roadside brush was completely shredded. Dust flew and leaves and branches fell, but there were no more shots and there was no other apparent shooter. Sam stood up cautiously followed by Perkin and Spaulding. He motioned to his soldiers and he ran forward with them to the shooter's position where they found two bodies—the soldier that Sam had killed and another who had been lying prone behind the cover of the brush.

When Perkin and Spaulding joined Sam, they saw that the massive captain was visibly upset. His face was pale as he shook his head. "They're just boys," Sam said as he rolled the bodies over and looked at their faces. "They can't be but fifteen tops. This one ain't ever shaved even." He motioned with disgust at the soldier he'd killed. Both rounds had struck the boy in the chest.

Perkin almost complimented his cousin for the shots—it was solid marksmanship—but seeing the look on Sam's face, he kept his comments to himself. Instead, he looked at the dead teenagers, looked at the bolt-action rifles they'd been carrying, and then looked down the road toward Velletri. As Sam's squad searched for more German soldiers, Perkin said, "They're clearly not snipers. They could hit a jeep but not much else. No scopes on these Mausers...no other Krauts that I can see. What do you reckon they were doing out here by themselves? Got cut off during the attack today and somehow moved undetected between 2nd and 3rd batts? Left as an observation post? I don't see a radio..."

"Came out to see the elephant for themselves, I'd guess," said Major Spaulding. "Thought they'd bag a few Americans and work their way back to their platoon, maybe?" Seeing that Sam wasn't buying his theory, Spaulding added, "Remember being a teenager? You think you're ten feet tall and invisible."

"I did just about every dumb thing a kid could do," said Sam as he grasped the uniform jacket of the soldier he had killed and began to drag the lifeless corpse to the side of the road. "But I was never this dumb."

"Don't sell yourself short. You're still pretty dumb," said Perkin cheerfully as he and Spaulding helped Sam with the second German soldier. He was less upset about the dead Germans than his cousin.

Sam sighed and said as he gave one last look at the bodies, "I ain't gonna argue. For the life of me, I ain't smart enough to understand how the Germans expect to win by facilitating the slaughter of their children. Why don't they just give up? This war's going to cost them two, maybe three, entire generations of boys, their dads, and their grandpas."

2140 Hours
East of Velletri, Italy

Three representative American soldiers of a single generation sat in chairs rescued from a destroyed house on the edge of the Able Company sector. Bill Spaulding had brought several cans of mixed fruit to Sam's command post, and he joined Perkin and Sam under the stars, the star shells, and the reflected illumination of murderous violence. Velletri and the southwestern quarter of the Colli Laziali lay between the soldiers of the Gun Club and the night battle currently underway between soldiers of the Allied Fifth Army and the German Fourteenth Army, but the lights from the distant fight were sufficient to see one another. Added to the distant light was the nonstop sound. Artillery boomed without pause and the Texans had quit trying to estimate the number of shells fired after the estimates surpassed fifty thousand.

The latest word to trickle through the rumor mill was that the great breakout along the left of the Colli

Laziali had all but failed. The Germans had slowed the push at great cost to themselves, but the advance, if any, would be measured in yards per day. Meanwhile, the cots at Hell's Half Acre continued to be filled by grievously wounded men who prayed for a rapid evacuation to Naples.

Twice since sundown, German gunners had shelled the woods housing Spaulding's battalion. Perhaps their artillery spotters had seen a prohibited campfire or perhaps they had triangulated a radio communication, but whatever their motivation, the shelling didn't last long, nor did it lead to casualties. Just strained nerves.

Sam was still disturbed by the events of the afternoon. He understood that a bullet fired by a child could kill as permanently as a bullet fired by a man, and he was crystal clear on where he stood with the concept of "it was either him or me," but it bothered him nonetheless. He wouldn't lose too much sleep over it, but Sam still wanted answers. "Bubba, how did we get here?" Sam asked breaking a long silence following Spaulding's rundown of the day's rumors.

Perkin knew where Sam's mind was at, and so while he was on the verge of saying, "We walked here, don't you remember?" he said instead, "You could make the argument that it goes back to the Teutoburg Forest…"

Spaulding interrupted and said, "Hmm…let me stop you right there, Professor. Is this before or after the time of Christ? And I only ask because…well, I know you."

"During," Perkin said enthusiastically. "It was 9 A.D. when the…"

Spaulding interrupted again. "That's what I thought. I would love to hear it…"

"I wouldn't," interjected Sam.

"…but I need to get some sleep. Can you skip us

through the ages to something a little more recent?"

Undeterred, Perkin nodded in the dark and said, "Of course. You miss the essence of the German question that way, but sure. I could start with the fall of Rome or the plague but in the interest of time, let's start with the Thirty Years War..."

"Oh Lord, Perkin, I can't think of anything I'd enjoy more than listening to a lesson on German history from, what was it? The eighteenth century?"

"Seventeenth."

"From the seventeenth century, but again, I'm not sure that you can cover four hundred years..."

"Three hundred," Perkin corrected. "This is the twentieth century."

"Yes, I suppose it is," Spaulding said patiently. "Regardless, I don't think you can cover three hundred years in the fifteen minutes before I try to get some sleep."

"I see," Perkin said. "While I have to say it hurts that you believe recreational sleep is more important than history as told by me, let me try. The event that brought us here—the triggering event—was a telegram that was sent seventy-four years ago in a resort town in what was then Prussia. But...it was the events of three hundred years ago that set the wheels in motion."

"A telegram from seventy-four years ago is why I'm here and not with Maggie on the ranch?" Sam asked.

"It's worse than that," Perkin said. "It was actually a ruined dinner party that led to three wars and tens of millions of deaths. The telegram was edited at the party. Boy, I wish Jim Lockridge were here. He would have been the guy to tell the story, but since I proofed his dissertation, I think I can do it justice...in fifteen minutes." Before his death at San Pietro, Jim Lockridge had been the 1st Battalion intelligence officer and a friend of Perkin's from the University of Texas.

"All right, Professor. The clock's ticking," Spaulding said as he threw away the remains of a wad of tobacco. "Best get started."

Perkin paused for a moment, collected his thoughts, and said, "Germany at the end of the Thirty Years War in 1648 was dramatically different than it is now. We've grown up in a world that had two German states: Germany and Austria. Two German states until the *Anschluss* in '38 that is. But it wasn't always like that. The Thirty Years War was the most devastating conflict in Europe until World War One. It started out as a religious conflict and ended as a political war with shifting alliances and changing tides, and the main battleground of the war was the territory occupied by the German duchies and princedoms. By the end of the war, with the Treaty of Westphalia, more than a third of the German people—meaning those that spoke German— were dead. Think about that…a third of the population. It was devastating—not just in demographics but in economy and commerce and arts, and well, everything. For the Germans, it was as bad as the Black Death three centuries before or even worse. Almost certainly worse than the Napoleonic Wars and worse even than World War One as a percentage of the population. Can you imagine the effect on the United States if the Civil War had lasted thirty years and killed one in three people? We wouldn't have recovered even by now. It might take another century and we wouldn't ever be the same people. I certainly couldn't enjoy Boston chowder like I do—although strangely enough it wouldn't change my feelings at all about the Manhattan style."

Perkin paused as a distant artillery strike found a rich target and there were several seconds worth of sympathetic detonations that echoed through the

Alban Hills. He took a drink of water from his canteen and said, "We think of Westphalia as ushering in the era of the nation-state, but that wasn't the case for the German people. Instead of one unified German nation-state, something that only Adolf Hitler was able to accomplish, there were more than three hundred little statelets and principalities. Some were Catholic. Others were Protestant. Some owed their allegiance to the French or later to British rulers or to the Pope or whomever, but no one answered to a single German king. And the boundaries constantly shifted as power grew and waned. In his day, Napoleon effectively put an end to the Holy Roman Empire and he consolidated many of the German states as he conquered territory and gave the lands and people to others to rule as vassals. So is it any wonder that there was a sense of insecurity among the German people?"

"I see what you're saying, Perk, but what does that have to do with us?" Sam asked.

"After Napoleon, the role of the Germans in Europe began to change. The Prussians under von Blücher had almost as much to do with Bonaparte's defeat at Waterloo as Wellington, and it was clear that Prussia was the rising German star and would challenge the preeminence of the Austrian Empire. But there was always that sense of insecurity among the Germans. You can see it in their philosophy in the last century— the fascination of the German philosophers with the role of the State and the march of History with a capital 'H.' Guys like Hegel and Marx. Philosophers of power like Nietzsche. Nationalists like Fichte. You can see it in their music and their literature. You can see it in the placement of their villages where one village is less than a mile or two from the next village. But you can also see it in their politics. The Germans crave security and they believe they can get it from a strong man. After the European revolutions in 1830 and 1848, some German conservatives took what they liked from the revolutionaries like pan-German nationalism, but they jettisoned the rest...the things we take for granted like popular assembly, free speech, and democratic institutions. But the politicians played on the fears the people had for uncertainty and insecurity, and no one was better than Otto von Bismarck. He was a strong man that the common German man could admire. Noble background. Invented social programs. World-class mustache. But beyond being a strongman, he was a brilliant and successful strongman, who once said that the issues of the day wouldn't be resolved by words, but with '*Eisen und Blut*.' Iron and blood. And he was a pan-German nationalist at a time when his boss, King Wilhelm of Prussia, wanted nothing more than to be the head of the Hohenzollern house and play golf or beat peasants or whatever with the other Junkers. He had no more use for Bavarian Catholics than I have for Aggies, or Sam has for hygiene."

Sam laughed in the dark but said nothing. In spite of himself, he was finding the subject interesting.

"This is fascinating stuff, Perk," said Spaulding sincerely. "But, I've got to get some sleep. We're probably on the move tomorrow. So, what about the dinner party?"

"I'm just coming to that. Bismarck fought three wars to unify Germany—I'll get to France in a moment, but they fought first against Denmark for possession of two small mixed German-Danish territories, and then a six-week war against Austria. It shocked Europe how efficiently Prussia cleaned the Austrians' clock, and it was a significant shift in the balance of power—it was their coming-of-age war like the Civil War was for us. While it meant the end of major Hapsburg influence in German affairs—as we know, they turned eastward with all the problems that brought—Bismarck was an unparalleled diplomat and he later brought the Austro-Hungarians in as junior partners with the German Empire. But beating Austria wasn't enough to bring all the German states around to Prussia, so Bismarck found the lever he wanted in what should have been a minor diplomatic spat with France."

"Which one was that?" asked Sam. "They had one about every weekend, didn't they?"

"Just about. This was the one about Spain. It turns out that royal intermarriage does less to improve the bloodline than one might think, and Spain had a queen named Isabella, who was meddlesome, mannish, and more than a little mad. The Spaniards gave her the boot in 1868, and then started shopping around Europe for a royal family to take the throne. No one really wanted it, but in 1870 they offered it to a Catholic cousin of King Wilhelm of Prussia named Leopold. That was the subject of Jim's dissertation—the Hohenzollern candidature of Spain. The French went as berserk as if someone put up a Catholic negro woman for exalted cyclops or grand goblin of the Ku Klux Klan."

Both Sam and Spaulding started to laugh, and Spaulding asked, "What'd they do?"

"They panicked. You see, the Germans aren't the only ones with insecurities. It's amazing, ain't it? What two oceans and decent neighbors can do for your self-confidence? Anyway, the French emperor, Napoleon III, was concerned with the emergence of a powerful Prussia to his east, perfidious Albion to his west, and now came the possibility that a German would sit on the throne of Spain. And not just any German, but a Hohenzollern. It didn't matter much to Napoleon that Leopold wasn't particularly interested in the job—apparently he thought the Spaniards were just as mad as their ex-queen—it was the potential threat that concerned them...the possibility that something bad might happen. The French spun themselves into a frenzy...the newspapers, the politicos, and even the man on the street were demanding war if Leopold accepted the throne. So, the French demanded that the Germans withdraw the candidature of Leopold and threatened war if they did not, and surprising everyone, the head of the Hohenzollern house, King Wilhelm, did just that. He withdrew Leopold's name. That's where it should have ended: a minor diplomatic spat which left the Germans slightly embarrassed and the French a little puffed up."

"But it didn't end there," Spaulding said.

"Unfortunately, no. The French weren't content with a small victory. They wanted to humiliate the Prussians and they wanted to weaken or destroy the drive towards German unification. So, while the old king was taking the baths at the resort town of Ems, the French sent their ambassador to demand that the Hohenzollerns renounce the Spanish crown for eternity. The ambassador, whose name was Benedetti, ambushed the king during his afternoon walk and made his demands. In response, the king said something to the effect of 'this issue is resolved, we've made our position clear, and we've got nothing more to say on the subject.' He was probably a little annoyed that the French ambassador ruined his walk, but it was all within the realm of good diplomatic decorum. So, here's where the chain of events started clicking that led to us here today. King Wilhelm sent a dispatch from Ems to Bismarck detailing his interaction with Benedetti and authorizing him to release the telegram to the press. If I remember right, when he got the telegram, Bismarck happened to be hosting a dinner party with the Prussian Army Chief of Staff, Field Marshal von Moltke..."

"He must have been pretty young in 1870," Sam said. "He was head of the German Army in '14, wasn't he?"

"Wrong Moltke. The Moltke you're thinking of was his nephew. A lesser general than his uncle, I reckon. Anyway, Moltke the elder was with Bismarck and they'd probably had a bottle of schnapps or two to wash down their *jagerschnitzel* by that point, and I imagine that the king's telegram was depressing for both of them. In fact, it ruined their dinner party. You see, Bismarck was already embarrassed and it was clear the French weren't done with the humiliations yet, so after checking with the old field marshal as to whether the army was ready, he edited the king's telegram before releasing it to the press. He didn't lie with his edits, he just omitted the part about the diplomatic niceties. When he was done, it looked to the French as if King Wilhelm had been rude and dismissive to the French ambassador, and to the Germans—all the Germans, not just the Prussians—it looked as if the French tried to poodle hump the king's leg. War was inevitable after that telegram was released. Bismarck even bragged about it: 'It was like waving the red flag in front of the Gallic bull.' They were at war within the week, and the combined German armies, minus the Austrians, crushed Napoleon at Sedan. And in January, 1871, the old king was crowned Kaiser Wilhelm I at the Hall of Mirrors at Versailles."

"And that led to the Great War?" Sam asked.

"Inevitably, I think. More specifically, the German decision to annex Alsace and Lorraine, two French provinces along the Rhine, made it inevitable. They were historically German territories that had been annexed to France by Louis XIV—if you look at a map, more than half the towns have German names. But that had been two centuries before. Foreseeing a big burr under the French saddle, Bismarck didn't want them...but von Moltke and the general staff insisted. Von Moltke said that Alsace and Lorraine were like a dagger pointed at Berlin, and the emperor agreed. It even kind of looks that way on a map. So, they took it, and in my opinion, more than the assassination of Archduke Franz Ferdinand and the cascading set of alliance implementations, World War One was about the redemption of Alsace-Lorraine. After the war, the territory was re-annexed by France despite the majority of the population having then grown up as German citizens, and that led to Hitler's revanchist claims that helped bring him to power. The lost territory— Alsace-Lorraine, full sovereignty over the Rhineland, East Prussia—was just as powerful a motivator for the German nationalists after the Great War as the lost territory had been for the French nationalists after 1871. You might have thought the fellas at Versailles could have foreseen that, but more than anything else, what brought the Nazis to power was the insecurity that ruled in the inter-war years—that German fear of disorder that goes back to the Thirty Years War. The loss of the war, rise of the communists and the beer hall brawls and street fights, the putsch, the crippling strikes, the hyper-inflation, the Depression, and above all, the sense that the Weimar Republic was too weak to hold the center, made it possible for the strongmen to march in and save the day. The Nazis were revolu-tionaries and as such were responsible for much of the disorder they later quelled but while the Germans may not have approved of their methods, they wanted order above all."

Perkin stood up and said, "There. No more than fifteen minutes. I'm going to check in with Sergeant Taylor and then get some sleep." He listened to the boom of the guns and pointed to a distant flash of light. "Boys over there are dying today because that telegram was edited three quarters of a century ago. It could have been any one of a thousand sparks that set it off, but that telegram was it. And while we're here because of it, we're also here because too many people valued security more than freedom. You gotta remember, Hitler didn't take power in a coup. The Nazis won elections and then kept power. But it didn't have to be like this. We didn't take this route, although we could have. I think the Great Depression was actually the great equalizer—it destroyed the rich and the poor nations alike. Germany was no worse off in '32 or '33 than we were, but we didn't go for authoritarianism or totalitarianism...no matter what Bear thinks of FDR. While there may be benevolent strongmen, Hitler ain't one of 'em. The Germans thought they were getting another Bismarck and in electing him, they wrote a check signing over their freedom, their destiny, and, as Sam said, the lives of entire generations to the most evil man to ever walk the planet."

2300 Hours
Rome, Italy

Douglas Grossmann cocked his head and listened intently. There were distant booms echoing through the hills of Italy, and while it sounded like thunder, Grossmann knew it wasn't. Romans could occasionally hear the distant sounds of combat if the atmospheric conditions were right, and it usually served to buoy their spirits at the same time as it depressed those of the Italian Fascists and their German masters.

Grossmann knew his clock was ticking—the war was coming his way. He wanted more than anything to be devoting his limited time to his warehouse project, which he had code-named Operation Monte Carlo, but the war was intruding in his life just as it had for millions of others. General Wolff had been receptive to his briefing earlier that evening, although there was a shadow of hesitancy in his eyes that Grossmann couldn't explain. Nevertheless, there had been a fruitful discussion on the resources needed, and the general had essentially given his approval on Grossmann's preferred course of action to arrest Pius XII and all senior Vatican personnel. Experts would move in rapidly to secure works of art and the Vatican library and archives would be catalogued and removed to Berlin for safekeeping. Grossmann had liked that proposal. Perhaps the presence of the most valuable documents in Christendom might lead the Allies toward second thoughts on the unrestrained bombing of the German capital. And if not, the world might remember that it was American or British bombs or Russian artillery that destroyed the priceless artifacts and not Doug Grossmann.

The sound of far-off artillery brought him back to his military duties. He was standing outside of the compound housing the villa of an affluent Roman family named Nascimbeni. The Nascimbeni villa was on the list given to him by the Gestapo, who had informed him that the owners were harboring Italian Jews. It did not require a lieutenant colonel of the SS to manage such an affair, but orders were orders. He would take the Jews into custody, and if the owners of the villa refused to contribute to Grossmann's retirement fund, they would be arrested as well. His orders were to show no mercy, but he intended to look for an opportunity to tidy up his finances through a little give and take with the Nascimbeni family.

He looked at his watch with the aid of a flashlight. It was time to go. He had asked for a full squad of SS troopers since the compound was so large, and he knew that everyone was in place. Major Kemmerling had remained at the SS headquarters to refine the Vatican courses of action, but he would bring additional troops if needed. They wouldn't be. Grossmann turned and faced down the street, turned his light on twice, and was gratified to hear the rumbling of the large truck. The compound had a large, heavy, steel gate, which would need to be knocked down. He'd then use the same truck to evacuate any Jews they discovered.

Grossmann lit a cigarette and waited for the truck. He had been wanting a smoke since he walked down the street to the compound but had refrained. No one would be running away now. The truck made its turn onto the street and Grossmann shielded his eyes as the driver turned on the lights. A few seconds later, the truck slammed into the heavy gate and with a screech was torn off its hinges and went flying. Grossmann had a whistle on a lanyard around his neck, and he blew it twice, but the whistle was superfluous. The sound of the gate was enough to get the troops moving to their positions throughout the compound, and their first act was to detain four private guards in the employ of the Nascimbeni family.

Lights came on inside the house, and Grossmann paused momentarily to view the splendor of the home. In the light of the truck, he saw a stunning villa of the Umbrian style—a three-story home with a yellow stucco exterior and magnificent balconies overlooking carefully manicured lawns. A white balustrade traced the perimeter of a rooftop patio, which Grossmann assumed was the owners' refuge on hot summer nights. He imagined that scores of parties had graced these grounds in happier times, and that the rooftop patio likely offered spectacular views of Rome to please the partygoers. *The party's over now...the party's over now.*

Grossmann leaned against a palm tree and watched as his soldiers quickly ran to a heavy iron ornamental door. After seeing the door was locked, a corporal attached a hook to the door's iron frame while other soldiers wrapped the rope tied to the hook around the steel bumper of the truck. Fifteen seconds later, the last barrier between safety and intruders was unceremoniously ripped from its hinges as well. Grossmann's troopers poured into the house, and seconds later he heard the inevitable screams. He debated between walking around the lovely grounds of the villa or seeing the interior of the house when a man's angry curse in Italian from inside the home was abruptly cut short. More screaming ensued, and Grossmann sighed. It was time to see the proceedings for himself.

2320 Hours
Rome, Italy

He strode slowly up the stairs leading into the villa knowing the terrorizing effect his entry would have. His jackboots echoed off the marble floors and he glanced down at small marble sculptures of horses' heads adorning the sides of each step. Grossmann assumed a bored demeanor knowing that he didn't have to be angry to intimidate the owners—the SS uniform, the peaked cap with the Death's Head insignia, and the jackboots were enough for that. Although he thought it a rather silly affectation, he carried a wooden swagger stick for no reason other than it gave him something to do with his hands. It wouldn't do for the inhabitants of the house to see him with his hands in his pockets.

He walked out of the entryway into a great room with high ceilings, mahogany-paneled walls covered with paintings more properly belonging in museums, and rich leather-bound furniture. Sergeant Fleischer was dragging an older man, in silk pajamas and a bathrobe, by the scruff of the neck down the stairs to the great room and the gray-haired man joined two women—mother and daughter by the look of their shared features. A harsh command given in German upstairs was followed by the sound of a hard slap and shortly thereafter seven more people joined Grossmann in the living room. Here were the Jewish fugitives. Grossmann saw four men and three women with Italian features who were all well dressed and had intelligent eyes reflecting fear and resignation.

The man in the silk robes started to protest, and without permission, Fleischer punched the soft man hard in the gut. Grossmann paid no attention to the gasping man writhing on the floor as he walked slowly around the room admiring the paintings. It was an unsubtle expression of power on his part and he enjoyed knowing that all the eyes in the room were on him. He spied a massive painting on the far wall that was clearly the masterpiece of the collection, yet Grossmann resisted the urge to head directly for it. He would take his time and he walked in silence as a patron might stroll through a gallery or museum. He paused at each painting and examined a diverse mixture of landscapes, still lifes, and portraits that he assessed to be from the late nineteenth or early twentieth century. The entirety of the collection seemed to be from the Post-Impressionism period, and while it wasn't to Grossmann's taste, he believed he was looking at a priceless collection of works from artists including Gaugin, Luce, Seurat, and Puccini. It was extraordinary.

The room remained in total silence as soldiers and prisoners alike wordlessly watched Grossmann as he approached the massive painting he had seen from across the room. The masterpiece of the collection was on a long wood-paneled wall, and had a broad light above it to illuminate the work. Grossmann bent down, plugged the light into a wall socket, and stepped back in amazement. He stepped back even farther to take it all in as he estimated the painting to be at least two meters by three meters. It was so large that it seemed to fit uncomfortably on the wall even though the room was large.

Although there were more than a dozen characters in the painting, the unknown artist had used light to draw the viewers' eyes to a woman in the center of the painting and to a man on her right. Grossmann examined the woman first. She was wearing a gold-trimmed blue gown with a gold tiara set on her head, and she was holding the hand of a man kneeling before her, who was not looking at her but rather up at the man on the right. The kneeling man held a feathered hat in his other hand, which was extended in supplication to the illuminated figure on the right of the woman. Grossmann examined that man—he was wearing the red cloak and ceremonial helmet of a Roman general, and he was seated on the edge of a golden chair while resting a foot on a tasseled pillow. The arms of the general extended toward the woman while he looked down at the kneeling man as if to say, "She's yours." Slaves to the left were bringing in vases and pots made of silver and gold and the supplicating nature of the kneeling man led Grossmann to think that she was being purchased.

Perhaps she was to be a slave, he thought, and the deal had just been struck. He looked for a signature and saw none, but he knew the painting itself was certainly worth hundreds of thousands of reichmarks—if not more. It was a superb specimen of the Romantic period and it felt like it belonged in a museum, not a private collection. Grossmann took yet another step back and looked at the painting again. There was something about the theme that he couldn't quite place, and he was on the cusp of remembering what it signified when another thought abruptly occurred to him. It was out of place among all the Post-Impressionists. He turned in thought and walked back to the others.

Grossmann strode directly up to the oldest man in the group and examined his prisoner. He didn't look like the Jews he had seen in Germany or Poland. There was nothing that differentiated this man from any other Italian other than obvious wealth. Like the other fugitives, he wore expensive clothes that didn't look like they had been worn daily or slept in and Grossmann concluded they must have been still awake when the raid began. Unlike every other enemy of the state that Grossmann had arrested, this man looked Grossmann in the eyes, and Grossmann had the sense that he was being judged by the man. It infuriated him for a reason that he couldn't explain. Without warning, Grossmann struck the man across the face with his swagger stick, leaving a bloody stripe on the man's cheek.

Ignoring the bleeding man, Grossmann nodded at the painting and said to two of his troopers, "Take it off the wall!"

When the soldiers lowered the painting to the ground, Grossmann looked at the wood paneling behind it. There were several rectangular patches of darker wood where smaller paintings had been hung for years. The large painting was a relative newcomer to the wall. It must belong to the Jews, he thought. *They're leaving it here for safekeeping, or they've used it to buy their safety.*

Grossmann turned, faced the people in the living room and said, "This painting is declared contraband art, belonging to the enemies of the Reich. It, and all other art in this house, are now under the protection of the German government. You..." Grossmann indicated the Jews with his swagger stick. "...will be deported to the greater Reich for further disposition." Grossmann pointed toward the door with the stick and nodded to Sergeant Fleischer.

The SS sergeant roughly pushed two of the Jewish women with his rifle and other soldiers began herding the rest toward the door. A woman, wearing a pale green dress, stumbled, twisted her ankle, and fell over awkwardly. Two men moved to help her, and Fleischer took a step backwards and leveled his rifle at the men. They froze, and watched as the crying woman began to get to her feet unassisted.

The Italian owner of the villa, the man in the bathrobe, was undeterred. Even though he was wary of Sergeant Fleischer, he moved to help the woman. She was already standing when he reached her side, and turning to Grossmann, he let forth a stream of invective. Starting with, "You have no idea who I am," the man screamed threats at Grossmann and actually took a step toward him before Fleischer thumped him hard against the side of his head with the butt of his rifle.

"Get everyone outside," Grossmann ordered.

Once outside, he gave orders to load the Jews onto the truck. As his soldiers complied, he turned to the owners of the villa. They, too, were enemies of the State and Grossmann was in no mood to negotiate a deal sparing them from prison. He would arrest the family, and then take what he wanted from the villa. He was about to issue orders arresting the family, when the daughter, a pretty woman in her late teens or early twenties, broke free and tried to run. She went no farther than a couple steps before she was tripped by one of Grossmann's troopers and fell hard on the ground. Grossmann had had enough. He unsnapped his holster, drew his Walther, and walked up to the woman still lying on the ground. Without hesitation, he shot her in the head while she looked up at him in terror. *In for a penny, in for a pound. This is more complicated if they're alive.* He turned to her parents. In the pale light from the truck's headlights, he watched himself in an almost surreal third person detachment while he brought the pistol up to the forehead of the stunned mother and pulled the trigger again. Two SS troopers held the father, and Grossmann put his pistol to the forehead of the man in silk pajamas and pulled the trigger a third time as the man protested feebly that he was a Fascist.

Grossmann's troopers stood in momentary silence, and then Fleischman asked, "What are your orders, sir?"

Grossmann looked at the three bodies as he holstered his weapon and said, "Radio Major Kemmerling. Tell him we'll need another truck. No, make it two."

2355 Hours
Rome, Italy

Grossmann lit a cigarette as he walked up the statue-adorned steps into the villa. He shrugged off the murder of the Italian citizens even as he noted the irony that the Jews were still alive while their protectors were dead. His orders were to use brute force, and he had. There would be no ramifications.

He walked to the back of the house to the kitchen where he ordered a terrified maid to make him a cup of tea. Grossmann sat in a chair in the kitchen and watched her steep the tea and pour it into a clean cup. He wasn't going to allow himself to be poisoned just after he had secured the haul of a lifetime.

Taking the tea with him, Grossmann wandered the house. Despite the preference for relatively modern art, Grossmann saw signs of old wealth in the home, and he wondered who Signore Nascimbeni had been. That he claimed in his last seconds to be a Fascist was meaningless to Grossmann. Every Italian who wanted a favor from a German officer claimed to be a Fascist, although most German soldiers had no more use for the Fascists than they had for any other Italian.

He idly went through Signora Nascimbeni's jewelry box. It contained only her daily wear jewels—he would tear apart the villa by morning and discover where she hid her most valuable items. A distinctive ring caught his attention and he whistled softly to himself as he picked it up. It had a very large round-cut diamond surrounded by small rubies and set in rose gold—the diamond was two carats at least, probably three, thought Grossman. To make sure it was real, Grossmann tested the diamond on the mirror, and then on a whim, scratched a swastika on the mirror. He put it in his pocket along with several other rings and diamond bracelets. The Nascimbenis wouldn't be needing the jewels any longer. A drawer in Signore Nascimbeni's dresser yielded several nice watches, and Grossmann took off his own watch and buckled on a brand new Rolex with a black face and a satisfying art deco look to it. Grossmann wasn't familiar with the model, but judging by the slight crease in the leather watchband, the Rolex looked like it had only been worn a few times.

Through the open window, he heard the engine of another heavy truck approaching. That would be Kemmerling, he thought, as he sat on the bed and held the Italian man's shoes against the sole of his boots. Too large. He threw the shoe in a corner and flopped back on the bed and blew out his breath. It had been a long day, and he still had more work to do before he could get some sleep.

Painted on the ceiling was a happy landscape of the Italian countryside, and it led Grossmann's tired mind back to the painting in the living room. It was a painting of a particular theme or movement, he knew, but it still escaped him. It would come to him eventually and he stood up and walked down a long hallway to the daughter's room. No sooner had he put the problem out of his mind than the answer came to him. The painting was *The Continence of Scipio*, although he still didn't know the artist. It was a literary and artistic theme from the Renaissance that told the story of General Scipio Africanus refusing a ransom payment for a young woman his soldiers had captured. Instead, Scipio returned the woman unharmed to her betrothed—an enemy prince—asking only that her fiancé and family be friends to Rome. The story of Scipio's generosity had inspired later generations to chivalry and was upheld as the standard for mercy in warfare.

Grossmann was smiling at the irony of mercy in warfare as he rummaged through the daughter's jewelry box. He pocketed yet another ring, this one with a light blue diamond, as well as a gold and silver necklace. He heard Kemmerling call from the first floor and he was walking out of the room to join him when a picture on the girl's wall caught his eye—it was a rare colorized picture in an olivewood frame. It showed the daughter he had killed, but at a younger age, perhaps thirteen, holding hands with another teenaged girl. Both girls were wearing matching sleeveless blue dresses with white stripes at the bottom and a white sailor's neckerchief around the neck. They were smiling broadly as they stood on the bow of a small yacht in a harbor ringed with distant palm trees. The girls were both beautiful and it was a striking picture that conveyed youth and innocence at the same time it showed wealth and privilege. With growing horror, his smile faded as he recognized the other girl...the beautiful companion of the young lady he had just killed was Antoniette.

Chapter Eight

May 29, 1944
0015 Hours
East of Velletri, Italy

Captain Sam Taft lay in a shallow trench that was a few feet away from a foxhole. He could have tossed a bedroll in a truck tucked under a tree or slept atop a nearby Sherman or even pitched a tent, but he wanted to sleep out under the stars and as alone as he could be in the immediate company of thousands of soldiers. The mosquitoes weren't too bad and he had scouted a sandy patch of ground that didn't appear to have any active ant hills nearby. He was using a gunnysack filled with sand as his pillow, and Sam had spent considerable time getting just the right amount of sand pounded into just the right shape. It was still uncomfortable, but was luxurious compared to other nights he'd spent since leaving home.

The killing of the German soldier still preyed on Sam's mind and was denying him sleep. Likewise, Perkin's story about Bismarck's ruined dinner party disturbed him, and lingering in the background of his thoughts was a disquieting notion that the long dead Germans of 1870 were no more culpable than the long dead French in creating the cascade of events that brought Sam from Texas to Italy. He sighed to himself as he wondered how that boy's family would cope with the news that their son was dead, and then he told himself that they would be no more grief-stricken than the American families that were losing their sons this very moment only a few miles distant. Sam sighed once more and closed his eyes. A few moments later, they were open again and staring at the sky.

The night was clear in a meteorological sense—there were no clouds overhead—but there was enough smoke and dust in the atmosphere from the days of combat that the stars lacked the crystal clarity he was hoping for. Many times during the war when Sam couldn't sleep, he'd look up at the stars and work his way through the constellations until he got bored and fell asleep. He would always begin with the North Star and then after he was done with Ursa Major, Sam would try to identify all the stars in Canes Venatici—the hunting dogs.

Sam had some luck—making the association with hunting dogs got him to thinking about various dogs he'd owned in his life, and for the moment, he forgot about the young soldier he'd killed earlier. Thinking of his dogs, he reflected sadly that none were alive any longer, although Maggie had recently bought a bluetick puppy that Sam had only seen in pictures. A Brittany spaniel named Ned and a Labrador retriever named Dixie had been his favorite dogs but they were long gone. The Brittany was a tireless hunter and a true gentleman of a dog who had slept on Sam's bed when he was in high school and would trot next to his horse for hours on the ranch. Dixie was the sweetest dog he'd ever known. She had severe shortcomings as a Labrador with a total indifference to retrieving and an abiding fear of water but despite these limitations, she had loyalty in spades and an abundance of affection. He had always felt gratitude toward the caveman who domesticated that first wolf pup, but Sam also believed the world would have been better served had the Almighty given man's best friend a longer lifespan.

Sam yawned but couldn't quite make the transition to sleep. His thoughts went from dogs to home and his mind ran over the letter he had received that morning. There was nothing earth-shattering about the letter. Some of it was business—a monthly rundown on the size of his herd, which was smaller than he expected, and an estimate of the production of his oil wells, which exceeded anything he had imagined before the war. Both factors combined with a promising cotton crop meant he was making money hand over fist and the truth was that it made him a little embarrassed and ashamed. The war was making Sam richer than he'd thought possible. Sam snorted at himself as he realized he was getting morose at what was objectively a good day—he had been the victor in a small skirmish and he found out he was getting richer. *What more could a soldier ask for?* he thought as he closed his eyes again.

In his last waking thoughts, he went over Margaret's letter one last time. Margaret had hinted that she had a present waiting for him when he returned but it was to be a surprise. Although he would never tell her, Sam already knew what it was. Old Perkin had written to Sam privately and asked his thoughts on the gift before Margaret had made the purchase—two thousand acres of Edwards Plateau wilderness along the Sabinal River northwest of San Antonio. Old Perkin wrote that the land crossed between Real and Bandera counties and was thick with whitetails, foxes, and even the odd mountain lion. Sam had written back to Old Perkin and said it sounded wonderful—and it did. As Sam drifted to sleep under the stars listening to the sounds of men killing and dying, he thought that maybe when he went to see his new property for the first time, he'd just leave the deer rifle behind and enjoy being alone with Margaret with no one else around for miles.

0230 Hours
East of Velletri, Italy

"Cap'n Berger…" The Appalachian tones of Sergeant Taylor interrupted Perkin's dreamless sleep and he was awake instantly.

Perkin sat up and reached for his Thompson. "What is it?"

"We had a patrol come back," Taylor said. "From Baker Company. They saw four tanks in a hull-down position in the no-man's land between us and Velletri."

"German tanks?" asked Perkin. There had been so much movement of the lines during the course of the day that no one was truly certain where the lines were.

"That's the thing, sir. They didn't get close enough to positively I.D. the tracks. They seemed to think there was a German patrol between them and the tanks so they came back and reported it. But they caught the profile of the tubes over a ridge in a flash of light. It appears they were pointed our direction."

"Well, let's work up a fire order."

Taylor shook his head. "There's some disagreement about where exactly these tanks are. The patrol leader pointed to three areas on the map."

"Oh. Well, that's unfortunate. Wanna go with me to check it out?" Perkin fumbled around on the ground looking for his helmet, found it, and stood up.

"Hell no, sir!" Taylor shook his head emphatically. "Absolutely not. But I brought my shit with me in case you insisted."

0245 Hours
Rome, Italy

Major Kemmerling walked to his staff car humming a drinking song. Kemmerling, at least, was in a good mood. He believed both he and Grossmann could retire off this evening alone, and that was even after making sure the front office received a significant share of the spoils of war.

Kemmerling was no expert, but he assumed the painting of Scipio was worth more than he could possibly make in a lifetime, and it was only one of more than two dozen works of art. *The Continence of Scipio* and a few select pieces were loaded on a separate truck destined for a warehouse that Grossmann controlled, while the other art went to the SS compound in Rome. Kemmerling knew that some paintings would eventually make their way into private collections of high-ranking Nazis, while others would be sold on the black market and the prize money divided. Kemmerling and Grossmann would get a cut of that money, but they had protected their equities with the seizure of the Scipio painting. As the art belonged to one of the Jewish refugees, it would not be insured by the Italian family that Grossmann had killed, and therefore could not be concretely traced back to Grossmann or Kemmerling and the night's events.

When Kemmerling had first seen the painting of Scipio, he whistled and smiled, but it was a smile that quickly faded as soon as he saw Grossmann's face. After hearing Grossmann's story, Kemmerling assured his boss that they would be able to manage the consequences. There was a discussion about burning the villa or just telling the truth—after all, Grossmann was merely following orders. But the connection to Antoniette Bernardi was an unknown variable that Grossmann didn't want to leave to chance. A large hammer and sickle was painted on the interior walls of the house with the blood of the Nascimbeni dead, and Grossmann helped Kemmerling spell and paint "Eat the Rich," "Fuck Mussolini like a Goat," and "Justice for the Workers" on the walls as well. For added measure, he put four bullet holes into the mirror with the swastika—one on each quadrant of the broken cross.

As soon as Kemmerling had what he needed from Grossmann's language skills, he told his boss to go home for the night. Grossmann was in a downward spiral of depression, and not even the discovery of a wall safe could turn it around, which when easily pried open with a crowbar revealed several kilograms of gold in a mix of bars and coins of various denominations and nationalities. The gold would never be reported to higher command, although some of it would be shared out among the hand-selected SS troopers present that night.

An Italian policeman who came to check on the noise was detained and then executed. His car and body would be dumped miles from the villa, and more blood was used to draw a hammer and sickle on his forehead. Kemmerling had considered bribing him with Rolexes but he assumed that the Italian would not remain quiet for long. With some genuine regret, Kemmerling killed the maid who had steeped Grossmann's tea, and with less regret, he ordered Fleischer to kill the four security guards of the villa. There could be no witnesses.

0330 Hours
East of Velletri, Italy

The conversation was whispered in the dark.

It had taken Perkin and Sergeant Taylor longer to find the tanks than expected, and once they had done so, it took even longer to identify the tracks as friend or foe. They were friendly. It had taken even more time to creep up close to the four Stuart light tanks, and longer still to get the attention of the lone sentry—a private from Ithaca, New York. The private woke his platoon leader who was a second lieutenant from Asheville, North Carolina.

The lieutenant, whose name was Enoch Everage, was a little groggy at first. He hadn't had much sleep in the past four days and was somewhat annoyed at Perkin who mistakenly kept calling him Lieutenant Average. After a few minutes of small talk including fielding a question from Perkin about the reportedly ideal climate of Asheville, he came around sufficiently to ask, "Tell me again. Why are you here, Cap'n?"

"You're in no-man's land out here. Are you aware of that?" Perkin asked patiently.

"What do you mean, sir?" asked Everage as he looked about in the darkness.

"There's about three miles between the 141st regimental line and the Krauts at Velletri. You're closer to them than to us, and as far as I can tell, you've got your barrels pointed towards me and not at the enemy. Y'all don't have any infantry support that I can see, so unless you've been ordered to remain at this exact spot, I'd recommend that you withdraw at least two thousand yards or so to the east." Perkin pointed back to the 141st lines and said, "Which is that way."

"Shit!" Everage said. "Are you sure? I mean, I

thought we were well within our lines last night when we bedded down. We've been doing everything from support to infantry to reconnaissance, and...shit...I guess we're lost. Goddamnit!"

Perkin laughed quietly in the dark. "Well, at least now you know you're lost. I'd relocate ASAP. There was a German patrol working through here earlier and they're probably taking your coordinates back for a fire mission or sending out a squad of bubbas with panzer-fausts. If you want, we'll escort you back through our lines."

Fifteen minutes later, they were out of no-man's land and watching the lights of a German artillery strike on the now empty ridgeline. As Perkin turned to head back to his bedroll, Lieutenant Everage grasped his hand in silent thanks. Although Perkin was tired, he walked with a smile in the darkness.

0615 Hours
East-northeast of Velletri, Italy

The tank destroyers moved slowly but it was a quick pace for the infantry that was in company with the open turret M-10s. Some soldiers of the company were riding on the tank destroyers, others were jogging alongside, and more were riding in the heavy trucks in the rear. Sam, Perkin, Sergeant Kulis, and Private Jimmy Cooper, Sam's radioman, rode in a jeep that was close behind one of the Wolverines. Kulis, who was driving, was careful to stay in its tracks.

As Sam looked out over the ragged skirmish line of his troops and the tank destroyers, he had a moment of panic as he saw Corporal Hodgson fall flat on his face some fifty yards to his left. Sam was pointing at the soldier and had whipped his head around to look for the shooter when Hodgson sprang back to his feet with an embarrassed look on his face. He had tripped over a rock. Sam laughed as much at himself as at the soldier who was already being teased by a friend.

The 141st was moving toward Velletri. The regiment had been alerted at 0430 hours, and was now moving forward to close the distance to the town. Major Spaulding had told his company commanders that major engagements were to be avoided—they would push forward with patrols until they met significant resistance, and then they'd move the main bodies of the battalions up behind them. The point wasn't to take Velletri in this push, but to be better positioned to do so when the order came.

So far, Sam had seen little indication of a German presence, but the patrols reported that German roadblocks weren't far ahead and it was Spaulding's intent to stop short of the German positions. One forward patrol from 1st Platoon reported seeing Germans pull back before the American advance, but Sam didn't put much stock in it. In his experience, the Germans had never given up ground without a fight. Ever. Consequently, Sam was expecting German contact before they had gone much farther.

They were no longer moving through countryside defined only by fields of wheat, vineyards, olive orchards, or pockets of dense woods. The Velletri-Valmontone highway was transitioning to a growing number of homes and small businesses where wire fences protected property from unwanted visitors. The highway crested and began a slight slope into a saddle that continued for at least one thousand yards before another crest took the highway leading into Velletri out of view.

Sam had Kulis pull the jeep into the parking lot of what Perkin identified as a store selling plumbing supplies. "Make sure no one's in there but Italians," Sam said to Kulis and his radio operator as he stood on the bumper of the jeep and surveyed the next thousand yards with his binoculars. Much of the company was now out of view behind the brush and homes along the roadside, and Sam realized that the road was particularly channeled by a string of buildings only a few hundred yards ahead of them.

"We're probably about as far as we're going to go," Sam said to Perkin.

"Yeah, I think so too. Judging by the map, if we push much farther, we're kicking off the battle for Velletri."

Kulis joined them at the jeep and said, "No one's there. The door was unlocked. No people, German or otherwise, but it looks like it's been looted. Ain't much of value left there."

Perkin looked for the radioman. "Where's Cooper?"

"Looking for a latrine. He said a place like this should have the only working toilet in…"

Kulis was interrupted by the short sharp crack of a grenade coming from the store. A cloud of smoke and dust rolled through the door, and Sam thought he heard someone say, "Awww…what the hell?" Sam and Perkin ran to the door of the building while Kulis ran to the side and began to work his way to the back.

Sam saw some of his soldiers watching from the roadside and he waved them in. As they ran up to the building and began to fan out, Private Cooper called out, "It's okay, sir." Sam entered first followed by Perkin. There were no enemy soldiers in the plumbing store. What they did find was a partially deafened radioman covered in excrement and white dust, who was simultaneously shaken, furious, and embarrassed.

When the soldier calmed down, he said, "I lifted the lid to the commode and seen it was full of shit with a pineapple grenade on top. There was a wire running from the lid to the grenade and I guess when I lifted the lid, it popped the spoon. Maybe. I don't know…I didn't wait long enough to examine it."

"You were lucky," Sam said.

"I think we disagree on that, sir."

"I think he was very perceptive to notice it was the wrong fruit," Perkin said.

"What?" asked Private Cooper with a look conveying both confusion and annoyance. Sam's look conveyed the same.

"Normally the U.S. Army dishes out shit with a cherry on top," explained Perkin helpfully. "I guess the Germans do it differently. Who would have thought about pineapples?"

Ignoring his cousin as he looked over the radioman from a distance, Sam asked, "You didn't catch any frags? You ain't hurt?"

"I don't think so, sir." The soldier looked himself over as well and then groaned. "This is the nastiest thing I ever seen. Ah, hell. I'm bleeding." Cooper lifted his shirt and there were a dozen small cuts on his back. He gingerly pulled out a shard of porcelain.

"Shit bombs should be outlawed if you asked me," Perkin observed. "Against the laws of nature…the whole thing stinks if you ask me."

Kulis started laughing as the soldier glared at Perkin. Between fits of laughter, Kulis said, "There's a pump out back. Let's hope it's working, but check it for booby traps first. That's got to be the funniest damn thing of the whole war!"

Sam shook his head as he tried not to laugh, and then said, "We're wasting time." He motioned to a medic who had been watching from a distance. "Help him get cleaned up. We don't want these to get infected.

Then y'all catch up to us. Kulis, stay with me and Cap'n Berger. You can work the radio until Coop gets back." As he walked back to the jeep with Perkin, he said, "Craziest shit I ever seen."

0625 Hours
East-northeast of Velletri, Italy

The three soldiers were still laughing a few minutes later as Perkin weaved through the riflemen and the tank destroyers on the highway. They wanted to get closer to the lead track and make a determination whether to proceed to the next crest or to dig in where they were. As often happens in war, the decision was made for them.

Unlike the short sharp crack of the hand grenade, the next explosion they heard was deep and powerful as the lead M-10 tank destroyer went up in a thirty-foot column of white flames that instantly incinerated the crew in the open turret. The right track was blown off the Wolverine yet it continued to roll down the road until it came to rest in the ditch to the right of the highway. Perkin put the jeep in reverse and began to back down the highway as the ammunition on board the Wolverine cooked off and the column of flame burned fiercer.

"In here! In here!" Sam shouted, and he pointed to a sunken gravel road to the right of the highway. Perkin spun the jeep onto the road, which was bounded to the left by a café that had signs nailed to a wooden telephone pole advertising its *panino, cotolette, caprese,* and *tramezzini.* The café was boarded up and looked as though it hadn't served any food to paying customers for quite some time. On the right of the sunken road was a small olive orchard and each soldier looked hard through the orchard for signs of German troops but saw none.

"Perk, will you and Eddie get up on that rooftop yonder and let me know what's out there? I'm going to see to the company." Sam pointed at a house at the end of the sunken road. He reached into the back of the jeep and pulled a handheld SCR-536 radio out of a green canvas bag and handed it to his cousin.

Perkin nodded, hopped out of the jeep with his Thompson, and as Sam was clambering into the driver's seat, he said, "Give us a couple minutes. Take care. Oh… here's Cooper." The radioman was dripping with water but was running full out for the jeep. Private Cooper jumped into the back and put on the headset of his SCR-300 and then he reached into the canvas bag and pulled out another handie-talkie and set it on his lap.

Perkin and Kulis jogged to the corner of the closed café and Perkin peered around the corner. Nothing. The house that Sam had pointed to was another hundred yards away and they ran bent over down the sunken road until the driveway ended at a three-foot-tall green metal fence set atop a short stone wall. A matching green metal gate was closed but not locked and as Perkin pushed open the gate, he observed the house. The bottom half of the house was also painted green, although a lighter incongruous color than the fence, while the second story was brownish stucco. A flight of concrete stairs led to a dark brown door, which was the only entrance to the house from the front other than several windows hosting closed metal persianas. They ran to the top of the stairs and Kulis paused before the brown door.

"Should I knock, sir?" he asked.

"See if it's unlocked," Perkin said. "But don't open it."

Kulis nodded. The exploding toilet was on both their minds. He pushed the lever down and leaned gently into the door. It was locked. He looked back at Perkin who shrugged. Kulis knocked hard on the door. There was no reply, and Kulis kept knocking.

Perkin was leaning back to kick open the heavy door, and he wasn't optimistic that he'd be successful, when he heard a woman's voice call out angrily, "*Basta!*" Enough. They heard the key turn from the inside, and when the door was opened they were faced with a bent over angry old woman with white hair and dressed in a bathrobe and slippers. Her Italian was too fast for Perkin to follow completely but he understood that she was tired of *Tedeschi* soldiers asking for food.

While Kulis took the handie-talkie from Perkin, the tall captain smiled at the old lady and said, "No tedeschi, signora. *Siamo americani* and we need to get to your roof." Turning to Kulis he asked, "How do you say roof?"

The anger faded from the old lady's face as her eyes filled with tears. She grasped Perkin's hand, kissed it repeatedly, and then pulled his face down to hers. She wrapped her thin arm around his neck and kissed him gently on the cheek as tears spilled down hers. She hugged him for a long moment and then took his hand again and pulled him into the house.

Perkin looked around the room. It was neatly kept with bookshelves lining the walls and two well-worn chairs sharing a reading lamp next to an art deco Marconi radio on a small table. Kulis had moved to a corner of the room and had his finger in one ear as he talked on the handie-talkie. Perkin looked for a staircase, didn't see one, and he gently detached his hand. In English, he said, "Signora, we need to get to your roof," and he pointed skyward.

She clearly didn't understand, and Perkin was on the verge of walking away and looking for the stairs himself when Kulis said, "I thought that we might need help, sir. Here, ma'am."

The young sergeant walked next to the white-haired lady and said into the handie-talkie, "Go ahead, Scott." Kulis held the radio up to the woman's ear, and he smiled when her eyes grew wide as she listened to an Appalachian-accented voice ask her in Italian to take the men to the roof.

"Si, si," she said to the radio and she took Perkin's hand again as she nodded her head vigorously. She led him through an arched door, and on the other side was a set of stairs. She pointed upwards and stood aside as Perkin and Kulis sprinted up the faded stone stairs two at a time. They reached the landing for the second story and there were two doors on either side of the landing, both leading to made-up bedrooms that obviously were reserved for grandchildren. On the back of the landing was a wooden ladder that was affixed to the wall leading to a hatch through the ceiling.

Perkin climbed the ladder, gratified that it held his weight. He was puzzled by the latch for a moment, turning the handle first one way and then the other until he felt a satisfying click. The hatch leading to the rooftop clearly hadn't been used in some time, and Perkin had to push hard to lift it. When it gave way and opened, dust and old leaves trickled down on Perkin as he climbed through the hatch and over the coaming.

In his limited experience in Italy, rooftops were of two varieties—either a tiled roof with a relatively shallow slope or a flat roof with a short wall. Perkin was happy to see that this was of the latter variety. The roof was painted the same color green as the first floor of the house and the wall was about twenty-four inches high and went around the perimeter of the roof.

Without waiting for Kulis, Perkin crawled to the wall facing west. He cautiously raised his head and looked over the wall. Spread out before him, he saw the still burning tank destroyer to his left and Able Company soldiers moving to positions to his front. Although there had been several M-10s accompanying the riflemen, Perkin couldn't see any of them now and he assumed they were trying to ascertain what had hit their lead track.

Perkin sat cross-legged and found that the wall was a near perfect height for him to rest his binoculars on while he surveyed the battlefield. He could only see forward about a thousand yards before the terrain dropped out of view. To his left and right were a scattering of houses, businesses, fields, and small olive orchards as the terrain gained in elevation to the north.

Perkin focused his attention on the horizon where the Velletri-Valmontone highway passed over a small hill. His binoculars helped but at that distance all he could see were vague shapes. Near the crest of the highway, he saw several figures running to the left and he tracked their progression with the binoculars. They were headed to a clump of trees not far off the highway. Perkin stared at the tree for a long moment, and then handed the glasses to Kulis.

"See the trees to the left of the highway?" Perkin asked as he pointed to the horizon.

"Yes, sir." Kulis handed the glasses back to Perkin and looked at their map. "Here?" he asked.

Perkin looked at the map as well. "Uh huh. Call it in to Bear, and have Cooper relay a fire order. I bet there's an 88 unlimbered over there, and that's what took out the TD. It might be a PAK-38 or 40, but the way that thing went up, I'm guessing it was an 88."

Sergeant Kulis talked to Private Cooper, and then set the handie-talkie down. "They're calling it in. Bear wants you to look to the northwest. Some fellas thought they seen something up there. Oh hey…look at that." He pointed back to the hatch. The lady of the house had brought up a bowl of strawberries and a carafe of water while they were looking off into the distance.

While Kulis crawled back to the hatch to get the strawberries and water, Perkin scanned the countryside to the northwest. He saw plenty of buildings and ample natural cover to hide an antitank gun, but if there was a hidden gun, he couldn't find it. Perkin set down the binoculars and as he ate a sweet strawberry, he traced a path from the burning tank destroyer to the northwest. There appeared to be only a narrow azimuth from the spot of the explosion to the countryside that wasn't obscured by buildings along the highway. Perkin ran his eye over that pathway a couple times and still didn't see where the round might have come from.

"Tell Sam that I don't…wait a second," Perkin said as he picked up his binoculars again and focused on a stone house that he estimated was about 600 yards away. "Did you see movement up there?"

"No, sir, I didn't. But I don't have Bear's eyesight or your binoculars, so I wouldn't," Kulis replied.

"Here, focus on that house." Perkin handed the binoculars to Kulis, and said, "I thought I saw something move."

The young sergeant stared hard at the house for several minutes, and then handed the binoculars back. The house was not unlike the one that they were currently on. It had a long gravel driveway with a southern face but it was set back farther from the highway. It boasted a more conventional color scheme as well as a better view—it was set on a small hill, which gave Kulis the impression that he was looking up slightly at the house. "Cap'n, I cain't be for certain, but I think there's a tube stickin' out from the far corner, that'd be the, uh, southwest corner of the house," Kulis said. "D'ya see? It kind of breaks up the color of the background some. I bet it's a PAK or somethin' and they wheel it out, shoot, and then pull it back in the excitement…" Kulis stopped to listen for a second and then said, "Here's our arty."

Indeed, the deep booms and the ripping sound overhead presaged the destruction of the clump of trees on the horizon. As Perkin watched the first spotting round impact, he commented, "They're short." He was about to pass corrections back to Sam when the artillery adjusted fire and the trees soon disappeared in a cloud of smoke and dust. He turned his attention back to the house and looked for the gun barrel. Perkin couldn't see it. While he kept his eyes focused on the house, he said, "Pass that house back to battalion. I think we ought to get some rifles and a bazooka team up there to take a look at it."

A couple minutes later, Kulis handed the handie-talkie to Perkin and said, "It's Major Spaulding."

After a short discussion, Spaulding understood Perkin's hesitation in calling in artillery and destroying the home without confirmation that there was indeed an antitank gun or a tank in the lee of the house. He told Perkin that he'd get a squad up there as soon as possible from either Able or Baker companies.

Perkin was setting down the radio when he heard Kulis say, "Damn! That was fast." Kulis pointed to an M-5A1 Stuart light tank that was working its way toward the house. Perkin watched as the light American tank weaved through an olive orchard four hundred yards behind the house. The small tank came to a stop and Perkin watched as the tank commander dropped back into the tank and closed the hatch to the turret.

The M-5 continued toward the back of the house. When it came within 150 yards, the tank stopped once again, and then rocked back hard on its tracks as it fired. Then it fired again. And again. The little American tank abruptly started moving again and its tracks tore up the soil as it turned hard and accelerated fast to its left. From the far corner of the house where Kulis had thought he'd seen a barrel, a gray and green German long-barreled Panzer IV slowly emerged. Despite the three shots fired by the Stuart, the German tank appeared undamaged and as it moved, it was rapidly traversing its turret to the rear to face the threat.

"Oh Christ!" Perkin exclaimed. Then he shouted at the American tank, "Run! Goddamnit! Get out of there!"

"Oh, he's done for," Kulis said. "That little popgun ain't got a chance."

The tank commander of the Stuart had different notions, however. He pulled his tank to the northeast corner of the house and moved away from the home to a standoff distance of about twenty yards. The tank commander opened the hatch and stood up to have a clear view. His head went back and forth between the two other corners of the house that he could see and he waited.

The panzer commander also had different notions. He was done with the battle. Perkin watched the panzer ignore the driveway and accelerate in a cloud of exhaust smoke through the yard toward the highway. As the turret faced rearward to cover its retreat, the tank moved slowly down a small incline toward the road. Perkin turned to Kulis to tell him to pass that information to Sam to see if he could get it in the hands of the Stuart commander but Kulis was already on the radio.

A few moments later—it seemed like an eternity—
the Stuart commander dropped down in his turret
again and closed the hatch. Before the hatch had
slammed shut, the small tank was already on the move.
He headed for the southeast corner of the house, and
the Stuart moved without hesitation past the protection
of the house and stopped in the front yard of the home
taking aim on the departing German tank. The panzer
commander had expected the Stuart to follow directly
behind, and the 75mm cannon of the German tank was
pointed toward the western side of the house. As he saw
the Stuart appear to the east and realized his mistake,
the German commander began to traverse his turret
again.

The Stuart fired its 37mm main gun for the fourth
time, and for the fourth time, the small American tank
found its target. This time, the shot had an effect. The
engine on the panzer started to pour out black smoke
and both the tank and the turret traverse came to a halt.
Slowly, deliberately, the Stuart fired one last round.

It penetrated just below the turret. More black
smoke poured from the stricken German tank, and
then Perkin saw the first flickers of flame. The hatch
flew open on the panzer, and a crewman scampered
over the side, dropped to the ground and tried to run
away. He was gunned down by the .30 caliber coaxial
machine gun on the Stuart.

A pair of hands showed from the hatch of the
panzer, and when the Stuart didn't open fire, the
German crewman quickly stood up. The American
commander signaled for him to come out and approach
the Stuart. As the German soldier came forward in a
smoking uniform, he looked over his shoulder for signs
that more crewmen would follow, but none did. The
German loader was the tank's sole survivor, and when

he realized he was alone and that they had been beaten by a light reconnaissance tank, he hung his head so the Americans wouldn't see him cry.

0745 Hours
East-northeast of Velletri, Italy

The last German defenders had been pushed back and the 1st Battalion had moved its lines to the crest of the highway. The crest really signified nothing new in their situation. They could see the town of Velletri as it rose on a hill a mile in the distance, but the German forces had probably withdrawn no more than the thousand yards they had just yielded. German artillery had twice shelled soldiers of the 1st Battalion, and everyone was rapidly digging in.

They were there to stay for the time being. Major Spaulding said that orders were in the works for a two-regiment attack on Velletri, and after the town was cleared, the division would move to replace the 34th Division on the line. There was no concrete timeline given, and no one was excited about either prospect, but there was work to be done in the meanwhile.

Perkin was gratified to discover that the artillery strike he'd called in had destroyed an 88mm Flak. It was partially limbered with the front wheels attached and the rear wheels lying in a mangled mess some twenty yards away and Perkin surmised they were preparing to tow the artillery piece to another location. He was pleased to see that this particular piece would never threaten anyone again—paintings on the crew shielding indicated that this gun and its crew were responsible for the destruction of 12 aircraft, 43 tanks, and 18 bunkers. Perkin wondered if the 88 was the source of the tank destroyer's misfortune or whether it had been the Panzer IV. The Germans had taken their dead and wounded when they withdrew but judging by the bloodstained ground there had been plenty of both. That also gave Perkin some degree of satisfaction.

As he was moving forward from the house, and after giving the old Italian woman a kiss on the cheek, he came across the M-5 Stuart that had destroyed the panzer. It was Lieutenant Everage's tank and his excitement knew no bounds. "Brother, my crew is so damn good, they never had a chance! That was our first tank! We snuck up on him and he couldn't hear us over his own engine. We hit his turret three times and didn't penetrate but we sure got him later!"

"You sure did," Perkin agreed with a smile. He knew from experience that after the adrenalin left the young lieutenant's system, he'd probably be nauseated, but what he was feeling now was a euphoria that few men unfamiliar with successful combat could comprehend.

Perkin took the German prisoner from Everage and wished the lieutenant good hunting, and he also made a mental note to write up the young officer and his crew for Silver Stars. A Stuart defeating a Panzer IV might not be unprecedented, but Perkin had never heard of such a thing. Lieutenant Everage might need further instruction in nighttime navigation but his skill and courage in combat were beyond question.

Perkin looked at the German soldier. His face and hands had flash burns and his entire body trembled uncontrollably. Sergeant Kulis offered the German a cigarette and the young enemy soldier gratefully accepted while a medic looked him over.

"I can put sulfadiazine on it, sir," the medic said. When Perkin raised an eyebrow, the medic explained, "Burn ointment."

Perkin spoke passable German but waved over

Private Pfadenhauer who was passing by, and said, "Howie, ask this boy his name."

Pfadenhauer had a brief conversation with the German soldier while the medic applied the burn ointment and said to Perkin, "His name is Gerhard Becker. He's nineteen and from Buttelstedt. I ain't ever heard of it. He says it's a country village north of Weimar. He's pretty scared and happy to talk, I think."

"We'll send him up to regiment in a minute to talk to their interrogators. I only have one question. Ask him if his tank hit our tank destroyer." Perkin looked closely at the soldier as Pfadenhauer asked the question.

The soldier shook his head and said, "It must have been a Flak cannon. We hadn't shot yet. We were waiting for the first tank to pass, then we were going to hit them from behind." The soldier looked at all the American troops busily digging in and added, "Staff Sergeant Keller just thought we'd catch a small reconnaissance when we set up this morning. We didn't expect all this."

Perkin was satisfied that Becker was telling the truth. Before he walked away, he said, "Tell him he gets to go home to Buttelstedt when the war's over. *Viel glück.*" Good luck.

1000 Hours
Rome, Italy

The Romans were looking a little too happy, thought Douglas Grossmann as he drank his second caffé corretto of the morning, the coffee remaining untouched. The sounds of combat had faded since it was a windy day, but many Italians had lain in bed the night before dreaming of their liberation. It was getting closer. The Allies knew it. The Germans knew it. And now the Romans knew it. It was in the air even if the wind was blowing from the wrong direction.

Grossmann was no longer interested in the affairs of the citizens of Rome. He was tired of the noise, the chaos, and the people. Even his café owner was getting on his nerves. He was obsequious as usual, but he had told Grossmann there was no more American whiskey to be found in Rome, and would grappa be sufficient? It wasn't. Not today. But Grossmann would have to make do. He grimaced as he downed the second shot and he motioned for the waiter to bring him another. "Bastard's probably saving my bourbon for the Americans," thought Grossmann and he added to himself in English, "Fuck him." Swearing was always more effective in English.

Unconsciously, Grossmann looked down at his hands and sighed. He had done what he needed to last night, but it would haunt him for the rest of his days. Not because he had killed innocent people. He had moved past that long ago. But because of what this meant to his life with Antoniette. He still didn't know who the Nascimbeni family was and what their relationship was to the Bernardis, but it was had to be close. Grossmann didn't think they were family—he had long ago investigated all of Antoniette's aunts and uncles to make sure they wouldn't be liabilities to him—but they must have been close family friends. Or acquaintances through the Fascist Party. Or perhaps the girl was just a schoolmate of Antoniette's.

They weren't *just* schoolmates though, thought Grossmann as he corrected himself. They were wearing matching dresses and holding hands, but more importantly, five or six years after the picture had been taken, it was still on the girl's wall. Antoniette was important to the girl he'd murdered and he wanted to know why.

Grossmann lit a cigarette and thought through his

options. He had no good ones, and the worst before him was telling the truth. If Antoniette knew he had murdered a family friend and for no better reason than whimsy—and Grossmann was honest enough with himself to admit that's what it was—his relationship with Antoniette would never be the same. Never. An out and out lie was problematic as well. She could read him better than anyone. If the subject came up, would he be able to maintain his composure? Would she see his guilt? He wasn't sure. Maybe a hybrid of fact and fiction would do it. He sipped his grappa and thought... *fact and fiction*.

1300 Hours
Rome, Italy

The chief of staff leaned back in his chair and looked at Lieutenant Colonel Grossmann. The boss's special projects officer looked like crap. There were bags under his eyes and while Grossmann was normally a dapper officer, he needed a shower and a shave. Moreover, the chief of staff wasn't even sure that Grossmann was sober.

"Colonel Grossmann, tell me about your operation last night," the chief of staff said.

Grossmann nodded, swallowed hard, and said, "It was straightforward up until the end. We went in, found the Jews that we were looking for, and we were preparing to truck the enemies of the Reich out and arrest the family that was hiding them, when the family resisted."

"How?"

"They were screaming obscenities, threats, that kind of thing. A young woman broke free and tried to run. I executed her. More threats followed. Then I executed her family and we deported the Jews to Fossoli for further disposition this morning."

"Okay. So far, so good. Why didn't you execute the Jews on the spot?"

"A couple reasons, sir. I wanted to make sure that we were showing progress to Berlin...you know, that our numbers were where they were meant to be." The chief of staff nodded approvingly. Grossmann continued, "Second, I thought we might give ourselves some deniability with the Italians. They didn't know the Jews were there, but if we killed them on the spot, it would come back to us. So, instead we slid them out at night and made the executions of the traitors look like it was done by communist guerillas."

The chief of staff leaned back in his chair and thought for a moment. He said, "All right. I'll make sure that if the cat-eaters broach the subject we deny involvement. But sometimes you intelligence guys out-think yourselves. There's nothing wrong with executing enemies of the Reich, so there's no need to cover it up. There are benefits to publicly enforcing order. It's what we Germans do. Ambiguity leads to complications."

"Yes, sir. I'll remember that. Did you hear about the contraband that we confiscated?" Grossmann asked. He wanted to avoid mentioning the Italian policeman they had murdered as well as the other Italian citizens.

"No. A good night?"

"Yes, sir. A considerable art collection that I conservatively estimate to be worth, I don't know...four to five million reichsmarks. I've made arrangements for a buyer to acquire some but the choice pieces should go to Berlin. And a wine cellar that, well, I was hoping you and I could split. It's remarkable."

The chief of staff brightened and clapped his hands together. "Oooh! Tell me about it!"

Grossmann smiled at the colonel's delight and said,

"French, of course. Great labels. Great. Some others I don't know personally but they look promising. Some spectacular vintages…Burgundies from '20, '23, and '34. Bordeaux from '28, '29, and cases of the 1934 Latours and Haut Brions—even a selection of the 1900 vintage, which I've never had but I understand is wonderful. Some promising Rhône wines—Châteauneuf-du-Papes of '11, '28, '29, and '34. Like I said, great. Also a mix of good champagnes and whites, dessert wines, etc. Some Italian wines with good reputations but I say we sell those unless you want them."

"No. I've had enough Chianti for a lifetime. I'll make you a deal. I'll let you have the Burgundies and Rhônes in exchange for the Bordeaux—assuming the numbers work out in your favor of course. We split the champagnes down the middle and you take what you want of the whites and I'll take the rest." The chief of staff smiled generously.

Grossmann almost laughed. He was being robbed of course, but he had already taken several cases of the best Bordeaux anyway. Besides, the meeting with the chief of staff had gone well. "As long as I get half of the 1900 vintage, you've got a deal, sir."

The chief of staff smiled even wider. "Done! I can't wait! Okay, back to business. I want you to go back to your quarters and catch a nap and get cleaned up. The general wants to see you tonight about your other project."

Grossmann was surprised. "Yes, sir. Is he expecting something from me? I don't think I owe him anything."

The chief of staff shrugged and said, "If you don't think so, then probably not, but he didn't say. Be back by 1800."

"Yes, sir."

1300 Hours
Southeast of Velletri, Italy

Perkin brushed off his uniform before he walked into the dairy's farmhouse that was still serving as the divisional headquarters. He'd been summoned to division but he hadn't been told who to report to or for what reason.

The house was not unlike most farmhouses that he'd seen in America except the exterior was stone and not wood, and the floors were tile and not wood. He walked into a mud room that had a modern washing machine with an electric wringer and he was surprised to see that it hadn't been stripped of its motor or wiring. Since the electrical power was out indefinitely, it didn't make any difference for the short term but given the looting in the dairy barn, it was one less thing for the owner to replace.

The mud room led to the kitchen where there was a large table with a half-dozen officers sitting around it. Lieutenant Colonel Miller, the division's G-2, was one of the men. He saw Perkin walk in, waved off the salute, and said, "Hey, Perk, come on in. How are you doing?"

"Outstanding, sir. How 'bout you?" Perkin nodded to the other men at the table and walked over to shake Miller's hand.

"Good, thank you for asking. Glad you're here. The general's finally approved your transfer to my staff," Miller said with a deadpan visage. Seeing Perkin's face fall, the intelligence officer started to laugh. "I'm just screwing with you, Perk, although I gotta say your reaction's a little disappointing. Most of the junior intelligence officers would be delighted to work under my tutelage."

Perkin laughed. It was rare that someone got one

over on him. He nodded his respect and said, "Since I'm always being told I have to be a mentor—are you sure you wouldn't be under my tutelage, sir?"

Miller rolled his eyes and said, "I forgot. You're the professor. Well, Professor, there's some coffee in the dining room yonder, and then if you head to the sittin' room in the back, there's them two civilian fellas that no one seems to know anything about but every time they show up they wanna talk to you. Come see me when you're done mentorin' the professional spooks, would ya?"

Perkin grabbed a cup of black coffee and walked back to the sitting room. The door was closed, and he knocked twice and entered. As he expected, George Hill of the OSS and Charles Ackernly of British MI-6 were waiting for him.

"Professor Berger!" Ackernly exclaimed with obvious delight. "How good to see you, my boy!"

"You too, Charles," Perkin said with a smile. Turning to the taller man, he said, "And you, George, how are you doing?"

"Great, Perkin." A strong breeze blowing off the cow lot lifted the curtains and Hill coughed. "The fresh air agrees with me," he laughed as he gasped. "Oh Lord, that's something, isn't it? Whew, this city boy has never gotten used to it."

"If Sam was here, he'd tell you that's the most wonderful smell in the world, and based on the aroma, he could tell you what the cows had for dinner."

Ackernly coughed out, "Maybe he should be the intelligence officer."

Perkin grinned and said, "Don't count on it. If we ever go to war with the Bovine Nation, Sam's likely to defect. He likes cows better than most people, I reckon. Dang, *that is fragrant*. Speaking of which, have either of you ever seen the effects of a pineapple grenade in a filled toilet?" Such a phenomena was beyond the experience of either man, and Perkin told them about his delightful morning beginning with the trek to find the tanks, the exploding toilet, and the truly remarkable tank battle that he'd witnessed.

"You lead an interesting life, Professor Berger," observed Ackernly with a smile. "So, old boy, we have some news for you."

"I thought that might be the case," Perkin said. "Grossmann?"

"Yes," said Ackernly. "We have an asset in Rome who is familiar with the Grossmann case, but not actively pursuing him. It appears that he's recruited a mob boss, who in addition to taking the king's salt from our asset has also previously accepted Yankee gold from none other than Lieutenant Commander Cardosi. This mob boss is named Occhiato, and he says Grossmann is preparing to hit the other crime lords in Rome at the end of the German occupation. Apparently, Grossmann's plan is to steal from the other mob families, sell the purloined goods to Occhiato, and then call it a day... probably in Switzerland."

Perkin thought for a second and asked, "How about that? That's very industrious of him, isn't it?"

"Yes, indeed. It's pretty industrious of the Occhiato fellow as well." said Hill. "Do the math. He has business arrangements with Jimmy, with the Crown's asset, and with Grossmann himself."

"Well, that's somethin' to think about, ain't it?"

"Yes, it is," said Ackernly as he loaded a pipe with tobacco.

"Do we know where his allegiance lies?" Perkin asked.

Hill shrugged. "His allegiance is probably to

the Occhiato syndicate, and to them only...but, he volunteered to Charles's man in the Eternal City that Grossmann had approached him. Our assessment is that he is inclined to our side, but like many Italians, he's going to go where the long-term money takes him."

"Is that why you came here? To let me know we have a triple-dealing mobster?" Perkin asked.

"Yes," said Ackernly. "Out of all of us, we still feel like you have the best shot at getting into Rome first. Grossmann's most likely long gone by then, but who knows? George and I gave you Occhiato's address a fortnight ago. We thought you should know this. It might be significant, but probably not."

"Well, the question is, how do we make it significant? How do we use this to our advantage?"

"I don't know if we can. Any suggestions?" asked Hill.

"I don't know exactly, but it seems unlikely that Grossmann will still be in Rome when we get there. He's a fool if he is. But, these mob families and their depots are another place to search for him when that time comes. There and Antoniette's apartment."

"True. We never held high hope that you'd be able to swing in and arrest him, but this is war. And war is defined by chaos. And chaos makes possible magical things like exploding toilets and victorious Stuarts all in one day," Ackernly said. "You never know."

"Well," Perkin said thoughtfully, "I wasn't going to arrest Grossmann to begin with, but that has me thinking. I want...above almost all things...to be the one to pull the trigger when Grossmann's in my sights. I think I've earned that right. But, I'm objective enough to know it's unlikely. The ends are more important than the means...so, I won't play Ahab to his white whale. Whether it's from the *Rachel* or Starbuck or Queequeg,

I can sleep at night just knowing he gets a harpoon through the heart."

"What are you suggesting, Professor Berger?" asked Ackernly as he looked at the young soldier with interest.

"Is it possible to get tasking back to either your asset or to the syndicate?"

Hill and Ackernly looked at one another and Ackernly said, "Yes."

"I can't bear the thought that he's going to decamp to Switzerland after killing Gianina and the Gildardino family...and after looting Rome five ways to Sunday on top of that. Tell our respective governments, it's time we put an end to this. Insist on it! Let's kill Grossmann! Let's have our men in Rome do it. Let's pay the mob to finish him off." Perkin looked at the two men standing before him. "Let's make sure that when the German Army retreats from Rome, he's left behind in pieces."

Ackernly looked serious and then the tension broke on his face as he smiled. "Assassination's a serious step, Professor Berger...but to play on your words, I think Colonel Grossmann's earned the right to be taken seriously. If our superiors agree, the order will go out as soon as possible, and if we can't come to agreement, maybe you can still acquire him in Rome."

"Nothing would make me happier."

1405 Hours
Southeast of Velletri, Italy

When Perkin left his meeting with the two intelligence officers, he found Lieutenant Colonel Miller still at the kitchen table. The other officers in his company had departed but Miller remained seated sipping from a tin cup of coffee and reading a month-old *Stars and Stripes*. "Look at this," Miller said as he slid the paper over to Perkin, who saw a picture of Joe Louis in a staff sergeant's uniform shaking the hand of a London cab driver. When Perkin looked back to Miller, the intelligence officer said, "What is the champ doin' in London? If he wants revenge on Schmeling and his kind, and I'm not talkin' about his two-minute match in '38, he should be here. Not London."

"I suppose the boys in London will get their chance soon enough," Perkin said. "Should be any week now, I'd think."

"I'd think so too, but that's not what I'm talking about. Schmeling himself is probably somewhere here in Italy…assuming he's still alive. I read a long time ago that he became a *Fallschirmjäger*. The First Parachute Corps is somewhere over those hills there." Miller nodded toward the Colli Laziali.

Perkin shook his head. "He was. But he was wounded in '41 and invalided out. We'll just have to settle for killing his comrades."

"Russia?" asked Miller.

"Crete, I think," said Perkin.

"Shoot. I was hoping to trade Schmeling's head for an autograph from the champ. Oh well. Perk, I got a question for you."

"You want to know how to meet women too?" Perkin asked innocently. "It's okay. I get that a lot."

Miller laughed. "No thanks, Professor. My wife told me before I deployed that I've already met all the women I need for this lifetime. No, I wanted to see if you're happy in your current slot as the battalion S-2."

Perkin nodded, "Yes, sir. There's no other place I'd rather be than in the battalion. Why do you ask? Were you serious earlier?"

"I'd like you on my staff but I need good guys at the regiments and battalions as well. No…it's not that. The

Old Man's aide-de-camp is going to rotate at the end of June back to the States for airborne training." Miller looked at Perkin closely. "The chief of staff asked all of us for a list of qualified company grade officers for the boss to choose from and you would be my recommendation. But I won't put your name forward if you don't want it. What would you think? And I want an honest answer."

Perkin said nothing for a moment. Then he shook his head. "Sir, I'll do anything for the general, but I don't think I'd make for a very good dog robber. And to be honest with you, I wouldn't want the job."

Miller nodded and said, "This is an honor, you know. It's recognition that you have the potential to be a general officer yourself—that, as our friends in the fleet would say, someday you might hoist your own flag. It's an opportunity to witness command at the highest levels and it's a building block in the career of an officer who is destined for bigger things."

Perkin whistled and said, "You sure know how to play on a guy's ego, sir, but Bill Spaulding tells me almost daily that it's unlikely I'll stay a captain let alone make major. Sir, I genuinely appreciate..."

Miller held his hand up to stop Perkin. "No. I understand. No hard feelings."

"Thank you, sir."

Miller leaned back in his chair and scratched his stomach—the very vision of a good old boy on the family porch and not indicative at all of one of the sharpest minds in the division. Miller said, "Your name actually came up this morning in a discussion between General Walker and General Truscott."

"Uh oh," Perkin said. "That could be trouble."

Miller laughed. "Paranoia's a good trait in intelligence, but no. No trouble. The general had a meeting with Truscott at 0700 this morning, and the Old Man said that one of his intelligence officers, a Captain Berger, first stumbled onto this route over Monte Artemisio, and Truscott said, 'Berger? Perkin Berger?' Naturally, it has to be one and the same—I don't think we have two Perkins in the entire U.S. Army, let alone the division—and the boss was pretty curious how the corps commander knows your name."

Perkin grinned and said, "I played cards with him while I was on leave on Capri."

"So he said. He also said, and I quote, 'I'm not sure if he's the best cheater I've ever seen or the luckiest son of a bitch in the world.' Then the subject got onto Helen and he decided at least you're the luckiest S.O.B. he's ever met. I'm not so sure you impressed him one way or the other but your girl sure made an impact. He said she was one of the most charming women he'd met since leaving the States. How is Helen, by the way?"

Perkin sighed. "She's back in England, sir. Breaks my heart. Say! If I take the dog robber job, any chance I could go to the old country and pick up some shortbread cookies or a pint of ale for the general's dinner? I'd get some for Truscott too if it helped."

"No chance at all. But, I'm going to offer you something almost as smashing as a trip to England as they would say."

"What's that, sir?"

"We have orders. At 1500, the general and the senior staff are meeting with the regimental and battalion commanders in the dairy barn. Since you had a hand in all this, I thought you might like to be a fly on the wall and listen in."

1455 Hours
East-northeast of Velletri, Italy

Sam lay on the ground under the extensive cover of brush that for a brief panicked moment he thought was poison ivy. Seeing Sam's reaction to the leaves, First Sergeant Donohue said to his company commander, "I already checked, sir. It kinda looks like it but it ain't."

"Thank God," Sam said. "That'd just cap Anzio off perfectly, wouldn't it? To go into battle with white paste smeared on your face." Assured that a severe rash wasn't in his near future, Sam picked up his binoculars and surveyed what he assumed was the new no-man's land between Velletri and the company.

"Beats the exploding toilet experience, I'd think," said Donohue as he looked through his own binoculars. "When I was in the Philippines we went out into the middle of nowhere for jungle training. There's about a million things that'll kill you in the jungle so we had some old Negrito feller who taught us how to survive out there. He knew everything about everything in the jungle. He could tell you which bugs you could eat, and which ones you cain't. He'd show us which vines had fresh water or which roots cured cancer or eating which snakes would make you virile."

"You ate snakes?" Sam asked.

"I don't need to eat no snakes to get virile, sir. I'm a white man from Texas," Donohue said. "But one night we're sittin' around the campfire, and the old Negrito's off hunting monkeys or dogs 'cause he was going to teach us how to barbeque either a monkey or a dog, and our sergeant stands up and pulls a bunch of leaves off some bush. He turns around and says, 'Everyone know what this is?' We didn't. He said, 'It's the toilet paper leaf, remember?' No one did, but it turns out it wasn't the toilet paper leaf, but more of a poison ivy kind of leaf. Except worse."

Sam squirmed uncomfortably and asked, "What happened?"

"We had to pay nearby villagers a dollar to haul him out on a donkey." Donohue started laughing, "He had to stay in a hut in the village for almost a week with his ass pointin' skyward. You know, you'd think an experience like that would sour a guy on the Orient, but it didn't. He married a Filipina girl from that very village."

"You don't say. You'd think a severely chapped ass would be an impediment to romance," Sam observed.

"You'd think that, but not in this case. But the sergeant's wife didn't want to leave the village and come live in Manila. So, he'd catch a bus up to Bataan Province every weekend he didn't have duty to see her."

"Bataan? Was he still there when the Philippines fell?" Sam asked.

Donohue stopped smiling. "Sir, I wish I could tell you that he got out but he was still there when I left in November of '41. He wouldn't have left anyway. You get these guys that fall in love with the Orient, and it seems like nothing short of a court-martial will get 'em to leave. He's probably dead now, the poor bastard."

"I wonder what happened to her?"

"Lord knows. If the Japs found out about her bein' married to an American, they'd probably either gut her or just turn her into one of their brothels."

Sam was silent for a moment and then he said, "This war's hurt an awful lot of innocent people."

Donohue nodded his head and said, "You got that right, sir. But that's not how the Japs see it...or the Germans for that matter. There ain't no innocents. There's only them and the enemy. Being in the P.I., we watched what they were doing in China pretty closely and it was just brutal. Just…well, it makes ya sick. Manchuria, Peking, Nanking…Nanking was the worst, of course. They raped tens of thousands and murdered hundreds of thousands of noncombatants. I don't know why we were surprised by Pearl Harbor or their attack on the Philippines after what they did in China. They're a mean little people, them Japs. Given my druthers, I'd rather be in the Orient killing them than here, but Uncle Sam in his wisdom decided that I should kill Germans."

"I'm glad Uncle Sam made the decision that he did, Top. This wouldn't be the same without you," Sam said dryly.

"Aw hell, sir. You say the sweetest things." Donohue laughed and said, "Speaking of killing Germans, how long have you been watchin' them Krauts settin' up that O.P.?" He was watching two German soldiers crawl through the brush about 600 yards ahead of them and off the highway by about fifty yards.

"Since we got here. They're not bad. Movin' low and slow. When'd you pick 'em up?" Sam asked.

"Just now. Whatcha wanna do about it?" Donohue slid his Garand forward and counted the clicks as he adjusted his sights.

"I'm gonna mortar the absolute bejesus out of 'em and send 'em a message on behalf of the Gun Club that they ain't welcome here," Sam said.

"That's an elegant message, sir. How 'bout we have every mortar in the company hit 'em at once?"

"That's even eleganter. Set it up, would you, Top? I'm gonna sleep right here until our message is delivered."

1500 Hours
Southeast of Velletri, Italy

Major General Fred Walker strode confidently into the barn. A large storage room adjacent to the chute leading to the milking room had previously held rusted iron wheels, unused milking equipment, rope, wire, and assorted tools which had been cleared out. The odoriferous room was now the division's briefing room. Some of the officers present were clearly uncomfortable with the smell, and Perkin smiled to himself as more than one officer coughed involuntarily. It wasn't a nostalgic aroma for Perkin like it was for Sam, but it didn't bother him much either.

Walker told everyone to find a seat and a few officers leaned against a sawhorse or the walls of the barn, and as Perkin was in the back, he sat on the top slat of a wooden fence separating the chute from the storage room. It had decades of crusted manure on it, but he was tired and wanted to sit. It had been a long day.

Bill Spaulding sat next to Perkin in the back, and they both leaned forward slightly as Walker began to talk. The first thing that both officers noted was the contrast between Walker today, and Walker at another briefing he had delivered back in January. The division then was being ordered to cross the Rapido River. It would be a traumatic catastrophe and Walker knew it. Today, he knew something else.

"Good afternoon, gentlemen," he said with a smile and he was answered with a chorus of "Good afternoon, General."

Walker continued, "We have our orders from VI Corps, and it's huge. We're going to break the Anzio stalemate wide open, and we're going to do it in the next forty-eight hours." Walker smiled again at the excited reaction from the assembled officers. "Several days ago, our intelligence team discovered that Monte Artemisio was unmanned by the enemy. No fortifications to speak of and less than a platoon in the aggregate spread across its entire mass. We've conducted extensive patrols across the massif and our engineers have completed several surveys. This morning I talked to General Truscott and this is what I proposed: That we fix the enemy in Velletri with an assault on the town while we conduct a two-regiment infiltration up Monte Artemisio into the enemy rear. Infantry will lead the way and heavy equipment to include artillery and tanks will follow."

Perkin watched as the officers before him smiled wolfishly. This was the redemption that the division needed and everyone knew it. They could feel it. It would be an historic assault and everyone wanted to be a part of it.

Walker paused to let the news sink in and then he said, "Gentlemen, yesterday I received word that we would be replacing the 34th on the line to the west-southwest of Velletri. It seemed to me that we were being asked to do the same as at Cassino. Hit the enemy where they want us to hit them…at their strongest point. Yet, we spent three months in the most intensive mountain training in the U.S. Army and it made no sense for us to fight a battle of attrition against the Caesar Line on the Anzio plain. So, I invited General Truscott to come here this morning. He was intrigued by our plan and took it back to his staff. Although his chief engineer nonconcurred—he said we were mad—Truscott agreed. So, here are the commander's intentions and then I'll turn you over to the G-3 for the specifics. The first thing I want to stress is that all commanders must remain flexible. When we're in the run up to execution, things are going to change and change quickly. Once we begin to execute this plan, it will change even quicker. Okay, the 142nd and 143rd infantry regiments will break contact with the enemy and pass far to the rear of the 141st, loop back around to their east, and then commence their infiltration tomorrow evening after dark. Before that, at dusk, the 141st will launch an assault on the town of Velletri with the intent of diverting the enemy's attention while fixing the forces he has garrisoned in Velletri. Although the 141st's attack is intended to be a diversionary attack, it will transition to an assault to liberate Velletri as soon as the other two regiments are in the enemy rear. Once we hold the high ground north of Velletri, the German position will be untenable not only in Velletri but westward along the width of the Caesar Line. Furthermore, the enemy lines of communication literally all the way to Rome will be in jeopardy." Walker's smile was replaced with a serious look as he finished with, "Truscott's last words to me were 'You'd better not fail.' I'm going to interpret that as 'I know the 36th won't let me down.'"

1800 Hours
Rome, Italy

Grossmann had taken a nap, although he had overslept and now felt worse for doing so. He had washed up and shaved, and while he felt the need for a drink, he refrained. A meeting with senior SS officer in Italy required as clear a head as possible.

An aide showed Grossmann into the general's office and at the general's bidding, he took a seat on the leather sofa opposite the general's favorite chair. When the general asked if he wanted a drink, Grossmann gratefully accepted. It was a superb brandy and he savored the fumes and the burn down the back of his throat.

The general didn't mention last night's operation—he never acknowledged Grossmann's side ventures. Instead, he clearly wanted to discuss the operation to kidnap the Pope and deport him to territory controlled by the Reich. When Wolff sat down he opened the folder that Grossmann had prepared on the operation. He flipped through it obviously refreshing his memory on the details and then he closed the folder. Then he did something unexpected. He led Grossmann into a discussion that could only be categorized as cordial small talk. For half an hour, they drank brandy and talked about the laughable proposition that people could adapt to drinking seawater, their common hometown of Darmstadt, and the likelihood of having to relocate. It was an enjoyable discussion for both men, and the brandy helped sooth Grossmann's nerves.

Finally, the general tapped the folder again and said, "Douglas, this is good work. You've taken care of all the aspects that I asked you to and then some. Fine staff work." General Wolff's words were complimentary but he looked troubled.

"Thank you, General," Grossmann said as he accepted another brandy. "But...you have a concern?"

"Ja. I find this whole matter concerning," Wolff replied. "I've given a lot of thought to what we discussed the other day. Do you still think that deposing his Holiness would be detrimental to the interests of the German war effort?"

"Absolutely, Herr General. Arresting Pius would be a mistake of the first magnitude. It will throw the weight of the Catholic world against us including allies like Croatia and Hungary. It could lead to civil unrest or worse in Austria and the southern states." Grossmann took another sip of the excellent brandy and said, "It's a mad plan. It must be stopped."

"Yes, but orders are orders." Wolff stood up and motioned for Grossmann to keep his seat. He walked to the office door and said something in a low voice to his aide and then sat down with Grossmann again. He looked at Grossmann with interest and said, "I think we've had enough to drink for tonight, Douglas. I have more work for you to do. We're going to figure out how to ignore those orders and save the papacy."

1845 Hours
East of Velletri, Italy

Sam sat down in the passenger seat of his jeep. Perkin was in the driver's seat, although they had not gone anywhere recently nor were they planning to. The jeep's seats were simply marginally more comfortable than sitting in the dirt while they ate more hash from a can.

"Do you have any more of those cookies?" Perkin asked.

"No," Sam replied. "You know I don't. Got any figs? Ripe ones?"

"No. Got any more peaches?" Perkin asked as he rummaged through an ammunition bag that had once been stuffed with cans of assorted foods.

"No. I got some hard candy in there from some old K-rations," Sam said.

Perkin waded through the stuff in the back and shook his head. "You must have eaten 'em. I can't...oh, here we go."

As Perkin split the candy between the two of them, he said to Sam, "I don't see why we have to be the diversionary assault. We're closest to the mountain."

Sam shrugged. "I'm sure the general has his reasons,

but it seems to me that you're right. We should get the fun of being up there."

A raspy voice behind them said, "Save me some of that candy." Bill Spaulding hopped into the back of the jeep and stretched out as best he could among all the assorted equipment that was scattered about. He took the last piece of candy from Perkin and popped it in his mouth as he said, "Of course the general has a reason. He's a military genius...unlike you two knuckleheads. Look, we're engaged more closely with the Krauts than either of the other two regiments and therefore it's easier for them to disengage. They're scrounging now to find other units to slide in there—maybe engineers or the forward regiments out of II Corps' advance. Meanwhile, we stay here on the Velletri-Valmontone road and make sure that nothing comes out of Velletri and threatens the flank and supply lines of the infiltrating forces."

"Does that mean that we're not part of the assault?" Sam asked.

"Nope. It just means that no one gets through us. We're the key."

"What do you mean, 'we're the key'?" asked Perkin.

"It means we unlock the front door. This road is the main line of communication into Velletri...that we have to hold in any case. The brunt of the assault will fall on our shoulders. I'm glad to see we're not going to spare the town by the way. We're going to hit Velletri hard with artillery and tactical air before we move in."

Sam and Perkin looked at each other and shrugged. The days had long since passed where they were inclined to take additional risk to spare towns or monuments. It was regrettable, but better than losing another American life.

"Good," said Perkin. "What do you want the boys

to do tonight?"

"Light patrolling and a lot of sleep. They won't have much after tomorrow."

1900 Hours
Rome, Italy

Grossmann looked at General Wolff. The SS general was a hard man, but he looked calm and composed. "What did you have in mind, General?"

Wolff lit a cigarette and winced as the smoke drifted into his eyes. "I was at Kesselring's headquarters this morning to catch their daily operations and intelligence briefs. Our days in Rome are numbered. Two weeks, maybe three at the most, I would guess. The British Eighth Army was savaged at Cassino but they've broken through. In typical British fashion, they're moving slowly. Thankfully. And because of that and thanks to the American decision to shift the Fifth Army focus to the western Caesar Line, most of what remains of our Tenth Army will escape. Ach...I don't know what Clark is thinking but it only delays the inevitable. We're moving more forces down from the north, but there's not much left to send. Luftwaffe...police units...that's about it. We'll have to regroup north of Rome, I think."

"And Rome?" Grossmann asked.

"The Führer's mind isn't made up yet. Part of him wants to save Rome for the architecture...make it an open city. Another part wants to level it to the ground... make it another Stalingrad."

Grossmann shivered involuntarily.

Wolff saw it and sighed. "My thoughts exactly. We will lose this fight. And soon. There isn't anything to be gained by deposing Pius except more enemies. Of course, if the Führer is adamant, we will fulfill our orders to the best of our capabilities."

Grossmann thought for a second. *If he was adamant?* "Herr General, the order has already been given, has it not?"

Wolff nodded. "It has. And I will take your excellent plan to Berlin tomorrow to personally brief Reichsführer Himmler and perhaps even the Führer. Except that my plane will have engine problems and I will not be able to take a flight tomorrow. Or maybe even the next. It is my intention to delay the implementation of these orders as long as possible. Perhaps until it is too late or until we no longer have the forces to do so. That is my contribution to saving the Reich. Meanwhile, this is what you will do."

For the next ten minutes, General Wolff laid out his plans for Grossmann, who as he stared at the general with growing concern deeply wished he could have another brandy. When he left the general's office thoroughly shaken, his concern was magnified when the general's aide escorted him to another office with a closed door. Grossmann had never been in the room but understood it to be an office for communications specialists.

Outside the door, the aide said, "Pardon me, Herr Colonel, this is not personal, but the general has to protect his position." He opened the door and gestured inside. "Do you know what that is, Colonel?"

Grossmann looked into the room and then back at the aide. "It's a Magnetophon," he said as evenly as he could. Grossmann shivered again involuntarily—he knew what was coming.

"Yes, sir. The general wants to be sure that he won't be Canaris'd." The aide walked over to the reel to reel tape recorder and turned a switch. In perfect clarity, Grossmann could be heard saying, "Arresting Pius would be a mistake of the first magnitude. It will throw the weight of the Catholic world against us including allies like Croatia and Hungary. It could lead to civil unrest or worse in Austria and the southern states. It's a mad plan. It must be stopped."

Chapter Nine

May 30, 1944
0530 Hours
East of Velletri, Italy

It was supposed to be a night where the soldiers maximized their sleep prior to a busy day. That wasn't the way it worked out. Sam was awakened twice during the night by German counterattacks launched out of Velletri—once against his company and another time against the adjacent Baker Company.

Both attacks were driven back with no cost to the soldiers from Texas other than lack of sleep. The counterattacks had become predictable, and the sally against Able Company had proved a disaster for the German attackers. A platoon-sized force was detected at 0230, and by 0245 had withdrawn toward Velletri. In addition to eight German soldiers who surrendered to Able Company, four German bodies were found by Sam's patrols an hour after the counterattack ended.

Perkin had spent the night talking to the German prisoners—interrogation was too harsh a term. The surrendering soldiers had turned out to be Russians, all but one of which had volunteered to serve the German Army from Nazi prisoner of war camps. One Russian soldier told Perkin that he had been taken prisoner during General Vlasov's defense of Moscow, and he had agreed to serve the German Army out of boredom. "Germans, Russians, Americans..." he said to Perkin in heavily accented German. "What's the difference? Teach me some English, give me a rifle, and I'll fight for you."

Perkin declined the offer but gave the soldier a pack of cigarettes to share with his Russian comrades. They had been cooperative in describing the German defenses of Velletri and offered their opinion that the German defenders of the town were sick of fighting, but would still fight hard out of a sense of pride and a desire for vengeance. "All they talk about," the Russian said, "was getting revenge for the bombings of their families in Germany. They no longer want to rule Europe or fight in the deserts or the snow. But they fear the Bolsheviks and they swore to kill any bomber crews they capture."

"I guess they shouldn't have started the war then," Perkin said.

"Da. It's been a bad war, I think." The Russian soldier thanked Perkin for the cigarettes and as Perkin was releasing him to an MP, he asked, "What will become of us? If we go back to Russia, we will be killed."

"I don't know, soldier," Perkin said. "You won't have to worry about it for a while. You're headed to America. You'll get good food and you'll be treated well."

The Russian shrugged and then observed dryly, "That's what the Germans told us."

Later that morning as the sun was showing its intentions of illuminating the battlefield for the new day, Sam and Perkin sat next to each other in an abandoned house near the rear of the Able Company sector. Sam's radio operator had moved closer to a window across the room in the hopes of improving his signal, and Sergeant Kulis was asleep on the floor.

"Well," Sam said, "we'll soon find out if those soldiers were telling the truth. Although it doesn't make much sense...an armored attack into the rising sun."

"Not how I'd want to do it either," Perkin said. "If they're just going to do a little fuck-you raid, I'd have been at it about twenty minutes ago at least and then on my way before..."

"Cap'n," interrupted Cooper. "First Platoon is reporting armor crossing to their front heading north and turning inward towards Second Platoon. Three tracks. No infantry. Second Platoon advised."

"Roger," Sam said as he looked through the window to his right. "Notify battalion. Ah...here we go."

Perkin was also looking through the window. He didn't see anything at first but he heard the engagement begin. Then he found the action through his binoculars. Three German panzers, Mark IVs by the look of them, had been moving in a line abreast when the 57mm antitank guns opened fire. The southernmost tank on the left went up in flames followed by a much louder boom. The middle tank stopped and began to reverse while the tank on the right fired its main gun to its left but Perkin couldn't tell at what target. Then he saw a flash of light and the third tank simply stopped moving— no additional smoke, no detonating ammunition, no panicked tankers pouring through smoking hatches. Perkin assumed that the fragmentation from whatever penetrated the hull killed the crew.

Another 57mm round was fired at the retreating tank but missed high. Yet another round went just in front of the tank, and then the German tank was gone. The second German counterattack of the day against

Able Company lasted less than five minutes.

"Let's get down there and take a look," Sam said.

In less time than the duration of the battle, Sam and Perkin drove up to the Second Platoon sector with Kulis and Cooper in the back of the jeep. They were greeted by Second Lieutenant Alex Ryan, who stopped them from approaching the two destroyed tanks.

"I've got a bazooka team tucked up in the brush close to the tank on the north. They picked off the second tank," Ryan said. "They don't see any further signs of German movement, but I'd hate for you all to be picked off by a sniper."

"It's y'all, Alex. Not you all. As in, 'Don't they teach y'all nuthin' up there in Idaho?'" Perkin said with a grin.

"Oh. My mistake. Allow me to correct that. I'd hate for Sam to get picked off by a sniper. And it's Iowa. Not Idaho."

Perkin laughed and looked at Kulis. "You want to come take a look at those tanks with me?"

"Hell yes," Kulis said.

"Sam? You wanna come? I'm going to take a peek at the one that didn't blow up and see how much ammo they have on board."

Sam shook his head. "No. I'm going to follow the sound advice of my lieutenant. I recommend you do the same, but since I know you won't, keep your head down."

0600 Hours
East of Velletri, Italy

Perkin and Kulis drove within thirty yards of the tank that had been destroyed by the bazooka team. There was a neat hole through the turret and Perkin was sure he'd find utter devastation inside the tank. He put his fingers to his lips as they approached the tank and he softly climbed on board. Just because they hadn't seen any signs of life didn't mean there weren't any.

The commander's hatch was open and Perkin quickly peeked in and withdrew his head, and then did it again. His third look was sustained. There was no life in the tank that he could see. He counted three bodies below him and looked down toward the driver and radioman. He couldn't see.

"Check the front compartment and see if anyone's alive."

Kulis climbed on the front of the tank and looked into the open driver's compartment. The driver was dead. The hatch was closed on the radio compartment where the radio operator doubled as the machine gunner. Kulis carefully lifted the hatch to the compartment, sticking the muzzle of his Garand into the gap as the hatch came up. More blank eyes stared back at him. "They're dead, sir. Looks like this fella bled out."

Kulis leaned in and pulled back the sleeve of the radioman. He was searching for a watch to give as a souvenir to the bazooka crew when the tank crewman blinked slowly and reached weakly for the knife on his belt. Kulis easily pushed the soldier's hand away from the handle of the knife and pulled it out of the scabbard himself. Kulis appraised the knife with an expert eye. It was a well-worn Hitler Youth dagger with an inlaid swastika on the handle and the words *Blut und Ehre* engraved on the blade. Blood and honor.

Kulis pushed the tanker's head back, put the tip of the blade to the soldier's neck, and slid the blade through his throat just under the jaw. He pushed hard until he felt the blade enter the spine, and satisfied that the soldier was now dead, he wiped the knife dry on the German's uniform.

"How's it coming, sir?" Kulis asked as he reached in and took the scabbard off the dead soldier's belt. For good measure, he took the *Gott Mit Uns* belt buckle as well. As he listened to Perkin count rounds aloud, Kulis checked the Germans for a watch but found none on either man. He rummaged through a kit bag belonging to the driver, took a high quality straight razor, and then claimed a folded red Nazi flag. He'd keep the knife, sell the razor, and give the belt buckle and flag to the bazooka crew. It was only fair.

"Just finished. Less than a half load. Fifteen A.P. and twelve H.E. rounds. Plenty of machine-gun ammo though. No food worth taking." Perkin climbed out of commander's hatch, jumped to the ground, and joined Kulis in front of the tank. "You wanna take a quick look at the other track?"

"Sure," said Kulis. He hopped behind the wheel to drive the fifty yards over to the burning tank but a little over halfway there they came across the first tank commander lying on his back in the field. He was a staff sergeant and was still alive, but it was apparent he wouldn't live long. The tanker's eyes stared without blinking or focus at the sky and he had horrific burns on his face and hands. Perkin bent down and straightened the soldier's leg which was doubled back under his body. Perkin winced as he felt the bones grind against each other but the German soldier had no reaction. Perkin looked back to the burning tank twenty yards distant and then down at the man who struggled for each breath. His entire body was quivering and his chest was shaking with the exertion of each labored breath. From the nervous quivering and the purplish hue to his face, Perkin guessed he'd suffered considerable internal damage. There was no way the German soldier could have walked or crawled from his burning tank.

"Hey, sir. Comin' in," an American voice said behind him. It was a tall lanky soldier from Able Company and he was carrying the bazooka tube. His partner was following closely behind.

"Chuck Carter!" Perkin said. "How the hell are you?" Corporal Carter had been with the company since North Africa and was a veteran of Salerno, San Pietro, and the Rapido River. He'd been wounded at the river and Perkin had visited with him several times at the clearing station in Mignano.

"I'm grand, sir. Did you see me and McCorvey smoke that panzer yonder?"

As Kulis walked over to the two soldiers from Able Company with the souvenirs he was willing to share, Perkin said, "I did. Great shot, boys. Do y'all have any idea how this bubba ended up over here?"

"Yes, sir," Corporal Carter said. "We was actually lining up on him but the A.T. gun beat us to the punch. This feller was standing up in the commander's cupola when they got hit. He shot straight out of the hatch like a cork out of a popgun. He went up about fifty feet or so and come down here. I never seen nothin' like it." Carter took his first look at the quivering German sergeant and exclaimed, "Oh, sweet Jesus! Is he still alive?"

Perkin looked at the shaking soldier and said, "Not for long." The intervals between the man's breaths were growing longer but the shaking continued.

Carter couldn't take his eyes off the quivering man and said, "Does he have any morphine, sir?"

Perkin looked but the soldier didn't have a first aid kit on his belt. He shook his head at Carter who knelt beside the dying man. After a moment's hesitation, Carter picked up the man's hand and recited softly in his ear, "'To everything there is a season, and a time to every purpose under the heaven: A time to be born, and a time to die; a time to plant, and a time to pluck up that which is planted; a time to kill, and a time to heal; a time to love, and a time to hate; a time of war, and a time of peace…I said in mine heart, God shall judge the righteous and the wicked: for there is a time there for every purpose and for every work.'" Carter closed his eyes, bowed his head, and prayed, "Our Father, this man's time has come. Take him into your embrace and judge him not too harshly for we are all wicked on this field. I beg you, Father, to pardon his sins and end his suffering. Amen." Carter took the German soldier's arms and crossed them over his chest and stood up. As he did so, a long sigh came from the wounded man. The quivering came to an end and he breathed no more.

0915 Hours
Rome, Italy

Lieutenant Colonel Douglas Grossmann sighed and stubbed out a cigarette in the ashtray on the table at his favorite café. He waved off a caffè corretto even though he desperately wanted a drink. He had a meeting to attend to shortly, which he dreaded. It would help to be sober. He hadn't even wanted to come here this morning but he needed the baker's help, which Signore Alessio had agreed to do, but it would cost Grossmann dearly.

Grossmann's head was down as he contemplated what he would say in his meeting and little came to mind. It would be awkward to say the least. As he picked at his cornetto and stared at the empty espresso cup before him, he missed seeing Antoniette cross the street. It was not until she was standing beside his table that he detected her perfume—a scent that tugged at his heart every time. He started guiltily but recovered quickly, his hidden panic replaced by a welcoming smile.

Antoniette smiled in return and allowed Grossmann to hold her seat for her as she sat down. She looked inquisitively into his face. "Douglas, are you all right?"

Grossmann didn't answer at first but snapped his fingers for the waiter. After he ordered a cappuccino for Antoniette, he said, "I am, my love. I'm just very tired. It's been a busy week. How are you, my dear?"

"Terrible, but better now that I'm with you," she said.

"What's wrong? Other than we're losing the war, of course."

His weak joke didn't have the desired effect. Antoniette's eyes grew moist and Grossmann noticed a small tremble in her hands as she picked up her cappuccino. Grossmann shook his head and said, "I'm sorry. That was in poor taste."

"Douglas, which will be worse for us? Communists or Americans?"

"Communists," Grossmann answered. "If we end up in an occupied Europe, it will be much worse under the Bolsheviks. Five years from now there won't be an American on the continent, but the Russians will never leave. As a member of the SS, I will probably be shot on the spot."

Antoniette allowed Grossmann to light a cigarette for her, and then she asked, "Did you hear about communist partisans killing a Roman family the other night?" Her face was intensely sad and it broke Grossmann's heart.

Grossmann had been prepared to admit that the family was killed during a German raid while excluding his own role in the affair—combining fact and fiction— but he rolled the dice and abandoned the story. She had already bought into their cover-up. He only had to maintain the illusion that it wasn't a German affair for a couple weeks at the most, and then he and Antoniette would be in Milan—or maybe even Switzerland.

"I did. It's kind of ironic actually," Grossmann said.

"It was terrible! How could it be ironic?" Antoniette said as her face flushed with anger.

"Wait! Did you know these people?" Grossmann asked seemingly incredulous.

"Yes! What did you mean? That it was ironic?" The anger was fading and was being replaced with puzzlement.

"Two nights ago...it was two nights, yes? Two nights ago, I was in Umbria commanding a raid on a partisan compound. Communists." Grossmann coolly lit a cigarette of his own and asked after he had inhaled deeply, "Who were these people that they killed here?"

Antoniette's eyes welled up and a tear spilled over onto her cheek. "They were my godparents. Signore Nascimbeni went to school with my father and worked for him for years and then started his own company with Papa's help. They had a daughter my age who was killed as well. We were the best of friends a long time ago. That could be my parents...that could be me. What kind of monster would do such a thing?"

0915 Hours
East of Velletri, Italy

Bill Spaulding drove with Perkin in the passenger seat. They were making the rounds between the company sectors, and Spaulding felt like driving. Stretched out in reasonable comfort in the back was Sergeant Kulis, who had his helmet pulled down over his eyes and was trying to get some sleep.

"So you think it was an act of God," Spaulding said with a smile.

"Doubtful. But I wouldn't be honest if I told you it didn't give me goosebumps," Perkin replied. "He said it was time for God to take him, and He did. Right then."

"But you said you were surprised that he was still alive when you found him, right?" Spaulding said. "It shouldn't shock you that he died then or any other time after you came across him."

"I know," said Perkin. "But it was amazing none-theless. It was an interesting dichotomy in any case."

"Dichotomy? Between what?" asked Spaulding.

"Between killing and kindness. A minute before, Carter was proud as a peacock about destroying a tank with five souls on board, and the next minute, he was holding the hand of an enemy soldier and praying with him." As Perkin said the words, he had an image of himself doing almost the same exact thing on Mount Sammucro six months before. "Maybe it's not that weird after all, but it was something to behold."

Kulis lifted up his helmet and joined the conversation. "Did you know Carter was a lay minister? He said that he used to minister to cowboys up on the Llano somewheres."

"Doesn't surprise me. He quoted scripture like a real Bible thumper," Perkin said. "It was impressive."

Kulis shrugged. "He left most of it out, you know. But to be fair, I don't think he forgot or anything, I think he just cut it down some. That's a long passage if I remember right."

Spaulding drove to the abandoned house that Sam was using for his command post, and he parked under the shade of a tree on the east side of the house. They ran into the building hunched over in case there were spotters or snipers nearby, and they found Sam on the second floor looking through the windows with his binoculars.

"Hey, boys," Sam said with a smile. "What's the word?"

"The word..." Spaulding replied with a dramatic pause, "...is do nothin' and wait. Division called the regimental commanders in for a meeting and we're to standby for adjustments. I'm going to head over to the regimental CP in a couple of minutes and wait there."

Sam yawned as he stretched. "Better you than me, brother. My boss's meetings are boring and last forever."

Spaulding laughed, "Ha ha. You should be grateful to have a succinct commander like me. Anyway, I came by to see if you needed anything or had any concerns."

Sam shrugged. "My only concern is what they tell you next. We're good to go, but thanks. We're set here. We can plug away at the Krauts all day long."

Spaulding nodded. "Good. I'll give you a holler when I know something so we can start the shit flowing downhill."

1130 Hours
Vatican City

Douglas Grossmann stood behind the last colonnade on the northeast side of St. Peter's Square. A few steps more and he would cross the line that divided the temporal realm of God from the realm of Caesar. As he stood there, he thought of the etymological connection between Caesar and Kaiser...and then of Caesar and Czar. Maybe the connection was that they were all gone now. No Caesar. No Kaiser. No Czar. Only the New Order of Europe and the Führer. One empire and one leader.

He looked at the black Rolex on his wrist and shook

his head sadly. It was time. Grossmann adjusted his fedora and his tie. It was better to be in civilian clothes rather than in an SS uniform, even if he was going as an unofficial representative of that New Order. He bent over and picked up a paper bag, which held the items that had cost him dearly that morning. Everything had been costly this morning, he thought. It was time, he told himself again, and he forced himself to take the first step. It was difficult. He didn't want this meeting. The second step was no easier.

Grossmann crossed over the painted white line that formed the boundary between Vatican City and Fascist Rome. It had been painted by German soldiers last fall and strictly speaking, Grossmann was not supposed to enter the Vatican property. But a message had been sent notifying the Vatican that General Wolff's representative desired a private meeting. It was to take place on the colonnade steps near the fountain to the north of the Obelisk.

At first, Grossmann didn't see him. He did notice two Swiss Guards carrying submachine guns standing on the designated steps. They were in proper military uniform, not their ceremonial uniforms, and when they saw Grossmann approaching carrying a paper sack they stiffened. It was not the bag that they reacted to, but the man. They knew Grossmann and he knew them. One of the two guards had assisted him only a few months before when he infiltrated the Vatican's cadre of priests and nuns who were helping escaped prisoners. The guard turned and said something in a low voice to someone behind him in the colonnade...and there he was... walking out of the shadows of Bernini's Colonnade. He was tall and imposing in his purple trimmed robes, and while Grossmann was used to a characteristic twinkle in the monsignor's eyes, today they were deadly serious.

"Hello, Douglas," said Monsignor Hugh O'Flaherty in his soft brogue. "I didn't expect to see you again. Certainly, not before your trial for war crimes."

**1135 Hours
Vatican City**

Grossmann was on the verge of walking away. He'd had a terrible day. Without question, the worst in his life. Now, a man that he respected greatly seemed disgusted by his presence. It was fitting, somehow, given how his morning had gone. Yet, he was an *Obersturmbannführer* in the SS and he was on a mission that might very well save this man's life. So, despite his internal turmoil, he took a deep breath and pointed to the stairs.

"Hugh...my purpose here is not to discuss my actions but I consider you a friend and if you want an explanation, I'll do my best. I'll tell you now that it won't satisfy you, but I'd ask you to bear in mind that I'm a soldier following orders. Listen to me: you must stay and hear me out. It's no exaggeration to say this may be the most critical moment in the Church since the Council of Nicaea." When he saw that he had O'Flaherty's rapt attention, he said, "May we have a seat and talk, please?"

O'Flaherty looked at his guards and nodded. One of the Swiss Guards stepped forward and in Swiss accented German said, "We're going to search you for weapons, Lieutenant, uh, Peabody." It was not a request, and the rank and name were said with contempt.

"It's Lieutenant Colonel. Peabody's fine," Grossmann replied in German. He allowed himself to be frisked—his Walther was in his staff car, which was parked on the other side of the line. He had brought his security detail with him and they were watching the meeting carefully through binoculars. Diplomatic protocols or not, they would not allow him to be harmed or removed from the meeting spot.

The Swiss Guard, satisfied that Grossmann possessed no weapons, nodded to Monsignor O'Flaherty and the two guards stepped back out of earshot.

Grossmann spoke first. "Hugh, I brought you a couple things." Grossmann reached into the bag and pulled out a large box that was wrapped and tied in a bow. He handed it to the priest who looked at him quizzically, but when Grossmann nodded in encouragement, O'Flaherty untied the ribbon and opened the box. The Irishman looked at the contents and for the first time the twinkle briefly returned to his eyes.

"Scones, me boy?" O'Flaherty said. He held up a jar and looked at the contents. "Bless me. Is this clotted cream? And strawberries. How could you possibly know my weakness, Doug?"

Grossmann smiled his first smile in hours. "I took a chance. You're an Irishman, Hugh. Scones and clotted cream might be a bit too English for you so it was a dicey call. But if it failed, I brought you this." Grossmann reached into the bag and brought out a bottle of Bushmills Whiskey. "Likewise dicey. I hope it doesn't offend you...this being a Protestant spirit."

"Well, if it were true, it might. Then again, probably not...some things transcend faith." O'Flaherty looked at Grossmann. "Douglas, I'm going to ask you some questions, and if you tell me the truth, I'll decide whether to accept your gifts and whether I should stay and listen further."

Grossmann nodded.

"First, who are you?"

"I'm a German intelligence officer. My real name's

not important."

O'Flaherty nodded and asked, "What happened in Avezzano?"

Grossmann sat for a long moment as he thought through the death of Father Carlo. He put his head into his hands and rubbed his temples before looking at O'Flaherty and answering honestly, "When I was told to come here today and speak to you, I told General Wolff I couldn't do it. That I would be asked this very question, and that even if our security protocols allowed me to answer, I didn't want to relive that...day. He told me that the treason I'm committing here is far worse than violating a secrecy act and as for speaking to you man to man, it was up to me."

"Treason, is it?"

"Yeah. I'll get to that in a moment, Hugh. Here's the...here's what happened." Grossmann's throat tightened and he took a deep breath. "My job was to develop an understanding of your underground railroad and trace it to the end, which as I discovered was the Gildardino home. When I was in the church in Avezzano, Father Carlo was helping an American officer escape who by damn bad luck knew who I was. I'm not entirely sure how, but he clearly recognized me. He was coming after me and I pulled out a pistol and Father Carlo just simply got in the way. The truth is I shot him by accident. The American ran off and I don't know what happened to him."

"What happened to Captain Mullen?" Timothy Mullen was an Australian officer who believed he was escaping occupied Italy with Lieutenant Peabody.

Grossmann looked in the priest's eyes and said as steadily as he could, "He was an enemy combatant. I had to kill him."

O'Flaherty shook his head in anger. "Had to?" The

Irishman looked ready to explode but he caught himself and said, "There are always other options, Douglas. Is that what happened to the Gildardinos?"

"Yes. They were killed. I didn't have anything... that wasn't my doing." Grossmann looked down at his hands. They were shaking and he'd never before needed a drink as badly as he needed one now. He looked at the bottle and unconsciously licked his lips. "In addition to them, there was an intelligence agent of the Allies that was killed there."

O'Flaherty noted Grossmann's hard look at the whiskey and he asked the German-speaking guard to bring two glasses. "Douglas, we know about some things. Obviously, we learned of Father Carlo's death and we learned about the death of the Gildardino family. But the man that was killed there was an Irish priest, not an intelligence agent of the Allies."

Grossmann looked at O'Flaherty with interest. "An Irish priest? Patrick Riley?"

"Yes, so you know he was a priest. He wasn't involved in your war." O'Flaherty's anger was palpable.

"Hugh, I swear I didn't know Riley was the man killed at the farm until this very moment, but you're wrong about his involvement. His brother is an intelligence officer in the British Army, and Riley was passing information back to him since before the British crossing at Messina. I had sent a team in September to arrest him when he was in...what was that town? Pisciotta. But he escaped."

It was O'Flaherty's turn to stare. "I was unaware of that, Douglas, assuming you're telling me the truth."

"I am, Hugh. Any other questions for me? We have some business to discuss."

"A couple...some things don't make sense to me. The safe house that you stayed at was never raided. I closed it, of course, but you had time to raid it first. Why didn't you?"

Grossmann shrugged. "Hugh, from my perspective, you're violating the neutrality of the Holy See, and in effect, your actions should be considered hostile to my country at a time of war. Having said that, there are two men walking this planet that I respect for their selflessness and you are one—I had the other arrested in February. I tell you that so you know I wouldn't have let my respect stop me from doing my duty. But had I presented the entire story, told the scope of your transgressions of neutrality, you would have presented the Führer with a *casus belli* against the Church, which would have led to actions I believe are contrary to the interests of my government. It almost certainly would have ended in your death. So, as much as I would have liked to have told the world that you had a safe house next to Gestapo headquarters, I felt it put too much at risk, your life included."

O'Flaherty said nothing. When the guard returned with the glasses, O'Flaherty poured two stiff drinks. There was no ceremony—no toasts nor clinking of glasses. O'Flaherty took an appreciative sip of his drink and Grossmann finished his in one gulp—an act noted by O'Flaherty.

"There's much more I'd like to ask you, Douglas, but I suppose I need to inquire why you wanted to see me."

Grossmann felt better. He didn't want to talk about himself any longer. Although the whiskey hadn't had time to take effect, the act of drinking calmed his nerves. "May I?" he asked of O'Flaherty. Without waiting for an answer, he poured himself another drink. He drank half and set down the glass. He definitely felt better on this most terrible of days.

"General Wolff has requested that I give a message to Pius," Grossmann said.

O'Flaherty shook his head. "Douglas, I can't arrange an audience for you with his Holiness. Certainly not today."

Grossmann laughed. "That wouldn't be in either of our interests, I'm sure. No, I need for you to convey it to the Pope."

"Is it a letter from General Wolff?"

"No, and you won't write it down either. There won't be any written record of this or it'll be my death warrant if we win the war. If we don't, I have that war crimes tribunal that you mentioned earlier to look forward to. Guess I'm damned either way, Hugh." Grossmann laughed bitterly as he thought through it all. "Oh hell. Those aren't even the worst revelations of the day. Okay... tell Pius that the Führer has ordered the SS to depose him. He'll either be interned in a concentration camp where he'll die, or he'll simply be executed. Maybe over there in front of the Obelisk, or in the Sistine Chapel under the eyes of God and Adam. The library, the art, the...well, everything is to be taken under the protection of the Reich, and those who oppose us will be executed. That means every cardinal, bishop, monsignor, priest, monk, and nun. All of them. You know what we're capable of doing. We'll slaughter the Swiss Guard. We'll kill the worshippers while they kneel before us. We'll kill the janitors, and for good measure, probably even the postal clerks. Neither sinner nor saint will be spared. A week after we start, there will be no indication that the Papacy even existed on this spot. And that's not all. Everything, including the holdings of the Vatican bank, will be liquidated and used to support our war effort. If it is the Führer's intent that the Catholic Church cease to exist, it will be as dead as the Roman

Empire—both extinguished by Germania."

1145 Hours
East of Velletri, Italy

Bill Spaulding addressed his company commanders in the shade of a grove of chestnut trees. A table had been set up to hold the necessary maps, and battalion cooks had prepared coffee and a stack of canned ham sandwiches for the soldiers.

"I wish I had something more concrete for you, but things are in flux. The good news is the entire 142nd and 143rd infantry regiments are in the process of completing their movement—I was told that the battalions and their supply train go back some ten miles behind us. As you can see..." Spaulding pointed south, "...the smoke-makers are working overtime. The chemical mortars have thrown thousands of smoke bombs all over the Anzio plain, and if the army doesn't die of asphyxiation first, they might remain undetected. Now for the rest of the news: the disposition of the 141st isn't firmed up yet. There are two schools of thought at VI Corps as to what we should be doing. One suggests that we should be motorized and sent to exploit any gap created by the 1st Armored on their drive through the Caesar Line. If I were a betting man, I'd say that came from echelon above corps. The 1st Armored has lost so many tanks that they ain't punching through the German lines today. The second school of thought is that we should assemble northeast of Velletri and wait for further developments. That makes more sense so we made a command decision this morning at regiment to proceed with that course of action. Our battalion is holding fast and 2nd and 3rd Battalions are being relieved in place by the 36th Engineering Battalion on our left. The 2nd and 3rd will then move behind us to the northeast. If we get trucked to support the tanks, they can be picked up there, but if our infiltration of the hills works, then they can encircle Velletri from the top."

"Sir," asked Sam, "what about the diversionary attack on Velletri tonight?"

"I don't know for sure that it's gonna happen—at least our part in it. If we get picked up and carted off to the west, we won't be in any attack on the town. But, we're going to keep planning just the same."

1145 Hours
Vatican City

Monsignor Hugh O'Flaherty stared at Grossmann. He shook his head in disbelief and said, "That's madness. You can't mean it."

Grossmann finished his glass of whiskey, then poured himself another. "Madness defines the world these days, Hugh. You would know that better than most, I suppose. I assure you, what I told you is the truth and I'm taking a terrible risk to tell you this. Certainly, the Gestapo has St. Peter's Square under surveillance and if they recognize me, things could become complicated and I don't want any complications. The truth is, I'd rather be just about anywhere in the world than facing you today, Hugh. But here I am."

The Irishman nodded and took another sip of whiskey as he thought. "So, if I understand correctly, the man who has been ordered to attack the Church is warning us of the impending attack. Why?"

"General Wolff and I both agree that such a course of action would be catastrophic. It doesn't further the war aims of the German Reich, and only adds millions more enemies to the already considerable list we face. It's my concern that Ireland and Spain might end their neutrality and actively assist the Allies. Access to Spanish airbases, Irish ports…" Grossmann sighed.

"What are General Wolff's recommendations, Douglas?"

"The general is doing his level best to delay implementing this plan until it's overcome by events but in the meantime, don't provoke the Führer. Two weeks or so from now, you'll be sharing this whiskey with General Clark, but until then, do nothing to antagonize Hitler. No public commentary on the war. No démarches. No pressure on the German bishops. I'd add that you should get the Pope out of here. Where? I don't know. Gandolfo isn't safe—there's too much fighting in the area, and don't go north like to Viterbo. If you can't get him out of Rome, hide in the catacombs or something with enough food or water for a couple of weeks." With something approaching a genuine smile, Grossmann added, "And for God's sake, don't put him in the safe house next to Gestapo headquarters. Something that poetic only works once in a lifetime."

1435 Hours
East of Velletri, Italy

The Germans had launched another counterattack—this time against Charlie Company. Sam listened to the sounds of combat, which were no more than a half-mile distant, and he identified American antitank guns and American M-1919 machine guns and the popping of rifle fire. Two booms he guessed were German tanks but he wasn't sure. Thick columns of black smoke miles to his west told him that the real fighting remained on the Caesar Line, and he said a silent prayer for his friends in that battle.

His soldiers were primed if the action came their way, but he doubted it would. No doubt German patrols had identified his roadblock on the Velletri-Valmontone road, and there was no point in them trying to break it. If the Germans left Velletri en masse it would be in the other direction—to the west—and toward safety of the Caesar Line. Not to the east—they simply didn't have the resources to either break out eastward or to threaten the flanks of the Valmontone attackers. This was nothing more than what Perkin called a "fuck-you attack." It kept everyone on their toes, but Sam didn't see it posing much of a threat. If they came for Able Company, they would regret it, Sam thought.

Twenty minutes after the counterattack began, it was over. Charlie Company had been even more successful than Sam had been that morning. They bagged another two tanks and captured a squad of infantry—with only two lightly wounded casualties. It had been a good day.

1900 Hours
Rome, Italy

It was a terrible day, Douglas Grossmann reflected as he lay on his bed in his small room at the Rome SS barracks. He couldn't face going to the apartment he kept in town and he wasn't interested in food or company. Grossmann had commandeered a bottle of Bismarck schnapps and he stared blankly at the wall as he drank and chain-smoked.

His mission to the Vatican had been a success. Monsignor O'Flaherty took his warning seriously and Grossmann believed that as soon as he left the Vatican City grounds, O'Flaherty went directly to Pius XII to warn him. What Pius did or didn't do past that point,

Grossmann no longer cared.

Twice, Grossmann picked up his Walther and twice he laid it on the bed beside him. Antoniette was out of his life, and he suspected he'd never see her again. She was furious. She threw an empty espresso cup at him, and then a fork and a knife. She threatened to do to him what he had done to the Nascimbeni family and the look in her eyes told Grossmann she meant it. It wasn't the crime. It was the lie. The lie had been working. He had believed that fortune was finally going to smile on him and he was going to get out of this terrible dilemma. Grossmann hung his head in shame as he thought about even promising to use his position to eliminate every communist in Italy. He would have too. He would have done anything to protect his relationship with Antoniette. Except tell the truth, he thought bitterly. *The most important person in my life and I wasn't man enough to tell her the truth.* He picked up the Walther again and for the third time checked to see if it was loaded. It was. He stared at the safety, sighed, and put the gun on the nightstand.

It turned out that she was deeply spooked by the killings. They were close friends to her parents, and although Antoniette hadn't seen the Nascimbeni family since Christmas, she still regarded them with deep affection. Vengeance on the communists would have only been a start, she was so angry. As Grossmann took another swig of schnapps from the green bottle, he thought he should have stuck with his fact and fiction gambit. Let the Reich take the blame while he bluffed it out that he had nothing to do with it. Not the crime but the cover-up.

Hours later as he smoked and drank alone on his bed, he thought that had he done so, had he simply talked her through the circumstances...had he just been honest, maybe even then, he could have explained why he was wearing the Rolex she helped her father buy for Signore Nascimbeni last Christmas as they spent the holidays skiing together on the Swiss border.

Chapter Ten

Two Days Later

June 1, 1944
0600 Hours
Velletri, Italy

    The push to the center of Velletri would resume in a few minutes. There had been a seemingly mutual pause while each side collectively caught their breath, although the fighting had not truly stopped. The diversionary attack against Velletri had begun thirty-six hours before and it had been less than a day since the diversion turned into a proper assault. Extensive minefields had held up their advance and the Germans had naturally prepared extensive defenses that were layered outside and throughout the town. It was difficult gritty work but the minefields were crossed and the outer layers penetrated. Men had spent hours penned under relentless mortar and machine-gun fire, and there would be no praying with enemy soldiers once the dogs of war had slipped into Velletri.

    Captains Perkin Berger and Sam Taft sat on the cobblestones of Velletri with their backs against the large tires of a deuce and a half that had quit running without apparent reason and refused to start. They shared some hardtack from K-rations and divided their remaining chocolate. Their bodies were running low on food and sleep, and they decided to eat what they could while they could.

"Tell me again what you heard about the infiltration," Sam said unnecessarily loud—his ears were ringing from a night of sustained gunfire.

Perkin took a drink of water first, and then capped his canteen. "Bill says it's been more successful than we could have hoped. He said the 142nd and 143rd have advanced some five miles into the Alban Hills and the engineers have been nothing short of heroic. They bulldozed a road up Monte Artemisio and we've got Shermans and Wolverines up there as well as 105 and 155mm howitzers. They're even beginning to conduct raids from the hills into the German supply lines miles behind the Caesar Line. It's going to collapse, and when it does, it's going to be fast."

"I'm stunned they left it unprotected like that," Sam said shaking his head.

"Me too. But we saw it almost a week ago. Division intel is saying we found a gap between two German corps and we're just chewing it up. If we don't blow it, they won't be able to recover..." Perkin saw someone he knew and called out, "Hey, Eric! Over here!"

Perkin stood up and pulled Sam to his feet, and they walked over to a tall black-haired man wearing a war correspondent's uniform. "Eric, I don't know if you remember me, I'm Perkin Berger. We met on Capri a couple months ago. This is the commander of Able Company, Sam Taft. Sam, this is Eric Sevareid."

The reporter, who looked as tired as any soldier, nodded at Sam, and shook hands with both Texans. To Perkin, he said, "I remember your girl vividly but you're just a hazy memory. How are you doing?"

"Outstanding," Perkin said. "I hope you're capturing all of this for the folks back home. This has been a long time coming."

Sevareid lit a cigarette and nodded. "So you think this is it? That it's all going to bust open?"

"I do," Perkin said confidently. "We're giving Clark the keys to Rome as we speak. And you can quote me on that."

"Maybe I will," Sevareid said. "Good luck to you. I'm headed up the hill in a little bit to watch the fireworks."

Just as Sevareid was walking away, Sergeant Kulis drove up in a jeep with Major Spaulding as a passenger. Spaulding hopped out of the jeep energetically, although he hadn't had any more sleep over the course of the past few days than any other soldier on the battlefield. He motioned with his head to the truck and Sam, Perkin, and Kulis joined him in the back as he laid out a map on the floor.

"Howdy, boys. How's everyone doing?" Spaulding asked when he had the map in place.

"We're all good," Sam said. "The boys are good. We're ready to go."

Spaulding nodded. "Great, 'cause we're going. The encirclement of the town is complete. We control all the lines of communication in and out of Velletri. Regiment wants to wrap this up by evening so we can get out of here and join the march to Rome."

"Is there a plan?" Sam asked.

"Of sorts," Spaulding replied. "We're going to kick off at 0630 and resume the push. We're going to squeeze Velletri from all sides and force them to collapse to the center. Use indirect fire as needed, just be mindful that as their lines shorten, we've got boys on the other side."

"What's the call on armor?" Perkin asked.

"All the battalion commanders have been asking for armored support so we're going to get it. Shermans and TDs. It's on us to keep the panzerfaust crews at a distance. One last thing," Spaulding said. "The faster we move, the harder it'll be for the Krauts to reestablish defensive positions. We're going to have to do this house by house but let's move fast and hard. Expect a lot of prisoners. Let's clear them out of the area as quickly as possible and keep pushing. Oh shit! That ain't necessary…" Spaulding watched as a passing Sherman tank swerved to run over the head of a dead German soldier. It looked as if Spaulding was going to chase down the tank, but he shook his head, spat tobacco juice onto the cobblestones, and continued, "Be mindful of any Italians you may come across but our needs take precedence. Use the tanks to destroy any hardened positions. There's no point trying to save Velletri—as far as I can see, there ain't much left to save."

Everyone nodded. Months of combat in and around Velletri had left the town a shattered wreck and the devastation was as bad as San Pietro and Cisterna had been. The Italians were looking at years of rebuilding, but the good news was that they could begin maybe as early as the next day. Many of the buildings within a quarter-mile radius of their position were furiously burning or had collapsed from artillery or aerial bombardment. Other buildings had been deliberately demolished and the debris pushed into the road to block or channel the American advance.

"Oh," added Spaulding. "We didn't roister yesterday. It's probably why that minefield held us up like that. Sergeant Kulis?"

"Sir?"

"What do we have to drink?"

Kulis opened a green canvas bag. He pulled out a

battered canteen, opened it, and sniffed at the contents. "I ain't sure. Maybe sambuca or raki?"

"Raki? Where the hell did that come from?" Perkin asked as he made a face. He didn't care for the anise-flavored drinks.

"Waller's the only one I know who drinks it. He said he got a taste for it before the war," Spaulding said, and then he started laughing. "Have you heard the story of Waller and raki? He was doing a memorial service with the Turks at Gallipoli and got assigned to a Turkish colonel as a liaison. The colonel introduced him to raki, which the Turks sometimes lace with opium. Waller woke up naked on the battlefield the next mornin' with a British corporal kickin' him in the ribs and tellin' him to get up. Waller said his commander was 'quite put out' and if it hadn't been for the war, he'd have never been promoted again."

The story tickled Sam, who was laughing out loud for the first time for several days. When he caught his breath, he managed to say, "He was lucky they didn't use him like a woman."

"He said other than an unfortunate sunburn and feeling crapulous the next day, he was fine, but he wasn't sure that the corporal didn't take pictures." Spaulding reached into his cheek and pulled out an exhausted wad of tobacco before saying, "What else is in that bag, Eddie?"

Kulis pulled out two more canteens and sniffed them both. "This one's a whiskey of some kind," he said. "I don't know about this one." Kulis took a cautious sip, grimaced at the result, and spat to clear his mouth. "It's some of that tequila Cap'n Taft got from the tech sergeant from Gonzales who whistles through his teeth all the time. It's worse than grappa."

"I like tequila," Sam said somewhat defensively as

he wiped away a tear from the corner of his eye.

"Me too," Perkin agreed. "We liked it so much that Sam and I founded the Tequila Mutual Admiration Society of South Texas back in '31, but it never caught on."

"Mutual admiration?" asked Spaulding with a grin of anticipation. "What's that mean?"

"We admired tequila. It admired us. We admired each other," Sam explained. "It was such a positive society, we thought it might actually end the Depression. Kind of an Optimist Club with booze."

"Well, that's somethin', ain't it?" Spaulding said as he motioned for Kulis to bring the tequila. "But, I don't recall the Depression ending way back then."

"That's because it didn't work. Not all experiments are successful, you know," Perkin said. "There were legal barriers to contend with too, but it might have had a chance if it hadn't come to a violent end."

"What happened, sir?" Kulis asked as he poured out tequila into canteen cups.

"Old Perkin caught us admiring tequila one day when we cut class to go fishin' and he wore us out. He said intemperate behavior among children would lead to the ruination of society. I thought that was an unfounded prejudice for years, but after seeing Jim Bob drink a bottle of wine in Naples, I have to agree."

"What was the legal barrier?" Spaulding asked as he sniffed the tequila in his cup.

"The un-American Eighteenth Amendment. Even if we'd been old enough, we couldn't buy it. We had to get it from an old Mexican fella in Gregory who made his own from agave squeezin's and hair tonic," Perkin said. "It's probably just as well that Old Perkin caught us. That stuff was potent. It might have given us a whole new meaning for our motto of '*Usque ad mortem bibendum.'"*

"I don't know what that means, nor do I care," said Spaulding. "Y'all ready?" When they nodded, Spaulding said, "I don't have time for a roister, but your touching story got me thinking about Gonzales. So, I thought I'd wear the professor's hat for a minute and remind y'all that we're the descendants of the 1st Texas Regiment. We go all the way back to the beginning of the Republic and before, and Perkin tells me that only the 7th Infantry is older than us on this battlefield today. Seeing as what we're fixin' to do to the Germans, 'Come and Take It' may not be apropos, but here's to the finest soldiers in the world, the 1st Texas!"

"The 1st Texas!" they all echoed as they downed the tequila and moved on to the morning's work.

0655 Hours
Velletri, Italy

Second Lieutenant Alex Ryan moved toward the sound of the guns. His squads were each methodically moving along three narrow, more or less parallel streets and he was in the middle trying hard to maintain command and control of his soldiers. The handie-talkies worked sometimes but not consistently, and there was no point in running wires as they planned to move quickly through the town.

The first day of the battle had been frustrating for Ryan and his soldiers. The Germans had laid extensive minefields, which were not unexpected but it took time for the engineers to clear the fields. Once a passage had been cleared, his soldiers had been the first in Able Company to make contact with the enemy on the out-skirts of town. It was a pillbox built into the side of a hill and unlike the pillbox on Monte Artemesio, this one was manned. Machine-gun fire from the pillbox pinned his soldiers until a 37mm antitank gun mounted in the back of an open ¾-ton truck was brought up behind their position. Ryan had no idea who the soldiers were, or to what unit they belonged, but they bounced up in their truck, which looked like a large jeep, and parked the truck in a ditch facing away from the pillbox so that only the barrel of the gun was above ground level. The three soldiers on the antitank gun simply fired H.E. rounds at the pillbox until the MG-42 quit firing. Ryan wanted to keep the antitank crew with his platoon but they were called elsewhere and Ryan watched the truck disappear with genuine regret.

A second pillbox was handled in a completely different manner. After Ryan's call to surrender was met with a burst of fire from the pillbox, a Sherman tank outfitted with a bulldozer blade approached from the blind side of the small concrete fortification and pushed dirt over the top of the pillbox. A large mound of dirt was piled on the top and against the exit to the pillbox, black smoke belching from the tank under the exertion. Through his binoculars, Ryan watched the three German soldiers' puzzlement turn to terror as they realized what was happening. They pushed futilely against the exit door and when they started screaming at the unseen dozer, their faces disappeared from Ryan's view as the Sherman began pushing the mound of dirt over the front lip of the pillbox. A few minutes more work and the pillbox was entombed under several feet of dirt and rock. Then the Sherman rumbled down the road toward Velletri. The tank could have blasted the pillbox but the crew apparently decided it would be more cost-effective to entomb the German defenders alive, or perhaps they were motivated by a sense of justice. Ryan didn't blame them. Hundreds of tanks had been destroyed in the breakout from Anzio and their crews had suffered terribly, but Ryan was certain he'd have nightmares about the Germans in the pillbox if he ever got to sleep again.

The whole experience was nightmarish. It wasn't that he objected to combat or killing. He had no taste for it like some soldiers, but he did object to unnecessary fighting. The town was encircled. There would be no breakout, nor would there be a task force sent to relieve the German soldiers in Velletri. It was either fight and die, or surrender. Those were the only two options Uncle Sam was giving them, and for the life of Ryan, he couldn't understand what purpose they served by fighting on. Some Germans were of a like mind, he knew. In his limited, albeit intense, experience of combat on Monte Cassino, he had seen very few German prisoners. Velletri was different. He'd sent plenty of enemy soldiers to the rear under guard, but there were still many—far too many—who wanted to fight on.

Ryan found a lateral alley and saw several of his soldiers kneeling at the end of the small road taking shelter behind a massive mound of shattered stone and brick at the corner of an apartment building. Corporal Hodgson saw him and waved him onward. Ryan joined Hodgson, who said, "This opens onto a big patch of land, maybe a half-acre or so, that's got nothin' on it except weeds and junk. Some of the boys were checking it out when the firing started."

"Where's it coming from? Casualties?" Ryan asked.

"This field is rectangular like a football field, but it ain't flat. We're in the bleachers at the one-yard line. We think there's a sniper team in the apartment building on the far side of that street yonder but I can't swear to it. Maybe at the other team's twenty-yard line. As for casualties, Private Warner was hit in the shoulder—a couple inches lower and he'd have bought the farm. He's behind a wall with a medic but we can't extract him and we can't move forward." Hodgson pointed in the direction of the street, but Ryan couldn't see the apartment building. He took a step forward to see for himself but was stopped by Hodgson and another soldier. "You oughtn't do that, sir. He knows we're back here," Hodgson said. "It's offset a little but he can see where this exits on the street."

Ryan looked to the roof of the building that he was leaning against and said, "Where's Private Froman?"

Hodgson pointed to the vacant lot and said, "He's hunkered down yonder behind some rubble. I hope he's movin' up to get a shot in but he might consider it more advantageous to stay put."

Ryan would have laughed if it hadn't been so serious, instead he agreed dryly, "Yes, he might." Froman, who was one of the three snipers assigned to Ryan's platoon, wasn't known as an aggressive soldier. Although he knew the answer, he asked, "Who's my grenadier?"

Hodgson pointed at another soldier. "He is."

The other soldier, a private from St. Louis, snorted and said, "Nice try. Want us with you or stay here, Lieutenant?"

"Stay here and be ready to move up. Okay. With me, Corporal Grenadier. Bring your stuff."

Hodgson was ready to go. They jogged back to the street that Ryan had come from and Ryan motioned for two of his soldiers to join him. They were next to a modern apartment building, a bland product of Fascist architecture, and Ryan cautiously stepped through the open door and looked around. There was an open stair-case but no elevator. It wouldn't have worked in any case—Velletri had no power. Lieutenant Ryan started to lead up the stairs but Hodgson grabbed his arm, pulled him back, and then pointed at another soldier. "You," he said.

The landing at the second floor had a blown-out window but the view was obstructed by a small tree that had been flowering two days before but was now nothing more than bare shattered limbs. The third-floor window offered an unobstructed view across the vacant lot and as Ryan cautiously looked out, he could see the building, but he had no idea as to the shooter's location. None of the windows on the building they were looking at had glass—neither did his for that matter—they had all been blown out by the concussion of repeated artillery. For that matter, Ryan thought, maybe the gunner wasn't set up in a window. Half of the apartment building was rubble, and perhaps the gunner was on a floor behind a collapsed wall…or perhaps he had already decamped and was setting up in another building.

"As soon as we find him, we'll start launching grenades from here," Ryan said. "Get set up while I go down to the second story and take a look from behind those tree limbs."

Hodgson nodded, rummaged through a bag he'd brought, and began adapting his Garand into a grenade launcher. He attached the M-7 launcher and locked it in place by clamping it down on the bayonet lug. He could have added the sights for the launcher but it was time consuming and he felt confident he didn't need it. After some cursing, he managed to force a rubber boot onto the stock of his rifle and then the rifle was ready—it took less than a minute. Hodgson pulled an olive-drab M9A1 high-explosive antitank grenade from the bag and set it on the floor. He then opened a small ammunition box, setting it on the floor beside the grenade. Hodgson extracted the en bloc clip from his rifle, ejected the chambered round, and inserted a blank cartridge from the ammo box. The grenade was attached to a tube which Hodgson slid over the top of the M-7 launcher. He was ready. The soldier from Tennessee looked at Ryan who had just returned. "Any luck, sir?"

"Not one hundred percent. On the right side of the second story there's a collapsed wall. That's the only place I think he could be. I looked at every single window and didn't see anything definitive, but if I were a sniper in that building, that's where I'd be."

"That's where I'd be too," said a deep voice behind them. Sam had been pointed upstairs by Ryan's soldiers who were still clearing the street below them.

Ryan had jumped when Sam spoke, but he recovered quickly. "Are you here to move me along, sir?" he asked.

"Something like that," Sam said. "We need to keep pushing hard. I understand the temptation to stop and methodically clear but we can't let one sniper hold up a platoon because it can hold up a company or a battalion. We need to stay abreast of the other units as best as possible."

Ryan nodded. "Yes, sir."

"I assume that you're going to lob grenades at the likely spots, right?" When Ryan said that it was, Sam said, "When you do that, I'll be downstairs and I'll lead your soldiers into the building. We'll clear it and then move on to the next. If we just plink at him with grenades, he'll move before we find the right spot."

Ryan shook his head. "No, sir! It's my platoon. I'll take 'em in."

Sam nodded in reply. "Good. I'll give you a couple minutes to get in place and then we'll hit that collapsed wall. When the first grenade hits, have your team plaster every window and then move up fast. I'll see what we can bring up to help." As Ryan headed out, Sam waved his radioman over and took the handset from him.

0715 Hours
Velletri, Italy

It was four minutes exactly when Sam gave Hodgson the order to fire. Hodgson came up before the window, knelt on one knee, aimed briefly, and fired. The kick from the grenade launcher was tremendous so most soldiers preferred to plant the butt of the rifle in the dirt. That had been Hodgson's intention when he put the rubber boot on his rifle, but the angle didn't work right and he shoulder fired it instead.

The antitank grenade flew in a graceful arc and hit the apartment building a few feet to the left of the pile of rubble that Hodgson had targeted. It was close enough. The remainder of the exterior wall collapsed back into the room and Sam's view of the room disappeared in a cloud of dust and smoke. Simultaneously, Ryan's soldiers started firing at the windows of the apartment building and began advancing toward the distant street. Little puffs of dust appeared on the exterior wall of the apartment building where soldiers missed the windows and hit the building, but it was nothing compared to the storm kicked up by a heavier gun, which opened fire a few seconds later.

An M-3 halftrack emerged from the shadows of the alley and moved into the vacant lot with soldiers jumping into its troop compartment. A crewmember of the halftrack stood behind an M2 .50-caliber heavy machine gun and he blasted the open room that was still smoking from the antitank grenade, then he went from window to window. The heavy rounds from Ma

Duece ripped into the window frames, and mortar, stone, and splinters flew back into the room and onto the ground beside the apartment building.

The driver of the halftrack sped up as the vehicle went up a short but sharp incline, and then it crossed the street to the apartment entrance. Soldiers from Ryan's platoon poured out of the back of the troop carrier and entered the building with Ryan in the lead. The remainder of his first squad quit firing at the windows and ran up to the building to join their comrades.

Sam watched from the building across the vacant lot with his radioman and Corporal Hodgson, and he nodded grimly as one of Ryan's soldiers appeared in the window on the third floor and gave Sam a thumbs-up. Seconds later, he watched as the same soldier and another man hoisted the corpse of a German soldier onto the windowsill and then tipped the body out of the window. The body did a half-rotation and then hit hard on the ground. As American soldiers walked past the crumpled body on the ground without sparing it a second glance, Sam and Corporal Hodgson picked up their weapons and headed outside.

0845 Hours
Velletri, Italy

The German defenses around Velletri continued to collapse inward as the battalions of the 141st Infantry Regiment and other assorted units advanced into the town. A dozen small hard-fought battles took place simultaneously as streets were cleared house by house. Soldiers from the Texas Division moved forward with tanks and tank destroyers, and the first real urban fight of the regiment was carried on in an improvised manner as communications broke down and the commanders invariably lost, regained, and lost again the command and control of units constantly on the move.

Perkin and Kulis had left the battalion command post and were headed toward Able Company. Major Spaulding wanted an update from Sam, but was unable to reach him by radio. They had spent much of the morning maintaining a plot of the known German positions but those were now overrun. After their maps had become out of date, they checked in with the regimental S2, but the regimental intelligence maps were more out of date than the battalion's. One interesting tidbit they picked up, however, was that corps intelligence was reporting that the Germans were still undecided about the threat posed by the infiltration in the hills north of Velletri.

It was undoubtedly good news, yet Perkin was focused on his own problems. He had Kulis stop the jeep and he asked directions to Able Company from a private with a handie-talkie who stood smoking on a street corner. Much to Perkin's irritation, the soldier pointed with his cigarette on a map where Able Company was, yet after weaving through a maze of streets and alleys, they found that not only was Able Company not there, but there didn't look to be any American presence at all.

Kulis looked at the buildings and the street itself. They were on a narrow street that snaked back and forth down a hillside. It was after following the slope of the hill past a hairpin turn surrounded by multicolored row houses that they had finally stopped to get their bearings. Besides being eerily vacant of people, the two-, three-, and four-story homes looked ancient to the Americans and the damage from errant artillery and air strikes strangely accentuated the age of the cobblestone street and its houses. As Kulis looked at the damage, he observed that despite the wreckage and the rubble, there were no signs of recent fighting—no telltale pock-marks on the standing buildings from small-arms fire, nor smoke or dust rising from the rubble. "Hey, Cap'n, are you thinking what I'm thinking?"

"If you're thinking of a whorehouse again, then no, I'm not. If you're thinking we need to go back and Patton-slap that private for getting us lost, then I'm with you." Perkin looked at his map—a Michelin tourist map that he took from an abandoned gas station—and tried to figure out where they were.

Kulis laughed as he put the jeep in gear. "You saw a whorehouse?"

"No, but…oh shit! Go back!" Perkin pointed down the street. Three German soldiers had emerged from another curve farther down the hill. Then three more. Perkin heard two rifle shots but had no notion of where they went.

Kulis completed his turn and gunned the jeep heading back up to the hairpin turn while Perkin kept an eye on the German soldiers. The leader of the soldiers pointed to a house and two soldiers ran inside. They entered a faded yellow four-story house that fronted the street below them but also backed up to the street above them. Perkin quickly realized that control of the house meant control of their avenue of retreat.

Kulis saw it too. "We're trapped," he said it in the same casual tone of voice he would have used to say, "I like pancakes."

"No," Perkin replied. "Go there." He pointed to a small dirt road on the other side of the turn. "Let's see where that takes us." Before they were out of sight from the curve, Perkin saw more German soldiers had joined the four still on the street and they were moving cautiously up the hill. Just to discourage them some-what, he fired a quick burst from his Thompson and was gratified to see the soldiers scatter.

The dirt road took them nowhere. It was nothing more than a driveway leading to an empty, packed dirt lot behind a row of houses, that served as a parking lot for those who had cars and a small area for the kids to play soccer. An old carriage house stood at the end of the lot, and Kulis parked the jeep behind it while Perkin weighed their options. The steep hill formed the back boundary of the remainder of the lot but the owners of the home had built small gardens up the side of the hill with an amalgamation of stone retaining walls and terraces. Only one garden looked like it had been tended to recently, the rest were overgrown with weeds.

The options as Perkin saw it were to either enter one of the houses and try to fight it out from there, or to try to escape from the back. It wasn't a difficult decision. Perkin and Kulis grabbed their weapons, packs, and a handie-talkie from the jeep and began to climb the hill using the little garden terraces as steps. It wasn't much of a climb but it was nearly vertical, and both men were beginning to breathe hard when they reached the top, except there wasn't a backyard to another row of houses like they expected. As they pushed through the weeds and the brush above the terraced gardens of the homes below, they found the moss-covered stone foundations of the houses above. As far as they could see to either side, there was no break between houses nor entrances to the homes—just sheer wall for at least ten feet up.

"Shit," Kulis hissed.

"Who the hell builds a house like this? Let's move your way, Eddie, and see if we can get around this."

They shuffled about twenty feet to their right and then Kulis stopped. There was nothing further to stand on. "We either go your way, or we stay up here in the weeds."

"Yeah, until they find us," Perkin said as he looked over his shoulder. There was no sign yet of pursuing Germans. He began shuffling to his left and they went past their original spot. After pushing aside brambles and crawling down a dip in their path and back up on the other side, he stopped. "There," he said as he pointed to a small concrete balcony on a house hanging precariously over their slope. Perkin estimated the balcony was about nine feet over their heads, and he saw it had a wrought-iron railing around it. There was a single wood and glass door leading from the house to the balcony, and Perkin could see a lacy curtain over the window of the door. It seemed so out of place in his present circumstances that he stared at it for a moment.

"Let me help you up first, sir," said Kulis. "I don't know if I could pull you up." He handed Perkin his rifle, which Perkin looped over his shoulder, and interlocked his fingers. Perkin put his boot in Kulis's hands and on the count of three, Perkin was lifted high enough to grasp the corner post of the balcony railing. While Kulis supported him from below, Perkin slid Kulis's Garand under the railing and then his own Thompson.

Perkin wrapped both arms around the post and as he dangled from the ledge said to Kulis, "Okay, go."

Sergeant Kulis grasped Perkin's leg and jacket and leapt lightly onto the top of Perkin's boot and scampered up Perkin's back until he could reach the bottom bar of the balcony railing. He swung over and seconds later was kneeling on the edge of the balcony helping pull Perkin up.

As they hopped over the balcony, Perkin whispered, "You did that really fast. Impressive."

Kulis whispered back, "We did two things for fun on the farm: climbin' trees and giggin' frogs down at the pond. I was the tree climbin' champion of Falls

County. I hope I never have to fall back on my frog giggin' skills."

Once over the rail, they knelt before the door. Although they still couldn't see anybody, Perkin assumed the German squad was searching for them and it was only a matter of time before the Germans entered the lot behind the row houses and discovered the jeep. He wanted to get inside and off the exposed balcony as quickly as possible.

Perkin reached up and tried the door. It was locked. As much as he hated doing so, he was forced to break the glass. He rapped sharply on it with the butt of his Thompson near the door handle and winced at the noise as the entire pane cracked and crashed to the ground. There was no point in reaching in and unlocking the door now. They duck-walked over the broken glass into the house and as they stood up, they saw a spartan home where everything of value had been removed. Maybe the owners took their pictures or mementos of their lives with them when they evacuated Velletri or they buried them in the yard—Perkin didn't know.

"Go check the front," he ordered and he walked to the kitchen and looked out the window which viewed the back. He had a good view of the little driveway leading to the carriage house and a clear line of sight to the windows at the rear of the houses on the street below.

"Sir, I think we're on the edge of our lines now," Kulis said as he walked into the kitchen. "There's no one out there. We went down this street a few minutes ago and if we cross that street yonder and go up the hill fifty yards or so, we're back where we started."

Perkin looked at Kulis and then back through the window at the neighbor's driveway below. "I'm not ready yet."

0900 Hours
Rome, Italy

Lieutenant Colonel Grossmann told Signore Alessio to leave the bottle and then leave him alone. The Italian had been seeking compliments for his scones, but Grossmann wasn't in the mood to give compliments. He looked at the distant smoky haze over the rooftops of Rome and as he listened to the distant echoes of the big guns, Grossmann wondered when the Allies would arrive. Grossmann really didn't have time for a drink and cornetti, but he would do as he pleased before he headed to the office...if he went.

Life was over, he decided. He had sent two notes to Antoniette, one to her apartment and another to her parents' villa. Grossmann had tried to explain that he had been following orders and the family had been harboring fugitives of the state...and then he apologized for lying. It had been his best attempt to come clean, to beg for forgiveness, but he'd known it would be inadequate. He was afraid it would be perceived as being weak, yet he couldn't stop himself. He had to try.

He'd heard nothing in return. As he took his third shot of an expensive brandy, an overpriced brandy to be truthful, he thought morosely that he'd never see Antoniette again. She had rejected him completely, and it was his own damn fault. He knew that.

Major Friederich Kemmerling walked up to the table, looked at the downcast Grossmann and motioned for Alessio to bring him a glass. He sat down and when Alessio brought his glass, he poured a shot and drank it silently. For five minutes, Grossmann and Kemmerling sat in silence and drank brandy and ignored their espressos. Finally, Kemmerling said, "I'm sorry about Signorina Bernardi, Boss. But there will be another.

There always is."

A flash of anger ran through Grossmann, and just as quickly it faded and was replaced by his sadness. There would never be another like Antoniette, he thought, but some last vestige of male pride made him nod. "Yes, Fritz. There is always another. Have you been to the office this morning?"

"Yes, sir. I just came from there."

"What's the word? Was I missed at the morning meeting?"

Kemmerling shook his head. "I told them you were working a problem regarding the Gestapo list, and you'd be in either later today or tomorrow morning. But... sir, you can't miss another day without it becoming a problem."

Grossmann nodded. "I'll be there. Any update on the Vatican?" He had told Kemmerling about his meeting with Monsignor O'Flaherty.

Kemmerling nodded. "We've seen them double the Palatine Guard—patrolling outside the Vatican walls and inside as well. The assessment is that they've added, very quietly I should say, another thousand soldiers or so. That'd bring them to four small battalions total, perhaps."

"Thank God for that," said Grossmann with a wan smile. "As hard as we're stripping the Rome units, we can make the argument that we're outmanned—although I could slaughter the whole lot of them with a platoon of Pomeranian grenadiers. What's the assessment of the military situation?"

Kemmerling shook his head and looked grim. "It's not clear. There are differing assessments coming from Kesselring's headquarters as well as from the Fourteenth Army. There's been some penetration by Clark in the Alban Hills but the extent of it is contentious. I talked to some of our analysts this morning and they think it's worse than either Kesselring or von Mackensen are saying."

"What do you mean?" Grossmann asked. "Are they falsifying the reports or are they just unaware?"

Kemmerling shrugged. "Fog of war, I think. You know, we've done so well in holding up the Allied advance that they maybe can't contemplate a breakthrough. I think they thought Italy would be like the first war forever—a meter here, a kilometer there."

"What's our assessment? At the headquarters?"

"The command staff says they have to take Kesselring's word that there is risk but it's contained. But who's that smart kid in the intelligence section? Sergeant Marquardt? His assessment is that the better part of a division—the Texas Division apparently—has penetrated behind the Caesar Line, and he's sharper than any of Kesselring's analysts. Add to that we've lost contact with the forces in Velletri. The army sent an armored column towards Velletri this morning and got it chopped to pieces. With the collapse of the Tenth Army position on the Gustav Line, Marquardt thinks it's probably catastrophic. We'll know in the next day or two but I hope we're wrong."

0905 Hours
Velletri, Italy

The Germans had yet to materialize and Perkin was beginning to believe they weren't going to aggressively pursue the two Texans. It was disappointing. Kulis had raised Able Company on the radio, and Sam was sending reinforcements to Perkin's position. It was looking as if reinforcements wouldn't be needed, but in any case, Perkin wanted to see how far into the city center they could penetrate on this road.

Perkin took a drink of water from his canteen always keeping his eyes on the window and the driveway below them. He passed the canteen to Kulis and when he was done, Perkin put it away. Five minutes earlier they had been running for their lives. Now, he was getting a little bored.

"We've got friendlies coming in, sir," Kulis said as he opened the front door.

First Lieutenant Frank McCarter walked in and smiled at Sergeant Kulis. "Hey, Eddie, hey, Perk." As McCarter joined Perkin at the kitchen window, he asked, "What y'all got goin' here?"

"Hey, Frank. We ran into a German patrol—a squad or less I think. We thought they'd follow us back here, but they evidently lost interest. This road out front winds down this hill and I think that this street ties eventually into Via Garibaldi. Once on it, we can track that south and then cross west towards the city hall at the Palazzo del Comune."

"Okay. I've got my whole platoon waiting to spread out. Sam is shifting his boundaries south towards us, and he's got armor movin' up to join us." McCarter felt his pockets looking for a pack of cigarettes and then accepted one from Kulis.

Perkin nodded and said as he continued staring out of the kitchen window, "Sounds good, Frank. How far behind is the armor?"

McCarter tilted his head, listened for a moment, and said, "I think they're coming up now."

Perkin could hear the squeal of the tracks and he smiled. "If it doesn't conflict with Sam's orders, I'd recommend following this road down the hill." Perkin pointed down the hill and said, "There's a yella house on that side of the road that may have two Krauts in it waiting to ambush us. As soon as it comes into view, have the Sherman pop an H.E. round in there and let's see what hap..." Perkin hissed, "They're comin' in now, Eddie. Like we talked about...standby."

Kulis ran to the side of the balcony door, knelt as he set his rifle down, and slid a grenade off a shoulder strap. He laid the grenade on the ground. Kulis took another grenade and prepared to pull the pin. He nodded to Perkin who said in a low voice, "Wait until I fire. Frank, take a window upstairs." McCarter headed for the stairs and as he passed the open front door, he waved for two of his soldiers to join him.

Perkin had seen three German soldiers cautiously come between the row houses on the dirt driveway. One German soldier pointed to the jeep's tire tracks in the dirt. They moved against the side of the building on their right, and one soldier ran back to the street and silently motioned to his comrades before coming back to the driveway. Two more soldiers joined the three on the dirt road and an NCO tapped two men on the shoulder and they moved cautiously into the driveway.

Perkin watched as the NCO looked over his shoulder toward the street like he was expecting more troops. The largest person Perkin had ever seen then walked confidently onto the driveway and moved toward the parking lot. He was carrying an MP-40 in his right hand, and strapped over his back was a panzerfaust— the German version of a bazooka. Perkin saw no need to wait any further. He aimed at the massive soldier's chest and fired a five-round burst.

Perkin was already lining up on the NCO when he saw the soldier he had just shot defiantly raise his MP-40 and begin firing at the house next to theirs. Perkin fired another burst at the giant soldier and it didn't seem to even register to the German that he'd been hit. Perkin inwardly shrugged and emptied the remainder of the magazine of the Thompson into the chest of the German soldier from a range of no more than forty yards.

He dropped the magazine and inserted another, and after waving away the smoke, Perkin watched the massive soldier stagger backwards and grasp at empty air trying to steady himself. His eyes found the right house as he sought out Perkin and with a look of utter hatred on his face, he dropped onto his knees and pitched forward dead.

0910 Hours
Velletri, Italy

Frank McCarter had no sooner arrived at a bedroom window when Perkin opened fire on the giant German soldier. It was a double-paned casement window that McCarter opened carefully. When he looked out, the German soldier was receiving his second burst and then third. McCarter took aim at the NCO who had dropped to one knee—McCarter wasn't sure if he'd already been shot or was just minimizing his profile when the grenades started to fall on the German soldiers below.

McCarter heard a grenade explode to his left and then another one went off closer to the driveway shattering a window on the bottom floor of the row house opposite the parking lot. It was too close for comfort for the NCO who shouted something at his soldiers and started to fall back. McCarter shot him twice in the chest and one of McCarter's soldiers put two more rounds in the German sergeant from another bedroom. Another grenade exploded and then McCarter heard Perkin shouting to cease fire, although no one was still shooting.

"Frank!" Perkin called out. "Come down here!"

McCarter bounded down the stairs and met Perkin at the front door. "Give me a squad of your boys, and then take the rest down the road and around. We'll meet you at the big guy. Don't forget about the yella house. Move quick!"

McCarter replied, "Yes, sir!" and headed out of the house. He motioned to his squad leaders and told one to report to Perkin inside. He gave a second squad leader his instructions, and told the third to remain with him. McCarter hopped onto the Sherman that had been assigned to him, gave the tank commander a quick rundown, and then hopped off.

The Sherman rumbled forward heading downhill, and the soldiers of McCarter's platoon followed in trail. Thirty yards down the hill and McCarter nodded to his second squad leader who in turn sent four of his soldiers into a pale pink house that looked to have a good view of the street as it wound downhill below them. Thirty yards farther and another four soldiers entered another house on the same side of the road farther down the hill. A little farther and the Sherman stopped, rotated its turret, and without warning fired at the yellow house. The assistant driver hit all the windows with his .30-caliber machine gun and McCarter watched with fascination as the tracer rounds screamed into the house.

He ducked as a second H.E. round was fired from the tank's main gun and then he almost clapped out loud as the tank commander joined in with his M2 .50 machine gun. In less than thirty seconds, the home ceased to be habitable as the second story collapsed bringing the third and fourth stories with it. The staff sergeant commanding the tank looked back at McCarter and when he pointed forward, the tank continued down the hill.

McCarter's attention was caught by small-arms fire to his left and he ran into one of the houses his soldiers had entered. A corporal at one of the windows turned and smiled broadly at him when he asked what was going on.

"We saw two fellas with a bazooka on that rooftop. They were goin' to try to pick off our tank, but they won't bother nobody. I popped one and Billy got the other." The corporal spit a long stream of tobacco juice on the marble kitchen floor as if to accentuate his point.

McCarter told them to stay in place and provide overwatch to his troops coming into view on the street below and the tank which had just navigated one of the cut back turns, and as he was running out of the house to catch up to his soldiers, he heard the corporal say to the private, "Goddamn, it's nice to be winnin' for a change!"

0920 Hours
Rome, Italy

A tactical aircraft screamed overhead just feet above the rooftops of Rome and while about half the people under its path instinctively ducked, everyone eventually watched it. Antiaircraft artillery in a Roman park opened up as the plane crossed overhead leaving Rome toward Velletri but the aircraft was moving too quickly for the crews to react in time. Change was in the air, and Rome could feel it.

"P-51?" asked Kemmerling who'd had to twist in his chair to see and thus only caught a glimpse of it.

"Maybe. Probably an F-6 variant of the Mustang conducting a low-level reconnaissance. I bet they're trying to figure out if we'll leave Rome as an open city."

"I suppose they'll find out soon enough. I wonder

if they'll learn before us," Kemmerling said with a sar-
castic laugh.

Normally, Grossmann would have come back with
an equally cynical rejoinder, but instead he said, "I
think I shall stay here all day and drink. Do you want
to join me?"

Kemmerling laughed as he stood up and said,
"More than anything, but one of us needs to be seen
at the office. I've left my uniform cap on my desk and
told the orderly to keep replacing the coffee in my cup
as soon as it gets cold, but I'll probably have to go over
the front office evacuation plan this afternoon with the
chief of staff."

Grossmann almost smiled in relief. He really
wanted to spend the day alone in his misery, and while
Kemmerling was normally jovial company, he didn't
want to be jovial. "You're a prince, Fritz. I'll see you
tomorrow at the latest."

Kemmerling was turning to leave when Signore
Alessio interrupted, "Excuse me, gentlemen. A
messenger brought this note for you." Alessio handed
Grossmann an envelope addressed to "Douglas" in a
woman's handwriting. Alessio bowed and walked away.

It was Antoniette's handwriting, and Grossmann's
heart stopped beating. He wasn't sure he wanted to read
it; he certainly no longer felt like being alone. "Hang
on a minute, Fritz." With a slight tremor in his hands,
he broke the seal and pulled a letter from the envelope.
He looked at Kemmerling with something approaching
panic, and he said, "I'm not sure I can read this."

Kemmerling looked at his boss with the sympathy
one feels for a friend who's lost a family member. He'd
never known a man so utterly controlled by his desire
for a woman. "You want me to scan it for you, sir?"

Wordlessly, Grossmann handed over the letter.

Kemmerling glanced at the contents, the tension draining from his face, and after a moment, handed the letter back. "I didn't finish it, but I think you'll want to read this, sir. I'm going to ask Signore Alessio to make us some sandwiches. I'll be back in a moment."

With a definite tremble in his hands, Grossmann opened the letter and read it carefully—it was dated that morning.

> *My love,*
>
> *I almost didn't get your note. Papa intercepted it and threw it away but my maid saved it for me, bless her. She comes with us to Switzerland!*
>
> *I don't know where to begin. I felt so betrayed when you lied to me, but I've given it some thought—I've thought of nothing else in fact—and I understand why you felt you couldn't tell me the truth. That they—I can't speak their names—could betray our cause so completely was such a shock and you must have known that it would be. Although I raged at you so angrily, I understand now that you were trying to spare my feelings. Next time, tell me the truth. Our love can withstand anything.*
>
> *My father has forbidden me to see you again. So, I will see you as soon as I can. My parents are making me stay at their home for the rest of our time in Rome—they won't let me stay at my apartment! But Papa is headed to Milan on Saturday night to make arrangements for the family—when he leaves, I'm*

going back to my place. Mother will be
understanding. If not, she won't be able
to stop me!

Meet me at our café Sunday morning
at 9:00 (pay Alessio what he requires to
open) and we will face the future togeth-
er. Tell Fritz to come so I can say hello
(or maybe goodbye for now), but then he
has to leave so we can be alone! If the
war intervenes, find me at our villa in
Milan or in Bellinzona. I will wait for
you—as long as it takes! Please be safe
and know that you are in my heart. All
my love, Toni

PS...don't try to contact me or he'll
make me go to Milan with him.

Grossmann read it through twice before his heart
started beating again. He pushed away the brandy bottle
and picked up his cold espresso and contemplatively
sipped it. When Kemmerling returned, the major was
looking at a man a decade younger with no apparent
concerns in life.

"Stay with me a little, Fritz, while I sober up. Let's
get some coffee and I'd like to go over Operation Monte
Carlo with you." Grossmann smiled his first genuine
smile in days.

Kemmerling looked puzzled. "Am I missing something? What's Operation Monte Carlo?" he asked.

"Our plan to take down the Italian mob as our way
of saying 'ciao' to Rome as we leave."

Kemmerling couldn't help but smile at Grossmann's
new enthusiasm. "I didn't know we'd named it. Why
Monte Carlo? Because it's a gamble?"

"Well, I won't deny it's a risk, but that's not what

I had in mind. In Coronado, before the war, there was a ship called the *Monte Carlo* and it was owned by the mob. They anchored it three miles out in international waters and it was a floating casino and brothel, which made a ton of money from the American puritans. In '37, it broke free and drifted towards the beach and it eventually sank next to the Hotel Del. I was in Heidelberg at the time, but I went back to California the summer before the war started and dived on the wreck. I found thirty silver dollars and always suspected there was more. That was big money at the time which I blew on a date where I didn't even get laid. That was my last time in America," Grossmann mused. "So, I named this Monte Carlo because I plan to end my time here by taking the mob's money once again, and instead of impressing my date with a nice dinner, I plan to buy my future wife a villa on a Swiss lake."

0920 Hours
Velletri, Italy

Perkin watched McCarter's handling of his platoon with professional admiration as they moved down the street. As the tank came to a point even with a team in a house, McCarter whistled and waved the team outside and had an equivalent number of soldiers move into the houses farther down the street. He repeated the process several times moving down the street and he always had a squad moving with the tank and a squad providing protection from the upper stories and rooftops of the houses.

Perkin and Sergeant Kulis had left the house the way they came in—by the balcony. They found six Germans on the ground. Four were dead, one was destined to join them shortly, and another was moderately wounded but had lost the motivation to fight. One of McCarter's medics was examining the wounded man while another soldier disarmed the German who would join a long line of walking wounded prisoners from the battle of Velletri.

The giant soldier was even larger in person. Perkin and Kulis stretched the corpse out straight and laid next to it for comparison. He didn't make it to the German's shoulder. "I'm almost six foot three," Perkin said. "He must be a foot taller than Sam even. I ain't ever seen anybody like that."

Sam drove up to check on McCarter's progress and he too was amazed by the German soldier. "This is the first superman I've seen in this war, Perk. Holy smokes!" Sam looked at a tight grouping on the German's chest. "How many rounds did you put in him?"

"A little less than a whole twenty-round magazine. The first ten or so didn't even bother him. He mostly looked annoyed...it's the same look Maggie has when you sing or try to kiss her."

Sam ignored the jibe and looked back at the dead German. "I could kill guys like this all day long...a lot more honorable than killing their children. Damn... look at the size of this fella's feet. Kulis do you want his boots? You could use 'em as overshoes."

"It's the dry season, sir. I don't need galoshes. Hey, sir? If you gentlemen are done here, some of the boys want to take a picture with the Giant of Velletri."

1345 Hours
Velletri, Italy

Sam moved cautiously up the stairs of another row house with Cooper, his radioman, following. The battle was largely concluded, but there were still outposts of

German soldiers that refused to surrender. Sam was going to oversee the elimination of this group, and then he would move on to the next.

His soldiers really had little need for his supervision. Velletri had been a laboratory of improvisation, and as far as Sam was concerned, his soldiers had performed brilliantly. He had seen soldiers from Able Company blast holes into German-held buildings with antitank grenades and bazookas, and in one case, blow a hole through a tile roof with a satchel charge and then drop grenades onto the upper floor of the house until the German surrendered.

The current problem was several German hold-outs in a row house on a street too narrow for armor. They were going to try the Canadian mouse-holing method, which Sam had learned about in Ortona at the beginning of the year. His soldiers knew of it, but with the focus on mountain training had never tried it before. Sam wanted to be there to see it in action.

He had entered the house next to the Germans' on the end of the street through a hole blasted by an antitank gun—the front door on the street might be exposed to grenades thrown from above and gunfire, and the Texans had learned the hard way that the doors and windows were frequently booby-trapped in any case. When Sam reached the third floor of the house, he joined Second Lieutenant Balzac and three of his soldiers. Balzac put his fingers to his lips and waved Sam over. In a whisper that seemed out of place on that noisy day, Balzac said, "They're just on the other side of that wall." Balzac pointed to the wall shared with the other house.

Sam nodded, and just as quietly said, "What are you planning to use as the munition?"

Balzac nodded to a soldier that Sam didn't know.

"This is Corporal Blackburn of the engineers. He's made up a reduced munition satchel charge...two sticks of dynamite. He thinks a regular satchel charge would be too much, so he whipped this up for me."

Sam walked softly over to Blackburn, who had joined the division as a replacement private last winter just in time to conduct a nighttime ascent of the Cassino massif in an ice storm. The corporal, a short muscular farmer from Maine named Blackburn, carefully hung the satchel charge on a hook on a plastered wall directly opposite where they had heard the voices. When Sam leaned in close to talk, the engineer cupped his ear to hear better.

"Don't you reckon this is goin' to blow back out instead of breaching this wall?" Sam asked softly.

"I don't know what it's going to do, sir. Well, it'll definitely blow back but this amount should blow a helluva hole here as well...I think. To tell you the truth, we don't have any doctrine for breaching walls in a house. Dynamite's not ideal, but it's all I've got now. Your boys wanted to go wait in that bedroom here and come across the landing after I blow this, but there may not be a bedroom when this is done so everyone needs to get out of the house. I've got it set with a pull ignitor and a fifteen-second fuse, but there's no guarantee we've got that long. Go ahead and get your men out, Cap'n, and I'll get the ball rolling."

Sam and the other soldiers exited the house through the hole and squatted against the stone wall of the house and covered their ears. A few seconds later, they were joined by a heavily breathing Corporal Blackburn who did likewise.

The explosion, when it came five seconds later, was louder than Sam expected and the whole house shook with the force of the dynamite...but no one hesitated.

They ran back into the house prepared to sprint up the stairs. Just as quickly, they ran back out. With a groan, the roof collapsed onto the third floor and stone, wood, and red tile cascaded down the stairwell.

"Stay here," Sam ordered as he motioned for Balzac to join him. They entered the house again, and Sam peeked cautiously up the stairwell, ready to run at the first sign of further collapse. He saw the stairs were impassable and most of the third floor no longer existed but he also saw that the wall had been breached. Rather than creating a mouse-hole, it was large enough for an elephant to pass through. Sam thought about tossing grenades up and through the hole, but the angle wasn't in his favor and he thought it more likely the grenades would drop back down on him.

"We're going to have to do this the hard way," Sam said softly. "I don't know if we got 'em or not."

Balzac nodded and said, "We got this, sir. We've been clearing houses all day long."

Sam stood back and watched from the corner as Balzac and his men ran down the street hugging the walls to the second house. Balzac and a corporal threw two grenades through the front window shattering the glass in the process. Immediately following the detonations, a large private kicked the door in and Balzac and his soldiers entered the house. A few minutes later, Balzac returned to Sam. Shaking his head, Balzac said, "Three bodies upstairs...killed by the dynamite. It's a terrible mess to leave for the homeowners."

Five minutes later, Sam was heading to another position two streets away. More German soldiers refused to surrender; they had set up an MG-42 overlooking a small square that boasted a broken fountain and no living grass. Once again, the casualties were light but Sam wasn't going to risk any soldiers to take out the recalcitrant Germans. He stood aside as a Sherman tank rumbled past him and moved onto the street fronting the park. There were no additional calls to surrender. The Sherman fired a high-explosive round at a corner of the house at the ground level and fifteen seconds later fired another round at the other corner of the house. It kept firing until the house collapsed, and the Sherman moved on to the next street where Baker Company was reporting more recalcitrance.

1805 Hours
Velletri, Italy

Perkin, Sam, and Kulis stood in the courtyard before St. Michael the Archangel's church, which was opposite the damaged town hall and they looked up at a pedestal holding a statue of St. Michael in the moment of his victory over Satan. The church, the pedestal, and the surrounding buildings were either reduced to rubble or heavily pockmarked with bullet holes from the intense fighting but with the exception of a broken arm, the statue looked intact.

"It gives me chills every time I see it," said Sam. "I never really paid much attention to this part of the Bible."

"Neither did I," said Perkin as he unconsciously touched his locket. He took his helmet off and wiped smoke out of his eyes with the back of his hand before saying, "I was familiar with the art and the historical significance, but I never really gave much thought to the meaning of the story or St. Michael or his role as the patron saint of soldiers. And yet here we are...in the midst of the greatest battle between good and evil in the history of humanity. While I've never been a big believer in saints and angels, I can't help but feel that St.

Michael has looked over us these past months."

"Someone's got to," laughed Kulis, who was even less impressed with saints and angels than Perkin. "We'd be six feet under today if left to our own devices."

A distant burst of machine-gun fire reminded them that the battle for Velletri was still being fought. Earlier that afternoon, the remaining Germans had launched a desperate bid to break out of Velletri to the northwest and the 2nd and 3rd Battalions had crushed the attempt in fierce fighting that was frequently hand to hand. Four hours after that counterattack, small skirmishes continued throughout Velletri. But as far as Perkin knew, the battle was over for the 1st Battalion. Its sector had been cleared, scores of German prisoners had been taken, and they were awaiting further orders. Casualties had been extraordinarily light although there had been killed and wounded.

A man in a shabby dark suit walked out of the plain church and blinked in the daylight. His black hair was turning white at the temples and he was extremely thin and tired looking. Although he had dried his hands, they were stained deep red with blood. He saw the three Americans and walked tentatively over to them. In excellent English, he said, "Excuse me, gentlemen. Are you Americans?" When Perkin told him they were, he said, "There are wounded German soldiers and Italian citizens in the church. Is it possible to make arrangements for their transfer to your care?"

"Are they disarmed?" Perkin asked.

"Yes, signore. The German officers who left them here took their weapons. Several of them will die soon without better care than I can give them. Can you please hurry? I'm afraid the fire from that apartment will spread to the church." The Italian pointed to flames from a furiously burning building behind the church.

Sam whistled loudly and waved over two medics from Ryan's platoon while Perkin and Kulis walked with the doctor into the church. It was dimly lit with candles and there was little natural light as the simple church had few windows and those had been optimistically boarded up. A dozen wounded German soldiers lay on the stone floor of the church, some on blankets but most simply on the floor. As he walked into the dark church, Perkin asked the Italian, "Are you a doctor?"

"Yes, although I'm not..."

Perkin interrupted, "You're not Doctor Frattini by any chance?"

The Italian stopped and stared at Perkin. "Yes. How could you possibly know that?"

"Because I've been looking for you," Perkin said with a broad smile. "My name is Perkin Berger. This is Eddie Kulis, your future son-in-law."

Kulis stopped short with a concerned look on his face and he mumbled something about helping the medics.

As Kulis scurried away, Frattini's confusion showed. He shook his head and said, "I don't understand."

"I met your family in the caves under San Pietro, and your wife and father-in-law took care of me after I was wounded. I promised Stefania a couple weeks ago that I'd kill every German I saw and bring her daddy home." Perkin laughed with delight. "I'm so happy to be able to do that. They're like family to me."

Frattini's entire body was trembling and he abruptly sat down in a pew and started to cry. Through his tears, he said, "I thought they were dead. The Germans told us San Pietro had been destroyed and that the Americans had killed everyone. I didn't want to believe it but other workers told me there was nothing left of San Pietro."

"There ain't much left of the town, that's for sure, but

they're building a new one. You won't find your family there though. They've bought a house in Presenzano." Perkin dug through his pack and found a C-rations can of beef hash. As he opened it, he said, "I'm guessin' you ain't eaten for a while."

Frattini pulled a battered tin spoon from his coat pocket and as he wolfishly ate the cold hash, he asked, "Three days. My goodness, this tastes wonderful. Please tell me everything you can about my family."

"Let's start with my favorite Frattini, Stefania. She's great. Since I first met her, she's grown like a weed and put on at least ten kilos—nothing like Uncle Sam's vittles to set someone right. I think she was on the verge of starvation when I met her but she's a healthy teenager now. Smart as a whip and speaks English better than half our soldiers."

Frattini's eyes welled up again. "What about that young man?" he asked as he nodded toward Kulis. "Did you say he's to be my son-in-law?"

"I was just joking. Stefania thinks so though. She's a determined young lady." Perkin laughed again, still delighted to have found Dr. Frattini.

Perkin's mood was infectious, and Frattini joined in the laughter. "Then I'd better get to know him," he said. "She can be very determined. He must be something special—she doesn't make friends easily."

"He's a good man," agreed Perkin. "So, where were we? Angela is good. She wasn't hurt by any of the fighting but I hate to say that your old home was destroyed. Angela's working for the British Army as a post-op nurse in Presenzano, although that hospital may be moving soon." Perkin stopped as a thought occurred to him. "Doc, these German boys are most likely going to be evacuated to Naples. I'll see if I can arrange for you to ride the ship back with them, you know…them under your care…and then we'll see if you can hop a supply truck up to Presenzano. We might be able to get you home in a couple days or so."

The doctor's eyes welled up again as he grasped Perkin's hands and thanked him profusely. They talked for several minutes more, then Dr. Frattini said he needed to check on some of the patients and he joined Sam's medics beside a seriously wounded sergeant from Königsberg. Perkin wandered around the church and was joined by a young priest who spoke no English.

After answering a question that Perkin believed was, "Is the fighting over?" they came to a fresco of a Madonna. He was about to inquire about the artist when the priest said proudly, "Francesco Grandi." Perkin started to say that he'd never heard of the man when he understood the priest then saying that they also had a painting by Antonio Carracci but it had been put away for safekeeping.

Before Perkin could ask who Carracci was, the priest hurried over to help Dr. Frattini lift a German soldier onto a stretcher. The weakened doctor and priest took a leg each while the German's torso was easily lifted by a massive soldier from Wizard Wells, Texas, who told the uncomprehending priest that "the waters back home would heal this here Kraut right up."

Perkin went in search of Major Spaulding and after finding him reviewing plans for the onward movement of the battalion to the Nemi area, he had the battalion clerk draft a set of orders authorizing the transport of Dr. Frattini to Naples and then on to Presenzano. Spaulding signed the orders after noting that he had no standing whatsoever to authorize such a thing, but by the time someone complained, he'd be in Rome.

2100 Hours
Rome, Italy

The chief of staff looked seriously at the assembled officers with his good eye, and glared at them with his bad eye. No one knew for sure which was the true mirror of his soul, but regardless, he had their rapt attention.

"Good evening, gentlemen. I'm sorry to have to call you in at this hour, but the situation on the ground south of Rome is deteriorating rapidly. For those who haven't heard, events in the Fourteenth Army sector will likely necessitate a withdrawal of all German forces to north of Rome."

After sobering up, Grossmann had spent the afternoon at the headquarters and he was aware of the unfolding catastrophe in the Alban Hills but apparently, some officers were caught by surprise. There was silence—no gasps or lamentations—but the shock and anger on many of the faces told Grossmann that this was unexpected news.

The chief of staff continued, "The Velletri garrison has surrendered to the Americans and there was an infiltration in force between the LXXVI Panzer Corps and the parachute corps in the Alban Hills. The Americans now control the high ground adjacent to and behind the Caesar Line. They moved heavy equipment onto Monte Artemisio and now can effectively contest the lines of communication between Rome and our forces south of the capital. General Wolff is meeting with Field Marshal Kesselring and his staff this evening, and we will be looking at any and all means to support the army. Do you have any questions?"

Grossmann spoke first. "Sir, what is Berlin's position on Rome? Is it to be an open city?"

The chief of staff shrugged. "Berlin's position is not yet known. When it is, it should come to Kesselring first."

"My recommendation is to make it an open city," Grossmann said.

A lieutenant colonel in the operations directorate, a fanatical Nazi, sneered at Grossmann. "Why? Why should the Italian cities be spared while ours are being reduced to rubble? The miserable traitors! We should burn it to the ground as an example to the rest."

Grossmann saw heads nodding in agreement. If nothing else, these fanatics would destroy it all, he thought. He would have done the same before Antoniette's note that morning.

"We gain nothing militarily from contesting Rome. We will inevitably be encircled and annihilated..." Seeing a protest on the fanatic's face, Grossmann hastened to add, "...not before we exact a toll on the Allies. But, we'll need those troops for fighting a delaying action in northern Lazio before we are prepared defensively in Tuscany and Umbria."

"We can fight the delaying action in Rome!" argued the other officer.

"Why should the Allies do that when they can move past Rome and engage us in Umbria?" countered Grossmann.

"What do we gain by making it an open city, Colonel Grossmann?" asked the chief of staff.

"German honor. The first time Rome was catastrophically sacked was by German soldiers. History mourns the fall of the Rome Empire. It doesn't celebrate the rise of the Visigoths. Leaving it open loses us nothing. Besides, Mark Clark might halt his advance long enough to have a victory parade through the city and have hot dogs with Pius." Seeing blank looks when he said "hot dogs," Grossmann clarified, "Bland American sausages."

The chief of staff nodded. "It's not our decision to make in any case. We have the plan prepared to defend Rome, and we have the plan prepared to evacuate Rome without a fight. Either way, our headquarters is moving north. I'll know more upon General Wolff's return." The chief of staff glared with his bad eye as he relayed his orders. "All staff elements will prepare to evacuate this headquarters. Should the situation stabilize on the Caesar Line, we can use this as a training evolution, but let's be realistic. The time to start is now. I think we have a minimum of forty-eight hours, but let's be ready to transfer classified material by this time tomorrow. This takes precedence over all other activity except direct support to military operations. That is all."

2130 Hours
Velletri, Italy

Perkin had decided to ride with Able Company, and he gratefully accepted Sam's helping hand to pull him up into the back of the deuce and a half. Sam sat behind the driver and Perkin sat opposite his cousin. It was the last truck of the company and after Sam did a silent head count, he slapped the roof of the cab and simply said to the driver, "Let's go."

They had marched to the outskirts of Velletri after the garrison surrendered, and Perkin struggled to remember what he had seen. He was so tired that he was afraid of forgetting it altogether, but some of the images were clear enough in his mind: a long column of German prisoners being marched in one direction, another column of American tanks and riflemen walking the other. The destruction of Velletri would always stay with him, but as much as he'd grown to care for some Italians, he was fairly callous to the fate of their homes. Better to destroy an Italian home than lose an American life, he reasoned, and when Sam had told him of the tank leveling the house protecting the German machine-gun crew, Perkin nodded approvingly.

As he had marched out of town, he had passed another church and crossed a mountain-fed stream over a stone bridge, which miraculously supported the Shermans and the Wolverines. It was a beautiful town once, he had thought, and no doubt would be again. He was surprised at the number of Italians he passed on the way out of town—he had seen very few during the past days of fighting. They had come out of cellars, bomb shelters, and churches, and the men and women wept at the sight of their shattered town. They picked up pieces of the red tile from rooftops and stared at it mutely before dropping it in despair. Not all Italians were despondent. Some were outright jubilant and the soldiers of the 1st Battalion were given hugs, kisses, and flowers by the women of the town who also spat and cursed at the German prisoners as they were marched away.

When they reached their assembly point at the edge of town, they ate their first hot meal for days. It was hash, but the soldiers wolfed it down before closing their eyes for a few moments sleep before the trucks arrived. At least they wouldn't have to march to join the rest of the division, and they feverishly hoped they wouldn't be going back into combat until the morning at the earliest.

Unexpectedly, Sam spoke to Perkin. "Lord, I'm glad to have that past us," he said. "Bill told me this thing is cracking right open and a couple days hard fighting and we'll be in Rome. Do you think that's right?"

"Have you ever seen the Germans give up fifteen miles in two days?" Perkin asked by way of reply.

"Nope, but I'm gonna stay optimistic. What was the craziest thing you saw in town, and don't bring up the exploding toilet...that was a week ago." Sam frowned in the darkness. That couldn't be right.

"It was three days ago, wasn't it? Maybe four?" Perkin yawned. "The craziest thing I saw was General Walker kicking a German soldier for lollygagging."

Sam started to laugh. "He didn't!"

Perkin joined in. "He sure did. I think he felt bad about it afterwards, but if a kick in the ass by a two-star is the worst thing to happen to that Kraut today, he's pretty damn lucky. What about you?"

Sam was silent for a moment. The worst thing he had seen was a Sherman that had been destroyed by an antitank gun. The cookoff of the tank's ammunition had thrown the entire turret up in the air, and when it came down, it was tipped forward nearly vertically. The 75mm barrel of the Sherman came through the open driver's hatch and impaled the driver, and the entire turret remained almost upright, held up by the barrel running through the tanker. It was the most gruesome thing Sam had seen in the war, and he would tell Perkin about it but not now.

Sam put the image out of his mind, rubbed the thick stubble on his chin, and said, "Well, it's not the craziest thing, but today I saw the best thing I've seen in this whole war."

"What's that?"

"These boys in victory, the 1st Texas. You know, this wasn't some cakewalk. It was a hard-fought battle, and they were the best they've ever been. And they know it! They're new men, new soldiers...even those who were on the river. You can just feel the difference. You can see it in the way they held their heads up after the fight. You can see it in the way they walk. Hell, these boys just came out of days of battle. Give 'em an hour's sleep, some hot food, and they're ready for more." Sam's voice rose with uncharacteristic emotion as he said, "There ain't a damn thing on the planet that can stop us now."

Chapter Eleven

Three Days Later

June 4, 1944
0200 Hours
Rome, Italy

    The jeeps paused before the last roadblock established by the Fifth Army. Once through the barrier, they would be past the protection of the Allies and on their own. Reconnaissance elements had already entered the city, but they would be the first soldiers from the 36th Division to drive through the Italian capital. The buildings of the eternal city loomed in the darkness but not a single light was to be seen. It was as if they were entering a ghost town.

    They were too tired to care.

    Ever since Velletri, Captains Sam Taft and Perkin Berger, and Sergeant Eddie Kulis had debated the merits of going into the city in search of Douglas Grossmann. They had discovered the massacre at the Gildardino farm last February, and had sworn to hunt Grossmann down over the graves of the Gildardino children. There was certainly no lack of desire on anyone's part. There was no inherent fear in hunting him down in a foreign city. It was a simple question of productivity. Sam had argued that Grossmann would be gone long before they arrived, and although Perkin and Kulis agreed intellectually, they argued back that if they didn't try, they'd never know.

The German Army had been routed. They had fallen back again and again, but the American advance led by the Texas Gun Club had been too fast for the Germans to establish defensive positions. The battalions of the pursuing Allied armies leapfrogged each other, keeping a constant pressure on the withdrawing Germans until the night before when the German Army broke before the suburbs of Rome. All nonessential equipment was left behind. So were the nonambulatory wounded. Thousands of German prisoners clogged the narrow roads and highways that the Allies desperately needed to continue their advance.

The final defenses outside of Rome had been overcome the night before with the ruthless elimination of the German soldiers who had drawn the short straws to man the machine guns in the face of two advancing armies, both questing to be the first to enter Rome.

Nine months before, Perkin would have been excited to be one of the first Allied soldiers into the first Axis capital to fall, but not this time. He, like his companions, was exhausted. They had survived on catnaps here and there, but hadn't had a full night's sleep in over a week. After Velletri fell, the battalion fought at Nemi and again at Marino, but had never stopped moving. Ironically, it was on this night when most of the soldiers of the Gun Club were getting some sleep. When they were told their advance was halting and they would enter Rome at daylight, they collapsed in the fields, vineyards, and orchards of the gently rolling plains southeast of Rome. On that night, tens of thousands of men slept hard under the stars, but not the team designated to head into Rome.

Permission to pursue Grossmann had been hard to get. Major Spaulding agreed with the plan. He knew enough about the Grossmann story to want him dead, but the regimental commander balked and only after much persuasion did he agree to send the proposal to division. The small operation was approved at the 36th headquarters by General Walker, but even a division commander lacked the authority to order troops into Rome ahead of the general advance. Corps had likewise approved but entry into Rome was a complicated political decision, and it had gone to the Fifth Army headquarters with a recommendation for approval. The senior intelligence officer on the Fifth Army staff had weighed in with George Hill by his side, and the plan had been finally approved at 2230 hours the night before.

Perkin looked at the assembled team. All were volunteers. One had begged to go, and technically, he was the senior officer present, although Perkin was in command of the mission. Captain Waller Finley-Jones of the Welsh Guards was senior to Perkin, but he was along as an interpreter and a guide. His father had been a diplomat assigned to Rome in the thirties, and Finley-Jones knew the city as only a teenager could have. In addition to the Welshman, Private Roscoe Pfadenhauer rounded out the five-man team. He was an expert marksman, fluent in German, and his coolness under pressure had been demonstrated countless times in his nine months in Italy.

The team looked back at Perkin and he nodded in the dim light to the second lieutenant of the 157th Regiment at the roadblock. Perkin leaned over from the passenger seat, spoke softly to Kulis, and the first jeep moved forward into Rome.

0330 Hours
Rome, Italy

Douglas Grossmann bolted upright in bed. He was disoriented and distraught. He'd been having a nightmare about the Ardeatine Caves, and the young Nascimbeni woman was there along with all the Italians he'd rounded up for execution. Mindful in his sleep how her murder had nearly ruined his life, he made the decision to spare her in the second chance of dreams and not execute her with the others. She watched in tears as Grossmann's soldiers marched in the victims in groups of five and made them kneel before the SS officers put bullets in the back of their heads. Row after row of Italians were pushed into the cave at bayonet point and then executed, and all the while, the girl protested and begged for mercy for the others.

Grossmann didn't relent. He couldn't. The orders for retribution came from Hitler himself. A Führer order knew no mercy. It was either kill or be killed. In his dream, the nightmare of the caves replayed in his mind just as his senses had recorded it months before. The noise of the pistols in the cave—the pleas of the victims. The smell of gunpowder, vomit, urine, and excrement—even the smell of the hot pitch he would pour over the bodies to hide his crimes. The look of terror in their eyes mixed with hatred and contempt. It wasn't until Grossmann personally executed a fifteen-year-old boy who had been snatched off the streets after the Gestapo prison on the Via Tasso had been emptied that the young Nascimbeni woman changed in the way of dreams into the younger Nascimbeni girl from the photograph.

The pleas for mercy morphed into taunts as the woman transfigured into the girl, and every execution was egged on by the thirteen-year-old version of the girl who screamed in English and German that Grossmann didn't have the balls to pull the trigger—even though by the time Grossmann had murdered the boy, he had already executed more than thirty prisoners himself. Each taunt was seemingly prophetic and it became increasingly difficult for Grossmann to pull the trigger.

Finally, the last row of prisoners was brought in. The hatred and defiance in the eyes of the victims was replaced by the sad resignation he'd seen in the eyes of so many Jews. They were pushed and beat into a kneeling position and the executioners stood behind them waiting for the order to fire. Grossmann stood behind an old woman, who reminded him of the mother of the priest he'd blackmailed. She was praying in a language that Grossmann didn't understand, and while he lined up his sights on the back of the old woman's head, he couldn't pull the trigger. To peals of derisive laughter from the Nascimbeni girl, he tried again to pull the trigger, but he couldn't.

"Do you think she will love a man who can't kill an old woman?" the girl called out as she laughed at Grossmann's failure.

Grossmann glared at her in his frustration, turned back to the old woman and tried to pull the trigger again. He couldn't, no matter how hard he tried. This led to another paroxysm of laughter from the girl.

"You're no man!" she cried in evil delight.

Grossmann lowered the gun and turned to face the girl, his anger building. He stormed over to where she was standing next to a pile of bodies and whipped her hard across the face with his Walther, the front sights leaving a wicked slash on her cheek. She grinned at

Grossmann and ran her index finger through the blood pouring down her cheek. The girl struck a coquettish pose and playfully licked the blood off her finger. She grinned even wider and taunted him again. "That's the best you have, little man?"

Shaking with rage and frustration, Grossmann put the barrel of his Walther against the temple of the girl and snarled, "Don't tempt me!"

The girl's face suddenly transformed to terror as her dark brown pupils slid to the corners of her eyes as if she were trying to see the gun. Tears welled up in her eyes and she begged, "Please don't kill me, Douglas," and the voice wasn't hers but was that of Antoniette's.

Stunned, Grossmann lowered the gun, and looked at the girl. The terror left her face and she burst into laughter again.

"You won't kill me," she said as if she were playing the most delightful game.

"Why won't I?" he cried.

"Antoniette won't let you. She'll kill you if you hurt me," the girl said as blood dripped on her sailor's neckerchief. "She loves me more than you." She pouted seductively. It was a look that Grossmann had seen Antoniette use many times to tug at his emotions.

"Lies!" He pushed the barrel of the gun against her forehead hard.

"You can't touch me!" The girl sneered, all signs of coquettishness gone. "Antoniette will protect me!"

"She can't! You're already dead!" Grossmann screamed as he pulled the trigger in frustration. The Walter jumped in his hand, and the girl slowly dropped to the floor of the cave with a small hole in the center of her forehead and a look of triumph on her face.

She lay on the floor with her leg bent awkwardly beneath her and the blood running off her pretty face, yet she seemed otherwise unharmed. Her calm had returned and she looked at Grossmann with black mocking eyes. Her last words before Grossmann woke up drenched in sweat were said with a sweet smile: "You shouldn't have killed me, Douglas. Antoniette will avenge me and you'll die alone and unloved…"

0330 Hours
Rome, Italy

"You're sure this is the right place?" Perkin asked Finley-Jones. "This is Villa Taverna?"

"Of course! I never forget an address," Finley-Jones said in the darkness. "Now, the last time I was here was '36 for a soiree that my father was invited to, but it's still got to belong to you chaps. It's sovereign territory, is it not?"

"I think so," Perkin answered, uncertain if that was actually the truth.

"Why are we at the ambassador's residence and not the embassy?" Kulis asked. "I don't think it's far."

"It's not," Perkin said. "But we got our reasons. You'll see in a minute."

"Let's get this done," said Sam. He looked at an ornate wrought-iron gate that sealed the driveway leading to the mansion. On either side of the gate was a six-foot stone wall. There was a guard shack built into the wall, but it had been abandoned and boarded up. Sam cautiously felt along the top of the wall and feeling nothing that didn't belong there, Sam pulled himself up and sat atop the wall. "Stay away from the gate. That's where I'd put a grenade if I was a surly Kraut soldier… and a tripwire across the sidewalk to the front door." Sam helped Perkin as he climbed over as well. The three remaining soldiers stood a respectful distance behind the iron gate to watch in the dim light provided by the blackout lights of the jeeps.

The short driveway led to a courtyard bounded by three wings of the mansion and in the center of the courtyard was a twenty-five-foot tall flagpole. Perkin reached the flagpole first—there was no flag flying— and Perkin unwrapped the halyard from the cleat. As Sam pulled the flag from his jacket, Perkin lowered the halyard and unclipped the hooks. Sam fumbled in the dark and almost dropped the flag. "Careful, now," said Perkin.

"I got it," Sam said as he snapped the halyard clips to the grommets of the flag. "Send it."

As Perkin ran the flag up the flagpole, Sam took a step back and offered a parade ground salute to the Lone Star flag as it began to flap in the gentle night breeze. When Perkin had tied off the halyard on the cleat, he saluted as well and then asked Sam, "Ready?"

"Yep." Sam hoisted Perkin up the flagpole as high as his arms would extend, and Perkin climbed even higher on the twenty-five-foot pole. "That ought to be high enough," Sam said as he looked at Perkin with his legs firmly wrapped around the flagpole.

Perkin ensured that the flag was tightly two-blocked against the hoist pulley, and pulled a bundle of bailing wire from his jacket. He quickly wrapped the wire around the pole, binding the halyard tightly to it. To be certain, he produced more wire and wrapped it tightly around the pole and halyard. When satisfied, he slid down the pole and wiped his hands on his uniform jacket and said, "Now for the next step."

Sam walked back to the wall and said to Kulis, "Eddie, there's a grease gun—an actual grease gun— wrapped up in an undershirt in the back of my jeep. Get that for me, would you please?" When a grinning Kulis, who finally understood what was going on returned with the gun and shirt, Sam said to Perkin, "Ready?"

"This was your idea. Don't you think you should be the one doing it?" Perkin said with a grin.

"Do you really want to hold me up? C'mon. Ready?"

"Okay, the feeling's just come back to my legs. Let's go."

Sam hoisted Perkin as high as he could again, and this time, Perkin stood on Sam's shoulders. They walked slowly around the flagpole while Perkin put several thick beads of axle grease running vertically down the flagpole. When they had completed the circumnavigation of the pole, Perkin tossed the gun to the ground but kept the undershirt, which he used to spread the grease as high as he could up the pole. When he dropped back down, he looked up at the pole with some satisfaction as he tested the immobile halyard. "I'd like to see the son of a bitch who can get that flag down now!"

As they left, Sam checked the gate for booby traps and found none, but they had to climb back over the wall as the gate was chained and padlocked. When they rejoined the others by the jeeps, a laughing Finley-Jones asked, "Didn't you have an American flag?"

Sam grinned in the dark and said, "Sure. But since this is where Mark Clark is liable to lay down his imperial head to sleep tonight, we wanted him to know who made it possible."

0345 Hours
Rome, Italy

Douglas Grossmann fumbled in the dark until he found his cigarettes and lighter. After his first deep inhalation, he began to calm down. His heart rate returned to normal and his breathing slowed. But the disquiet…the fear and the anger…remained.

The dream about the Ardeatine massacre was an occasional visitor, but fortunately, it didn't strike him every night. He'd never go to sleep again if it did, but this dream was more realistic than the others. On the few nights he'd relived the killings, it was always as a detached third person observer. This time he saw it in first person as it actually occurred, hearing the pleas, giving the orders, pulling the trigger, smelling the hot tar as he hid his crime. He shivered in the darkness and then thought about the Nascimbeni girl. She had no business being in that dream. It made him angry in the illogical way dreams affect people. It was wrong of her to try to put a wedge between Antoniette and him. The threats and taunts still stung as he smoked his cigarette.

There was no sense trying to go back to sleep, he thought. Sleep would never come again after a dream like that. He briefly thought about going downstairs to the SS canteen and seeing if there was anything left to eat or drink, but he knew there wasn't. The last SS truck had pulled out of Rome the night before…then he corrected himself. Almost the last truck. He had one heavy truck and two staff cars reserved for his purposes.

Operation Monte Carlo had been a bust. All the planning in the world couldn't compensate for an obstinate chief of staff, who felt that the pressing demands of the withdrawal took precedence over the extracurricular activities of the general's special projects officer. Since the German Army needed every man and every last vehicle to support the withdrawal, Grossmann and Kemmerling's plan to hit the mob warehouses had to be curtailed. They had made the decision to raid just the largest depot yesterday morning with their sole truck, but when they arrived, the warehouse was empty. Not a scrap remained. They moved to the next family's warehouse and found that it too was empty. They had questioned a shop owner from across the street of the second warehouse, and he claimed to have no knowledge of the mob's presence in the first place. Was it possible their interrogation of the gangsters had yielded false results or had Occhiato betrayed them? Or was moving their stock merely a precaution before the arrival of the Allied armies? Grossmann didn't know.

They had one true treasure left, and they were keeping it close to them. Grossmann had crated *The Continence of Scipio* and the other works of art taken from the Nascimbeni house, and he would sell them at discounted rates in Northern Italy, Switzerland, or Germany. He would have to unload it quickly, before Antoniette saw it in his possession, but the Nascimbeni art was their nest egg. It was worth more than the entirety of any black-market warehouse, he was sure. His treasure was already loaded in the sole truck remaining to the SS in Rome, and shortly after 0900 hours, it would leave Rome with Antoniette and him.

He hadn't seen Antoniette yet. Grossmann had left countless notes at her apartment, but the doorman said she hadn't been seen for over a week. He was afraid of trying to contact her at her parents for fear her father would take her away. It had taken every strand of will-power remaining to stay away from her home but he would have to trust that she would show up at their café. Whether she was prepared to leave or not, he didn't know. But he wouldn't leave Rome without her.

0450 Hours
Rome, Italy

The three officers walked softly down the hallway along marble floors to the apartment they believed belonged to Douglas Grossmann. They had no expectation that he was in the apartment waiting for them—their silence was a courtesy to the sleeping residents of the apartment building.

The building had not been difficult to find, and Perkin was gratified to discover the addresses that separated Grossmann's apartment from Antoniette's and the address for the mob family that was Lieutenant Commander Cardosi's contact were all within a five-mile radius. They decided to check out Grossmann's first, for no other reason than it was the closest.

The night doorman to the apartment building burst into a dance of joy when he saw the American and British uniforms, and it was with great difficulty that Captain Finley-Jones was able to quiet the man long enough to show him a picture of the German officer.

As he wiped away tears, the man nodded furiously and said that this was Herr Schmidt, a German businessman who had maintained an apartment in the building for several months. "But he's not here now," the doorman said. "I helped him load a suitcase and several cases of wine into a Mercedes-Benz just two days ago."

Disappointed, Perkin asked, "So you haven't seen him since?"

"No, signore. His young lady came here looking for him earlier tonight, and I had to tell her the same."

Perkin showed the doorman a picture of Antoniette and was gratified to see the recognition on the doorman's face. "Si! A lovely young lady," said the doorman as his face darkened. "But not very nice. She went up to his apartment after curfew and left a few minutes later."

They had obtained the keys to Grossmann's apartment from the doorman in exchange for two cigarettes, and Kulis and Pfadenhauer remained with the jeeps.

When they opened the door to the apartment, they found it was nicely furnished but empty. The bed was made, the armoire was emptied with the hangers neatly pushed to one side, the cupboard was devoid of food and wine…but lying on the countertop was an opened letter. Perkin glanced at it and handed it to Finley-Jones to read aloud:

> *My Dearest Antoniette,*
> *I hope this finds you in time. I'm at the barracks until Sunday, which is the latest that I can stay. I've left notes at your apartment and I pray that one of them finds you. Pack your clothes and we will leave together. Signore Alessio is opening the café for us, and I'll meet you there. I'll make sure we have a bottle of that wonderful champagne before we start anew in the north. Love, Douglas*

Finley-Jones looked at Perkin and raised his eyebrows. "So the daft bugger's in love and still in Rome, eh? They're leaving today." He turned the letter over and said, "It's her response."

> *My Darling,*
> *I'm so sorry I haven't been able to see you. Papa is watching me like a hawk, and wouldn't let me leave the house tonight without an escort. I had to threaten the chauffeur to take me here! I will see you tomorrow at the café, but I may be late. I must stay with my parents tonight, and I won't be able to get away until morning. I won't keep you waiting*

for long but I need to go to my apartment
and pack. Wait for me and we'll leave
together! All my love, Toni

"Well, ain't that somethin'?" Sam said. "I wonder where the café is? Maybe we could get them both."

"Unless the doorman knows, there's no way of telling," Perkin said. "However, he always comes back to the girl. Let's see if we can stake out her apartment and see if she goes to him or he comes to her."

0730 Hours
Rome, Italy

Antoniette Bernardi's apartment building was less than two miles from Douglas Grossmann's flat. They were in similar upscale neighborhoods east of the Tiber River and not far from Vatican City. Antoniette's apartment was on a short and narrow cross street between the Via del Corso and the Via del Babuino. The small expedition had driven down her street while it was still dark and they decided there was no way to do close surveillance in front of the building without being detected. There was, however, a hotel on the Via del Babuino that had a courtyard for parking that offered a view down her street although the front of Antoniette's building was partially obstructed by trees.

The courtyard was devoid of vehicles, and as far as Perkin could tell, the hotel was devoid of inhabitants as well. A new sign on the door leading to the lobby from the car park said in effect that the hotel was closed until the liberation. They parked the jeeps behind several palms in large pots, and closed a picketed gate leading to the street. It didn't totally obscure the jeeps from the street view, but it was the best that they could do.

"How come we've seen so few people?" asked Private Pfadenhauer.

"Rome has a curfew," said Perkin. "They're off the streets by 2000 hours, and curfew doesn't lift until 0700. And the Italians are late sleepers. Most of 'em ain't up yet. I suspect we'll see about a million of 'em before tomorrow night."

"What about that skirt, Bernardi? Didn't the doorman say she came lookin' for Grossmann at 2100?"

"There are rules and then there are rules. There are always exceptions for women that beautiful," Perkin said as he looked down the street with binoculars. "Don't you remember her?"

Pfadenhauer laughed and said earnestly, "I think about her almost every night, sir. It's going to cost me some sleep if I have to kill her."

They sat and waited. A few people walked past without noticing the Americans tucked away in the courtyard of the small hotel. Just before 0800, the door opened to the hotel and a sleepy-looking man in slippers and wearing a threadbare bathrobe let a small dog out into the courtyard. He glanced to make sure that his gate leading onto the street was closed when he saw the two American jeeps and five Allied soldiers staring at him curiously. His eyes grew wide when Sam got out of the jeep and sat cross-legged on the ground to pet the dog, which jumped playfully in Sam's lap. He had never seen a man so large in his life.

Perkin and Finley-Jones approached the Italian, and seeing that the man was about to call for someone in the hotel, Perkin put his fingers to his lips. The call to the hotelier's wife made it no farther past a deep inhalation of breath and the man nodded and whispered something in Italian to Perkin.

"He asks if we would like some orzo," translated

Finley-Jones.

Perkin had tasted the ersatz coffee before and had no love for it. "Please thank him but tell him…"

"Hey, Waller," Sam interrupted, "I got some coffee beans in my pack. Ask him if his missus would make us all some coffee. I got some sugar too. Tell him if he's quiet and doesn't let on we're here, I'll leave some coffee and smokes with him when we go." Sam didn't smoke, but he'd found from long months in Italy that cigarettes were sometimes a more reliable currency than lire or greenbacks.

A few minutes later, a very thin middle-aged woman came to the door of the hotel and stood beaming at the party of soldiers. She had obviously been warned by her husband not to make a sound so she clasped her hands over her heart and then silently blew a kiss to each of the men. A few minutes after that, she came to the door again and beckoned to Finley-Jones. They held a whispered conversation and she went back inside, leaving the door open.

"Her name is Maria. She says we'd better drink the coffee inside. People are so starved that their sense of smell is heightened and if we drank the coffee outside, we'd have a hundred people around us in five minutes."

0850 Hours
Rome, Italy

The entire party had moved indoors, and Perkin and Sam were sitting in an upstairs bedroom that gave a second-story view of Bernardi's street. Signora Nervetti had come upstairs twice to check on them and refill their coffee, and on the second trip, she stayed to talk. She had been in the hotel business all her life—the hotel had belonged to her parents—and she spoke passable

English, although it was a little rusty.

"When will your army come?" she asked anxiously. She understood that her current guests were an advanced party of some sort.

"They're already entering the suburbs in the south," Perkin answered. "I would think that they will be here by noon or earlier."

She started to cry, but she controlled herself quickly. "I'm sorry," she said. "I should be...*come si dice*...laughing. It is a good day."

"Has it been hard?" Sam asked.

Afraid she would start to cry again, she simply nodded. Then, a little more confident, Signora Nervetti said, "People are dying...uh...starving. The food is rationed, uh, very much, even though the German Army has a large stockpile at Giardino del Lago—less than a kilometer from here. They are not as fat as they used to be but we are starving. We get one hundred grams of bread per day. That's a roll. It used to be 150 grams but they...uh...cut it two months ago. It's not even made with flour—dried chickpeas, rye, cornmeal...maybe sawdust. One hundred grams of meat per month. There was a monthly pasta ration which we sometimes get but sometimes it is stolen by the Fascists or the Nazis. No vegetables. No salt. No soap. Sometimes chicken but seldom fish or meat in the markets. I paid two hundred lire for a kilo of meat in the Trastevere black market. They said it was beef. Maybe it was horse or mule or donkey. It wasn't cat though." She started to cry again, and Perkin was getting up to comfort her when she pointed out the window and said, "We closed because no one has money. No one travels. Last month tram fares doubled—who can go out? No one. But they can! See them in their fancy car? They have food. We have none."

Sam and Perkin's eyes followed her finger, and less than a hundred yards away, Antoniette Bernardi was getting out of a gleaming black Isotta Fraschini limousine and walking into her apartment.

0910 Hours
Rome, Italy

Douglas Grossmann sat at his usual table with Major Kemmerling. His handpicked SS troopers were seated inside the café, and were eating as well. It might be their last meal for some time and Grossmann felt obliged to buy them breakfast and pay Signore Alessio to prepare sandwiches for them.

Grossmann was getting nervous. The sounds of distant gunfire—ever-present for months—had completely ceased, and Rome was deathly silent. The Romans were mostly afraid to leave their homes until the Allies arrived. The German departure had more been orderly and less lethal than most Italians had anticipated, yet German soldiers executed Italian citizens for no greater offense than being in the wrong place at the wrong time. Most Italians were content to wait a few more hours for their liberation. Still, the silence was unnerving.

It wasn't just the lack of noise that had Grossmann on edge, however. He was tired, and still deeply disturbed by the dream that continually replayed in his mind. Grossmann's anger at the taunting and derision he'd received still burned fiercely even though he knew it was illogical.

Most of all, Grossmann was on edge because he didn't know whether Antoniette had truly forgiven him or whether he was being played like he'd seen her manipulate countless other men. He didn't know whether he'd see her that morning. He didn't know whether she'd leave Rome with him. He didn't know whether they'd have a life together, and that was all he truly wanted.

Seeing Grossmann's leg bounce nervously under the table, the gleaming jackboot flashing in the morning light, Kemmerling said quietly, "It's okay, my fellow Lilliputian. She'll be here in a few minutes. She's always late." Kemmerling watched as a black limousine drove past their corner on a side street, and asked, "Doesn't her father have an old, what's it called? Fraschini? A black one?"

Grossmann, who had his back to the side street and hadn't seen the car, said, "Yes. Antoniette doesn't like it. Her father's got a Mercedes that she prefers. Why?"

"I thought I saw one drive by." Kemmerling nodded with his head toward the side street.

Grossmann looked around expecting to see Antoniette walk up to the café. She didn't emerge. He stood up and said to Kemmerling, "I'm going to check."

Kemmerling nodded, even as he inwardly sighed. "If that's her, I'll say good morning and then I'll join the troops inside. Then we'd best be leaving."

Grossmann didn't hear him. His thoughts were solely on Antoniette, and he hurried to the street corner unconcerned about how it might look to his soldiers inside the café. He peeked around the corner hoping to catch a glimpse of her as she came up the sidewalk, looking to surprise her as she walked by. When he saw no one in view, he walked out onto the side street and watched as a black car drove off in the distance. He walked twenty yards toward the disappearing car before he stopped, confused, in the middle of the street.

It must not have been her, he thought disappointedly. As he cursed to himself, Grossmann heard the squealing of tires as another car came around the edge

of the piazza behind him. As he turned toward the
noise, his heart leapt as he saw a black Mercedes, which
immediately made the turn onto the street fronting the
café. In a second it was out of sight. It must be her.
Grossmann began to walk back and quickened his pace.
He didn't want to keep her waiting. Then he heard the
guns.

His first thought was for the safety of Antoniette.
She had arrived just in time for Allied soldiers to attack.
As he was running for the shelter of the café, he heard
the gunfire more closely. It was the sound of MP-40s,
the machine pistols used by the German military,
and which his SS troops were carrying. But the firing
seemed to be from outside, not inside the café where
the SS men were having breakfast. *What is going on?* he
asked himself.

0915 Hours
Rome, Italy

Perkin and Sam sat up simultaneously as they heard
the gunfire. Perkin walked to the open window and
looked out cautiously. He saw nothing. No soldiers, no
civilians, no vehicles on the road.

"That's close," Sam said as he joined Perkin at the
window. "A few hundred yards. Half a mile, tops."

They were joined by Kulis a few minutes later who
came upstairs to announce, "There's small-arms fire to
the north of us."

Perkin nodded. "We heard it too. Let's keep an eye
out. Is Signore Nervetti in place?"

"Yes, sir. He's watching the back side of her apartment," Kulis said. They had explained to the hoteliers in
general terms why they were in the neighborhood, and
Nervetti had told them that Bernardi's building had

another exit on the street to its rear. He volunteered to walk his dog down that street and keep an eye out for either Antoniette or a blond man.

0915 Hours
Rome, Italy

Grossmann drew his Walther and ran to the street corner, hugging the exterior of the café. The gunfire stopped and tires squealed again and he heard a groan from inside the building. When he walked under the awning, confused and with a pounding heart, his boots slipped on the bloody stone floor. It had been a massacre.

Major Kemmerling was dead. It looked like he had been shot no less than a dozen times from no more than a few yards. The exit wounds on his torso looked as if he were turning to see the car behind him, and the look on his face strangely suggested familiarity.

With a sick heart, Grossmann walked over the broken glass of the door and the windows and he assessed the carnage. Alessio was dead from a single bullet to the forehead. Two of his three troopers were dead and only one, Sergeant Fleischer, remained alive. He had been shot through his upper chest, and there was no exit wound. Grossmann went behind the counter, pulled out a fresh towel, and put it over the wound. Unless there was internal bleeding, Grossmann thought the soldier would live.

He helped Fleischer to his feet and they walked past the dead and out the door in the sunlight. "We have to get out of here in case they come back," Grossmann said.

There were three vehicles parked on the far side of the street and Grossmann looked at them weighing his options. "Let's take a staff car. I have to see about

Antoniette and then we can come back and get the artwork."

"Fuck that cat-eating bitch!" snarled Fleischer. "And fuck the art as well. We need to get out of this city, Colonel. I've had my suspicions about you since I joined the staff. You're not a soldier, you're nothing more than a thief. You're derelict in your duties…to yourself, to the SS, to the Fatherland, and to the Führer!" He angrily shrugged off Grossmann's support and started walking stiffly toward the staff car. "Get moving, Colonel!"

On a different day, Grossmann might have been stunned but not this day. He drew his Walther again, and shot Fleischer in the back of the head. He stood in the street trying to decide whether to take the truck with the art or one of the staff cars. *It doesn't matter now*, he thought, and he stepped over the twitching body and headed to the staff car with his belongings.

0925 Hours
Rome, Italy

Douglas Grossmann parked the car and left the motor running. He walked past a man and his dog on the street and was gratified to see the man scurry away. He didn't care about witnesses, he relished the fear. Grossmann entered the back of Antoniette's apartment building and walked up the marble steps as silently as he could. He was sick at heart as he had come to the only logical conclusion during the drive from the café. Antoniette had tried to have him killed. It was why she had requested Fritz join them at the café, and why she was late. It explained why the Isotta Fraschini had driven past the café and not stopped. Someone, maybe even Antoniette, had done a drive-by, confirmed that he was there, and then radioed the hit team. He didn't know whether he could ever bring them to justice, but if it was in his power, at least Antoniette would pay for her betrayal.

Betrayal, it was. Grossmann had been betrayed by the woman he loved and trusted. It was what the Nascimbeni girl had prophesized in his dream... Antoniette didn't love him and she would avenge her friend's death. *Well, after a fashion, she had*, he thought. She was responsible for the death of *his* best friend, and the death of his soldiers. An eye for an eye. She was responsible for the coming ruination of his career—he would never be able to explain the loss of his men. She had probably even stolen their savings in Switzerland.

Grossmann's face was flushed from humiliation. He'd been used all along by Antoniette. She'd taken advantage of his love and he thought again he had been betrayed. All the plans they'd made together were...*what? For her amusement? For the money?* He paused before her door and drew his SS dagger from its scabbard. He hardly ever carried it but on this occasion, he had wanted to wear it for Antoniette...show it off. The razor-sharp knife had been given to him personally by SS Reichsführer Himmler when he joined the SS following Admiral Canaris's arrest. Grossmann read the inscription, *Meine Ehre Heißt Treue*...My Honor is Loyalty...and he thought without conscious irony that he alone was loyal and he alone had honor.

Grossmann contemplated kicking the door down or simply using his key. He knocked instead. Grossmann heard the clicking of her heels on the marble floor of her entryway. He took a deep breath and waited. The door opened and there was the most beautiful woman he'd ever known—glossy black hair, a perfect light-olive complexion, black soulless eyes capable of the warmest empathy. *All lies*. His heart skipped a beat as she beamed at him, and he remembered the warning he'd received from a colleague a year before: "She will dangle your desire before you for an eternity—until you either kill her or yourself in despair." As he recalled the taunts and curses from the night before, he grabbed her roughly by the neck and pulled her toward his dagger, her screams drowning out the echoes of her greeting: "There you are, I was just…"

0930 Hours
Rome, Italy

Douglas Grossmann stumbled toward the door of Antoniette's apartment. After he killed Antoniette, his knees had buckled and he nearly vomited. He had sat on her bed with his head in his hands waiting for sanity to return. It did not come for several minutes. The sane voice in his head was screaming that something was wrong, but Grossmann couldn't put his finger on it. He took several deep breaths and told himself he had done what he had to do. *It was necessary…her or me.*

He couldn't bring himself yet to look at her body or the growing pool of blood on the floor. The shock in her eyes was the last memory he would have of her life, and he stood unconsciously to go. Grossmann poured himself a glass of her brandy and as he gulped it down, he looked around her apartment one last time. He had been sitting next to her open suitcase on the bed and he hadn't recognized it for what it was. With the first quiver of doubt, he realized she was packing to leave, but he told himself that meant nothing. She had to leave Rome regardless. Resting on top of her clothes was a small rectangular object carefully wrapped in pink tissue paper. With trembling hands, he pulled away the paper and saw a framed picture of the two of them—a

picture taken on her camera by Signore Alessio on the
magical day she had told him she loved him.

0930 Hours
Rome, Italy

Sam, Perkin, and Kulis walked softly up the last
flight of the white marble stairs. They halted on the
landing, and before a lovely wrought-iron door. The
door itself was a work of art, although its beauty was
lost on the three men.

Perkin held up his hand to stop his team behind
him and he cautiously peeked around the corner of the
landing. Before him was a long empty hallway dotted
on either side with heavy wooden doors each leading
to a luxury apartment. Thanks to Jimmy Cardosi and
his underworld contacts, they knew which apartment
Grossmann would have gone to, and Perkin silently
motioned for his companions to follow him. He slipped
around the door, raised his Thompson submachine gun
to his shoulder, and walked as softly as he could down
the richly carpeted hallway.

Sam and Kulis mimicked his movements. They both
carried their M-1s in a ready position: cheek against
stock, and rifle butt against shoulder. No safeties were
on any of their weapons, and fingers rested with gentle
competency on triggers.

Sergeant Kulis had been paying attention to the
iron numbers mounted on the doors to either side of
him, and he knew they were getting close. He gently
put his hand on Perkin's shoulder; when he had Perkin's
attention, he held up two fingers and mouthed the
words, "Two more on the right." Perkin nodded and
halted his party when they were still twenty feet from
the apartment doorway. In the softest whisper he could

manage, he said, "Sam, you kick the door in and move to the side. Eddie, toss a grenade in. I'll move in first."

They had all dreamed of this moment for countless days and nights, and while their dreams had seen themselves capturing and interrogating their prey or making him beg for his miserable life, they all knew subconsciously that those dreams were silly flights of fantasy. Their history with Grossmann had been far too costly for such indulgences.

Sam would kick the door down, and then they would kill everyone in the apartment without mercy.

0930 Hours
Rome, Italy

Before Kulis could reach for a grenade, the door to the apartment opened and Grossmann stumbled out. He didn't see the three American soldiers only yards away from him—he turned and stared back into the apartment, and it seemed to Perkin that the German officer was staring at the floor. There was more. Perkin saw blood, still wet blood, on Grossmann's field gray uniform, and his boots were tracking blood into the hallway.

As he stared at the floor, Grossmann groaned and put his hand on his holstered Walther.

"Hold it!" shouted Sam. "Don't move!"

Grossmann jumped at the sound of Sam's deep voice, and he stared at the three Americans in the hallway. He took his hand off the pistol and slowly raised his hands shoulder high. For the longest time, he remained silent as he looked at the soldiers before him. Finally, he glanced to his left, at the floor in the apartment, and then looking back at the Texans, he said in a curiously formal way, "I would be grateful if you would explain

how you came to be here. You're Taft, right? And
Berger? And I saw you in Ogliastro, Sergeant, but you
were a private then. I'm sorry I don't know your name."

Kulis said, "You have a good memory, Colonel. My
name is Kulis…from Rosebud, Texas. Colonel, is there
anyone else in the apartment? What's on the floor that
you keep lookin' at?"

Grossmann looked to his left again and shook his
head. "There's no one in there, Sergeant. Who's the
officer in charge?"

Perkin spoke for the first time. "I am."

"Will you tell me how you came to be here?"
Grossmann asked again.

"We've been tracking you for some time. Since the
bombings in Naples," Perkin said. He had not lowered
his weapon.

"I was following orders," Grossmann said as he
looked at Antoniette's body again. "I thought you were
infantry. Are you with the OSS?"

"No." Perkin felt he had more to say about Naples,
but the conversation was strange and unnatural. Instead
he asked, "What's on the other side of that door,
Douglas?"

Grossmann looked into the apartment again and
swallowed hard. "The love of my life. I just killed her."

"You killed Antoniette?" Perkin asked. Grossmann's
eyes welled up, but he contained the tears with effort.
Seeing this, Perkin knew he was telling the truth about
the apartment but he still kept his Thompson pointed
at Grossmann's chest.

"You know her?" asked a surprised Grossmann.

"Of course," Perkin said. "Why'd you kill her,
Douglas?"

"That's not for you to know, Captain Berger."
Grossmann looked at the apartment floor again. "What

are your intentions here?"

There was another long pause. In all of the day-dreams he'd had about gutting Grossmann, he'd never contemplated this situation...having a calm but surreal discussion with Grossmann. Perkin had a binary set of options in front of him, one of which entailed killing the man. He looked to Sam, who nodded, and then to Kulis, who did the same. Setting aside his cherished dreams, Perkin said, "We're going to disarm you, Colonel, and you will be remanded in Allied custody awaiting trial for war crimes."

Grossmann tilted his head and looked at Perkin curiously. "What war crimes?"

"We're not playing that game, Grossmann," Sam said harshly. He was willing to give Perkin the benefit of the doubt and accept his change of plan, but only barely. He thought of Gianina's death in Naples, and he could still hear the screams of the victims in the collapsed post office. It wasn't long before his thoughts went to the children of Gildardino family who were tortured and murdered, and Perkin had told him that Grossmann was responsible for the murder of hundreds in Rome, if not more. Sam had a deep well of forgive-ness, but the well was dry for Grossmann. However strongly he craved vengeance, Perkin's ache for it was an order of magnitude more compelling and Sam marveled at Perkin's restraint in the face of such evil. Sam shook his head and said, "You can play twenty questions with the prosecutors."

"No. That's not going to happen," said Grossmann simply in his neutral California accent. "You know...I swore I would kill Captain Berger for the murder of my friend Mark Gerschoffer, and Antoniette wanted you dead, Captain Taft. You embarrassed her in Ogliastro, and she begged me to do it. It sounds like a petty reason to kill someone, but I always promised that I would. It seems unlikely at this juncture, but... *aut viam inveniam aut faciam*."

Grossmann saw the recognition in Perkin's eyes, and before the German intelligence officer could drop his hand to his Walther, Perkin killed Douglas Grossmann.

Epilogue

Two Months Later

August 14, 1944
0900 Hours
Pozzuoli, Italy

The long column of soldiers snaked across the pier and back toward an assembly area where thousands more soldiers waited for their turn to embark on dozens of navy LSTs, properly called a Landing Ship, Tank. The day was shaping up to be hot and dusty, not unlike the day they had landed at Paestum eleven months before. This would be their last day in Italy as a division and the excitement was palpable.

Major Perkin Berger stood in line behind Captain Sam Taft and Lieutenant Colonel Bill Spaulding. Every staff issue that was brought to Colonel Spaulding while they inched forward was gleefully referred to Perkin with the words, "Take it to the XO." Perkin had been the battalion's executive officer for five weeks—when he had been promoted in a personal ceremony by Major General Fred Walker before Walker's return to the United States to assume command of the army's infantry school at Fort Benning, Georgia.

Standing in front of Sam was First Lieutenant B.G.E. Beams, who had been in hiding in the Umbrian countryside since February. His liberation had come only two weeks before, and it had taken considerable staff work on the part of the new executive officer to get Beams returned to Able Company. While in hiding, an Italian dentist had made a set of dentures for the soldier who had lost most of his front teeth during his escape from German captivity, and while his toothless lisp was gone, his smile was now awkwardly dominated by exceptionally large stark white teeth.

"If we do a night landing, you'll need to keep your mouth shut," Sam observed. "Those things probably reflect moonlight."

"B.G.E. stands for Big Glowing Eaters," agreed Beams amiably. "So Kulis was tellin' me about Rome, Sam. Why do you think he stabbed that woman? Kulis said she was the prettiest tail in all of Europe."

"They say that looks ain't everything," Sam replied. "And her personality exhibited shortcomings."

"They're wrong," Beams said. "Look how far my looks have got me." He offered a blinding smile as evidence.

"Stop doing that," Spaulding interjected. "You'll ruin my night vision for a month." Spaulding let loose a long stream of tobacco juice on the pier before saying, "Perk's got a theory on Grossmann, if you want to go to the source." Spaulding pointed at Perkin with his head.

"Am I allowed to talk to your exalted selves anymore?" Beams asked. Without waiting for an answer, he said, "So what do you think it was about, Perk? I mean, your lordship."

Perkin laughed. Despite his administrative nightmares of the past weeks, he was in a good mood. "That's the thanks I get for gettin' you back in the Gun Club?

I swear, this job was oversold to me. Now I gotta spend our time at sea figuring out how to get the army to recognize Sergeant Kenton's marriage to the soon to be Italian mother of his child."

Beams shrugged and then grinned. "I tolt him that if the army wanted him to have a Dago wife and little spaghetti eaters, it would have issued him some, and he said it was my fault for makin' him escape in the first place. I ain't even gonna dignify that with a response, so how about it, Perk? What's the story with the skirt?"

Perkin thought for a moment and said, "It seems that the Italian mob had tried to assassinate Grossmann just minutes before we ran into him. This crime lord, Occhiato, had accepted a contract job on Grossmann and he even tried to get us to pay him for killing Grossmann. It wasn't Grossmann, but apparently, his deputy and several of his troopers that got themselves killed by the mob. My working hypothesis is that Grossmann blamed Antoniette for some reason, although I can't for the life of me fathom why."

"You should have asked him," Beams said.

"I did. He wasn't inclined to tell us."

"Eddie said he spoke some Latin to you, and you shot him for being pretentious."

Sam started to laugh and said, "If that was a shooting offense, the professor would have been dead a long time ago. No, he said he'd sworn to kill us, and what he said in Latin was he'd either find a way to do it or make one. After I translated for Perk, he shot him in embarrassment because Grossmann knew more Latin than him."

Perkin smiled but said nothing more. He felt no guilt over Grossmann's death. He actually felt a great degree of satisfaction, but he didn't want to joke about it either. He thought back to the day as he had many times, and wondered again what would provoke Grossmann to kill the girl. He didn't put much faith in his working hypothesis but he didn't have any other answers.

Sergeant Kulis had searched the body and the room which hadn't offered up any answers but had proved to be a considerable source of what Kulis called "prize money." He asked the officers if they wanted anything of Grossmann's, and when they said no, he kept Grossmann's Rolex for himself. He pressed the Walther on Sam, saying since it had been pointed at him in Avezzano, it was only fair he kept it. Sam reluctantly agreed. Kulis gave the dagger that had killed Antoniette to Private Pfadenhauer, and when he searched Grossmann's car, he quietly pocketed two diamond bracelets, a stunning diamond and ruby engagement ring, and another ring with a light blue diamond. Several thousand dollars and two thousand pounds sterling were also found as was a considerable amount of gold. At Perkin's encouragement, the money was divided up between the two enlisted men with a significant portion given to the Nervetti family at the hotel and several weeks later, a much larger portion was given to the Frattini family in Presenzano. Perkin suspected that the money might be counterfeit but as it looked good enough to him, he kept his concerns to himself.

The Gun Club had pursued the German Army north of Rome and finally been pulled off the line in late June and returned to the Gulf of Salerno. It was an emotional division that said goodbye to General Walker in a ceremony in Paestum, and then they headed to the Neapolitan port of Pozzuoli for embarkation with the 3rd and 45th Divisions on amphibious assault ships. Another landing was in the works, but they were leaving Italy. For good. No one knew where they were headed, but everyone knew that the landings would be tough. It didn't matter. They had been redeemed as a division and were ready for anything.

They reached the brow of the ship and it was Perkin's turn to walk up the gangway to the quarterdeck. He hesitated briefly, took one last look around from Italian soil, and stepped forward toward whatever distant shore awaited.

Author's Note

Many outfits deserve the credit for the whole operation, but those of us who were present will always remember the men of the 36th, climbing silently in the night behind the enemy, armed with little but their American competence and a personal faith in their quiet, retiring general who had never let them down. If Generals Alexander and Clark received the key to the city of Rome, it was General Walker who turned the key and handed it to them.

Eric Sevareid

The first landings at Anzio and Nettuno took place on January 22, 1944, as the Gun Club was being destroyed on the Rapido River. The attack across the Rapido River was intended to draw German reserves in the Rome area down to the Gustav Line while Allied forces landed in their rear. The amphibious assault at Anzio was a plan championed by Winston Churchill, who had also championed a similar landing at Gallipoli in the Great War with similar effects. I think Churchill may have saved Western Civilization but neither Gallipoli nor Anzio were his finest hours.

The first VI Corps commander at Anzio was Major General John Lucas, who was less than enthusiastic about his mission. Mindful of Lieutenant General Mark Clark's warning not to stick his neck out, Lucas gave orders to consolidate the beachhead rather than seize the distant high ground of the Alban Hills...or cut the lines of communication between German-held Rome and their forces at Cassino. It was a decision that ultimately cost Lucas his job, but, in the opinion of many military historians, probably saved his corps from certain destruction. The Germans reinforced their positions faster than the Allies, and had Lucas attempted an early move on Rome, it is likely that his corps would not have survived. A breakout was attempted by Lucas in the days that followed. It failed. Multiple German counterattacks aimed at destroying the lodgment like-wise failed, and months of soul-destroying stalemate set in.

The decision to deploy the 36th to Anzio in May seems to have been made at the last moment. The division trained extensively for mountain warfare and as of the end of April expected to join the II Corps movement up the west coast of Italy between the mountains and the sea through Formia, Gaeta, and Terracina. It wasn't until May 2 that General Walker had an indication that Anzio might be in the cards for the division, and the actual decision wasn't finalized until May 14. The division was landed during the night of 22/23 May, and was committed to battle a week later.

Between their landing and commitment to battle, General Clark, the Fifth Army commander, made one of the most controversial decisions of the war. His orders from General Harold Alexander were to cut Highway 6, the same Victory Road running past previous battlegrounds at San Pietro and Cassino, at Valmontone and block the German Tenth Army's retreat from the crumbling Gustav Line. Sixth Corps was to be the anvil to the hammer of Lieutenant General Oliver Leese's Eighth Army.

Clark concluded that course of action posed an unacceptable risk, namely, that the British Eighth Army would get to Rome before his Fifth Army. In breach of orders sending the VI Corps to the east of the Alban Hills and blocking the main avenue of escape of the German Army, Clark ordered Major General Lucian Truscott to shift his attack to the west of the Alban Hills along the Appian Way (Highway 7), in what Clark believed was the quickest route to Rome. The depleted 3rd Infantry Division was tasked with the taking of Valmontone and was the sop to Clark's conscience and his orders.

Sixth Corps intended for the 36th to replace another severely depleted division, the 34th Infantry Division, on the assault on the Caesar Line west of the Alban Hills on May 31, 1944. Major General Fred Walker convinced Truscott and Clark that an infiltration behind the Caesar Line, over Monte Artemisio, had a better chance of success in breaking open the German defenses. The night ascent of Monte Artemisio by the 142nd and 143rd Infantry Regiments was one of the most audacious and successful operations conducted by the U.S. Army in the Second World War. The German line began to crumble almost immediately and the victory that had eluded the Allies for four months at Anzio came within days.

It wouldn't have been possible without the outstanding performance and ingenuity of the division's engineers. A road was bulldozed over Mount Artemisio over the course of the night of 31 May – 1 June, which allowed the 36th to get heavy equipment—tanks and artillery—to the mountaintop by daylight. It was a feat that the senior engineers at VI Corps and Fifth Army said couldn't be done, and yet they did it.

While the 142nd and 143rd Infantry Regiments were stealthily climbing Monte Artemisio, the 141st Infantry Regiment had the unenviable task of taking the town of Velletri. Urban warfare, which would define much of the post D-Day war in Europe, was still a relatively unknown task for the U.S. Army. In doing research for this book, I found that army doctrine was virtually nonexistent for urban warfare and what little there was ran counter to much of what would later be adopted (the discouragement of the use of armor in prewar doctrine, for example).

Many incidents were taken from the pages of history and adapted to my story such as the massacre of the Ardeatine Caves, and according to General Wolff, the slow-rolling of Hitler's order to invade Vatican City and depose Pius XII. Many of the small skirmishes used in this book also came from the pages of history such as a Stuart light tank prevailing over a Panzer IV outside of Velletri; the killing of the giant of Velletri by a U.S. officer with a Tommy gun; the German tank commander shooting from his turret like a cork from a champagne bottle; and General Walker kicking a sluggish German soldier and immediately regretting it.

The division fought for nearly another month and advanced far along the Tuscan coast before being pulled off the line south of Pisa. Walker left the division in early July to take command of the Infantry School at Fort Benning, Georgia. Walker's performance at Anzio was exemplary, and arguably should have earned him a corps command, but it wasn't to be. He was the oldest division commander in the army, and the army preference was for younger officers (Walker turned fifty-seven a few days after Rome fell). More than age, the tragedy at the Rapido River probably cost Walker any further combat command. Walker believed that Clark waited until the division's success at Velletri before relieving him for the failure of the Rapido.

After saying farewell to the general who had led the division since 1941, the Texas Gun Club received replacement soldiers and then embarked on amphibious assault ships for their landing in Southern France, which seems to be where we'll next find Sam and Perkin.

Mark Bowlin
Flower Mound, Texas
February, 2017

About the Author

Commander Mark Bowlin, USN (Ret.) is an eternally optimistic Texan who believes that one day, maybe not this season, but soon, the Dallas Cowboys will return to the Super Bowl—and as players, not spectators. He likewise holds the wholly understandable opinion that Texas is truly God's country, and that cold beer and Texas barbeque is truly superior to champagne and caviar in every respect.

Mark was a soldier in the Texas National Guard before being commissioned as an ensign in the United States Navy. Mark has lived in Wales, Japan, Italy and Iraq and served in a variety of billets—ashore and afloat—in the United States and overseas. His awards include the Legion of Merit, and Defense Meritorious Service Medal, among other personal, unit, and campaign awards.